PRAISE FOR THE BREATH OF GOD

"This debut suspense novel…explores the universality among all religions.
As with many contemporary thrillers revolving around a spiritual quest,
the novel contains chases, murder, and romance. Verdict: This tale is for fans
of Dan Brown's thrillers as well as readers who enjoy visionary fiction."

—LIBRARY JOURNAL

"Jeffrey Small explodes on the writing scene with his first novel and this book has
Best Seller written all over it! *The Breath of God* is a riveting novel that grips the
reader from the first chapter and does not let go until the last paragraph. Fans of
the *Celestine Prophecy* (James Redfield), and *Conversations with God* (Neale Donald
Walsch) will place *The Breath of God* right alongside these books in their library!"

—FEATUREME2 REVIEWS

"Jeffrey Small, a Harvard/Yale/Oxford-educated speaker on religion and spirituality,
makes an impressive literary debut with a thriller…Small's themes, such as the
common ground of the world's religions, are timely."

—ATLANTA MAGAZINE

"This meticulously researched, thought-provoking masterpiece is filled with high
adventure and intrigue. Based on an actual document from 1887, Small's stunning
debut reveals the impact of such a find. RT Rating: 4 1/2 stars TOP PICK!"

—RT BOOK REVIEWS

"A spellbinding novel, full of suspense as well as the thrills of a lifetime.
Very hard to put down. It also brings religion to the forefront of the reader's mind,
no matter what faith he or she follows, raising questions that have not been asked
before, as well as bringing other parts of the world into the living room.
Not to be missed. Excellent reading."

—BOOKLOONS.COM

"*The Breath of God* is sure to create controversy while exploring the plausibility
of an ancient legend that could tie the world's religions to each other. Mr. Small
paints a colorful and realistic depiction of India that reflects the multi-faceted
environment of daily existence in that country. A must-read for those that love
suspense and mystery; also for those who wish to expand their knowledge
of the world's religions, check out this novel."

—UNIVERSAL LEARNING SERIES RADIO

"First-time novelist Jeffrey Small has created a thrilling adventure tale that spans cultures and religious traditions while also exploring fundamental spiritual truths. If you enjoy reading a fast moving mystery with the added bonus of a challenging investigation of religious beliefs then this is the book for you."
—STEVE FLOYD, CEO August House Books

"In this gripping tale—played out against an intriguing international setting— East meets West, mystery meets romance, the human spirit meets the divine spirit and the reader meets a novelist of the first caliber."
—THE HONORABLE RAYMOND SEITZ,
Former US Ambassador to Great Britain

"From the very first pages, *The Breath of God* will draw you in! Jeffrey Small's masterful storytelling will take you from Himalayan monasteries to the American Bible Belt in a heart pounding adventure filled with twists, turns and shocking revelations that will rock the foundation of traditional Christianity. This gripping roller coaster of a novel will keep you guessing until the very end."
—DARREN MAIN, Author of *Yoga and the Path of the Urban Mystic*

"A page turner! From the first sentence to last word this book kept me captivated. A combination of religious/mystery/historical/modern-day thriller, I found it to be just about unputdownable...The descriptions of place are so well written I almost felt like I was actually there. The thriller aspect had me racing through the pages to find out what was going to happen next. A fascinating tale of what can lurk behind blind faith and what is possible if you open your mind."
—BROKENTEEPEE.COM

"Jeffrey Small skillfully maneuvers this spectacular historical mystery between the Indian subcontinent and the American south, where Evangelicals go to war against a scholar's tantalizing discovery. You'll be fascinated by the stunning connections between the world's faiths that Small unveils against today's background of savage religious hostilities."
—PARUL HINZEN, ArtsCriticATL.com

THE

BREATH

OF

GOD

Also by Jeffrey Small:

God as the Ground of Being: Tillich and Buddhism in Dialogue

A NOVEL OF SUSPENSE

THE

BREATH

OF

GOD

JEFFREY SMALL

WEST HILLS
ATLANTA · SAN FRANCISCO

PUBLISHED BY WEST HILLS
a division of Hundreds of Heads Books, LLC

Cover photograph by ©istockphoto.com, ©Clipart.com
Cover image © Anegada ARTs
Author Photograph by Kelsey Edwards

All of the characters and events in this book are fictitious, and any resemblance to actual persons, living or dead, is purely coincidental.

ISBN-13: 978-1-933512-86-0

Printed in Canada
10 9 8 7 6 5 4 3 2

TO ALISON AND GABRIELLA.
THANK YOU FOR MAKING THIS POSSIBLE. I LOVE YOU BOTH.

AUTHOR'S NOTE

Although this novel is a contemporary work of fiction, I have based it on extensive historical research. The primary settings in India and Bhutan exist, and I have tried to capture them as accurately as possible. Russian journalist Nicholas Notovitch, whose explosive discovery in the Himalayas in 1887 serves as the basis for this story, was a historical figure. He published his findings in 1894 before being publicly condemned and silenced for the heresy he proposed.

PART ONE

THE SPARK

"In the beginning was the Tao. All things issue from it; all things return to it. Every being in the universe is an expression of the Tao. The Tao gives birth to all beings, nourishes them, maintains them."

The Tao Te Ching, 6th century BC

"In the beginning was the Word, and the Word was with God, and the Word was God. He was in the beginning with God. All things came into being through him, and without him not one thing came into being. What has come into being in him was life, and the life was the light of all people."

The Gospel according to John, AD 1st century

CHAPTER 1

⚬⚬⚬

PUNAKHA VALLEY, BHUTAN

"THE NEXT ONE WILL BE the most dangerous."

Most dangerous? Grant Matthews spat out the remnants of the Himalayan river water he'd just inhaled on the last rapid, a Class IV.

"You good?" Dasho, his Bhutanese guide, called to him in accented English.

"Just need to catch my breath."

The current slowed as the Mo Chhu, the Mother River, widened. Grant balanced his paddle on top of the neoprene spray skirt that kept the icy water from entering his kayak and shook out his arms. He needed to stretch his legs too; the yellow boat barely accommodated his six-foot-two frame.

Dasho approached him with powerful strokes. "Monsoon season just passed. Chhu very fast now."

Grant pushed his helmet back, brushed his wet hair out of his eyes, and studied the guide's tanned face, his wide cheekbones. "So, how does a Buddhist monk become a river guide?"

When he arranged his trip to Bhutan, he'd asked his travel agent to find a tour guide familiar with the country's many monasteries. Grant hoped to find what he'd been searching for hidden in one of them. When the agent told him that Dasho, a former monk, led tours and kayaking expeditions, he knew he'd found a kindred soul.

"Father died two years ago," Dasho replied. "I was only son with three sisters and a mother. Left the monastery to provide for them."

So he lost his father around the same age I did, Grant thought, estimating Dasho to be in his early twenties. He then quickly shrugged off the memory of his sophomore year in college: his once invincible father—the great reverend—and his scandalous death. He lifted the paddle off his lap and swept it through the water.

"I'm sorry."

"No sorry." Dasho smiled. "I could be farmer." He pointed with his paddle across the river.

The valley rose gently from the riverbank in tiered fields planted with wheat, peppers, and beans. A lone sun-wrinkled farmer worked the plants with a wooden hoe. On a hill beyond the fields, a strand of Buddhist prayer flags fluttered on forty-foot-high poles. The snowcapped peaks of the Himalayas framed the picture in the distance.

"So you traveled through India before coming to the Land of Thunder Dragon?" Dasho asked, alluding to Druk Yul, the name the Bhutanese used for the tiny Buddhist kingdom nestled in the Himalayas between India and Tibet.

Grant nodded. "Research for my PhD."

As soon as the words left his mouth, a rush of anxiety flooded his body. *My unfinished dissertation*, he thought. The members of his dissertation committee at Emory University in Atlanta, even his mentor Professor Billingsly, were skeptical when he'd first outlined his research plans five years ago. The story he proposed to track down was only a legend, they'd said, but Grant was determined to unravel the ancient mystery.

He'd just spent a week in the cold, barren moonscape of the northern Indian Himalayas near Kashmir. Several monks at the Himis monastery in Ladakh had become suspicious of his inquiries there. A hundred years earlier, similar questions had brought unwanted attention from the West to their isolated monastery with devastating consequences for the questioner. Grant planned to handle Bhutan differently.

He grinned at Dasho. "I much prefer your milder weather and lush landscapes."

"We measure progress by gross national happiness instead of gross national product." Dasho beamed. "And you tackle toughest river?"

"I like the challenge. Learned in college on some big water."

"You Americans enjoy pushing everything to extreme." Dasho chuckled.

"Ah, that's the secret to our progress."

Progress, he thought with a hollowness in his gut. He wasn't making much, and he was running out of time. Bhutan had hundreds of Buddhist monasteries, and he could only afford two weeks in the country. The tenuous lead he'd received at Himis from the one monk he'd befriended didn't specify which monastery in Bhutan might hold the treasure.

"What you are searching for was moved long ago," the elderly monk had whispered.

"Where?" Grant had asked, glancing down the cloistered hallway to make sure no one approached.

The monk had shrugged. "Certainly to another Buddhist monastery. Probably Bhutan."

In the two days he'd been in Bhutan, Grant had already visited three major monasteries, one in Paro, the city he'd flown into, and two in Thimpu, the country's capital. In each he'd approached several monks, but not a flicker of recognition had passed over their faces when he hinted at what he was looking for. Grant shook his head. This kayaking trip was an indulgence he couldn't afford, even if he'd worked the past month without a day off.

He should have finished his dissertation last year. The extension he'd received on his scholarship would run out in the spring, and he was tapped out. From the moment he'd graduated from high school, he'd been on his own financially. His father had rejected his choice of college and his academic interests. He'd worked to pay his way through undergrad at the University of Virginia and now grad school at Emory with a combination of teaching assistant jobs and late nights waiting tables.

Grant pulled his paddle through the jade water. Sweat began to drip inside his black wet suit. *What if I can't find it?* The fear nagged at him, but he wouldn't give in to doubt. He couldn't let the skeptics in his department at Emory prove him wrong.

He increased the pace of his paddling. The water was getting more tumultuous, and his body responded naturally. His mind, however, was still immersed in his strategy for tracking down the truth. He stroked the paddle with his whole body, his blood surging through his veins as if powered by the energy of his resolve to return to the search. Tomorrow he would visit the monastery in Punakha, a few miles downriver from where he paddled. Of the monasteries he'd targeted, Punakha's was the largest, but he willed himself not to get his hopes up.

"Whoa," Dasho called from behind. "Who you racing?"

Grant paused to let his guide catch him. Soon the river picked up speed as the crop fields on each side transitioned into progressively steeper banks. Ten minutes later, the two kayakers were encased inside a gray granite canyon, bumping over the small rapids that occurred with increasing frequency. Only a few trees managed to grow from the sides of the craggy cliffs, their exposed roots clinging to the walls like a rock climber's fingers searching for holds.

Just ahead, Grant saw that the river narrowed again and then dropped out of sight beyond a grouping of boulders. "Follow me, my friend," Dasho said, paddling into an eddy near the right cliff wall. The guide raised his voice over the noise of the falling water ahead of them. "Meet Laughing Buddha."

Grant pointed to the large boulder in the center of the river. "The Buddha's head?" He enjoyed the creative names paddlers used to describe the rapids, falls, and various obstacles in their rivers, like kids finding animals in the shapes of the clouds.

"The water flows on sides of rock are Buddha's upheld arms, and four-meter fall beyond that is Buddha's body." Dasho added with a grin, "And if you hit wrong way, he will laugh as you flip."

"Four meters?"

"Class five. Lots of water this week. Don't take many tourists to Laughing Buddha."

Grant felt a twinge of regret for letting his ego rather than his brain fill out the questionnaire about his kayaking experience. Most of his kayaking had actually been on Class III rapids with the occasional IV thrown in for terrifying effect. Now he faced descending the most difficult navigable rapid; the next highest classification, a VI, was considered too dangerous to run.

He examined the cliff walls at the river's edges—too steep to pull the boats out and walk around. "How do we approach it?"

"See right fork? We take that. At top of fall, paddle hard as you can, and lean back. If you go vertical too soon, you capsize." Dasho made a flipping gesture with his hands and winked. "No problem for you. Just follow me."

Dasho spun his kayak, facing the rapid. He yelled over the roar of the falling water, "One more thing: careful when you land. A boulder under high water makes large hole; don't get caught inside."

Grant paddled two quick strokes next to his guide. For the first time, he could see over the rapid. The smooth sheets of water at the top of the fall churned into a foamy meringue as they spat over the edge of the rocks and then tumbled into a turbulent frenzy at the bottom. Grant wasn't sure what made him more nervous: the twelve-foot fall ahead of him or the swirling whirlpool where the water pounded into the river below.

He'd seen a number of hydraulics over the years, but this one was by far the largest. When water cascaded over a large rapid, it would occasionally strike submerged rocks at the bottom that caused the current to recirculate on itself, creating a whirlpool or a hydraulic, as paddlers called them. Rafters and kayakers stuck in hydraulics often had to be pulled out. Both he and Dasho carried throw bags with thirty feet of rope each. He hoped they wouldn't need them.

"I watch for you at bottom," Dasho said. Taking long smooth strokes equally on both sides, he guided his kayak through the water straight for the right fork.

Grant caught his young guide's mistake as soon as he made it. Dasho glanced over his shoulder just before reaching the top of the fall to yell his final words of encouragement, "Don't forget to have fun!"

A slight error, really, but as Grant had learned, any misstep under dangerous conditions had a way of compounding itself, like an avalanche picking up power as it gathered snow on its slide down the mountain. The slight twist in Dasho's body caused his kayak to drift off center, just a few inches to the left. The powerful current then exacerbated the problem, pushing him further off his line. Dasho was quick to recover, digging in on the left side of his kayak, paddling ferociously. The bow of his boat swung to the right just as he crested the fall.

He'd overcorrected and his maneuver to straighten his kayak cost him much of his forward momentum.

Grant held his breath, watching from the upper pool. Dasho hit the churning water below nose-first at a steep angle. Grant flinched as the kayak flipped. His guide's body twisted unnaturally when it slapped the water. A queasy feeling spread through Grant's stomach.

"Roll, Dasho. Damn it, roll!" he shouted, but he knew his voice couldn't be heard over the thundering water.

The pale underside of the blue kayak spun in the whirlpool as water pummeled it from the fall above. Dasho should have either rolled or exited the kayak by now, but Grant saw no sign of him. His guide was either trapped or unconscious. In either case, he needed help.

Grant knew he had to descend the rapid quickly. A checklist of his options flashed through his mind. Landing on top of the other kayak would create a whole new set of problems. A glance to shore confirmed his earlier assessment—no way to go around. His only choice: time his fall just right.

With a firm, two-handed grip, Grant lifted his paddle in the air and let his boat drift forward slowly. *Another few seconds*, he guessed, watching the boat below. His heart pounded as if he'd been paddling hard, although he had yet to move. *Just a second more*. His breathing quickened.

Now.

The moment Dasho's kayak spun to the left, Grant sank his paddle deep into the water. His arms and back burned with his effort. He hit the rapid dead-on. The roar of the water and his own pulse drummed in his ears. Pressing his feet into the kayak's plastic footrests, he leaned his long torso into his last strokes. The drop came so quickly, he didn't even register it until he felt the splash of his impact.

Grant squinted through the cold Himalayan spray.

There!

Dasho's boat bobbed upside down only a few feet away. Four quick strokes and he bumped against it. The turbulent current now rocked his own kayak; he was caught in the same hydraulic that trapped his guide. Grant fought back the chill of fear that crept up his spine. If they were both to live, he had to focus on the task ahead. He formed his plan. First, he would right Dasho, and then he would worry about getting them out of the swirling hole.

Gripping his paddle in his right hand, Grant grabbed for Dasho's kayak with his left. His fingers slipped on the wet hull. He tried a second and then a third time with the same result. He needed a new plan. Leaning as far to the side as he dared, he searched the frigid water for any hold on the boat's underside. He took rapid, shallow breaths to avoid sucking in the water that splashed around him.

He felt the lip of the kayak's opening. The spray skirt was attached, which meant that Dasho was still inside. He clenched his numb fingers around the narrow lip. Bracing his legs against the walls of his own kayak, Grant jerked his left arm upward while he torqued his body to the right.

Dasho's kayak started to roll. A rush of triumph surged through Grant.

Then a gush of current from the hydraulic hit Grant's kayak on the rear quarter, twisting him unexpectedly. He struggled to compensate for the jarring movement while maintaining his balance and his grip, but the water overpowered him. His hand was ripped from the other boat.

He flipped.

Upside-down and spinning underwater, Grant opened his eyes. He couldn't see through the turbulent green. His lungs ached. And, he realized, he no longer held on to his paddle. The urge to panic threatened to consume him faster than the frigid water enveloping him.

His only hope was to follow his training. As he'd practiced many times, Grant tilted his ear to his right shoulder, bent his torso to the same side, and then swiveled his hips forcefully. Nothing. He attempted his roll again, but the current was too strong.

His vision darkened. Grant knew he only had seconds before he blacked out. He recalled his final option—a wet exit. Reaching both hands to the top of his kayak, he grasped the neoprene loop where his spray skirt attached to the kayak's opening and pulled toward his chest. It released. He gripped the sides of the opening and pushed himself out of boat. The moment he was clear, his PFD, the personal flotation device, shot him to the surface.

Air.

He gasped deeply, then choked on the spray permeating the air around him. A second later, he caught a clean breath. He was going to be okay.

After a few more cautious breaths, Grant's head cleared. *Dasho.* His guide's kayak still bobbed upside down a few feet away. Grant kicked hard, swimming toward the other boat. Just as he reached his goal, the whirlpool sucked him under.

Instinctively he grabbed his knees, tucked his chin, and curled into a ball. Grant remembered that somewhere underneath the cold water, large rocks created the hydraulic, and colliding into them would worsen his situation. He had no choice but to have faith in his PFD and the circulating current to re-gurgitate him back up. A few seconds later, he shot to the surface again. Breathing carefully but deeply, he surveyed the standing waves around him. Dasho's boat had spun farther away to the other side of the waterfall, and his own kayak was nowhere to be seen.

With a tightness in his chest, Grant realized that he could never swim against the current and reach Dasho. His arms were losing sensation, and his legs were slowing. Adrenaline would keep him going for another minute, but then hypothermia would win. Grant realized that to save himself from drown-ing, he had to get out of the hydraulic. He'd have to find a way to reach Dasho from the other side.

To escape the whirlpool on his own, he would have to execute a technique he'd only read about: the elevator maneuver. He recalled that the hydraulic's current was strongest on the surface; even the best swimmer was no match for its power. Underwater, however, once the initial undertow subsided, an opportunity existed to push through the whirlpool. The key to the maneuver lay in allowing the whirlpool to suck him under, like pressing the down button on an express eleva-tor, and then at the deepest and weakest spot, to swim out of the water column. If successful, he would pop out ten or fifteen meters downstream.

Moments later the whirlpool jerked him under again. Rather than resisting, Grant curled into a fetal position as he shot downward. This time he felt no fear, his mind strangely clear but for the immediate task before him. The moment he felt his momentum slow, Grant kicked as hard as his numb legs would allow while pulling with his arms. He made progress, but tired quickly. Then, his foot struck something solid—the underwater boulder causing the hydraulic.

A thought occurred. *Why not use the rock to push myself out?*

It was the wrong idea.

Planting his right foot on the rock for leverage, he pushed with the last of his energy, but instead of launching himself downriver, his foot slipped on the polished surface of the rock and wedged itself deep between the boulder and another rock beside it. Grant didn't have time to register what he'd done. A rush of current twisted his body. He couldn't possibly hear the cracking of his shin over the muffled roar of the water in his ears, but he experienced the splitting of his lower leg as a white light that flashed through him, as if he'd been struck by lightning.

Grant realized he was going to drown.

A cold blackness closed in around him. After the initial flash of agony, he no longer felt the pain in his leg, nor did he experience the burning in his lungs. Even the roar of the water faded into the darkness. Grant's body went limp. Enveloped in a cool cocoon, he slipped into peaceful dream. He dreamed of flowing like the river, as if he and the water had become part of the same substance.

CHAPTER 2

⁓

BIRMINGHAM, ALABAMA

A GUITAR RIFF RIPPED THROUGH the bank of speakers suspended over the stage. Each of the five thousand audience members stood, some on their tiptoes for a better view, most with arms in the air, and all bathed in the colorful stage lights that washed over them. Tears rolled out of the closed eyes of more than a few women in the front rows.

Brian Brady grinned at the crowd, enjoying the frenzy he'd created. Sweat ran from his silver streaked hair down the sides of his tanned face. God, he loved this. Twenty years, and he never tired of the rush of the crowd's adulation.

In synch with the drummer punctuating the end of the song, Brady raised both arms, embracing his people. He called out hoarsely through the wireless microphone attached behind his ear, "Let me hear you one more time!"

In unison the congregation responded, "Praise Jesus!"

"Who's down with JC?"

"We are!" they screamed.

"If you are on the Lord's team, what are you?"

"Saved!"

"If you are out of Christ, what are you?"

"Condemned!"

"We, the Army of the Righteous, shall bring light to the darkness," Reverend Brady proclaimed in his smooth southern baritone, punching his fist in the air to the cheers of the congregation.

He lowered his arms palms down. Then he grinned at the crowd, showcasing his newly bleached teeth. "Can we chat?" He took a folding chair from a techie who rushed from backstage to meet him.

"You go, Reverend," a voice called out from the middle of the congregation. A chorus of laughter sprinkled through the church.

Brady settled his two-hundred-pound frame into the chair, alone in the center of the stage. He straightened the lapel on his Armani suit, black with a fine blue pinstripe. The band Rapture stood behind him stage right; opposite them the thirty-member choir stood on risers, their crimson robes blowing from the powerful fans hidden offstage. Surveying the audience as they anticipated the topic of this Sunday's sermon, Reverend Brady spoke in the disarming tone he used to connect with his people, as if he were sharing iced tea with each of them alone in their living rooms.

"I am troubled, my friends. I'm troubled with the corruption of our once great nation." He paused, allowing the thought to sink in. When he spoke, he did so deliberately, enunciating each syllable so that the echo in the cavernous New Hope Church of God wouldn't muffle his words.

"Corruption in our country takes many forms: the eradication of religion from our schools, our children's fascination with the occult in the *Harry Potter* and *Twilight* books, sex and violence in our television shows, politicians who care more about saving their elections than saving their constituents."

Leaning forward on the edge of his seat, he continued, "But today, we will talk about Satan's more subtle temptations. My friends, I'm here to warn you that sin targets not just the unfaithful. It targets you as well."

Murmurs spread through the congregation. Brady immediately noticed the man in the front row who sat ramrod straight, perched on his seat like a cobra waiting to strike. His crew cut was sprinkled with signs of premature gray, the deep crease between his eyes adding to the illusion of age beyond his years. The stage lights brought out the worst of the man's eczema: the top layer of skin on his face was flaking away, exposing the red flesh underneath. Brady paused to give thanks to the Lord for his own flawless complexion.

"Now, I don't wish to cast stones at anyone . . ."

Brady rose from his chair, descended the marble steps to the front row, and placed a hand on the shoulder of a midthirties blonde in a pastel cotton dress that complemented her athletic physique. Brady scanned the aisle to see where his camera guy was kneeling and turned his body to block any shot of the eczema man sitting two seats away. He was always conscious of who was being projected onto the giant screen suspended over the stage.

"But last Thursday evening, when I was picking up some groceries, I noticed Barbara Howell here coming out of the yoga studio in the shopping center off Montevallo Road."

Barbara gazed up at the reverend as a child might look at a parent, knowing she was in trouble but unsure of the nature of her infraction. Brady smiled at her indulgently. "First Corinthians instructs us that our bodies are temples of the Holy Spirit. By exercising, we honor God, who created us in his image. Now, I know Barbara strives to live according to the ways of our Savior, but"—he paused, holding his index finger in the air—"even well-intentioned activities can be fraught with sinfulness, if we are not vigilant."

At the word *sinfulness* Barbara's expression grew more concerned. The entire congregation watched her, as Brady knew they would. "You may think that yoga, with its stretching and breathing techniques, is a peaceful way to exercise and relax after a hard day's work. But don't be fooled. Yoga is not Christian. Yoga is Hindu in origin and practice. Of course, these teachers won't portray it as religious at first, but one day you're touching your toes, and then before you know it, you're chanting in Sanskrit, trying to find God within yourself."

Reverend Brady's grip tightened on Barbara's shoulder. He looked from her to the vaulted ceiling forty feet above them, increasing the volume of his voice. "God, our Father almighty, creator of the universe, and judge over all mankind: these so-called yogis would have you believe that the supreme being is located in a breath or in a flower." He shook his head in disgust. "But we know better, don't we?"

"We do," the congregation replied in unison.

"You tell me, what is the one and only path to God?" he shouted.

"Through our Lord Jesus Christ," they responded.

Brady lowered his voice again. "If it were possible to reach God through self-discovery, then why would he have sent Jesus to us?"

The reverend looked into Barbara's reddened eyes and brushed her tear-streaked cheek. "I don't fault you, dear. The devil comes in many disguises. In Second Corinthians, chapter eleven, verse fourteen, Paul writes, 'Satan himself masquerades as an angel of light.'" Brady prided himself on his facility with the holy scripture and his ability to come up with a verse to fit any occasion.

"From the beginning of time, Satan has targeted the fairer gender. Just as Eve succumbed to the temptation of eating the forbidden fruit from the tree of knowledge, women today flock to these yoga centers, seeking to find themselves through meditation and other Eastern practices that promote self-knowledge. But hasn't that fruit been tasted before? These practices will not lead you to God; they will not erase your sins. They will only open your hearts and your minds to dark influences. Our apostle John says in chapter one, verse ten, 'If they come any to you and bring not this doctrine, receive him not into your house.' Whose house do you want to be in, Barbara?"

In a whisper she replied, "God's house."

Pulling her out of her chair and to her feet, he asked, "Are you ready today, Barbara, to reaffirm your belief in Jesus as the only way to everlasting life?"

"I am."

Brady raised his hands in the air palms up, and Barbara mimicked him. "In the name of our Savior Jesus Christ, you are forgiven, Barbara Howell. Follow in the Lord's path, and you shall receive his grace." Relieved and drained, she collapsed back into her seat as a runner might fall to the curb in exhaustion after crossing the finish line of a race.

Climbing back onstage, the reverend addressed the whole congregation. "Today we have witnessed the courage of one woman. Do you also have the courage to accept Jesus?"

"We do!" they shouted.

"These are precisely the dangers I discuss in my humble little book." Brady glanced at the giant screen above the stage that displayed a ten-foot-tall projection of the cover of his recently published book, *Why Is God So Angry?* Under the bold lettering of the title, and the even larger type of his name, was a picture of Brady gazing upward at a wooden cross suspended in a dark, foreboding sky. "Thanks to your support, we now have over three hundred thousand copies of the book in print." The crowd erupted in cheers. "And that's only four months after being published!"

Brady paused to allow the applause to die down. Then he began to quote from the first chapter of his book: "The calamities our country has faced in recent times—the hurricanes along our coast, terrorism on our soil, the collapse of our economy—are punishments directed at our *formerly Christian* nation, which, like the Jewish people in the Old Testament, has lost its way from God. The evils of our permissive society have turned us into a modern-day Sodom and Gomorrah: drugs, abortion, promiscuity, and"—he raised his voice—"our so-called tolerance of other religions that encourage the worship of false idols that have polluted the minds of our citizens." Brady lowered the pitch of his voice but increased the volume even more. "We have forgotten the warning of First Timothy, chapter two, verse five: 'For there is one God, and one mediator between God and men, the man Christ Jesus.'"

The screen above Brady flashed from his book cover to a three-dimensional computer rendering of a town square centered around a huge church. "This lesson today underscores the importance of the greatest undertaking this church has ever attempted. Of course, I'm referring to the ongoing construction of the New Hope Community. Just twelve miles from here and twenty-four months from completion, our new church is truly evidence that the Lord is smiling down on us. Our community will be a place where you and your children can live and grow in God's image, a sanctuary of hope away from the evil influences of other religions. Our new gym will offer Christian stretching classes," he said, winking at Barbara, who smiled up at him, "set to the sounds of our own gospel choir. Your kids can learn martial arts, but they will bow before the Ten Commandments posted on the walls, not some self-proclaimed sensei spouting confusing Zen statements."

He softened his voice. "I feel so humble to be in the presence of each of you. For you are the ones making God's plan for our community a reality. Your generous contributions to the Lord have made this dream possible. And we are so close. We are so close, but we are not there yet. I must ask each of you to look deep inside yourselves and ask whether you can give just a little more. We don't want to shortchange God's vision. I hope that when you get a phone call next week from our volunteers, you will do what you can."

Reverend Brady moved to the altar in the center of the stage. "Please take a moment with me to pray silently as we ask for God's guidance with this holy project."

Brady knelt at the altar, turning his back on the congregation, who dutifully bowed their heads. A stillness fell over the sanctuary. After three minutes of silence, interrupted only by a few muffled coughs, Brady rose just before the audience grew restless and turned to face his people. His eyes remained closed. Tears streamed down his face. He opened his arms wide, palms upwards. "Can you feel it?" he cried. "The power of our prayer. Can you feel it? The presence of God is here, today, right now. Can you feel it?"

An elderly man in a wheelchair at the back of the church proclaimed in a voice that seemed too strong for his frail body, "God is with us! Hallelujah!" A number of people joined the reverend in his tears.

"Something special is happening here today," Brady cried out. "We are witnessing something sacred and holy. Come to us, Lord Christ!"

With his last exclamation, the people erupted into a chorus of *amen*s and *praise God*s. Brady opened his eyes and surveyed the upturned faces in their ecstasy. The man in the front row had cinched his eyes closed, while his chapped lips mouthed a silent prayer. Leaning on the altar railing, Brady bent over and removed his black Ferragamo loafers. He presented his shoes to the crowd. "We are on sacred ground here today. Let us not soil it with our dirty shoes." As the five thousand rustled to remove their shoes as well, Brady knelt again in prayer, but this time he faced the audience. His shoes lay on the ground in front of him.

After the rustling quieted, Brady opened his eyes and said, "Praise Jesus." Without waiting for a response, he picked up his shoes, stood, and walked past the band off the stage.

Once he disappeared through the side curtains, the stunned congregation erupted into the loudest cheers Brady had ever heard. The band and choir took their cue and launched into "Cruising with Jesus," one of their popular rock-inspired songs. Backstage, Brady strode past the lighting and sound technicians who hovered over their control boards. He stopped by a bank of video monitors overseen by a thin, balding man in a charcoal suit. Brady took the towel the man offered and wiped his face.

"I was really good today, William, wasn't I?" Brady said more as a statement of fact than as a question needing an answer.

"It was one of your best. You owned them," replied William Jennings, director of operations of New Hope.

Brady smiled at his number two as he tossed the damp towel, stained with tears, sweat, and smudges of bronze foundation, back to him and continued walking down the corridor.

CHAPTER 3

PUNAKHA, BHUTAN

IN THE DARKNESS, GRANT COULD HEAR soft voices speaking in a language he didn't understand. He became conscious of an unfamiliar smell: some sort of incense infused in a musty atmosphere. He shifted his weight; his arms felt heavy, as did his head. Gradually, the light returned, as if someone had slowly turned up a dimmer switch on his temple. He lay on a lumpy cot in a small room with a stone floor and sand-colored plaster walls. A pair of candles burned on a simple wooden desk by a narrow window. A second smaller table by his bed contained a carved wooden bowl and a hand-hammered tin cup.

Three men stood by the door, whose heavy timbers, painted a kaleidoscope of reds, yellows, and blues, provided the only color in the drab room. The men stopped speaking and turned their heads toward him.

"Where am I?" Grant croaked. His swollen tongue filled his dry mouth. He tried unsuccessfully to raise himself on his elbows. "What happened?"

The men approached his bed. Grant recognized two as monks because of their robes, sandals, and shaved heads, but the third was dressed in a *gho*—a plaid, knee-length woolen robe whose sleeves were rolled into cuffs exposing a hint of a white shirt worn underneath. On his feet the man wore leather shoes and argyle socks. Grant had first encountered the traditional Bhutanese garb on his arrival at the Paro airport. How many days ago, he was no longer sure.

The man in the *gho* responded in heavily accented in English, "Don't try to move." In answer to the confused look on Grant's face, he said, "My name's

Karma. I am the Punakha *drungtsho*—the town's doctor. You suffered a complete fracture of your right tibia. Worst I've seen."

For the first time, Grant became aware of his right leg, elevated on a folded blanket. He touched the rough plaster cast that ran from his hip to his toes. Then he glanced at his watch, a digital sports model with a waterproof band of rubber. The push of a button gave him the barometric pressure, altitude, and temperature—all for under a hundred dollars. Grant's favorite feature, though, was the tiny radio receiver that kept the time and date precisely set to the second. He was never late to an appointment.

When his eyes focused on the date, he shouted, "Four days!"

"You've been unconscious," Karma told him. "Should have died on the river from loss of blood, but your wet suit acted as a compression bandage and restricted the bleeding until these two rescued you." He nodded toward the monks.

Grant turned to catch a better look at them. The older one was dressed in a neatly wrapped orange robe that fell to his ankles. Judging from the salt-and-pepper stubble sprinkled across his shaved head, the monk was in his late fifties. His face was angular, with prominent cheek and jaw bones that joined to a point at his chin. The monk studied Grant with black eyes that were Asian in character but wide in shape, and placed close together. His unblinking gaze should have been disconcerting, but for a reason Grant couldn't explain, he found it comforting. His younger companion, who couldn't have been much over twenty, had a rounder face with a mixture of Tibetan and Chinese features. Several inches shorter than the older monk, and wearing crimson rather than orange robes, he was skinny in a still-filling-out sort of way.

"Thank you," Grant said to all three men, his fingers tapping his cast. "But what . . ." As if a projector in his head had suddenly come to life, the recent events replayed for him: the river, the rush of the cold water, grasping for his guide's kayak, the panic of being trapped underwater. From the corner of his eye he spotted his PFD on the floor by the table. Instinctually, he touched the wool blanket covering his chest. He guessed what had happened. When he blacked out from the breaking of his leg and lack of oxygen, the current must have pulled him free of the boulder. The flotation device would have shot him to the surface.

"My guide, Dasho?" he asked, dreading the answer he already knew.

The older monk approached the bed and rested a warm hand on Grant's shoulder. He answered in precise English with an unexpectedly clear British accent. "I am sad to report that our brothers found his body downriver from the *dzong*. He was upside down, still in his kayak."

Grant swallowed back the acidic taste of bile that rose to the back of his throat. If he hadn't requested to go on the most challenging section of the river, Dasho would still be alive. *Maybe if I'd tried harder in the hydraulic?* The friendly guide had been supporting his family.

As if reading Grant's thoughts, the monk added, "You couldn't have saved him. His neck was broken."

Grant broke eye contact. He didn't find comfort in the information. To distract his thoughts, he glanced around at his spartan surroundings.

"Is this some kind of hospital?"

"My apprentice and I found you lying on the riverbank about a mile from here," the elder monk replied. "We carried you to the closest building where we could provide help—to the Punakha Dzong."

The leftover haze vanished from Grant's mind. The Punakha Dzong was his next stop. He remembered driving past the imposing five-hundred-year-old fortress rising from the peninsula where the Mo Chhu and the Pho Chhu joined. Constructed in traditional Bhutanese style, its massive inward-sloping walls of whitewashed stone starkly contrasted with the intricately carved and painted wood molding around the windows and doors—in the same style as the painted door to his room, he realized. A colorful cornice anchored the pagoda-style roof.

He recalled Dasho's explanation that although the dzongs were originally forts built to protect the country from invaders who crossed the imposing Himalayan range and attacked from neighboring Tibet or India, today they served a dual purpose: to house both the local government offices and the country's Buddhist monasteries. Evaluating the furnishings in his room, Grant guessed that he must be in the living quarters of the monastery.

The monk who spoke English so well held out his hand. "I am Kinley Goenpo, the senior monk here during the summer season, and this is my student, Jigme." Jigme bowed from the waist but remained silent.

"Grant Matthews. Thanks so much for rescuing me, but . . ." Grant struggled for the right way to express his concern. "Shouldn't I go to a hospital—have a surgeon x-ray my leg?" He again drummed his fingers on the gray plaster.

The doctor shook his head. "Kinley and I debated the idea of moving you, but the nearest hospital is in our capital city, Thimpu, a three-hour drive over the mountains. My little office in town wouldn't provide you any more help than I can offer you in this room. Fortunately, your leg sustained a clean break, though a severe one. If you stay off it for the next six weeks, it should heal nicely. You'll go home with just a scar as a souvenir of your adventure."

"Six weeks?" Grant felt the blood drain from his already pallid face. He still had many monasteries to investigate, and then he had to be back at school in ten days. His palms began to sweat.

Karma shook his head. "Any movement before your leg stabilizes risks permanent disability."

"I shouldn't have even gone kayaking," Grant mumbled, feeling sorry for himself and guilty for his role in Dasho's death. Grant glared at his cast as if the sheer force of his gaze would fuse his bones together. His original plan had been to spend just an hour or so in this monastery, to let his guide ask the monks some questions, and then move on if the legend about a boy named Issa didn't ring any bells.

Kinley lowered himself to the edge of Grant's bed. "I understand your frustration. We will work with you to make your stay as comfortable as possible."

Grant craned his neck to search the room. "Did you find my stuff? I had a dry bag in my kayak—my credit cards and cell phone."

"My brothers who found your guide's body also found your kayak," Kinley replied. "It was empty."

Even though the room was cool from the September breeze flowing through the open window, Grant felt flushed with heat. He pushed the quilted blanket covering his torso to his waist so that he could breathe more easily. He looked down to find that he was wearing an off-white cotton shirt; the monks must have dressed him. The material was coarse, and Grant felt it start to scratch his skin.

"Can you lend me a phone? I need to call my professor and let him know what's happened." He owed his mentor so much. Grant refused to worry, much less disappoint him. Billingsly had gone to bat for him with the Emory admissions committee. He still recalled his professor's words verbatim from seven years ago: "Grant has one of the best analytical minds I've seen. Harvard was foolish to reject him because of that incident."

The elder monk shook his head. "Oh, there are no cell phones in the *go-emba*, the monastery, but if you give the number to Karma, he can call anyone you wish when he returns to town."

Grant flopped his head on the thin pillow. "I suppose email is out of the question too?"

Kinley shook his head. Grant thought he detected something in the monk's eyes. *Is this amusing to him?* Grant stared at the fine lines crisscrossing the beige ceiling. Bedridden in a jail cell of a room in a remote monastery with some monks who were enjoying his predicament. For the first time since he'd woken, Grant became aware of the throbbing pain in his leg. He also realized that his left shoulder was bruised, and he had a pounding headache behind his temples.

"What about the bathroom?" he asked, not sure he wanted to know the answer.

The doctor chuckled and bent over to retrieve a battered metal bedpan from the floor beside the bed. "I brought this from town."

Grant wiped his palms off on the sheets. Accepting this situation for six weeks was out of the question. He needed to devise a plan.

"Pen and paper?" he asked the men.

"That we can do," Kinley said, nodding to the doctor. Karma reached into his black bag—the kind of doctor's bag that Grant had seen in old TV shows but didn't think were used anymore—and produced a ballpoint pen and a blank prescription pad.

Grant wrote Harold Billingsly's office number at Emory and the name of his hotel in town, the Zangdho Pelri, and handed it to the doctor. "Room one-oh-eight. If you don't mind, I have a backpack with my clothes, and my laptop is on the desk."

Before Karma could respond, the door to the room opened. A third monk, a boy no older than ten or eleven with a perfectly round bald head, dressed like Kinley's apprentice Jigme in a crimson robe, entered carrying a steaming cup centered on a tray.

Kinley took the cup from the boy and patted his shoulder in a fatherly way. "Thank you, Ummon."

After the boy bowed to the older monk and left the room, the doctor emptied the contents of a small envelope into the cup. "Drink this," he said. "It will ease your discomfort."

Grant sniffed the cup, wondering what sort of herbal concoction he was about to consume. He took a sip. *Just a little bitter.* He hoped the effects would kick in quickly. After Grant finished the tea, the doctor left, but the two monks remained, watching him silently.

"I appreciate your help, but really you don't need to stay." Grant focused on the notepad on his lap. He drew a line down the center of the page and wrote at the top of the left column "Options." At the top of the right he wrote "Plan of Attack."

Kinley sat on the edge of the bed, his hands folded in his lap.

"Grant, you are experiencing the *dukkha* of life."

Without looking up from his notepad, he responded, "Suffering." He resisted the temptation to glance at the monk to gauge his surprise at Grant's knowledge of the Pali word: it was the language of the ancient Buddhist canon. Grant enjoyed near-photographic recall of the texts he'd studied. His comparative religions class had been six years earlier, but he still remembered the basic tenets of Buddhism as if he'd read them yesterday.

"Yes, that's the common translation, but not entirely accurate," Kinley said without missing a beat. "Actually, *dukkha* means *out of balance*, like a cart with a broken wheel."

"So you're saying that my life is out of whack right now." Grant put his pen down and looked Kinley in the eye. "I could have told you that."

"Indulge me in a story," Kinley began, as if he were telling a fable to a group of children gathered at his feet. "A farmer in the foothills of the mountains had a beautiful horse that ran away. The farmer's neighbor stopped by to console him on losing such a magnificent animal, but the farmer surprised his neighbor by saying, 'Who am I to judge what is an unlucky event or a fortunate one?' The next day his horse returned, bringing with it a herd of similarly beautiful wild horses. The neighbor returned and said, 'You were right yesterday not to wallow in your loss. Look how fortunate you are now with all these horses.' But the farmer surprised him again by repeating his comment from the previous day, 'Who am I to judge what is an unlucky event or a fortunate one?' A few weeks later the farmer's son fractured his leg while trying to break in one of the new horses. Of course, the neighbor returns to offer his condolences again, certain that the farmer cannot be unaffected by his son's injury."

"Let me guess," Grant intervened, resisting the urge to roll his eyes. "Even with his son lying in bed, his leg in a splint, the farmer repeats his previous response, 'Who am I to judge what is an unlucky event or a fortunate one?'"

Kinley grinned and rested a hand on Grant's cast. "The following week the army came through the farmer's village, drafting men to go to war, but they passed over the farmer's son because of the broken leg."

"Well, I'll be safe then, if the Bhutanese army comes looking for soldiers," Grant said. He added a smile so the monk who had just saved his life wouldn't think him rude. *But really*, he thought, *I need time alone to work through my predicament.*

"You are a student?" Kinley asked.

"Grad school. I'm ABD, sorry, all but—"

"Dissertation," Kinley added. "I spent some time in a Western university."

Grant raised his eyebrows. "Well, that explains the accent. Which one?"

"When I was a young monk, I often asked questions my elders felt were out of place. Spent quite a few hours in extra cleanup duty. The senior monk suggested to my parents that my taking a break from the monastery would be better for everyone. Fortunately, I earned the highest marks in my class and was given the rare opportunity to attend Oxford on scholarship."

"Oxford? Impressive." This gentle monk who had saved his life was also a scholar?

Kinley shrugged. "Once I finished, I returned to Bhutan and to monastic life. And you? You didn't travel to the East on a spiritual quest?"

Grant shook his head. "My PhD is in religious studies, but my interests are strictly academic—historical." *Unlike my father's,* he thought. Grant's sole regret concerning his father's death was that he hadn't had the opportunity to prove to him the many ways in which the preacher was wrong where religion was concerned.

"You believe that the nature of religion lies in history?"

Grant's eyelids were becoming heavy from the effects of the doctor's tea, but he willed them open. His body wanted nothing more than to go back to sleep, but this Oxford-educated monk intrigued him. "I'm interested in the early development of Christianity during the first century, and"—he hesitated for a moment as he pondered how to phrase the next part—"how contact with other cultures may have influenced this development."

"What kind of influence?"

"I've been tracking several apocryphal stories." Grant remembered his promise to himself not to reveal too much. In spite of Kinley's Western education, Grant knew that the culture of these monasteries was insular and cautious of outside disruptions. Finding what he was seeking would certainly cause a disruption. He decided to use an example from his first trip to India, rather than his most recent. "For example, some evidence suggests that in fifty-two AD, twenty years after the death of Jesus, the apostle Thomas sailed to India. A small Christian community on the coast in Kerala traces its founding to Thomas and the several churches he established before he was martyred."

"Have you found what you came for?"

Grant shook his head. "I'm still missing a key piece of my research, which is why I'm ABD." He closed his eyes, giving in to the weight of his eyelids.

Kinley rose from the bed. "Sometimes we find not what we are looking for, but what we should be looking for."

Through closed eyes Grant noted that the pain was fading from his body. Whatever was in the tea was working. He heard Kinley's voice as if from a distance. "And I wish you good fortune on your search for the story of Issa."

Grant's eyes snapped open.

The monk responded to the look of shock that Grant knew was plastered over his face. "You spoke aloud at night during your period of unconsciousness. Gave us quite a fright at times."

Grant's pulse quickened. *How much did I say?* He'd planned to reveal that name carefully, especially after the monks at Himis clammed up at the mere mention of the Indian saint.

"Ah, yes," Kinley continued, "the legend of a boy on a journey through India seeking answers to his questions, much like you."

Grant forced his face to relax. "You know the story of Issa?"

"Rest now. Karma's medicine will help you sleep until tomorrow." Kinley bowed from his waist and left the room in a flurry of orange robes. His apprentice, who had been standing so quietly in the center of the room that Grant had forgotten he was still there, followed him out.

Grant wanted to call after Kinley. Did the monk know the importance of the Issa story, that it could answer one of Christianity's great mysteries? *A mystery that would challenge everyone's assumptions of how the religion came to be.* Could it be possible that the evidence he'd been searching for—the evidence that his colleagues at Emory didn't believe existed—was here in this very monastery? Despite the flurry of questions swirling in his mind, the narcotic effects of the tea finally won the battle, and Grant slipped into unconsciousness.

CHAPTER 4

GATEWAY BUSINESS PARK
BIRMINGHAM, ALABAMA

TIM HUNTLEY'S FINGERS stabbed at the keyboard. He used only the first three digits of each hand, but he entered code so quickly that the lines scrolled down the twenty-inch monitor as fast as he could read them. For the past three hours he'd sat military straight, immobile from the wrists up. He'd found the glitch in the program at five AM. Now it was just a matter of working around it. His coworkers had spent most of the past week searching for the bug. That was when his boss called him onto the project. Only he was smart enough to fix the issues the rest of them couldn't understand.

He heard their voices as they filed into the cubicles, laughing and recounting their Saturday night activities. Tim always arrived first to the single-story, red brick building. He slept four hours a night. Only weak-minded people needed more than that, he knew.

"Yo, Tim. Bring the pics?" Johnny Meckle poked his fleshy pink face over the front of Tim's cubicle. Johnny regularly complained to Tim about his difficulty in meeting the "hot babes," as he put it. Tim tried to explain that if he washed his hair, lost some weight, and stopped talking about his programming prowess, he might have better luck. Johnny was two years older than Tim, but he followed his younger colleague around like a groupie. He hadn't changed at all since grade school. The two had been friends when they were kids, until Tim was forced to move away during his sophomore year of high school—after the trial that changed everything.

"Check your email," Tim replied.

"That's what I'm talking about! Hey, y'all, come look at this."

The other six staff members of Information Systems Group gathered around Johnny's cubicle.

"Ewww!" drawled Elizabeth, a twenty-six-year-old data clerk who stood a full head taller than Tim and wore oversized glasses that made her look like a giant bug from a sci-fi movie. "What *is* that? A pig?"

"A wild boar. Tim shot it when we were hunting yesterday." Johnny's face, illuminated by the monitor's blue hue, was giddy with excitement. "Just look at those tusks." Johnny gesticulated with both hands. "Must be six inches. He could have killed us, if he'd charged. Right, Tim?"

"Sure." Tim returned to his work, but he had difficulty concentrating with the stares of his coworkers. The hair on the back of his neck stood on edge.

"Tim was in the Special Forces, you know."

"So we've heard." Elizabeth flipped her dirty blond hair and proceeded to her cubicle.

"Yeah, Afghanistan, Iraq, places like that," Johnny told the remaining five.

Tim tried to look busy, wishing his officemate would shut up. He was starting to question whether reconnecting with him had been a mistake. Tim had moved back to Birmingham two years ago. Two decades had passed since they'd seen each other, but Johnny was easy to track down. He was living in the same neighborhood they grew up in and saw his parents every Sunday night. The only good part about the reunion was that Johnny had turned Tim on to the New Hope Church. Tim hadn't missed a single Sunday since moving back to Birmingham. He sat in the front row every week. Now, however, he regretted having told Johnny about his military experience. Most of what he'd done was classified, but he had a few spectacular stories of mayhem from the front lines to share. But Johnny had been a loser when they were kids, and he was an even bigger loser now. Unfortunately, Johnny was the only one who'd hunt with Tim. At least hunting and blowing up homemade pipe bombs in the woods made time with Johnny tolerable.

Tim opened the metal drawer under his desk and removed a tube of Chapstick from the five he kept handy. His lips were cracking again. Even though he'd applied lotion to his face and arms before he left the house, the itching began to crawl across his skin. His fucking eczema.

"Tim can't talk much about it, though. Top secret stuff and all," Johnny continued. "He was showing me some of the techniques they used to take down the terrorists. Our hunt was just like a real military op, right, Tim?"

The sides of Tim's neck flushed. Without looking at the others, he knew they were watching him with skeptical expressions. Judging him.

"Yeah, something like that," Tim said. He began typing again.

Why did Johnny have to broadcast everything told to him? Tim began to have reservations about including Johnny in the plan he'd been hatching. Johnny was a true believer, but he was dumb. Yet Tim couldn't accomplish the plan on his own. Tim had been taking precautions, playing down his military experience, for example. He'd even kept a lid on his political and religious ideas around the office—ideas that had gotten him fired from his last job in Little Rock.

Tim had never been at home in the business world. The military should have been his career. And it had been, until a misunderstanding with his sergeant. The accusations. The bullshit. The early discharge handled quietly so that the Army would avoid embarrassment with one of its elite spec ops intelligence operatives. Having to return home to live in the apartment above his mom's garage had been the ultimate insult. He knew in his bones that God had greater plans for him. Now he was stuck in a glorified warehouse in the dark with these other losers, working in the back office for a medical data processing company. He could do his job in his sleep, but the pay was good, and he needed the money for his plans.

"Hey, Tim, buddy," a voice from behind him said.

Johnny ducked into his cubicle, while the others hurried to their stations.

Tim swiveled his chair to face Duncan Summers, vice president of ISG, his boss. Duncan towered over Tim, who remained seated. Even if he'd stood, at five foot six and a half, Tim would only have reached Duncan's goatee. Tim's relative height disadvantage to his boss didn't bother him, though. He knew that his muscular build was far superior to the taller man's. He'd snapped the necks of men taller than Duncan.

"Just reviewed your code on the new financial modeling package. Nice work solving the compatibility problems with our reports. We'll implement it in November—two months earlier than planned." The slap on Tim's shoulder radiated a heat that rose to his face. "Great job, big guy!"

"No problem," he replied.

Tim swung around to his desk. He removed the cap to a ballpoint pen. While he used one hand to scroll through the window of code on his screen, he used the other to scrape the edge of the cap across his forehead where the tingling was quickly developing into an itch. He worked the pen cap along the permanent crease between his brows. His mother had offered to pay for Botox during his last trip to the dermatologist for his eczema. She'd said he was "too young for such worry lines," but the last thing he wanted was to look like his frozen-faced slut of a mother. Though she'd never remarried after his father's death, she'd always brought home plenty of men. Anyway, he thought, his face gave him a serious look, and that's what he was: a serious man.

"So, how's the project going?" Duncan was still there, leaning down, his cheery voice now inches from the back of Tim's head. Tim could feel the humid breath on his neck.

"Fine."

"Great. Just great. Keep it up, buddy."

Tim paused the scratching of his forehead. Out of the corner of his eye, he caught Elizabeth peeking around the edge of her cubicle, her nose wrinkled in disgust. He opened the metal drawer an inch and dropped the pen cap inside. For some reason, Duncan still hovered over his shoulder. His boss seemed suspicious, checking on him.

Then a delicious thought sprang to his mind. A thought that caused him to lick his chapped lips, tasting the waxy strawberry flavor. A thought that caused him to forget his itchy skin.

Duncan was close enough to stick with the eight-inch commando knife Tim kept in the back of his desk drawer, behind his Chapstick. In seconds he could gut his boss, just like he'd done with the hog after he'd shot it. *Would Duncan's innards stink as bad as the boar's had?*

But then, Tim knew that killing his boss wasn't part of God's plan for him. No, God had something much bigger in mind. After three months of preparations, all the pieces were finally in place.

CHAPTER 5

———✧———

PUNAKHA DZONG, BHUTAN

I'VE GOT TO GET OUT OF HERE, Grant thought as he dropped the handmade wooden crutches on the stone floor. Supporting his weight on his quivering left leg, he placed both hands on the bed, twisted his body, and swung the bulky cast up and over the thin mattress. He collapsed on the bed, grunting from the exertion as well as the throbbing in his lower body. His T-shirt was soaked through the back, and he'd only crutched down the narrow hallway once. Karma had finally acquiesced and allowed Grant to use the crutches for the fist time that morning, three weeks since the accident. According to the doctor, Grant was a week ahead of schedule, but that wasn't good enough for Grant.

Karma had spoken to Professor Harold Billingsly several times, updating Grant's concerned mentor on his condition. Billingsly offered to fly over to help with Grant's recovery, but Grant had relayed, through Karma, that he'd prefer the professor use his efforts to obtain funds to extend Grant's dissertation deadline, again.

Grant knew that Billingsly didn't hold out much hope. Most of their colleagues believed he was on some kind of Holy Grail search. Their lack of faith didn't discourage him, though. Like his father's admonitions when he was younger, their resistance only made him want it more.

He pushed himself into a seated position, folded his thin pillow in half behind his back, and took his laptop from the table. The doctor had been beyond helpful, bringing him his laptop, making the necessary calls to cancel his credit cards, and retrieving his passport from the hotel's registration desk, where he'd left it for safekeeping the day of the kayaking trip.

While Grant waited for his computer to boot up, he reflected on the hours he spent each day talking with his new friend Kinley. The monk entertained him with ancient Bhutanese tales. Grant's favorite was one about the Buddhist master who flew on the back of a tiger to a mountainside cave. Their conversations were often like epic tennis matches with ideas being hit back and forth like a ball crossing the net at Wimbledon. Kinley continued to enjoy Grant's frustration, however, getting that same twinkle in his eye every time Grant complained about the vagueness of a particular parable or a koan—his Buddhist riddles with no real answers.

Grant imagined Kinley was trying to shock his mind into sudden understanding, but they approached their main topic of conversation, religion, from two very different angles. Whereas Kinley emphasized the importance of one's personal experience of one's religion, Grant viewed this approach as putting too much emphasis on subjective psychological states. The mystical, in his opinion, was only a step away from the supernatural. Instead, Grant believed that the historical and cultural study of religion better explained the competing doctrines of the various religions of the world. Grant had been raised in the church, his father a preacher, but ever since his teen years, he'd rejected the emphasis on the supernatural that was too often present in his own tradition.

What Grant understood now was that he was tantalizingly close to uncovering the key to his research and his future career. After his initial shock at having disclosed in his sleep his reasons for being in Bhutan, he'd been rewarded when Kinley told him several stories he'd never heard before about the mysterious Indian saint Issa. Grant could barely contain his excitement, but when he asked Kinley how he knew these stories, Kinley avoided answering. Yet something in the way Kinley told the stories caught his attention. It was as if Kinley were speaking from firsthand knowledge.

Grant recalled when he first learned the legend of Issa during his second year of graduate school. Russian journalist Nicholas Notovitch, who was traveling in northern India near Kashmir in 1887, made an extraordinary discovery at the Himis monastery in the town of Ladakh—the same monastery

Grant had visited before coming to Bhutan. The ancient manuscript he saw told the story of Issa, who left his home as a teenager to explore the secret wisdom of the sages in the Himalayas. It was said that these wise men knew the mystery behind life and death. After Notovitch returned to the West and published a translation of the text, the original disappeared from the monastery. Notovitch was then portrayed as a fraud and pilloried by the academic community, and the story faded into obscurity.

Grant had wondered if anyone had ever followed up on this disappearance, and he made it his quest to uncover whatever became of the text, but none of the scholars he consulted could recall any further investigation. The whole story had been buried. Based on his original research and the tip he'd learned in India, Grant hypothesized that the Issa manuscript had been moved to another Buddhist monastery sometime after the publication of Notovitch's book in 1894, in order to prevent the world limelight from shining on bucolic Himis. The thought that the treasure may have been moved to Bhutan—to this monastery even—started to torture him. He needed to be up, mobile, and investigating the grounds.

Grant deliberated over whether to come right out and tell Kinley how important the Issa story was to him. But as kind as Kinley had been, could he really trust him? He suspected that Kinley knew more than he was saying, and he was different from the monks at Himis. As an Oxford grad, he understood the workings of Western scholarship, and he had to realize the effect that the Issa legend would have on millions of people. Grant would keep working on him.

A gentle knock on the door interrupted his thoughts. "Come in."

Kinley entered, dressed in neat orange robes and carrying a small fern in a clay pot. "Since you cannot venture outside yet, I brought some of it to you."

"Who knows when I'll be able to climb down those treacherous steps of yours. I can barely hobble down the hallway." Grant was grateful for his friend's attention to the small things, but it was not his style to be over-complimentary.

Kinley placed the plant on the wooden desk by the small window. "Old buildings in Bhutan used ladders between floors because they took up less space than true steps. When our people began constructing staircases, they built them like the ladders to which they were accustomed, steep and narrow."

"How did you carry me up here?"

"You were unconscious." Kinley chuckled.

Something on the fern caught Kinley's eye. He bent close to the plant, tilting his head. He then extended his hand, gently touching one of the leaves. Next, Kinley brought his fingers to his face, rotating them as he studied the curiosity. After a minute, he walked to the window, extended his hand, and waved it slowly. Once his ritual was complete, he turned to Grant. "Ladybug," he said.

"Oh." Grant shrugged. He watched the monk pinch off a couple of dead leaves from the fern and then turn the pot so that the fullest side faced the bed.

"Making lists again?" Kinley asked.

Grant placed the laptop back on the table. He knew he shouldn't take the bait, but he said, "I can't just lie here all day long and watch my breath." Grant admitted to himself that he'd been enjoying learning the tenets of Buddhism in much greater depth than he'd studied at Emory. In addition to filling the long days, his lessons with Kinley had stimulated his insatiable intellectual curiosity. But he found many of the meditation exercises Kinley suggested pointless. "I mean, I have to *do* something," he said, a sentiment he'd shared more than a few times.

"What is it you have to do?"

"Well, my research for one thing." He resisted adding that his research was directly related to the Issa legend, which Kinley seemed to be keeping from him, but then he suspected that Kinley knew exactly what he was talking about.

"And when you achieve that goal, what next?"

"Simple. I'll set new ones, just larger. Publish books. Tenure."

"This will bring you happiness?"

"Without our goals and the plans to reach them, we would still be chasing antelope across the savannah." Reaching forward, he tucked a blanket underneath his cast to elevate his leg. It was starting to throb.

"You are in pain today."

"I do have a broken leg that is set in this nineteenth-century-looking cast." Grant knew Kinley well enough by now to know he could poke fun at the rudimentary cast that made his leg look like a log swaddled in tattered sheets.

But rather than smile, Kinley narrowed his eyes and said, "I wasn't speaking of your leg."

Grant remained silent.

Kinley paced the room, his hands clasped behind his back. He moved not with the nervous energy characteristic of pacing, but with grace, like a dancer gliding across the floor. "One day a student came to his master and asked, 'When the leaves fall from the tree, what then?' The master replied, 'The body is exposed in the autumn wind.'"

Grant knew better by now than to try to dissuade Kinley from delivering one of his koans. He sighed deeply and turned to Kinley.

"Do I bore you?" Kinley asked.

"Look, I've been lying here for weeks."

"You are a superb student, Grant, but your problem is not that you are missing information. You don't need to be taught more. You need to be taught less. You don't need to think more, you need to learn to think less."

"Pretty anti-intellectual of you. Not what I'd expect from an Oxford grad."

"Buddhism is not just about learning the teachings of the Buddha. It's not about believing in a doctrine. The Chinese have a saying—"

"I'm sure they do," Grant quipped, picking at the plaster on his cast.

Kinley chuckled and continued, "The finger pointing to the moon is not the moon."

Grant began to respond and then closed his mouth. After a moment of contemplation, he said, "The teachings and doctrine are not the ultimate truth, they are just a sign pointing in the direction of the truth?"

Kinley smiled. "You want to know more about Issa, correct?"

Grant's heart rate accelerated, but he kept his face passive.

"Issa too struggled with the teachings he learned on his journey through the Himalayas. What he learned differed greatly from what he'd been taught as a child in his homeland. Although his sharp mind quickly comprehended the essence of the teachings, it was only after he practiced what he learned for many months that he reached enlightenment."

Kinley paused when he reached the desk by the window, staring at the fern. "One particular story . . . but my memory is fuzzy on the details. Over twenty years have passed since I read the manuscripts."

"Manuscripts!" The word escaped Grant's mouth in a gasp. "You've seen writings about Issa?"

"We have several."

"Here in the monastery?"

An electricity originating in Grant's core spread through his body. He felt it send pins and needles to his hands and feet.

The monk nodded. Grant thought he detected a spark in his dark eyes. Did his new friend understand the magnitude of what he claimed? Grant longed to talk to Kinley about his theories, but he wasn't ready yet. Instead, he indulged himself by playing out the scenario of how he'd be received back home. All the problems he'd faced since his undergrad years. He could regain the respect of the board, which had admitted him only because of Billingsly. This was the kind of discovery that happened once a generation. He would have his pick at tenure opportunities—Harvard, Princeton, Yale.

The thoughts swirled in Grant's mind like a tornado picking up debris. If Kinley was right, then Grant's theory about Nicholas Notovitch's discovery a hundred and twenty years ago would be proved. Grant's professors at Emory, even Billingsly, all regarded Issa as just one more in a series of quaint legends, but something about the story had always resonated with Grant, something about the teenager searching for answers that eluded him. Grant sided with the common people he encountered in India who believed in the popular legend of Issa over the majority of Western scholars who rejected it. Grant thought back to his own upbringing in his fundamentalist household: the teachings that other religions were the dark work of Satan, that three-quarters of the world's population was going to hell because they didn't "believe in Jesus"—the "my God versus yours" attitude that made Christianity seem like more of an exclusive country club than a religion based on love and tolerance. Now Grant had an opportunity to show the ultimate fallacy of this line of thinking. He would uncover the mystery that would show not just a compatibility among the world's great religions, but a direct historical link.

Then another thought stopped him. He sat up straighter. Kinley referred to *manuscripts* in the plural, but Nicholas Notovitch wrote about a single *text* he'd seen at the Himis monastery, a large book written in Tibetan with an ornate cover.

Trying to keep his voice even, Grant asked, "May I see the manuscripts?"

Kinley shook his head. "Not possible. They are located in our library, on the top floor of the *utse* tower. Even if you could climb the steps, which you can't in your condition, the library is off limits to outsiders."

Grant felt as if his mind were moving in fast forward and the rest of the world was in super-slow motion. Even Kinley's words seemed to be drawn out too long. How could he be this close and not see the texts?

"But—"

A knock on the door interrupted his protest. Kinley opened it. "We will talk about this subject another time. Now we must eat." Jigme entered as silently as ever, carrying a wooden tray with three steaming bowls of food and cups of tea.

Grant stared at the two monks. Kinley couldn't just drop a revelation like that on him and then not allow him to see the evidence. *I've got to convince him to allow me access*, he thought. But watching the elder monk pass the bowls from Jigme's tray, Grant knew that the discussion had ended. As much as he needed to see the Issa writings, he feared appearing too desperate. Surely over time he would be able to reason with a man like Kinley—an Oxford grad who valued the Western world enough to have pursued his education at one of the greatest universities—that there was value in helping Grant complete his dissertation at the very least. *Not to mention the impact it would have on the masses.*

Grant took a deep breath and said, "Three o'clock already? I'm starved. I don't know how you guys eat just two meals a day." He thought he detected the corners of Kinley's mouth turn up ever so slightly.

For most meals Grant ate some kind of vegetable—green beans today—smothered in a bland white cheese sauce with a hint of ginger and served over a bed of coarse red rice. Jigme and Kinley ate the same dish, but theirs also contained several bright red peppers that bled into the cream sauce. Only once did Grant make the mistake of tasting one of these peppers in the hopes of adding some flavor to his food. His lips burned for the next half hour.

The three men continued their meal in silence, Grant sitting upright on his bed, while the two monks sat with legs crossed on the stone floor. Grant observed the peculiar way they ate, deliberately chewing each bite like they were grinding wheat into flour. Watching them chew for a full ten minutes after he'd finished, Grant could no longer contain his impatience. "Okay, I get that by living in a monastery you immerse all aspects of your lives in your practice. Mindfulness, right? Everything you do—cleaning, walking, and even eating—you take your time, but doesn't doing everything so deliberately get old?"

Kinley set his wooden bowl on the floor and answered, "Meditation for us is not just sitting and watching the breath or chanting a mantra."

Grant picked up his laptop from the side table and set it on his lap. He was in the habit of taking notes whenever Kinley launched into something interesting. The monk continued as Grant opened a blank document and began to type.

"Twenty-five hundred years ago, a young man traveled to Sarnath in India, where he spent several days observing the Buddha and his disciples. Confused about the nature of their practice, the young man approached the Buddha and asked him what exactly it was that the monks practiced. The Buddha smiled at the young man and said, 'We sit, we walk, and we eat.' The young man became animated and responded, 'But Master, everyone sits, walks, and eats!' To which the Buddha replied, 'Yes, but when we sit, we know that we are sitting. When we walk, we know that we are walking. When we eat, we know that we are eating.'"

Grant stopped typing. *Clever*, he thought, *but simplistic*. "I get it from an intellectual standpoint, but how is that really different from what I just did? I know that I just ate too, only faster."

Kinley stood, poured two cups of water from a pitcher on the table, and handed one to Grant, keeping the other for himself. "What is water?" he asked, holding up his cup.

The uneven but smooth surface of the tin cup felt cool in Grant's hand. He glanced at the water inside. "Two hydrogen molecules for every one oxygen."

"True, but look deeper. What is water?"

Grant raised his cup and made a show of studying it. He'd figured out the monk's game. He might not agree with the conclusions, but at least he understood. He rattled off, "Water is a liquid now, but it can also change to a gas or a solid. Water doesn't smell or taste by itself, but it can take on the characteristics of the substances within it, just as it can mold into any shape of container."

"Yes, but what is water?"

Grant continued without hesitation, "It's sixty percent of our bodies, and seventy percent of the earth. Water carves canyons, yet sits atop the tallest mountains. It's the origin of life on earth. Without it, we would all die. But with too much," Grant said with a sweeping gesture to the cast on his right leg, "we also can die." He grinned at Kinley, particularly pleased with his last insight.

"Yes, but what is water?"

Grant sighed. He didn't like being stumped. But what answer did the monk want? He stared at the tin cup for several moments and then closed his eyes. He reviewed the lessons he'd learned over the past three weeks. Kinley always brought the discussions back to the personal, to some internal insight. Then it occurred to him. He was thinking about water in general. Instead, he thought about the specific water in his cup.

He began slowly with his eyes closed, "This water was carried here by Jigme, but it originated in the river outside the dzong." The same river, he realized, that had caused him to be in that bed drinking the water. "Before that the water was runoff from the mountain snow, and before that it was vapor molecules in a cloud." He let his mind drift farther back in time, his eyes still closed. "Before the vapor was evaporated into the air by the sun's energy, those molecules were again water, part of some distant ocean or lake." He thought back to the many generations of cycles the water he now held in his hand had been through. These molecules had traveled around the world for millions if not billions of years. Then Grant understood. "And when I drink the water, then all of that history, that energy, will become part of me too, just like the food we ate."

The sound of clapping hands caused him to open his eyes. "Quite impressive. That is looking deeply," Kinley said. A mischievous smile spread across his face. "But there is still more. What else is water?"

Grant frowned, finally out of ideas.

"Drink." Kinley motioned to Grant's cup.

Grant opened his mouth to speak. Kinley cut him off. "No talking. No analyzing. No thinking. Just drink."

Grant looked from Kinley to Jigme who sat silently with a bemused expression on his face as if he had been through this lesson before himself. He drained his cup. The cool, crisp water flowed over his tongue, leaving a faint metallic flavor from the tin container.

"That is water!" Kinley exclaimed.

Then the monk raised his own cup, as if to toast Grant. Without warning, he tossed his water onto Grant's head. Wetness ran down his hair and soaked into his shirt.

"Hey, what are you doing?" Grant sputtered.

"And that is water," Kinley replied.

Grant heard him laughing until his orange robes disappeared at the end of the hall. Jigme gathered the empty dishes with a wide grin on his face and followed his master, leaving Grant wiping the water from his eyes.

CHAPTER 6

EMORY UNIVERSITY
ATLANTA, GEORGIA

TIM HUNTLEY FELT the excitement course through his body. His gloved fingertips drummed to an imaginary beat on the steering wheel.

The rebroadcast of Reverend Brady's sermon crackled over the AM station on the van's radio: "Yes, my children of New Hope, you, *the Believers*, will be saved. But do not let down your guard, for Satan is manipulative. Carry the strength of your faith in front of you like a sword against those who blaspheme against the Word!"

Tim checked his rearview mirror and noted the headlights that were still about fifty meters behind him. The reverend's voice continued over the radio, "In chapter twenty-four of Leviticus, we see the fate of these blasphemers: 'One who blasphemes the name of the Lord shall be put to death; the whole congregation shall stone the blasphemer. Aliens as well as citizens, when they blaspheme the Name, shall be put to death.'"

Stones. Tim smiled to himself. What would Moses have done with the firepower produced by modern technology? "Aliens as well as citizens," the Bible said. Tim had heard variations of this sermon many times. His usual thought was *which blasphemers should go first?* Tonight he knew. Tonight would be the night that he redeemed himself for his past sins. God had so many grand plans for Tim, and this night was just the beginning.

The Army had trained him well. After excelling in the elite combat training he'd received at Ranger school in Fort Benning, his unique intellectual talents were finally noticed and he was selected for INSCOM, the Army Intelligence and Security Command, where he specialized in cyber ops. Tim was a natural with a computer. In another life, he might have been a software mogul, but Tim loved the Army. In the fifteen years he'd spent there, Tim not only got to direct drones at his nation's enemies, locate insurgents through their cell phone calls, and hack into enemy computer networks, he'd been born again. His life since his father's murder had been directionless, but once Tim found God and the Army, his life had purpose. Everything changed again, however, when his career was taken from him.

On this evening, Tim understood that for every setback, God had planned an even greater return.

The hours at the call center job he'd taken when he'd first returned from overseas three years ago had sucked, but the pay was decent. His long-range plans developed slowly, but as they began to crystallize in his mind, he realized that he would need funds to accomplish his goals. He may have left the Army, but he was still a soldier—only now he was working for a higher power than the U.S. government. He was a soldier for God. But then one day, six months into the job, his company announced that their call center was moving to Chennai, India. They offered to retrain many of the employees but told Tim he wasn't "a good fit going forward." His penchant for emailing the other employees his political and religious ideology had resulted in more than one reprimand from his manager. He was happy to leave behind the bureaucracy of the call center, not to mention their bullshit sensitivity training classes. *Shortsighted idiots, all of them*, he remembered.

He had next moved to Birmingham to take a job working in the IT department of the UAB Hospital. That job lasted eight months after similar misunderstandings, plus accusations of missing medications and supplies. But those accusations were never proved.

Tim glanced at the glowing dial of his watch. Just under three hours. Not bad for sticking to the speed limit. The last thing he needed in his moment of glory was for the police to catch him speeding in a stolen van, especially one that contained a two-hundred-gallon plastic tank filled with ANFO in the stripped-out rear passenger area. He and Johnny had stolen the black minivan just after midnight from the long-term parking lot of the Birmingham-Shuttlesworth

International Airport, driven it to their hunting trailer in the woods in the Sipsey Wilderness Area, removed the rear passenger seats, and then installed the tank. This had taken just under an hour, just as Tim had rehearsed it several times. Tim had been hesitant about including Johnny in his plans, but the simple doofus was good at taking orders. Even better, he was a true believer—a lifelong member of Reverend Brady's New Hope Church.

Unlike others Tim had teamed up with over the years, Johnny sat with rapt attention as Tim explained the things that weren't taught in churches because the ministers were afraid of offending the fragile sensibilities of their congregations. Just yesterday, he had explained to his groupie the tenets of British Israelism. Like much of his knowledge, Tim had uncovered this fascinating tidbit during the hours he spent every evening researching on the Internet while others slept.

Tim recounted for Johnny how, after the ten lost tribes of Israel were freed from their captivity by the Assyrians, they migrated to Europe rather than returning to Israel. Therefore it was people like him and Johnny—white American Christians, through their European forefathers—who were the original Old Testament Jews that God had picked as his chosen people. Those who called themselves Jewish today were actually the progeny of Cain. When Tim had read this account, he knew in his heart its truth. He had always felt that he was chosen, and now he understood the history behind that feeling.

After Tim had read Reverend Brady's new book for the second time last month, he emailed the minister links to this same research. Brady's book had spoken to Tim, especially the predictions that the End Times were near. When Tim read the chapter about the Book of Revelation predicting that the rebuilding of Babylon would occur before the Second Coming, a chill had crept along his spine. Ancient Babylon was located in modern-day Iraq, and Tim had been part of an operation in that area and had seen firsthand the American efforts to rebuild the city. An hour south of Baghdad, the U.S. military had established Camp Babylon early in the occupation. Tim had been shocked to learn that the huge palace behind the high wall in the center of the city was Saddam Hussein's attempt to reconstruct Nebuchadnezzar's palace. He had relayed all this to Brady in subsequent emails, but he hadn't yet received a reply. The reverend was a very busy man.

Tim glanced in the rearview mirror at the tank in the back of the van. He had practiced for the past two weeks getting the mixture of ammonium nitrate and fuel oil, or ANFO, correct. The recipes Tim had downloaded from the Internet each differed on the proper ratio of fertilizer to fuel. He knew that fertilizer alone, which he'd been accumulating and storing in a mini-warehouse for the past three months, could be detonated with a blasting cap, creating a powerful explosion. But pure fertilizer tended to absorb moisture, making detonation unpredictable. His mission wouldn't tolerate unpredictability. Adding the fuel oil in a precise amount solved that issue. He wished that he'd had access to C-4 like he did in his Army days, but he was confident that the ANFO would be just as effective.

Reaching to the dashboard for his smartphone, which also doubled as a GPS receiver, Tim noted that the blinking dot of his destination was just a few blocks away. The campus streets were quiet, as he'd expected them to be at four AM on a weeknight. When he slowed to turn onto Clifton Road, he again caught the headlights in his rearview mirror. The vehicle tailing him followed his turn into the heart of the Emory campus.

He clicked the radio off. He needed to concentrate. Passing the sign for the Rollins School of Public Health, he took the immediate left onto Michael Street and then parked the van on the right curb in front of the complex of beige buildings that made up the main campus of the Centers for Disease Control. He immediately cut the ignition and the lights. Tim glanced into the rearview mirror and smiled. Johnny was no longer behind him. He'd turned his Ford truck onto Houston Mill Road where he would wait, just as Tim had instructed him to do. If they were being watched, no one would've guessed that they worked together.

Tim clicked off the phone and stuffed it into his pocket. From the backpack, he then removed the electronic timer. He'd preset the timer for one hour. Tim then searched the floor of the front seat for anything that might have fallen out of his pack.

"No evidence left behind," he mumbled. The heat from the explosion should incinerate everything, but those FBI forensic guys were crafty.

Next Tim leaned between the two front seats and attached the electronic timer to the two wires coming from the large tank. Building the timer had been child's play. When the red LED lights on the timer reached zero, an electrical pulse would travel from the battery across the wires to the detonation charges duct-taped to the container of ANFO. The results would be spectacular.

He reached a gloved finger for the green button on the timer. Then the itching started. At first Tim felt a slight tingle on his left forearm. Quickly it spread to his right. His fucking eczema. He'd applied his lotion when he'd suited up earlier, but it didn't matter. The tingle morphed into a full-fledged burn. Tim imagined the scaly surface of his skin cracking like clay mud drying in the summer sun. The desire to scratch became overpowering, but he didn't have time for that. The streets were clear and the buildings dark. Clenching his jaw, he stabbed at the timer.

1:00:00.

59:59.

Before opening the van door, Tim confirmed that the van's interior dome light was off.

57:48.

57:47.

Stepping into the night, he blended into the shadows in his black cargo pants and black wool sweater. He was well-concealed, but what was he thinking wearing wool? He pulled off his gloves, stuffed them in his pockets, and raked his fingernails across his forearms as he hurried by the buildings that housed the CDC.

Atlanta was such a target-rich environment of sinfulness—strip clubs, adult bookstores, CNN, Hindu temples and Islamic mosques, the multiple liberal universities—that deciding which of these to hit first had been difficult. He'd ultimately picked the CDC because of the agency's global research on women's health and reproductive issues, which Tim understood was a code for abortion. Then there were the various genetic experiments and the research into Ebola and smallpox as potential biological weapons that he was sure also occurred there. *This quasi-governmental organization is an abomination,* he thought. These arrogant scientists were playing God, even though they didn't believe in him. That its main campus was embedded in the heart of Emory University, one of the most liberal schools in the Southeast, was an added bonus. He would show them. His mission's purpose was not loss of life but something more powerful: *fear*.

Tim picked up his pace, continuing to block out the itching with sheer force of will. Tonight would start a new and more purposeful chapter in his life. He found Johnny's pickup around the corner, just where he'd told his childhood friend to park. Johnny might be a doofus, Tim thought, but he was reliable.

English Literature Professor Martha Simpson woke up and reached for the cell phone on the bedside table. She squinted against the glare of the blue light to read the time: 4:45 AM. The man sleeping next to her lifted a corner of the flannel sheets and rolled it tightly to his chest. Using her phone to light her way, she found the armchair in the corner of the room where her midnight blue suit lay folded. As she quietly dressed, she studied the figure snoring under the bunched-up blanket.

Harold Billingsly, holder of the distinguished Winchester Professorship of Religion, was the first man she had dated since her husband had died suddenly of a heart attack last year. She'd been determined to take things slowly and was surprised to find herself here in his town house in the center of the Emory campus on the night of their fourth date. She knew that Harold had been divorced for three years, and his distinguished looks and engaging demeanor had intrigued her for years. He'd been sweet to her after Arthur's death, and their relationship developed naturally. Still, she felt uncomfortable having slept with him so soon. Martha was unsure what relationships in your late forties were supposed to look like.

After she kissed Harold on the forehead, she tiptoed down the hardwood steps to his front door. The cool autumn air woke her fully. She wrapped her red pashmina around her neck and headed down the sidewalk toward the Michael Street parking deck, where she had parked the night before. She was anxious to make it back to her apartment to tend to her cat, who surely would be wondering where she was. She'd have plenty of time to prepare herself for the day's classes.

CHAPTER 7

—⟨∞⟩—

PUNAKHA DZONG, BHUTAN

G RANT TAPPED HIS FINGERS on his cast while he pulsed his healthy left foot
to the same imaginary beat. He felt as jacked up as he used to feel when
he chased NoDoz with Red Bull while studying for exams. But today he'd only
consumed a single cup of tea with his ten o'clock breakfast an hour earlier.

He lay on a granite knee wall, which surrounded the single tree in the center of the dzong's flagstone courtyard. The journey down the tall, narrow steps
from the second floor of the monastery had taken every bit of his energy, but
he was pleased that he'd been able to make it down three days in a row. The
October sun cast a golden glow behind his closed eyes. Grant tried to pay attention to the path his breath took as it entered his nostrils and filled his lungs,
like Kinley had taught him, but his mind wasn't cooperating today. Not only
did the chatter of a British tour group taking pictures inside the dzong distract
him, he had too much to think through.

After a week of not-too-subtle requests, he'd finally convinced Kinley to
show him the Issa manuscripts, and Grant thought that surely today would be
the day. Grant knew that his new friend was risking a lot by taking him to the
library, which was off limits to foreigners. Unfortunately, Kinley had insisted
that the texts remain there. Bhutan had stringent laws against removing cultural artifacts from the country, with the penalty being a long prison term in
a primitive jail cell. In an attempt to preserve its bucolic Buddhist culture and
to avoid the pitfalls Nepal had experienced, the government even strictly limited the number of tourist visas granted each year. Grant was confident he

could work around this problem. Maybe he would lead a group of distinguished scholars back to study the texts.

Even through his closed eyes, Grant could picture the nearby utse tower, rising from the courtyard like a watchtower overlooking a fortress. Similar to the rest of the dzong's architecture, the tower's stone walls were stark white, accented with hand-painted wood molding in vibrant reds and yellows, but unlike the other buildings, this tallest one was capped with a gold dome. And the library on its top floor possibly held the treasure Grant was banking his career on. If authentic, the texts would answer one of the great puzzles of the New Testament, and that answer would alter people's understanding of Christianity. A small voice in his head told him that such a revelation would be disturbing, even threatening to many people, but that wasn't his concern. His job was to uncover the historical truth.

The anticipation began to build within him. Soon it ran hot through his veins. The possibilities spun in his head: *These must be the texts related to the book that Nicholas Notovitch uncovered more than a century ago.* He imagined the shock that Professor Billingsly would display when he called to explain the discovery. Early on, Billingsly had encouraged Grant to pursue other topics for his dissertation, but once Grant had made a decision, no one could shake him from his course. Now he would finally show his mentor that his pursuit hadn't been in vain.

Waiting for Kinley to finish teaching his morning class to the younger monks was difficult for Grant, but lying out in the sun was far better than being confined to the small cell of a room he'd been living in all these weeks.

"That doesn't look very comfortable," said a female voice with an American accent.

Grant opened his eyes and blinked from the midday sun. When his vision adjusted, he noticed first the mass of curly black-as-night hair draped around a Nikon camera lens.

"Often sleep in monastery courtyards?" she asked from behind the camera.

Propping himself on his elbow, he knocked on his cast. "Not too mobile right now."

Now that he was upright, she was no longer backlit by the sun. He immediately noticed her unusual sense of style: hiking boots, black sweatpants with an expensive-looking violet silk scarf twisted around her waist, faded tie-dyed T-shirt under a lime green fleece, and various multicolored beaded bracelets on both wrists. No watch.

"Make the cast yourself?" She laughed as she continued to photograph him.

"I might as well have." He smiled and pulled off a dangling chunk of plaster that had peeled from his picking it out of boredom. "My medical options were somewhat limited. Broke it kayaking on the Mo Chhu."

"Impressive."

"Not really." He cast his eyes to the stone pavers on the ground. "My guide died." The pain of his failed rescue attempt still weighed on him most nights as he struggled to sleep.

"I'm sorry." She lowered the camera, reached out with her free hand, and touched his cast. A smile spread across her face. "Bet it's hard to go to the bathroom."

Grant paused, unsure how to respond.

She extended her hand. "Kristin Misaki, by the way."

Grant shook it for a moment longer than he should have, reveling in his first touch of the opposite sex in many weeks. Her grip was stronger than the delicate bones in her hand suggested, and he noted that she didn't release his hand until he did.

"Grant. Grant Matthews."

"Well, Grant Matthews, what brings you to the other side of the world, other than the superb medical care?"

Grant gave a vague description of his research in India, delighted to have a young, attractive woman for company. As he spoke, she hopped onto the knee wall and sat cross-legged next to him. He noticed a two-inch-wide strand of burgundy hair nestled in among her natural jet black locks. Like her hands, her face suggested a delicate bone structure, but she held his gaze as confidently as she'd held her grip. Her eyes shone with an intense blue that one might find in a person of Scandinavian descent but were shaped like the Asian heritage her last name implied. While the hair and the clothes said "artsy" to him, not his type—too much unpredictability and drama—she was stunning. He tried not to stare.

When he finished describing his journey, she asked, "So, religious studies PhD—planning on becoming a priest?"

"Me, a minister?" He laughed. The image of his father immediately popped into his head: the flushed face berating his parishioners about the consequences of their sins and frightening them with his mythology of the End Times with the same sanctimonious tone he used to hound Grant at the dinner table. He forced the memory out of his mind.

"No, I'm strictly an academic. Research and writing. Maybe teach some, if I can get around my whole public speaking problem." The words slipped out before he could stop them. Something in the directness of her gaze made him forget about his internal censor. Admitting a weakness like that was not the way to impress a woman.

"A speaking phobia," she said, as if turning over in her mind what this said about him.

"Oh, it's not a phobia, I mean, I'm not even that bad at it. I just prefer one-on-one discussions where I can delve into the issues deeper with a person."

She smiled at him like she wasn't totally buying it.

He decided to change the subject. "So, Kris, how did you end up here?"

"I'd prefer you not call me that. Only my sister called me Kris."

"Sorry, Kristin," Grant said, taken aback. He noted the use of the past tense but decided not to pry.

She tossed her hair from her face and toyed with one of the silver elephant earrings that dangled from ears that, to Grant's surprise, only contained a single piercing each. "Travel writer."

"Professionally?"

"Freelance for several magazines."

A writer. So, he was correct. The artsy type. "Must be a tough life, never in one place for long."

She shook her head. "Don't have to answer to anyone, and I can pick up and go at a moment's notice."

"Isn't it lonely?"

"Never needed someone to take care of me." She winked at him. "Plus, I meet interesting people everywhere."

"Sounds liberating." Actually, Grant couldn't imagine a life so unstructured.

"We have something in common." She touched his forearm. "Before coming here, I was in India too. I'm doing an article for *Vanity Fair* on Eastern religious rituals and celebrations." She moved her hand to his cast, where she tweaked a bit of the torn plaster. "Late as usual for my deadline, though."

Grant found the final piece of information unsurprising—attractive and creative, but disorganized. Then he remembered the state of his own work.

"Here, take a look," she said. "Photos of my travels." After fiddling with a few buttons on the back of the Nikon, she handed it to him. "Hit the right arrow to scroll."

Grant stared at the three-inch LCD screen. Although the image was small, the rawness of the emotion grabbed him. An Indian girl in her early teens gazed at him. Her face was feminine, beautiful but smudged with dirt. The expression in her eyes, however, affected him most—a melancholy resignation, the result, no doubt, of having grown up in conditions he couldn't even comprehend. The subsequent photos all featured girls and young women—some introspective portraits and others just details: a hand with dirty nails but intricate henna designs painted on it, the back of a woman whose sari was flowing in the wind like a colorful sail while she bent over to wash her laundry on the banks of a river. He and Kristin had both just traveled in the same country, but she had seen a completely different side of it than he had.

Grant was unexpectedly moved. When he handed the camera back, their fingers touched. Her skin was smooth and warm. "You could be a photographer," he said.

"Just a hobby. I take some shots for my articles when the magazines don't send a professional along."

"So after India, you came to Bhutan?"

"I traveled here to report on the annual Thimpu Tsechu." She brushed her hair from her eyes again. "Heard of it?" She continued without pausing for a breath or an answer. "A festival of elaborate costumes, masks, and dances in Bhutan's capital city. Then I hooked up with a tour group to come here to check out the dzong; it's the country's largest, you know."

As he observed her speak with her hands as animatedly as with her mouth, a realization struck him. This attractive woman and her expensive digital SLR camera could be the answer to one of his conundrums: documenting the discovery that he couldn't take with him.

But he immediately questioned whether he could trust sharing such an important archaeological find with a woman he'd just met. And a journalist, no less. Then he realized that he didn't have to trust her fully, or even confide in her, to get her help. He took a chance. "When you were in India, ever hear of an ancient saint named Issa?"

She shook her head. "Even in my writing, it's difficult to keep straight the bewildering array of Hindu gods and goddesses. Part of your dissertation research?"

"Related to it. The library here may have some manuscripts helpful to me." He didn't need to reveal the true importance of Issa to enroll her in this project. "Want to meet a friend of mine? The monk who runs this place is in one of the temples right now."

"Sure." Kristin surveyed the courtyard. "Looks like my tour group abandoned me anyway."

Grant saw that the only other people in the courtyard were local villagers. He recalled Kinley mentioning that some Bhutanese holy man was visiting the monastery to give blessings in the main temple that day. Kinley had invited Grant to watch, but Grant had thought a breath of fresh air would do him more good than participating in the superstitious ritual.

Kristin zipped her camera into the small daypack slung over her shoulder and jumped to the ground. "Here, give me your hand."

"No, I've got it." Grant attempted to stand, but the weight of his cast swinging off the wall caused him to stumble. He would have fallen to the ground, but she caught him without flinching.

"Sorry about that." His face flushed red. As she straightened him onto his good leg and handed him his crutches, he caught the scent of her hair.

She put her hand on his upper arm. "Might as well earn some good karma by helping out a cripple."

Her teasing felt comfortable to him, as if they'd known each other much longer. Enjoying her touch, Grant led her to the perimeter of the courtyard, which was enclosed on all sides with the two-story dzong building. The top floor contained dorm rooms like his, while the elaborately painted woodwork and large decorative doors on the first floor led to the various temples in which the monks worshipped. Now that the time was upon him, he felt his stomach twist.

With his crutches clicking against the stone pavers, Grant fell behind three elderly ladies with sun-weathered faces. The women walked hunched over from decades of tilling fields. Each carried items of food—bags of rice, fruits, even soup cans—in one hand and Buddhist prayer necklaces made of sandalwood beads in the other. Grant noticed that each woman's lips moved silently as she walked.

"Like praying over rosaries." Kristin nodded toward the ladies.

"You Catholic?" he asked.

"Raised that way."

"But no longer?"

"Not since my sister's death."

"I'm so sorry," Grant said quietly. He contemplated sharing the story of his father's death, but then he quickly shut off that idea. He never discussed that event with anyone.

They followed the women, climbing five stone steps at the end of the courtyard. A pair of ten-foot-tall carved doors, finished in a metallic gold, flanked exterior walls that depicted a mural done in luminous primary colors: an epic battle raged between sword-wielding gods and fiery demons. The women removed their shoes and disappeared inside the temple. Kristin stooped to unlace her hiking boots, while Grant kicked the single sandal off his left foot.

Kristin tilted her head. "What's that?" A rhythmic beating of drums and chanting spilled out of the open doors.

She walked inside the temple, and he followed. Inside, the pungent smell of incense wafted across the room to greet them.

"It's the Mantra of Compassion," he said a little louder than he intended. The harmonic chant of twenty young monks dressed in crimson robes echoed throughout the cavernous two-story hall. Grant had heard the same chant drifting up to his room many times over the past weeks: "*Om mani padme hum.*"

She put her finger to her lips, so he leaned into her. "It's Sanskrit. Originated in India, but it migrated to Tibet. A form of meditation for the monks." He couldn't believe how intoxicating it felt to be close to someone he'd only just met.

"What's it mean?" she whispered in his ear.

"My friend Kinley translated it as 'the jewel in the lotus of the heart.' I think it has to do with the idea that the light of the divine burns inside each of us."

"Beautiful."

"I guess so." His eyes lingered on her face, then followed her gaze around the temple. The rectangular hall was supported by twenty-foot-tall bronze-coated wooden columns around the perimeter of the room. Above them, a balcony circled three of the four sides of the hall. Above the balcony, an elaborately carved and painted wooden ceiling mirrored the decorations on the wood trim on the exterior of the building. On the right end of the room where the balcony ended, six monumental statues rose from behind a stone altar. Grant recognized the one in the middle, the tallest at two stories in height, as the Buddha. The only light came from windows placed high in the second story and from the candles along the altar.

The chanting rose from the monks seated on reed mats in a rectangular formation in the center of the room. With the exception of the young boy, Ummon, whose shy smiles Grant had become fond of whenever the boy brought his morning tea, the monks were mostly in their teens or early twenties, like Jigme, who also sat among them. Every other monk held a drum attached to a twenty-four-inch stick. They beat the drums in unison with a second padded stick while they chanted with their eyes closed. Two elderly monks sat at one end of the rectangle, blowing into long wooden wind instruments that reminded Grant of Swiss alphorns.

Grant could feel the bass reverberation of the drums within his core, and the harmonic voices of the monks filled the air with a weight almost as heavy as the atmosphere of candle smoke and incense. If Grant hadn't had something more important on his mind at that moment, he might almost have found the effect calming.

"That's him." Grant nodded to the only monk in the center group dressed in orange robes. Kinley had explained that orange designated his position of honor as the senior monk present at the monastery. Kinley paced around the group holding a string of prayer beads, which he would periodically shake in front of any of the young monks who drummed out of rhythm from the others.

Grant had to restrain himself from hobbling over to Kinley and begging to be taken to the library. Over the past week, he'd offered to help the monk strategize how to sneak him in, but Kinley had only changed the subject. Then a troubling thought occurred to Grant. *Would Kinley use the villagers' activity in the monastery as an excuse to delay the unveiling of the manuscripts again?*

Grant watched the stream of villagers pass by the seated monks and head to the far left end of the temple, the opposite end from the giant statues. The locals lined up in front of an oversized throne, upholstered in a luxurious purple velvet and perched on a platform six inches above four simple wooden chairs that flanked it. They stacked the food they brought next to a small altar on the side of the platform. Then Grant saw the figure sitting on the throne.

CHAPTER 8

———❦———

EMORY UNIVERSITY
ATLANTA, GEORGIA

ENGLISH LIT PROFESSOR MARTHA SIMPSON pulled her pashmina tighter around her neck. A brisk wind had picked up since she'd left Harold Billingsly's house. Fortunately, the parking deck was just around the corner. She glanced over her shoulder, checking that the maple-lined sidewalk behind her was still empty. She might have been more cautious about walking alone on the city street if it had been midnight, but at five AM the streets were deserted. The only vehicle to be seen was a white van parked across the street by the CDC buildings. *Probably the cleaning crew*, she thought.

Picking up her pace, she recalled the lecture she and Harold had attended the previous evening. She'd found Professor Browning's comments on Leonardo's use of chiaroscuro in *The Virgin of the Rocks* particularly interesting, but she guessed that Harold had gone just to be nice to her. Art history wasn't his passion like it was hers. He'd attended the lectures and museum trips because they excited her. She was lucky to have found a man who was as caring as Harold was. Sure, he was ten years her senior, but at her age that no longer mattered.

Although they had only been on four formal dates, they had known each other for years through various faculty functions. She'd even sat in on some of his lectures. He was an engaging speaker and a first-rate theologian. Lately he'd been excited about a new project that had piqued her curiosity when he told her he couldn't reveal any details about it yet. For some reason, it had to remain secret, but he'd promised she'd be the first to know. Martha wasn't religious herself, but she respected Harold's passion and his views. She was also looking forward to the following weekend, when they had plans to go to his cabin in the mountains of western North Carolina. The fall leaves would be at their peak then, and she was excited to spend some time lounging by the fireplace with him.

She opened her purse, a colorful Vera Bradley, and removed the round tin of Altoids. Trying to pry the lid open, her fingers slipped, and the container of mints tumbled to the sidewalk.

"Darn it!"

The can rolled across the pavement and stopped at the edge of the grass. *At least it didn't open.* The last thing she wanted to do at this hour was to collect a hundred little candies from the sidewalk. She bent over and reached for the tin.

The wall of heat hit her as unexpectedly as if she'd stepped onto the street and was struck by a speeding truck. The invisible force picked Martha up off her feet, sucking the breath from her lungs. The thunder of the explosion rang through her head. Then the dark night around her erupted into an orange inferno, engulfing her world.

Strangely, she didn't experience any pain.

CHAPTER 9

─◦◦◦─

PUNAKHA DZONG, BHUTAN

RECLINING ON THE THRONE at the far left end of the temple was a rotund monk about thirty years old. Unlike the crimson-robed monks Grant had seen during his stay, this monk wore orange, just like Kinley. *Who is this other senior monk?* Grant wondered. He immediately worried about how this development might affect Kinley's ability to take him to the off-limits library.

In spite of his impatience, Grant stood by Kristin and watched as the villagers received a ritual blessing from the orange-clad monk. When the villagers approached the throne, they prostrated themselves three times on the wooden floor. Then they rose, covered their mouths with their left hands, and bowed their heads in front of the holy man. He reached out with a lemon-colored staff and touched their heads while mumbling a blessing with the bored expression of an assembly worker in the middle of his shift.

"Reminds me of when I was thirteen," Kristin whispered in his ear, her hair falling on his cheek, "dressed in a frilly white confirmation dress, which made my mom happy. I knelt at the altar in the cathedral. When I bowed my head, the bishop blessed me."

Grant turned to face her. "You know, many rituals of the Church and its monasteries were patterned after the monarchies they existed under."

"So the bishop's pointy hat is like the king's crown?"

He nodded. "The bishop, as well as the most senior monk here, also carries a pastoral staff, just as the king would carry a royal staff; each wears unique royal robes; each sits on thrones elevated above their minions; subjects kneel in deference to them and bring offerings in the form of tithing to the Church and taxes to the king."

Ten minutes later, the drumming from the young monks in the center of the temple ceased. While the blessings from the holy man on the throne continued, Kinley nodded to the students, who opened the Buddhist textbooks lying beside them. Grant knew that the books were four inches wide by twelve inches long and printed in Tibetan, and that each page contained a single verse from an ancient Buddhist text, which the young monks would repeat until they knew it by heart. He'd seen Jigme's textbook on several occasions. As he and Kristin stood there, a few, including Jigme and Ummon, turned to smile at them, but most stole curious glances at Kristin.

With the students occupied, Kinley strode over to the temple doorway where Grant and Kristin waited. Grant tried unsuccessfully to suppress his excitement.

"You must be feeling better today." Kinley gave Grant's arm a fatherly squeeze.

"I can climb steps safely now."

"Ah, but I see you've brought a lovely friend to visit," Kinley said, bowing to Kristin.

He's avoiding me, Grant thought.

"Well, if Grant won't introduce me," Kristin said, extending a hand. "Kristin Misaki."

"Kinley Goenpo." The monk bowed again, taking her hand. "Japanese?"

"My father's family was from Okinawa, but my mother is pure New England Catholic."

"The combination suits you well."

Kinley smiled. Grant noticed that when Kristin shook the monk's hand, she used both of hers in a familiar embrace. He recalled the thrill he received in the courtyard when their hands touched for a moment longer than was necessary. *She's the touchy-feely type*, he thought.

Grant opened his mouth to suggest that they move outside where they could speak in private, but Kristin spoke first. "Who's he?" She pointed to the throne.

"Lama Dorji. He arrived today. He's the fifth reincarnation of a holy lama who lived several hundred years ago. These people have come to receive a blessing from him."

"Will he be staying here long?" Grant asked.

"Only until the Je Khenpo arrives in two weeks."

"Who's Jay Kembo?" Kristin asked.

Kinley chuckled. "No, the *Je Khenpo* is the head abbot of the *dratshang*, the central monk body; he's our country's spiritual leader, and a friend. Soon, he and several hundred monks will move from the Thimpu Dzong in our capital, where they're based during the summer, back to Punakha. Our lower altitude provides a more temperate climate in the winter months. Lama Dorji and I usually meet a few weeks before to go over logistics."

Grant felt the handles of his crutches become slick with the sweat from his palms. First, some reincarnated holy man had drawn crowds of villagers into the monastery and next hundreds of monks would be returning. He might only have a brief opportunity for Kinley to sneak him into the library.

Then he sneezed. The incense that had seemed pleasant ten minutes earlier now seemed to restrict his oxygen intake. A number of the villagers turned their heads and stared at him.

"Excuse me," Grant said. "Maybe we should step outside?"

Instead of following his request, Kristin stepped further inside the temple, stopping at the wall on their left. She brought her face right up to a section of the mural that covered the wall's entire fifty-foot length. "Hey, this looks familiar."

Kinley moved to her side. "A poor country's version of stained glass."

"Sarnath," Kristin said. "India. A temple there has a similar mural. Down the road from Varanasi, where I was writing my last article."

"Yes, that one is also lovely." The monk waved a hand across the fresco. "The life story of the Buddha."

A coughing behind them drew their attention. Grant felt the stares. Turning his head, he saw that the lama had paused his blessings and was now glaring across the hall toward them. Kinley exchanged a look with him that Grant couldn't interpret, but he felt distinctly uncomfortable.

"Maybe we should move," Grant said.

The lama gestured to the three of them with his staff.

"We're being summoned," Kinley said.

Kristin started off with Kinley in the direction of the throne. "I've never met a reincarnated lama before," she said over her shoulder to Grant, as if that was why she had traveled to Bhutan.

Unsure of the proper protocol when he reached the altar in front of the lama, Grant bowed as best he could without falling over his cast. Kristin did the same beside him. Lama Dorji was indeed about Grant's age but much shorter and at least forty pounds heavier. His round face with its smooth head sat on top of his orange robes like a small pumpkin resting on a larger one.

The lama dipped his head in Grant's direction but ignored Kristin. "So you are the American Kinley Goenpo has permitted to stay in the *goemba*?" He spoke in a singsong voice that was higher-pitched than Grant expected.

Grant opened his mouth to respond but closed it when Kinley rested a hand on his shoulder. His friend replied, "Grant was near death when Jigme and I carried him here, *la*." Kinley said, adding the formal *la* as a sign of respect.

"You are better now, no?" Lama Dorji asked Grant.

"I'm mobile now. The doctor says I can leave soon."

Lama Dorji turned to Kinley. "The preparations for the Je Khenpo and the *dratshang*?"

"I scheduled the juniors to clean the dormitories Friday, *la*."

"What about these disruptions?"

"Disruptions, Lama Dorji?"

"This American and"—the lama flicked his hand toward Kristin—"this woman. I know the temptation that cavorting with these foreigners must hold for you. After all, you did leave the order to study in the West."

When the lama grinned at Kinley, Grant heard Kristin inhale sharply beside him. The lama's teeth were deeply stained and his gums oozed a bright red saliva, giving him the appearance of a vampire in the midst of a kill. The plate on the narrow altar in front of the lama revealed the source of the blood: three leaf-wrapped betel nuts. Grant had seen some of the other monks chewing these around the monastery. Kinley had explained that the betel nuts acted as a stimulant and that they were used much in the way some Westerners chewed tobacco, but in place of the dark, leafy spit produced by tobacco, the betel nut produced a crimson red juice that permanently stained one's teeth over time. Kinley never cared for them, and, he explained, the Buddha taught that if the mind was under the control of narcotic substances, truly transcending one's thoughts and emotions would be impossible.

Kinley returned the lama's smile. "During Grant's recovery, I have taught him a little of our ways. He's beginning to understand the dharma."

"Is your role here to teach Westerners?" The lama's bloody grin vanished. "Their culture is too undisciplined to master our teachings."

Grant felt his face flush. *Is the lama accusing me of being lazy?* Even though the content of their studies differed, Grant put as much energy into his work as these students did. Even in the month he'd been stuck here, he'd made the most efficient use of every minute. When he wasn't sweating through the physical therapy exercises his doctor had prescribed, he was taking notes on Kinley's teachings or brainstorming how he would rewrite his dissertation once he saw the Issa texts. Kinley's grip on his shoulder intensified, indicating that he should keep his mouth closed and let the lama speak. "Look at the dedication of these young ones." Dorji waved to the students, many of whom now watched the two orange-robed seniors and the Americans. "Do you believe that enlightenment can be obtained with a few mind tricks and fancy sayings?"

His voice steady, Kinley asked, "Do you remember the story of the blind men and the elephant?"

A look of irritation flashed across the lama's face, but he did not respond. Kinley continued, "One day, the Buddha asked his students to imagine a group of blind men being led to an elephant and asked to describe it based on touch. One man might grasp the tail and say that the object was a rope; a second might disagree, feeling the leg and claiming it to be a tall column; a third might run his hands along the elephant's side and declare it to be a wall; and the last man might examine the trunk and exclaim that, no, the object was a hose."

Grant suppressed a smile. Kinley had explained to him several times how the Buddha taught that there was more than one path to approach his teachings. He could think of more than a few people from his father's church who could have used this lesson.

"Although you may be the elder in this lifetime, Kinley,"—Lama Dorji shifted in his throne—"I am the fifth reincarnation of Guru Tashi and the senior assistant to the Je Khenpo."

Grant noticed that the lama did not respond directly to the point of Kinley's parable. The rest of the temple was silent, listening to this exchange that seemed calm on the surface and yet had clear undertones of a power struggle that Grant imagined had been brewing for some time.

"I meant no offense, Lama Dorji, *la*." Kinley bowed his head. "I only wanted to illustrate the point that these young Americans have creative, curious minds. They learn differently than our students, and their independent nature may lead them to grasp a different part of the dharma elephant than we do."

"You spent much time away from our culture in your younger years, yes?" Lama Dorji popped a betel nut into his mouth and crunched it between his teeth.

Kinley replied in the same even tone, "I learned a great deal when I was away, but I chose to return to Bhutan, and I am here at the monastery now of my own accord."

"Do you know why we are the last independent Buddhist kingdom in the Himalayas?"

For the first time, Grant thought he detected a tension in Kinley—a slight stiffening of his posture and an edge to his voice that he'd never heard before. "A hundred years ago the only entrance into our country was on horseback or on foot over treacherous mountain terrain. Today we are but a two-hour flight from China and India, the two most populous countries in the world. Through the Internet, our children experience influences beyond our control. It is no longer possible to isolate ourselves from the world."

"So we disregard our traditions?" Dorji reclined further in his throne.

Kinley shook his head. "Why can't we embrace our heritage and open our minds to other Buddhist traditions at the same time? Feel the different parts of the elephant and decide for ourselves which works best."

For the first time, Grant better understood Kinley's teaching methods. Although Grant's knowledge of the differences among the various schools of Buddhism was limited, he had been curious about Kinley's use of koans, which were part of the Japanese Zen tradition, not his own.

"Different teachings?" Lama Dorji shook his head. "Why teach what is inferior? We practice Vajrayana, the highest form of Buddhism." He pointed at Grant and Kristin with his staff. Grant was acutely aware that all eyes in the temple were upon him. The lama's voice took on a tone that was almost sad. "Kinley, I know your intentions are pure, but I fear that your time in the West has polluted you. Those kinds of influences are the reason we choose the monastic life. We isolate ourselves from the temptations of the material world, an existence that the West"—the staff pointed at Grant and Kristin wiggled back and forth—"upholds as their ideal."

Kinley was immobile but for the breath going in and out of his chest. Then he bowed deeply from the waist. "Yes, Lama Dorji, I understand you clearly, *la*."

Grant stared at his friend. *That was it?* He couldn't believe Kinley would just give up.

Lama Dorji leaned forward in his throne and snatched another betel nut from the plate. "You are fortunate the Je Khenpo favors you."

"I am fortunate indeed." Kinley bowed again and then took Grant's arm to leave.

"You, Mr. Matthews," Lama Dorji said, surprising Grant by using his name. "Now that you have healed, I expect you will leave the monastery tomorrow. You will find a suitable hotel in town."

Grant felt a pressure on his chest that made it difficult to take in as much oxygen as he needed at that moment. Afraid of what might come out of his mouth if he spoke, he merely nodded and let Kinley lead them toward the sunlight pouring through the open temple door.

"And Kinley," the lama called across the temple when they reached the door. Every monk young and old watched. "If I were you, I would be careful about who you spend time with." He pointed his staff at Kristin. "You wouldn't want your brothers to get the wrong idea. Talk can spread quickly in the *goemba*."

Once they were outside in the warm afternoon sun, Grant said, "How could you let—"

"To continue the discussion would have served no purpose other than to cause more conflict and to feed my own pride."

"His insinuations don't affect you?" Kristin asked.

Kinley shrugged. "I felt frustration, but I didn't fight it. Instead I let it take its course, flowing through my body. I watched it as I might watch a log float down a river until it disappeared around a bend."

Grant shook his head. Kinley had explained this technique of watching one's emotions and destructive thoughts like one might watch a movie playing inside one's body, but he'd dismissed it as quaint. Such a practice might bring temporary relief, but then he would be resigning himself to a life of always surrendering to other people.

Kinley continued, "Lama Dorji means well. He wants the best for our young monks, just as I do, but he and I have had different life experiences: his life has been shaped by the insular monastic environment, while mine has been influenced by my travels and education. I realized that I was not going to change his opinion today. Further debating my position would only inflate my own ego and bring suffering to us both."

Kinley stopped walking when they reached the tree in the center of the courtyard. He glanced at its bare branches. A smile passed across his lips and his eyes crinkled in the corners. "Anyway, I had already made my decision. This conversation merely solidified it. We can no longer give in to the isolationism that religion often fosters. It is time that the story of Issa becomes public. Tomorrow morning we shall go to the library."

"You're serious?" Grant asked.

"And, Ms. Misaki, please join us, if you can. Your camera will be useful. We won't have much time."

CHAPTER 10

─◆◆◆─

BIRMINGHAM, ALABAMA

REVEREND BRIAN BRADY PORED over the construction plans spread out on the cherry table that could seat twelve comfortably. At the opposite end of the dining room that Brady's wife had decorated in a sea green Venetian plaster, William Jennings, director of operations of New Hope, and Carla Healy, the church's new controller, huddled over a stack of financial spreadsheets. Brady admired the brilliance of his design. The New Hope Community would be his crowning glory, his testament to the power of God's will to accomplish the difficult. The project had brought him the spotlight of recognition from his evangelical brethren. Brady was now one of the leading candidates in the upcoming election for the presidency of the NAE, the National Association of Evangelicals.

Brady had known since the day he had given his first sermon in a small church on the outskirts of Mobile that he was meant for something greater than Alabama. Most men would have been content with the success he'd already experienced as the pastor of Birmingham's largest megachurch, but as the head of the NAE, Brady would rise to national prominence. He could become the next Billy Graham, ministering to presidents and tending to the faith of millions. Eighteen months ago such a goal seemed a distant fantasy, but then he had announced the ambitious plans for the New Hope Community, and now his book, *Why Is God So Angry?*, was the number one best seller in the country.

The current NAE president, Jimmy Jeffries, had not had an auspicious term. The country had further declined under his leadership, and the power that the evangelical movement used to wield in politics had waned to its weakest point in thirty years. Brady would change all that. Rarely was an incumbent president challenged, much less defeated, but Brady knew that his momentum in the organization was building, and Jennings was working to ensure that it would peak right before the April election.

Brady admired the architectural drawings on the large sheet before him: the New Hope Community. What began three years ago as a search for land to build a larger and more modern church had morphed into a six-hundred-acre mixed-use development. The current master plan included not only the new church, which had grown from its current 100,000 square feet to over 250,000, but also a community center, athletic facilities, a new seminary for 650 students, an eighteen-hole golf course, over 200 single-family residences, 350 apartments, and 300 town homes. A retail center with a grocery store, shops, and restaurants completed the development.

For years Brady had dreamed of building a community of the faithful. A community that would literally be centered around the church that he'd placed in the middle of the town square. His architects had visited Charleston and Savannah for inspiration from old southern architecture.

In the New Hope Community, the faithful would gain strength and support from each other, as well as worship, shop, and dine together—all without the corrupting influences so rampant in society today. The development would have its own cable TV system and movie theaters, playing only appropriate inspirational programming. Likewise, the Christian bookstore would carry titles similar to Brady's book that would strengthen rather than confuse the people. Jennings had referred to the concept as Christian Urbanism, a take on the popular New Urbanism developments springing up around the country. Brady loved the term and immediately adopted it as his own. New Hope would be the model for how to turn around the problems of the country. Once Brady unseated Jimmy Jeffries, he would be in position to bring his vision to the nation.

Brady peered across the table at Jennings. His number two was dressed in a gray pinstriped suit that hung loosely from his limbs and a white dress shirt that had stray threads showing around the neck and cuffs from being laundered too many times. A long, sharp nose protruding from a pale face combined with an even longer neck gave him the appearance of an ostrich outfitted in Brooks Brothers. Brady shook his head and then brushed a fleck of lint from the sleeve of his own midnight black Armani suit. He then adjusted the French cuffs on his pale pink shirt so that they peeked out from his jacket sleeve just the right amount. He'd tried to tell Jennings that a low-budget appearance invited low-budget offerings, but his number two just didn't have the flair for style that he had.

Brady tapped his fingers on the table. Jennings and Carla still had their heads stuck in spreadsheets. Brady couldn't tolerate those things. Fortunately, he had Jennings. The growth the church had experienced under the Brady-Jennings partnership surpassed even Brady's lofty expectations: a few hundred members twenty years ago to over ten thousand today. The combination of Brady's charisma and passion for the scripture and Jennings's organizational abilities and attention to detail, along with God's blessing, had worked a miracle.

"These delays are getting annoying. Do we start grading for the town square next month as planned?" Brady asked. They could finish the accounting later.

Jennings looked up. "The bank's attorneys have agreed to the final changes in the loan documents. We should close next month on the first hundred million. Then we'll be able to pay down the line of credit we used to buy the land and fund our initial construction."

"Good. Everything's going according to God's will." Brady gestured to the site plan in front of him. "Let's talk about the layout of the retail center. I was thinking that maybe we should move these restaurants—"

"Brian," Jennings interrupted, "we spoke about this yesterday. Today we need to focus on the financial issues. You can indulge your creative side on Thursday with the architects, but for now we need to reexamine our costs."

"I thought we finished the value engineering last week. Didn't you say that the money from the banks was a sure thing?"

For the first time Carla spoke up. "Yes, Reverend, the loans should come through, but we still need to meet certain fund-raising covenants. I'm concerned that we've tapped out most of the large donors, and the smaller ones have slowed significantly." She pushed several sheets of legal paper in front of Brady.

Not bothering to look at the papers, Brady stared at his new employee. He recalled her resume: a twenty-eight-year-old MBA from Auburn, Carla had worked at a midsized Birmingham accounting firm before tiring of the corporate life and deciding to put her education toward a more worthwhile endeavor. Jennings spoke highly of her skills, but Brady had been reluctant at first because she was an Episcopalian. He didn't even like to think about the blasphemy that was occurring in that church: first women and then gays at the pulpit. Always the practical one, Jennings had persuaded him that they needed more firepower, as he put it, to handle the financial complexities of such a large development.

"Won't the million a month we pull in from our regular donations make up for any slowdown in the capital campaign?" Brady asked her.

"We take in eight hundred seventy-five thousand a month, but our current expenses are just over eight hundred, and that assumes our expenses stay flat, but they've been steadily rising. Just this year our general and administrative expenses are up twelve percent, our homeless shelter sponsorship expenses are up seven percent, and our outreach program is up twenty-five percent."

"Well, we can't cut any of those things," Brady replied. "Certain expenses are necessary to run the church. You have to spend money to make money, Carla. And our outreach programs are doing God's work. If we can't reach out and spread the message of Jesus Christ, then why are we here?"

"I anticipated you might say that, Reverend, so I've taken the liberty of putting together another option." Carla slid a second spreadsheet in front of Brady, which he also ignored. "We should consider phasing in some of the development at the New Hope Community over a longer period of time." She slid a copy of the same spreadsheet to Jennings, who wrinkled his brow as he studied the numbers. "Now, I'm not suggesting that we cut out anything on your plan," she added quickly, "but by delaying some of the projects until the home sales generate substantial income—"

"Delay our development!" Brady boomed. "Child, you don't understand the concept behind Christian Urbanism. Every aspect of this development works together harmoniously, each part supporting the other."

"Reverend, if you would humor me for a minute and just look at the plan." She held up the spreadsheet so that he was forced to take it. "What I propose is to start construction on the church, golf course, and phase one of the town homes first. As this phase sells out, we construct the next one, and when the golf course is completed, we open the adjacent residential lots for sale. This timing allows us to use revenue from the sales to fund the later development, and thus lower our debt."

"But what about the seminary, community center, theaters,"—he leaned over the table toward her—"the restaurants?" He stabbed at the site plan with a finger. "They're fundamental to the entire concept of the faithful living, worshipping, and playing together."

"Once we have seventy-five percent of the residential areas built and sold, then we have the critical mass to support the retail. Let's see," Carla said, brushing her flat brown hair out of her face as she studied the projections in front of her. "We could start construction on the retail phase in about four years."

Brady's face reddened before he exploded. "Four years! But I've promised the congregation an entire community, not just some houses and a church. This option is not acceptable." Brady turned to Jennings. "William, certainly you're not in agreement with this?"

Jennings removed his half-moon reading glasses from his long nose and spoke calmly. "Carla, your numbers here do not account for the income from the reverend's book sales."

With the two older men staring down at her, Carla's neck reddened. "We won't start receiving the first royalty checks for another couple of months, and by then sales may begin to taper off." The volume of her voice dropped to the point where both men leaned in toward her. "I just felt that the revenues from that were too speculative to be a basis for the millions in fixed costs that this project will take."

Brady glared at the young accountant. *The problem with these mainline Protestants*, he thought, *is that they don't have true faith anymore.* Carla put her faith in numbers and computer models, but computers couldn't decipher the will of God. God spoke through prophets, like his one and only son Jesus

Christ, and at times through his faithful servants, like Brady himself. Brady never had trouble falling asleep at night. He guessed Carla did, judging from the dark circles under her eyes. He didn't feel the stress of the unknown or the impossible because he had faith that God would provide the answer.

"I don't mean to be pushy, sir. I just don't want New Hope to turn into another PTL fiasco," she said.

"PTL?" Brady sputtered. "How could you even begin to compare what we're doing to that buffoon Jim Bakker?"

Jennings quickly chimed in, "Carla, I know you didn't mean any offense by that comment. But you're new here. We've been in difficult situations before. No one believed we would raise the money to build the current church either. It's only a matter of timing. We just need to make sure that the book continues on its course. Rick Warren made tens of millions off of *A Purpose Driven Life*. I believe the reverend's book can do the same."

Carla sighed. Brady placed his hands on her petite arm. She obviously didn't see the light he saw. "Carla, are you familiar with chapter twenty-five of Matthew?" he asked.

"Not off the top of my head."

"A man leaves on a journey, putting his servants in charge of his property. He gives the more capable servant five silver coins, and to another less capable servant he leaves one coin. The servant with the five coins invests the money, earning five more coins. The other servant digs a hole and buries his coin in the ground. When the master returns, the first servant brings him the ten coins and receives praise. The other servant then gives his master the original single coin back, explaining that he was afraid to lose the money so he buried it. Chastising the second servant for being lazy, the master then takes the servant's single silver piece and gives it to the first servant, who had ten pieces, saying, 'For everyone who has, he will be given more, and he will have an abundance. Whoever does not have, even what he has will be taken from him.'"

Brady removed his hands from Carla's now sweaty arm, leaned back in his chair, and placed his fingertips under his chin. "So you see, our greatest danger is not in going forward with the project, but in taking the path you recommended."

Carla stared at the table while Jennings gathered the spreadsheets and handed them to her. "Thank you, Carla. We can talk further when I return to the office."

Carla avoided the eyes of both men when she left the room. Brady shook his head. "I told you when you wanted to hire her, William, that a fancy education is no match for faith in the Lord."

Jennings winced at Brady's reprimand. Brady knew that his number two didn't like to be questioned on operational issues, but sometimes he needed to be reminded of who the boss was.

Jennings considered his nail-bitten fingernails for a moment and then nodded. "One negative attitude can foster dissention among many others. Negative energy is a virus we cannot have spread through our organization at this critical time. I'll take care of it."

"What will you do?"

Brady knew that Jennings would bring Carla around. He'd heard the stories of Jennings's reprimands of employees who didn't perform up to his expectations. Brady was happy that Jennings relished that role. Every organization needed a disciplinarian, but Brady was too beloved to fulfill that role himself.

"Simple." Jennings tucked his reading glasses into the inside pocket of his jacket. "I'm going to fire her."

CHAPTER 11

---⸙⸙⸙---

PUNAKHA, BHUTAN

---

*H*OW OFTEN DOES A PERSON *face a moment when he knows his life is going to change forever?*

This question played in Grant's mind as he gazed up at the decorative windows of the six-story, whitewashed-stone utse tower. The low morning sun cast a long shadow of the tower across the flagstones, like a giant sundial representing to Grant the time to grasp his destiny. He thought about the answer to the two-thousand-year-old mystery that might be revealed in the tower above him. He thought about the draft of his dissertation stored in his laptop, which was in the small backpack slung across his shoulders. He thought about the redemption this discovery would bring to him. He mentally reviewed the checklist he'd been writing the past week—documenting the find, emailing the photos and text to Professor Billingsly, arranging for the professional translations . . .

Then he caught up with the mental movie he'd been replaying in his head all morning. Kinley had taught him to monitor what the monk called the cycles of unproductive thinking he claimed Grant was prone to, the repetitive rehashing of future events in his mind. Grant released the breath he held tightly in his chest. The brisk breeze tossed his hair just as it swayed the naked branches of the tree in the center of the courtyard beside him. He continued to breathe, and he relaxed. But then other thoughts intruded: What if all this buildup was for nothing? What if the Issa texts were not as old as Kinley said? What if Notovich's critics were right? What if the story of Issa was nothing more than a legend spun by the creative mind of some Indian writer centuries earlier?

The footsteps behind him saved Grant from continuing that line of thought. His breath quickened when he saw Kinley and Kristin hurrying toward him. Dressed for the cool autumn day, she wore a red fleece over jeans with various multicolored patches that she'd obviously sewn on herself. Her camera was slung over her shoulder. Kinley strode with his hands clasped behind his back, while Jigme followed a step behind.

"So we're really doing this?" Grant whispered to Kinley.

"We cannot allow religious isolationism to govern our actions. But you do understand that what we are doing carries certain risks?"

Grant tried not to imagine what a Bhutanese jail cell looked like. But then they weren't planning on taking anything other than pictures. Surely they couldn't go to jail for that? He nodded. "This is too important not to try."

Kinley smiled. "Exactly what I would have said at your age."

"How are you going to get us up there?"

"Lama Dorji left for a neighboring monastery early this morning. We must hurry before he returns." He turned to Jigme. "Dawa will be sitting inside by the door to the stairs. Please occupy his attention."

A few minutes later, Jigme exited the utse with another monk who appeared to be in his late sixties. After they disappeared around the side of the building, Kinley hustled Grant and Kristin to the stone steps at the foot of the tower's entrance.

"What do you guys have against putting your doors on the ground floor?" Grant asked under his breath.

Kristin took his free left arm, wrapped it around her shoulder, and assisted him up the steps. Grant was proud of the milestone he'd reached that morning—graduating to a single crutch—but he didn't protest the help. He felt the same thrill he'd experienced the day before just by putting his arm around her.

They entered the building through a set of bronze-coated doors. Kinley surveyed the courtyard behind them and then closed the heavy doors with a thud. Inside, Grant noted that as in the other temples in the dzong, a worn wooden floor stretched from one mural-covered stone wall to the other. A single chair stood by a closed door.

Grant nodded to the door. "Top floor?"

Kinley nodded. "The sixth."

Grant started for the stairs while Kristin rushed to keep up with him. When he reached the sixth-floor landing, sweat dripped from his hairline. Kinley brushed by Grant, materialized a ring of keys from under his robe, and unlocked a set of carved doors at the end of the short hallway. The double doors creaked loudly, causing Grant and Kristin both to wince. Grant entered the shadowy room last, stooping to avoid cracking his head on the low frame. Kinley then parted a beige curtain from the room's single window, allowing the sun to pour in.

In the weeks he'd spent imagining the library, Grant expected it to be grander. The room measured twenty by thirty feet and had the musty odor of a closed space that hadn't felt fresh air in years. Dusty Tibetan-style books, narrow and long like the ones he'd seen the students use in the temple, were randomly stacked on crooked shelves and in various piles on the floor throughout the room. He looked around with the eager expression of a miner prospecting for gold in an undiscovered mountain vein.

"Let me see," Kinley said, stepping over several piles of books. "Twenty-two years ago, I was the assistant librarian in the dzong. That's when I first discovered the texts about Issa." The monk ran a finger along one of the shelves, wiping up a line of dust. "Not much has changed." He disappeared around a bookcase at the far end of the room, mumbling to himself.

"How can we help?" Kristin whispered.

"Oh, no help. Around here somewhere," he replied from the other side of the bookcase. "This library doesn't get used much. We keep the current texts downstairs."

The sound of books crashing to the ground startled Grant. "Are you okay?"

"Found it." Kinley reappeared carrying by iron handles a simple pine box the size of a small suitcase. He placed the box on a laminate table that looked like it had been salvaged from a 1970s garage sale but which sat on an exquisitely handwoven carpet.

Grant and Kristin took two of the four wooden chairs around the table. Grant noticed that Kristin sat cross-legged in the chair like she had on the knee wall the previous day. While Grant gazed at the simple box, she reached across him and touched it, as if trying to glean its contents from the texture of the wood. Grant eyed her slender fingers and short but manicured nails as they traced the grain of the wood. As alluring as she was, her need to touch everything reminded him again that she was too much a free spirit.

When Kinley lifted the lid of the box, which had neither lock nor latch, Grant held his breath. He rose from his chair and peered into the open container.

Grant's first reaction was surprise—more Tibetan-style books, seven, stacked on each other. Eighteen inches long by three or four inches wide, the books were individually wrapped in silk cloths of various faded colors. He recalled Notovitch's description of the book he found at Himis: it was larger with an ornate cover.

Kinley lifted a green, silk-wrapped book. He blew off the fine layer of dust from the silk and then slowly unwrapped the book. The cover was heavy and sturdy, woodlike, and the book was as thick as it was wide—about four inches. Kinley opened the cover using the silk so that the oil from his hands would not touch the book itself.

"Well?" Grant said, craning over the table from the edge of his seat.

Kinley stared at the first page for a long minute, then turned to the second page. Grant noticed that the pages, a beige color, were much thicker than normal paper, not really flexible, and seemingly handmade. Each book contained twenty pages at the most.

"Aha," Kinley said, when he turned to the third page. Grant saw some squiggly writing in faded black ink. He bolted out of his chair to stand over Kinley's shoulder.

"It's Pali!" Grant said.

"What's Pali?" Kristin asked.

"An ancient language"—he squinted at the text—"somewhat similar to Sanskrit."

"Can you read it?" she asked.

He shook his head. "Only rudimentarily. I took a year of Pali and Sanskrit, but I had three years of Tibetan: that's the language of the texts I was expecting to find." He turned to Kinley. "Do you have any idea how old these are?"

Kinley flipped a few of the thick pages. "First century, if I'm reading the words correctly."

First century! Grant's mind raced. Judging from the thick pages, it appeared possible, but he feared to hope too much.

"They do look pretty old," Kristin said. Grant flinched when she reached a hand toward the open book.

Kinley gently guided her hand to the table. "I grew up reading the Buddhist canon in its original Pali."

Grant knew that Pali was the language of the ancient Buddhist canon, and it was still in use in first-century India when Issa supposedly lived. The book that Notovitch had seen in the Himis monastery, however, was written in Tibetan, a language that developed centuries later. As part of his research, Grant had theorized that the Notovitch book, if it existed as he believed it did, was like the Gospels from the Bible. The oldest copies of the Gospels in existence were copies of copies of copies written more than two hundred years after the originals. More significant was the fact that the Gospels were written in Greek, although Jesus would have taught his apostles and his followers in Galilee in Aramaic. For decades after his death, stories of Jesus would have circulated first among his followers in Aramaic, and then later they would have been translated into Greek and then written down in various forms. Matthew, Mark, Luke, and John were not apostles of Jesus who had known the historical man, as was the common but mistaken belief. They were men who were part of the later Jesus community who compiled the stories that were in circulation about him and composed the Gospels.

Similarly, Notovitch's discovery appeared to be a Tibetan translation and compilation of earlier sources, sources that would have been in the original Pali language that was in use during Issa's travels in India. Grant had not imagined in his wildest dreams that he might uncover the original writings that Notovitch's book was based upon. He'd assumed those would have been long destroyed or lost, just as the original sources for the Gospels had long ago disappeared. As he stared at the narrow books on the table, he felt his heart pounding in his ears.

"Will someone at least tell me what we're looking at?" Kristin asked.

Kinley replied, "These books detail the journey of—"

"Issa," Grant interrupted. "The Indian saint I told you about yesterday. According to legend he left his home as a teen to seek a secret wisdom from the sages in the Himalayas."

"Secret wisdom. I'm game."

She sat back in her chair but glanced between Kinley and Grant, as if she suspected they were holding back on her. Grant knew that she was smart, and he made a decision to tell her the truth if she asked directly. Part of the problem was that she'd shown up unexpectedly, and he had a carefully laid-out plan for the release of this discovery. *She's a journalist*, he reminded himself.

"So these texts were written by . . . ?" she asked.

Kinley answered, "The monks in India who taught Issa. They were impressed by an unusually bright and receptive student, a student who became well known years later. You see, controversy followed young Issa wherever he went, even after he was martyred."

"Issa was killed?" Kristin asked.

"A story for another time," Kinley said, glancing at Grant. A short time after Kinley had revealed the existence of the texts to him, Grant had realized that the monk knew the truth behind Issa's identity. He'd mentioned to Kinley that until they were published, it might be safer for all of them if this fact remained secret.

"These silks, Kinley?" Grant asked, changing the topic.

"Only a hundred years old or so; they were added later to protect the books, and are changed by the librarian when they deteriorate." Grant noted that many of the other books on the shelves around them were wrapped in similar silks.

"If Issa lived in India," Kristin asked, "and these texts were written in a monastery there, what are they doing here in Bhutan?"

"For several hundred years after Issa's death, the texts remained in the monasteries where they were written," Kinley explained. "But then, as

Hinduism began to reassert itself over Buddhism as the dominant religion in India, the books were collected and sent to a monastery in Tibet. During the nineteen fifty-nine revolt by the Tibetans against their Chinese occupiers, the monks boxed up the contents of their libraries and secretly sent them out of the country with the Dalai Lama, just before the Communists suppressed the dissenters. The various texts were divided and sent to monasteries throughout Nepal and Bhutan,"—Kinley gestured to the shelves of books surrounding them—"where they have sat to this day, largely forgotten."

"What about the book that Nicholas Notovitch saw in the Himis monastery in eighteen ninety-four?" Grant asked.

Kinley shrugged. "In the days before the printing press or computers, it was the practice of the monks to copy by hand the ancient texts."

"As was the case with Christianity."

Kinley nodded. "My guess is that the monks at some point translated these books"—he pointed to the narrow books on the table—"into Tibetan, as they did with thousands of others, and then sent the manuscript out to Himis, where Notovitch saw it."

"But that manuscript is no longer there."

"Yes, a mystery indeed."

Grant considered the treasure laid out on the table before him. While the disappearance of Notovitch's discovery had always been the mystery Grant sought to solve, it was now irrelevant. Grant had evidence of much greater importance. He had the original texts documenting the existence of Issa.

"Does Lama Dorji know about this?" Kristin asked.

Kinley shook his head. "We have other interesting writings in here as well, but if they do not relate directly to the Buddhist canon, then he sees them as a distraction from our mission." He gestured to the shelves around him. "So they sit here for hundreds of years collecting dust."

Grant was beside himself thinking about the ramifications of these texts. That such a treasure could remain sitting in the monastery forgotten was beyond something his curious mind could relate to. "Kinley, you know that these texts need to be in a university or museum, where scholars can study and analyze them."

"I do, but Lama Dorji will never give his permission, and the Je Khenpo will need to be persuaded." Kinley rested his fingertips under his chin. "Something I will consider."

"Would international pressure from academic institutions persuade the Je Khenpo?"

"Possible. It would have to be handled delicately." The monk turned to Kristin, who was craned over the table studying the writing. "The camera?"

"Oh, yeah." Kristin glanced to Grant as if she were going to ask, *What was so important about Issa that these books deserved to be in a museum?* The anticipated question never came. Instead, she unzipped the case from around her Nikon and removed the lens cap.

Kinley closed the wooden cover of the narrow book and lay the silk next to it. Kristin took pictures from several angles using both a flash and the sunlight that splashed across the table from the single window. Using the scarf, Kinley gently turned the pages as she photographed them.

The whole time she photographed what must have been more than a hundred pages of text, Grant shot numerous glances to the closed library door. *How much time do we have?* His ears were alert for any sound of a person climbing the steps, but he only heard the clicking of the camera.

When Kristin finished, he turned to Kinley. "Will you translate for us?" His fully charged, thin white laptop was open in front of him. His fingers quivered above the keyboard. The three years he'd spent studying Tibetan would be of no use to him with these texts. Until he returned to Emory with Kristin's photographs, he would have to rely on Kinley yet again.

"I am ready," Kinley said, turning to the first page of the first book, "but are you prepared?"

"Prepared? For heaven's sake, Kinley. This has been all I've thought about for the past five years. It's hard to even contemplate."

"That's what I want you to consider. When we walked up to this room, how many steps did we climb?"

Grant felt the familiar frustration with his new teacher rising. "Six floors, must have been well over a hundred steps, but I don't see what climbing steps has to do with anything." Grant folded his hands in his lap.

He knew the more anxious he appeared, the longer Kinley would draw out his lesson.

"To reach this room, to read these manuscripts of Issa, you had to climb many steps," Kinley said patiently. "Each step brought you closer to this table, but once you used a step, you left it behind. You left it not in a disparaging way that the lower step was now beneath you, but instead you left it knowing that it had served you well, a necessary step to get where you are today."

A stillness settled over the room as Kinley stared at Grant, obviously waiting for his reaction. Even Kristin, who seemed to always be toying with the objects around her, sat quietly.

"Okay." Grant thought back to one of Kinley's earlier lessons and the cup of cool water that the monk had dumped on his head. "If I hadn't been raised in a fundamentalist household, if I hadn't gone to grad school, if I hadn't broken my leg on the river, then I wouldn't be here today." He squinted at Kinley. "So I need to be more respectful, or maybe forgiving, of my own past, even the painful things, because those events have brought me to these manuscripts?"

Kinley nodded. "Our lives are interconnected with the actions that came before as well as our environments, but there is still more."

"There always is."

Kinley pressed on. "A Chinese Zen teacher once said, 'When you are full of doubt and uncertainty, even a thousand books of scripture are not sufficient; but when you truly understand, even one word is too much.'"

Grant pondered the saying for a moment. "These texts are nothing more than yet another step in my journey?" *But how can that be?* he wondered. If Kinley's translation contained the same revelation that the Notovitch's manuscript did, then this was the type of find an academic experiences once in a lifetime if he or she is lucky. He imagined the effects it would have on the history of religion.

"And as with your previous steps, someday you will move beyond this one too." As if reading Grant's mind, he added, "As a historian, Grant, you might be adept at discovering the *what*: what happened in Issa's short life."

"Of course." *Isn't that the point?* he thought. In this case the *what* answered a crucial question that had remained unanswered for two thousand years.

"The *what* can be useful, yes, just as the *how* that scientists teach us can be." The monk caressed the silk covering the first book. "The importance of these texts goes beyond history. You are missing a bigger mystery here."

Grant scrunched up his brow. *How can that be?*

"The *why*," Kristin said.

Kinley nodded. "Just as Issa uncovered an ancient wisdom on his journey, Grant, you must do the same with these texts. Ask not just what, but why. Religion is not about what has happened in the past, but about what is happening to us in the present."

Grant sat without moving, his gaze on the table in front of him. He was suddenly struck by a memory from his early adolescence. A memory that seemed entirely out of place at this moment: he was lying in bed late at night, praying that the divine light would shine on him and remove his doubts so that he could believe just like the others around him did. He looked at the faded black lines of the ancient text in front of him. Then he raised his eyes, looked between Kinley and Kristin, opened his mouth to speak, but then closed it without saying anything.

"Let us see how good my ancient Pali is, shall we?" Kinley opened the first book.

Grant's fingers flew across the keyboard as Kinley began to translate the story of Issa.

CHAPTER 12

⸎

RAJASTHAN, INDIA
TWO THOUSAND YEARS AGO

H<small>AD HE RUINED</small> his life?

Staring into the glowing embers of the campfire as he lay on his reed mat, Issa couldn't push the question out of his mind. In leaving on this journey, he had gone against the wishes of his parents and teachers. But he needed to find the answers. Now, he wasn't even sure of the questions. Thoughts swirled in his mind much like the hot, red sand had swirled around his legs as he had walked alongside the caravan earlier that day.

An unfamiliar noise from the far side of the camp startled him. His heart racing, the teenager sat up.

Silence.

The other dozen men slept peacefully around him. Probably nothing to worry about.

Issa settled back on his mat, tightening the wool cloak around his bony shoulders against the cool desert wind, the *ruach*. Breathing deeply, he found comfort in the aroma of roasted wood. Why had he been so jittery? Maybe it was the strange land, the different customs. Far from his own people, he now slept beside Egyptian beer merchants and Chinese spice peddlers.

When he had crept out of his parents' modest stone dwelling that night many months ago, he had felt full of confidence. His parents expected him to follow a life he wasn't ready to accept. Although he enjoyed the attention of the families who knew of his reputation and brought their daughters to meet him, he had too much to learn, too much to experience before he was ready to marry. He was only fourteen, after all.

A loud grunt followed by a wet snorting sound returned Issa to the present. That was it—the noise that had startled him earlier. The camels.

The animals had acted strangely the last few nights. Camels did not rank high on Issa's list of God's creatures. Loud, smelly beasts, they enjoyed biting his shoulder if he ventured too near during the endless daily walks. Keeping outside biting range didn't guarantee escaping their displeasure, either; they would just as happily spit a glob of warm mucus down his neck. When the merchants traded the more civilized horses for the camels last month, they had told Issa that these disagreeable animals could not only carry heavy packs on their large hump through the searing desert heat but could also remember the exact path walked months earlier. Tonight they just kept him awake, and tomorrow he faced yet another day in the scorching sun, shuffling across the endless red landscape through dried grasses, thorny bushes, and scraggly trees.

Once the camels settled down, the night stilled. Even the insects decided to sleep. As Issa stared at the heavens dotted with the faint light of countless stars, the questions played again in his mind. He squeezed his eyes closed and pushed away the doubts. He knew he was destined for something larger, but what, he wasn't quite sure. He had made the right decision, he repeated to himself.

As a child, he had enjoyed listening to stories from the merchants who traveled through his village, bringing tales from the East, along with their brightly colored silks, brilliant stones, and pungent spices. These men radiated an energy that eclipsed their gruff and uncultured mannerisms, an energy absent from the teachers who didn't appreciate Issa's unique perspectives.

He was a smart, if sometimes unruly student. He may have asked too many questions, but what was the point of learning if not to question? Unfortunately, his elders saw his probing as disrespectful. During his travels, he would find the answers he sought.

Another sudden bout of coughing and spitting came from the camels. Issa jolted upright. Brushing his matted black hair from his face, he peered into the dense night. The camels were only thirty paces away, but he couldn't make out their dirty beige coats in the darkness.

Manu, the newest addition to their caravan, stirred on the other side of the fire. A native of this land, he would know what disturbed the animals. But Manu just grunted and rolled over. Issa debated waking him, but one look at the man's forearms—larger than both of Issa's lanky legs together—as well as the crescent-shaped knife strapped to his belt, convinced Issa to let the beefy man sleep.

Issa took some comfort in knowing that if anything unusual happened, the four porters would check on the animals. Not hearing their voices, he relaxed onto his mat. The porters were accustomed to the habits of these beasts, since they slept next to the smelly creatures for warmth, unlike the merchants, who were permitted to sleep by the fire. Difficult fate these porters had: carrying the sacks that didn't fit on the backs of the camels, cleaning up the campsites. The merchants barely acknowledged their presence. Issa tried to strike up conversations with the porters, but they seemed to be made uncomfortable by the attention, and he was unsure how to proceed. Issa's father was only a *tekton* by trade, and making tables and doors didn't provide enough money for the family to afford even a single slave.

Issa's thoughts were interrupted by a baritone roar that froze him to his sleeping mat.

The merchants around him jumped from their slumber. The sounds that followed terrified the teenager. A guttural snarl clashed with the camels' roaring. When his temporary paralysis subsided, Issa sat and strained to see, but he couldn't make out the struggle. Then a noise followed that Issa hoped never to hear again: a shriek that sounded neither human nor animal. The wail pierced the crisp air and vibrated through to his bones.

Manu, the first of the merchants on his feet, grabbed a half-lit log from the fire in one hand, drew his knife in the other, and raced toward the camels. As soon as he could will his legs to move, Issa followed the other men. When they reached the roaring camels, Issa slowed, expecting to find the source of the animals' distress where they were tied, but the terrible scream originated from ahead. He heard the porters' shouts from the same direction. Confused,

Issa followed the merchants. When he pulled to a stop beside the others, his breath heaved in his narrow chest. Then an involuntary gasp caught in his lungs. His eyes locked onto a sight that would be imprinted in his memory for years to come.

Issa had never seen a tiger before, only heard tales, but he knew instantly from the faded stripes on its white coat what it was. Three of the porters waved their arms and yelled at the beast. Manu stepped into their midst. Growling, the tiger backed away from the crowd, eyeing the flaming torch in the large man's hand. Issa glimpsed what looked like a tattered log in the tiger's powerful jaws as it retreated to the desert shadows. The fur around its face appeared matted and wet. The beast had stolen something from their camp. *Will Manu retrieve it?* he wondered. But the largest merchant stood his ground, watching the tiger carry its prize to its lair in the mountains that defined the horizon. The tiger gone, Issa looked at Manu's wide, dark face, whose deep crevices seemed canyonlike in the glow from the torch. He showed none of the fear that Issa felt.

Although the danger had passed, Issa realized that the shrieks continued. He focused on the semicircle formed by the men. Then he saw the source of the inhuman cries. The fourth porter, a boy, no more than a year or two older than he, lay clutching a mangled stump just below his right hip. The rest of his leg was missing. In its place, a thick pool of blood soaked into the dirt.

Issa's stomach turned. In a moment of awful clarity, he realized that the tiger, targeting the smaller prey, must have grabbed the porter while he slept next to the camels and dragged him a short distance. The porter's leg had been torn from his body.

As abruptly as the terrible sound had begun, the porter's screams stopped; his mouth now moved wordlessly. Issa looked to Manu, who watched the scene with a grimace on his face, or could it have been a smirk? The boy needed immediate help to stop the bleeding, or he would die within minutes. *Why is his countryman just standing there?* Issa scanned the other faces in the group. No one moved.

Unable to speak from the shock of the attack, the boy began whimpering like a fox caught in a trap. His right hand, covered in blood thickened by the dusty red dirt, grasped at the remains of his leg; his fingers searched through the torn flesh.

Issa could no longer contain his anxiety. "You've got to help him!" he pleaded in a voice that came out higher-pitched than he wanted. Speaking Greek, the common language of the traders, presented a challenge for him. Manu cocked his head in Issa's direction and raised the makeshift torch in the direction of the boy's voice. Confronted by the grimace of the large man, Issa stretched up to the full extent of his awkwardly growing frame and held Manu's gaze without blinking.

"Who are you, boy, to tell me what to do?" rumbled the voice out of the massive chest in a jumbled Greek worse than Issa's. Breaking the teenager's defiant stare, Manu glanced toward the porter. "He's just a *Shudra*. In two days' time, we pass through a village where we pick up another one." Cutting his eyes back to Issa, his lips formed a wide smile that showcased his twisted and missing teeth.

The hollowness in Issa's gut grew. He searched the faces of the other merchants. "Will no one help this man?" he asked.

None moved.

Issa tried again. "He's traveled with us for months, carrying our bags and cleaning our camp. We cannot let him die on the side of the road like an animal."

The merchants stared at Issa in silence, as if he were now a greater curiosity than the porter with the missing leg. *Why does no one care?* For a moment, Issa thought he recognized a glimpse of something in the faces of the three uninjured porters. Hope? But they remained uncomfortably silent.

Only the eyes of the boy, whose tear-streamed face contorted in agony, would meet his. Issa made his decision. Ripping off his tunic, he tore the right sleeve from the garment. He knelt next to the porter and placed a shaky hand on his clammy forehead. Issa's touch seemed to provide strength to the boy, and a clarity appeared in his eyes that had been absent before. "Be strong. I will help you," Issa assured him, sounding more confident than he felt.

He had no experience in medicine, but he had once watched his father dress the broken leg of a sheep that had fallen into a ravine. Stopping the bleeding was the first priority. Next, he would have to clean the wound to prevent the rot that would certainly kill the porter even if he were to survive the blood loss. With uncertain but determined hands, Issa wrapped his torn sleeve around the stump where the leg had been. Blood quickly soaked through the cloth with no sign of slowing. Technically this man's blood was unclean, but there was no way Issa could stop the bleeding without dirtying his hands in it. Taking a breath, he grabbed the cloth and pressed it into the bleeding flesh. Everyone in the group, except Manu, Issa noticed, jumped at the shriek that came from the dying boy. Startled but undeterred, Issa kept his hold firm.

"You will live," he reassured his patient, although again he was not as confident as he tried to sound. The bleeding slowed, but every time Issa let go, the blood started flowing again. He didn't know how much blood a man held in his body, but too much had spilled on the ground. Then an idea came to him. He quickly removed the makeshift bandage from around the torn flesh and retied it a couple of inches above the end of the stump. After a few attempts, he perfected his tourniquet, stopping the flow of blood. The porter was now unconscious but still breathing.

Sweating from his effort, Issa gestured his blood-soaked hands at the other porters. "Bring me some wine and oil to pour on the wound." The strength in his voice propelled one of the men to run to their supplies, returning in a minute with two flasks. Together they cleaned the wound. Issa then ripped off his other sleeve and wrapped it around the end of the stub. He admired his handiwork. The boy would live.

"Help me carry him back to the camp," he commanded the other porters. "We must move him carefully."

The three porters gathered around the injured boy. The one who had helped to clean the wound caught Issa's eye and smiled shyly. When they prepared to lift their patient, a baritone voice called to them, "And what happens in the morning, when we leave camp?"

Manu towered over Issa.

Issa hadn't thought that far ahead yet. He'd just saved this man's life. Certainly they could find a way to transport the porter to a village where he could recover.

Manu continued, "Anyway, what use is a one-leg *Shudra*? How will he carry our sacks?"

Confident in his rightness, Issa stood. "How can you speak of this man as if he were no more than one of your camels? He lives now. We can save him."

"He's no better than a camel, if he cannot work."

"He's one of your countrymen, your kin."

"Boy, you understand nothing. This servant isn't my kin. He's nothing but a *Shudra*, the lowest caste. His place in life is to serve, to carry, to clean: to do jobs that are unfit for higher castes. I'm *Vaishya*. It's not a merchant's responsibility to care for a servant. Nor is it your concern what happens to him." Manu leaned so close to Issa that the teenager could almost taste his foul breath. "You paid us to take you to the city of the great sages. Until we get there, keep your ideas to yourself. I've grown tired of listening to your mouth every day."

"But he is a human!" Issa shouted, his voice cracking.

"A man who will die here in desert."

"He will not die. I have saved him tonight and will again tomorrow."

"We're two days' walk from the next village. How will this man get there if he cannot walk? Villagers will not care for him. He has no way to pay for food or shelter if he can't work."

The solution came to Issa after a moment's contemplation. *Men can be so shortsighted*, he thought. *If only they would learn to open their minds.*

"Simple," he said. "We tie him on one of the camels and divide the camel's load among us. The empty sacks," he continued, pointing in the direction of the camp supplies, "we can use to spread the weight around. When we get to the village, I have a few silver pieces left I can give them to care for the man."

Issa looked to the rest of the group for support. They in turn looked back and forth between him and Manu, as if watching a Roman athletic contest. Only from the porters did he sense encouragement. But Issa knew he would eventually talk sense into even these dim-witted merchants. His quick mind and quicker tongue may have brought him trouble among his teachers, but these gifts would serve him well in the world. He didn't expect the burst of laughter from his adversary.

"What do you think we are, boy? Camels?" Manu said through his guffaws. "You don't expect us to carry these supplies. Why do you think we have animals and *Shudras*?" The other merchants were now smiling along with him. "I think you've had your fun."

A chill passed through Issa when he spotted Manu's fingers grasping the braided leather handle of his sharp blade. Then, handing the glowing log to one of the porters, who needed two hands to hold it, Manu pushed past Issa, nearly knocking the teenager off his feet.

Regaining his composure, Issa grabbed the thick shoulder of the man, who knelt beside the unconscious porter. "What do you think you are doing?" Issa asked, trying to lower his voice.

Manu's smile vanished. "I'm ending this game, boy, and then going to sleep." He drew his knife and glared at Issa's hand on his shoulder. "If you want to keep that, you move it quickly."

Issa withdrew his hand and searched the faces around him. They couldn't let this happen! But the other merchants only looked on with curious detachment, while the three porters gazed at the ground. Manu grabbed a fistful of the injured boy's hair, lifting his head off the ground. The porter's eyes fluttered open, and he gazed upward with grateful recognition at the teenager who saved his life. Issa struggled to fight back the nausea that rose to the back of his throat. He was helpless to prevent the inevitable.

In one efficient movement, Manu drew the long curved blade across the porter's throat, just as he might kill a lamb before a feast, or a sacrifice. Issa wanted to close his eyes, but he couldn't abandon the doomed boy's gaze, which widened to surprise as his last breath gurgled through the gash across his neck.

Manu stood, towering over the teenager. Issa's fight drained out of him, just as the life drained out of the porter. Manu said, "Starting tomorrow, you carry the *Shudra's* burden until we reach village and buy another one." He then wiped the bloody knife clean across the side of Issa's pants before turning toward camp and settling back onto his mat to sleep.

CHAPTER 13

HOTEL ZANGDHO PELRI
PUNAKHA, BHUTAN

THREE HOURS HAD passed since Grant had sat transfixed in the utse tower library as Kinley translated the stories of Issa. Before they left, Kinley had signaled to Jigme from the window to distract Dawa again while they made their escape. After they descended the six long flights of stairs, Kinley left to tend to the junior monks while Grant and Kristin caught a silver Land Rover taxi from the dzong into Punakha. The small town consisted of two-story wooden buildings with shop space on the ground floor and apartments on the top. With the wind blowing dust down the main street, Grant thought that Punakha appeared like an Old West town in the States, minus the tumbleweeds.

Kristin's dark hair, which earlier had been pulled back into a loose ponytail, fell freely around her shoulders. Again, he caught a whiff of her shampoo as the two hunched over his laptop in the cramped business office at her hotel, the Zangdho Pelri, the same hotel he'd stayed at before his kayaking accident. The office was nothing more than a windowless room that doubled as overflow storage for the adjacent gift shop. The screeching from the office's dial-up modem and the long minutes it took to log on to the Internet would have grated on Grant's nerves a month ago, but today he was thankful to have access to any kind of technology.

From the moment Kinley opened the first book in the dusty library, Grant's life had taken a new direction. He now better understood Kinley's Chinese parable about the man and his horse. A horrible accident had indeed turned out to be an incredible stroke of good fortune. Thoughts now raced through his mind so quickly he barely had time to register them. He imagined the shock waves that would reverberate throughout the academic world when he released the Issa texts. After listening to Kinley's translation, Grant was confident that the books were indeed the primary sources that were used to compile the Tibetan version Notovitch had seen. But what moved Grant even more than he had expected was the richness of the stories about Issa. Although he'd read Notovitch's account many times, the stories that Kinley relayed contained a level of detail and a personalization of Issa that Grant had been unprepared for. The pressure on the Bhutanese government to allow the documents to be studied would be immense, and Grant felt confident that he would play the lead role in the project.

"So," Kristin said, interrupting his daydreaming, "if this Indian saint is as historically significant as you claim, you're not uncomfortable emailing the entire translation to your professor?" Kristin pulled the memory card out of the portable card reader that she'd used to download the three hundred and fifty pictures into Grant's laptop, clicked it into a small plastic case, and zipped it into her camera bag.

"I trust Professor Billingsly completely, and I'll need him to line up resources the moment I arrive in Atlanta. Seven years ago, I was rejected by the graduate program at Harvard because of an irregularity in my file." A shiver passed through his body. *"Irregularity" is putting it lightly*, he thought. He pushed the memory of his greatest humiliation out of his head. "I worried that my application to Emory would follow the same path, so I set up a meeting with Billingsly, one of the senior faculty members in my area of study. We bonded immediately. After I explained the circumstances behind the note in my file, Billingsly went to bat for me in front of the admissions committee. I returned the favor last year when the position for one of the college's deans opened up. I organized a petition of recommendation that over one hundred students signed."

"Did it work?"

"Unfortunately not. Harold is an articulate and open-minded teacher, although our philosophical views often differ." Grant thought back on the many times he'd debated theology with Billingsly, who always took the more traditional Christian view, while he himself took the skeptical one. "The job went to someone connected in the fund-raising circles at Emory. Money, more than teaching, drives university politics."

"Oh no." She lowered her camera bag to the floor, reached for his laptop, and danced her slim fingers across Grant's illuminated keyboard. "Crashed again."

The slow and intermittent connection had already been lost twice before. The files were simply too large for the outdated technology. Grant decided instead to send only the Word file he'd transcribed. He would just bring the pictures back with him. With the originals on Kristin's flash memory card and a copy on his laptop, he felt comfortable waiting the few days until his return to Atlanta.

"Isn't it unusual for a professional writer not to travel with a computer?" Grant asked, as he watched her reboot his laptop. He'd been surprised when Kristin had opened her backpack and revealed three spiral-bound notebooks in which she wrote her articles. *Who uses pen and paper these days?* he wondered.

"I just prefer the tactile sense of writing longhand. It's like I'm more connected to my work. The electronics sap my creativity. Besides, once I've done the writing part, all I need is an Internet café or hotel computer where I can type in the story and email my editor. I can travel without worrying about someone stealing my laptop or having to recharge it."

Grant checked the screen. The translation of the texts had gone through. It would be waiting for Billingsly when he woke up. "I wish I could get Billingsly on the phone. Can't wait to hear his reaction."

Grant had placed four phone calls already, but the ten-hour time difference had made communicating difficult. He also knew that the professor spent long weekends at his cabin in the mountains of western North Carolina, where he had no cell phone service. Anyway, Grant would be home in three days. Then the real work would begin.

He reviewed the steps that had to occur before he could publicly announce his find. The photos Kristin took would have to be analyzed and the Pali text professionally translated. He would have to write an article on the background of the discovery. Two months' work, he estimated. And then his life would change. As he evaluated his mental checklist a second time, a voice intruded in his thoughts—Kinley's admonition about his endless ruminations on the future. Grant pushed the voice away. This time was different. He needed to make sure he was prepared to hit the ground running the moment he landed. Kinley's Buddhist mind tricks were useful when he needed to relax, but relaxation was the last thing on Grant's mind.

Then he noticed that Kristin had shifted the intensity of her stare from the computer to him, as if she were trying to read his thoughts. Her fingers absentmindedly toyed with the plaster on his cast. He held her gaze, mesmerized by her blue eyes, so unusual on a face like hers, and yet so captivating. They were the only two Americans in this place, and months had passed since he'd last been with a woman. He thought back to Holly, the brunette business student with the spiky hair and the temper to match, and Michelle, the blond theater major, before her. Dating students was uncomplicated: they didn't want to move in with him or call him every second of the day. His research had to be his priority.

"So what's the dating situation like, traveling from one place to another?" He tried to sound casual.

She moved her hand from his cast as if she'd just been caught touching something she wasn't supposed to touch. "I'm not really looking right now."

"Oh no, me neither," he added quickly. "Work, you know." He watched how her midnight black hair curled around her delicate ear. Hadn't she been flirting with him since they met yesterday? Then he reminded himself that she wasn't his type anyway. He had too much to think about without complicating his life further.

She shifted her gaze from him to the computer. "Look, Grant, I know these texts are important to your research, but what are you holding back? The stories Kinley read to us moved me. Issa's experiences made me question my own spirituality." She turned to him. "When are you going to tell me the truth about Issa?"

Conflict tugged at his mind. He'd been vague with Kristin on purpose. How could he trust someone he'd just met with this revelation, a journalist, no matter how intelligent or beautiful she was? But she was instrumental in his bringing back proof of the texts, and for a reason he couldn't put a finger on, he felt a connection to her. He'd promised himself that he wouldn't lie to her if she asked him directly. He took a deep breath and began to tell her about the two-thousand-year-old mystery of the missing eighteen years in the life of Jesus of Nazareth—the period of time from when Jesus appeared in the Temple in Jerusalem at age twelve until his ministry began at age thirty, a period about which the Bible was silent.

As the truth began to dawn on Kristin, her blue eyes widened. "Are you telling me," she asked, "that Issa is Jesus?"

PART TWO

THE FLAME

"I am the source of all things, and all things emerge from me . . . Infinite are the forms in which I appear. I am the self, seated in the heart of all beings; I am the beginning and the life span of beings, and their end as well . . . I am the source of all things to come."

The Bhagavad Gita, 5th century BC

"I am the Alpha and the Omega who is and who was and who is to come."

The Book of Revelation, AD 1st century

CHAPTER 14

⌘

BIRMINGHAM, ALABAMA

Tᴉᴍ Hᴜɴᴛʟᴇʏ sᴄʀᴜʙʙᴇᴅ his body with the thin washcloth in the motel room shower. Usually he was careful not to irritate the skin on his arms and face when he showered, lest he aggravate his eczema. This evening his body stung from the soap penetrating the cracks and crevices of his skin. But as hard as he tried, he couldn't wash away the sin. Ever since he'd been a teenager, he'd struggled with his unnatural desires.

When he stepped out of the bath, his arms and face began to itch before he even had a chance to apply the cool lotion. He prayed he was alone so as not to be confronted with the sickness of his actions. Bile rose to his throat when he heard the throaty voice outside the bathroom door.

"You about finished in there, honey? I need to freshen up. Business, you know."

Tim wrapped the towel around his waist and marched into the bedroom. The prostitute smiled at him from the edge of the bed, the tanned, youthful face glowing like a signpost to hell.

But it wasn't Tim's fault. He'd been unfairly tempted. He'd been tired and distracted. He'd returned home from Atlanta just before seven AM. He'd only had time to take a quick shower before launching into a sixteen-hour workday. Though he hadn't slept in almost two days, the hooker's tight jeans and low-cut shirt were too much. Even Jesus had been tempted by Satan.

But Jesus had resisted.

Usually Tim resisted too. But every so often, maybe once a year, the temptation proved too great. Like that fateful night, late in the latrine in the barracks in Fallujah, Iraq, when he and another soldier had thought everyone else was sleeping.

"So, sweetie, when do I get to see you again?" the man-boy asked from the bed.

Tim's fist flew out like a serpent striking its prey. The first two knuckles of his right hand connected with the side of prostitute's nose, snapping it as if it were made of balsa wood.

An instant relief washed over him.

"What are you doing?" the man shrieked in pain, as his hands flew to his face.

Tim cocked his fist a second time, but the prostitute grabbed his clothes with bloodied fingers and bolted for the door. *Just as well*, Tim thought. *Who knows what kinds of diseases reside in that man's blood?*

As he dressed, he began having second thoughts about punching the man. He should have killed the whore instead. Just as he should have killed the private who'd come on to him and caused him to be discharged from the Army. Both men had unfairly tempted Tim. Suddenly the image of Reverend Brady flashed into his mind. *What would the reverend say if he knew?*

Tim knew exactly what the reverend would say because he broke out into a clammy sweat every time he heard the baritone voice quote Leviticus: "If a man lies with a man as with a woman, both of them have committed an abomination; they shall be put to death."

Tim was strong, and he truly believed, just as the reverend said he should believe. Why then would God allow him to suffer like this? Even the bombing hadn't gone according to plan. There weren't supposed to be any casualties. All the talk in the office that day had been about the bombing in Atlanta. The nonstop news coverage focused more on the story of the death of Professor Martha Simpson than on the effects of the bombing on the CDC. The news reports said that only the exterior of the building was damaged. They hadn't used enough ANFO. Tim knew that the mixture was unpredictable and wished again that he'd had access to a real explosive like C-4. The work at the agency would continue, although with much higher security. Tim and Johnny hadn't spoken a single word about it and had ignored each other all day. Tim had promised Johnny that there wouldn't be any casualties, and the last thing Tim needed was to have Johnny flip out.

Pulling on his boots, Tim recalled one of Reverend Brady's sermons. Often in the Bible, sinners, like the Prodigal Son, were rewarded twice over for coming back to the flock after having sinned. The prodigal son's father had welcomed him back with open arms, as did God. Tim no longer had a biological father to welcome him back. The memory of the shotgun blast still echoed in his mind. He recalled the smell of gunpowder as he ran down the stairs of the house his family had lived in back then. His father lay in a crumpled heap on the floor of the den, his mother standing behind the body holding a black twelve-gauge. Years before, Tim had learned to block out the nightly arguments his parents had, turning up the volume of his stereo so he wouldn't have to hear their screaming. But nothing was loud enough to block out the sound of the shotgun—then or now. He told the police about the arguments, and he elaborated about the beatings his mother suffered at the hands of his father. The police concluded the shooting was self-defense, and then he and his mother moved to Little Rock.

Tim had always wondered whether he'd done the right thing by lying to the police. As loud as the nightly arguments got, Tim's father never actually laid a hand on his mother. But if he'd told the police that, then he would have lost both his parents that night and been put in some foster home. He knew his father had suspected the truth about his problem as much as Tim had tried to hide it, and he knew that the suspicion disgusted the old man. Every night his father read aloud from the family Bible before they sat down to dinner. In the year before his death, right after Tim turned thirteen, his father would concentrate on passages, like Leviticus, that described the abominations of promiscuity and homosexuality. Tim often had trouble sleeping at night. His father was pious and controlling, and Tim felt no affection for the man who never shared any affection toward him, and yet he wasn't ready to be an orphan. After his father's murder, Tim watched his mother drink to excess and bring random men into their Little Rock home. Maybe foster parents would have been the better choice.

As he stood up from the motel bed, Tim's mind cleared. As if he could hear Reverend Brady's comfortable voice speaking from the pulpit, he understood the real lesson. The father in the story of the Prodigal Son was metaphorical. It didn't matter that Tim's own father was dead; his destiny would be the same as the son's in the story. God would welcome him back. God had a plan for Tim: a plan much more spectacular than the Emory bombing, a plan of redemption. Tim wasn't sure of the details of this plan, but he knew that he would be given the chance to prove his worthiness, and his sins too would be forgiven.

Feeling better, Tim strode out of the motel room. He would head back to his apartment and spend the rest of the night online. Maybe he would find a clue to God's plan for him there.

CHAPTER 15

NEW HOPE CHURCH
BIRMINGHAM, ALABAMA

WILLIAM JENNINGS FOLDED his arms on the red leather covering of his walnut desk and hunched toward the computer monitor. His office was smaller than Brady's, not even half the size, but it was richly appointed with mahogany bookshelves filled with theological tomes and a thick beige carpet. At almost eight in the evening, he was the only one left in the New Hope offices, as was often the case. The hallway outside his door was dark, and the only light in his office came from the Tiffany desk lamp and the LCD screen. The fluorescent lights in the ceiling were too bright for his eyes. Jennings thought better in the dark.

His carefully laid-out plans were showing signs of stress. Firing Carla had made his job managing the finances of the construction more difficult, and it would take weeks to find a suitable replacement. His boss's unpredictability was exhausting. If he could rein in some of Brady's more self-indulgent tendencies for the next few months, they could get past the current financial difficulties of the New Hope development. Then the minister would become the next president of the National Association of Evangelicals during the spring election. Brady loved the limelight and was good at basking in it. Without Jennings's strategic thinking, organizational abilities, and attention to detail, however, Brady would be nothing more than a charismatic small-town pastor. Theirs was a good partnership. Jennings had no desire for the public adulation that Brady so enjoyed. He sought something more important, influence—influence to make a difference in the world. But they had several hurdles to get over first, the primary one being money.

Over the past twenty years, Jennings had watched the country go soft in the name of tolerance, multiculturalism, religious pluralism, diversity, and all the other euphemisms they came up with for turning away from the gospel. Even the focus of some of his evangelical brethren was being distracted from their true mission. A few of the pastors in the NAE had begun to take up the hysteria of environmentalism, a cause Jennings knew was contradicted by Genesis, which explained how God gave man dominion over the plants and animals. Other churches wasted resources on mission trips to Africa to minister to so-called Christian converts there who still practiced witchcraft and magic, practices which Leviticus clearly said should be punished by death.

Jennings knew that if Brady could become president of the NAE, then they could bring the organization back to the power it had wielded in the 1980s. The popularity of Brady's book—*one of my better ideas*, Jennings thought—demonstrated the frustration many Americans felt for their deteriorating country: their worries about the future and the hunger they had for understanding God's will. After the NAE election, Jennings would have the ear of the politicians. He would become one of the most powerful men in America. He would leave the TV and public adoration to Brady. The years of his being subservient to Brady's ego would be worth it; he would be in a position to influence U.S. policy for a generation. He would reverse the damage being done that was leading his beloved country on the path to Armageddon.

Jennings clicked on his email icon and began to scan the messages. He kept in constant communication with the other church leaders who would help to elect Brady, feeding out tidbits of information that would keep Brady in their minds. An email with an unusual heading caught his eye. Opening the message, he pored over its contents, reading it twice just to make sure he understood its implications. Then he pushed back his leather chair and templed his fingers under his chin. *This could be a problem.*

CHAPTER 16

—— ∞∞∞ ——

ATLANTA, GEORGIA

AFTER THIRTY HOURS OF TRAVEL, driving first to Paro and then flying to New Delhi, Paris, and finally on to Atlanta, Grant unlocked the door to his off-campus apartment, just three miles from Emory University. He thought he was used to the cast after five weeks, but lugging it around the airports and squeezing into the coach seats on the long flights had been uncomfortable to say the least. Fortunately, they'd given him an exit row, since he was incapable of bending his knee. He planned to see a doctor in a few days to have the cast removed, and he couldn't be rid of it too soon. He leaned the backpack containing his clothes and laptop against the black futon in the living room. To his left stood a circular table with two dining chairs and beyond that the small kitchen. To his right, a sliding glass door led to a deck overlooking the woods behind the complex.

"Bedroom's there." He pointed to the door directly ahead of him. After a moment's hesitation, he added, "I'll take the couch."

"That works," Kristin said.

He'd been pleasantly surprised when she'd agreed to travel with him to Atlanta. After he revealed the true importance of the Issa texts in the business office of the small hotel in Punakha, she could barely contain her enthusiasm for getting involved. He had to admit that he'd delighted in her awe upon learning that Issa was Jesus of Nazareth.

"Didn't Jesus live and teach in Galilee?" she'd asked with an intensity in her gaze that drew him in.

"He did during his ministry," Grant replied, "which began around the age of thirty and lasted about a year. But one of the great mysteries of the Bible is what Jesus was doing before then. The Gospel of Luke describes Jesus' appearance at the Temple in Jerusalem at age twelve, where he impresses people with his knowledge of scripture and his eloquence, but then the Bible is silent about his whereabouts until the beginning of his ministry."

"You're saying that nearly twenty years of Jesus' life is completely unaccounted for in the Bible?"

"The only mention of his life during those two decades comes again from Luke, which reads, 'He increased in wisdom and stature, and in favor with God and man.' So you see, these texts could be the most important biographical information on the life of Jesus that exists."

"But wasn't Kinley trying to tell you something about this being about more than history? We heard about Issa learning certain secret teachings. I can't shake the feeling that we're supposed to understand something—a bigger message maybe about these teachings."

Grant waved his hand. "I respect Kinley. I've learned a lot from him, but this is my area of expertise. Don't you see? These Issa texts go to the very heart of who Jesus was. Was he receiving his messages from God directly, or was he a man whose revolutionary teachings were derived from his studies of Hinduism and Buddhism?"

"What about the virgin birth stories? I thought that Jesus was born the way he was because that's how God made him."

"That's what the authors of those stories wanted you to think. The majority of biblical scholars believe those tales to be later additions to the Jesus tradition, part of the myth that grew up around Jesus after his death." Grant grinned. "And if Jesus was somehow divine from birth, why don't we have a history of miracle stories from the first thirty years of his life, instead of only the final year?"

"But if Issa really is Jesus, and he did travel to the East, wouldn't *those* stories be known?"

"Actually, the legend of Jesus traveling through India as a teenager, while not well known in the West, is widely believed in India. Do you remember hearing me mention the name of a Russian journalist, Nicholas Notovitch?"

She nodded.

"Notovitch published a book in 1894 entitled *La Vie Inconnue de Jesus-Christ*, or *The Unknown Life of Jesus Christ*, detailing his discovery of a text at the Himis monastery in the mountains of India. The book created quite a stir for a few months. It described Jesus, or Issa, traveling to India with a merchant caravan while in his teens. He studied first Hinduism and then Buddhism before returning to his own land. But immediately after Notovitch published, several academics denounced him as a fraud. One professor claimed Notovitch had never visited Himis, while another wrote to a lama there who denied such a text existed."

He added, "Scholars agreed that either the Russian fabricated his story or the mischievous monks at the monastery were having fun at his expense. The entire matter was essentially dropped, and in a world before TV or the Internet, the incident quickly disappeared from memory."

"And that was it? Why didn't someone go and check out his story?"

"After the rebuttal articles came out," Grant said, "most academics assumed Notovitch's report was false, and reaching a remote Himalayan monastery a hundred years ago would have been an arduous trip to find nothing. However, several other independent sightings of the text over the next twenty years were recorded, but for some reason, the press never pushed those stories."

"So what happened to the text?"

Grant shrugged. "We don't know. That's why I went to India in the first place. Maybe the lama who ran Himis was afraid of the attention the manuscript could bring. He may have sent it elsewhere. We've seen firsthand how insular monastery culture is, fearful of outside influence." Grant had a sudden mental image of Lama Dorji on his throne. He was a monk who would need little provocation to make the Issa texts disappear if it meant keeping foreigners out of his library.

She squeezed his arm. "So this is the basis for your dissertation?"

"It is, but most academics, by the way, discount the theory."

"Well, if Jesus didn't travel to India, then where was he during those missing decades?"

"The majority of scholars, including Professor Billingsly, assume Jesus grew up in his hometown of Nazareth, learning his father's woodworking trade. But similar to the legend of his travels to India, other apocryphal stories arose that claimed he traveled to what is now Wales with his uncle, while others tell of him growing up in Egypt."

"Hold on." Her grip around his arm tightened. "Why is he called Issa and not Jesus in Kinley's texts?"

"In Islamic texts like the Koran," Grant said, "Jesus goes by the name of Isa, with one *s*, but in Buddhist and Hindu literature, he is known as Issa."

After she'd pelted him with additional questions for another hour, she accompanied him in the taxi back to the dzong later that afternoon to collect his belongings. When they returned to the hotel, they ate together in the small, brightly lit restaurant with checkered tablecloths. They'd stayed up talking well past midnight. As they separated to their own rooms, she'd said that she was in no hurry to return to New York and she wanted to meet Professor Billingsly. With her journalistic contacts, Grant thought she might be useful in helping to convince the Bhutanese government to allow the texts to come to the States. Before they left the country, he and Kinley decided that Grant would begin to lay the groundwork at Emory for the release of the texts, while the monk would speak to the Je Khenpo. Since Kinley had neither phone nor email access, they would have to communicate through Karma, the doctor. Although Grant had been anxious to return to Atlanta, he was surprised how choked up he got saying good-bye to Kinley in the monastery courtyard.

Although the three days of travel that followed, along with the ten-hour time zone change had been exhausting, traveling with Kristin made the trip pass quickly. Talking with her felt different from talking with other women. They moved from one topic to another with an ease that was never interrupted by uncomfortable silences. Even if she was more free-spirited than he was accustomed to, her inquisitive mind and exotic looks intrigued him. He wondered if she felt the same. She gave him mixed signals. She looked at him and touched him as if she were attracted to him, but then at other times, like in the business office, she seemed more distant. Indecision was one of his major pet peeves.

After dropping her backpack on the floor of his living room, she strolled to the built-in bookcase that took up the entire wall opposite the futon. Other than the TV in the center, books filled every shelf. She ran her fingers across the spines. "You alphabetized these?" she said.

"By category." How else would he be able to find the one he was looking for?

Next, she lifted one of the six framed pictures displayed in front of the books. Each picture was in an identical black frame. "This impresses the girls you bring over?"

The one she'd picked showed him surrounded by spray, screaming with exhilaration as he descended a rapid on the Chattooga River. "Kayaking," he said, feeling himself redden. He took the picture from her and placed it next to the one of him scaling a rock wall in Tennessee. Conscious of her stare, he said, "Thinking about my adventures helps me unwind after work."

"I'll unpack," she said. She grabbed her backpack and headed for the bedroom.

"There's some room in the closet, if you want to hang anything up, and I'll clear out a drawer for you."

"No need."

He watched through the open door as she unzipped the bag and proceeded to upend the contents on the floor by the bed. He shook his head. He felt suddenly overwhelmed by how moody and disorganized she was.

He sat on the futon and opened his laptop. When his email inbox popped up, he gasped.

"What the hell!" he yelled at the screen as he scrolled through over two hundred messages.

Kristin raced into the room. "What?"

"No. No. No!" He lifted his computer off his lap. The urge to hurl it across the room and through the glass doors was overpowering. Instead, he dropped it onto the futon.

"Grant, what's happened?"

He rotated the screen so she could see the list of emails, most from university professors and biblical researchers around the world. All had either the words "Issa" or "Jesus" in the subject line. He punched at the keyboard with his index figure, opening one of the messages. Reading over him, she rested a hand on his shoulder.

"Kinley's entire translation of the Issa texts, the one I emailed Billingsly"—he fought back the burning in his throat—"has been posted online."

CHAPTER 17

---⊷∞⊶---

NEW HOPE CHURCH
BIRMINGHAM, ALABAMA

"LOOK AT THIS BS," Reverend Brady mumbled to himself.

The Birmingham newspaper headline read, NEW HOPE COMMUNITY IN FINANCIAL SCANDAL. Brady settled his ample frame deeply into the leather chair in his church office.

Decorated in an English gentleman's style, the office was spacious to allow for meetings with his parishioners. Brady's favorite touch was the Flemish painting hanging on the wall behind his chair: Jesus, with the cross on his back and thorns cutting into his scalp, struggled up the Golgotha hill as the tendons in his legs and shoulders strained under the weight of his effort. Clouds obscured the sun, casting dark shadows on a background of twisted, leafless trees and distraught followers, but a single ray of light illuminated Christ's face as his eyes looked ahead to the top of the hill. Despite the immense burden of the cross, his face expressed a sea of calm. Brady liked sitting under this painting when he met with people, so that every time their eyes drifted upward, they would be reminded of Christ's acceptance of his own sacrifice, just as they might be asked to make a sacrifice on behalf of the church.

Turning the page of the newspaper, he thought how Satan had an easier time in the modern world. Through print, television, and the Internet, the Evil One could reach millions of corruptible minds. Brady recalled the teaching of John 8:44, that Satan was "the father of lies." Clearly he used the media as his pawns. Why else would they jump at every chance to condemn prayer in schools, to lobby for the removal of the Ten Commandments in public spaces, and to promote other, heathen religions?

These godless reporters had been digging for dirt the moment he'd announced the plans for the New Hope Community. And now, after two years, this was what they came up with? Brady turned the page, shaking his head as he read about his own limited partnership interests in one of the developers building the town homes in the community. Just because he was a clergyman, why shouldn't he have the same right to make a living as anyone else? Anyway, the entire concept was his dream, with God's guiding hand, of course. The following page detailed the "severe funding crisis" the project faced, claiming that contractors were threatening to stop work if late bills weren't paid.

As he thought about the effect the article could have on his campaign for the presidency of the NAE, his stomach began to constrict as if it were attempting to fold in on itself. The surge in support from his fellow evangelical ministers had come after the dual home runs he'd hit with the ground breaking of the New Hope Community and the popularity of his book. The election was only a few months away, and he couldn't afford any negative publicity now that his popularity was peaking. Brady envisioned the trips to Washington he would make as the man who could deliver the votes of millions of Christians. Senators and congressmen would bend over backward for him, and the national news media would cling to his every word.

Who was the lowlife reporter's anonymous source? Brady fumed. Then it came to him; he hadn't trusted that Carla woman for one second. She was one of those typical accounting types. They never understood the bigger picture, and yet they had access to his most personal data—his checkbook. He hadn't heard from Jennings about how she'd taken being let go, but he imagined it hadn't been pretty. She was one of those uppity MBA women, the type of woman Brady simply couldn't tolerate. Brady's other employees had more respectful attitudes. They saw him for what he was: the visionary leader of the church. She just didn't fit in.

A knock echoed through the mahogany office door. "Enter," Brady said.

Jennings hurried inside without saying hello. He thrust several printouts in front of the reverend. Brady looked at his number two without glancing at the papers. Brady noticed that Jennings had opted today for his ill-fitting charcoal Brooks Brothers suit instead of the frayed blue one.

"Yes, William. I've read the article already. What are you going to do about it?" Brady tossed the newspaper to the floor in disgust.

"The article?" Jennings said, momentarily confused. "Oh, that trash? Our attorneys already called the editor and threatened a libel suit. Your partnership interests are completely legal."

"Legal or not, it's the perception of unbecoming behavior we need to fight. The last thing we need is this kind of publicity."

"It'll blow over," Jennings said with a dismissive wave of his hand. "The paper won't risk a follow-up story after our attorneys finish with them. Not why I'm here, though. Have you read your email today?" Jennings jabbed a clawlike finger at the first sheet of paper he'd tossed at Brady.

Brady surveyed the printed copy from an academic website of a society of biblical scholars. "Why do I care what these egghead professors have to say? You know that most seminaries today don't teach the true word of our Lord. That's why we're building the New Hope Seminary—to teach the literal word of God, not some unbeliever's wishful thinking about what he wants God to say."

"I know that, Brian, but to fight these types, we need to understand their positions." Jennings rolled a ballpoint pen from one finger to the next in rhythm with his rapid speech. "These professors are more dangerous than the atheists and agnostics. Every time one of them writes a new historical Jesus book, it sets us back. People who should be listening to you are intoxicated by these professors' academic credentials and the pseudoscience behind their distorted views."

Now Jennings was speaking his language, Brady thought. The reverend understood better than most that once the mystery and the magic were taken away from the Bible and people were allowed to interpret it in any way they chose, the Good Book lost its power and authority. That was why his own book was so effective: it took the dire predictions in the Book of Revelation and showed how these predictions clearly were coming true today. Brady reluctantly began to scan the article.

"What the . . ." Turning the page, Brady's eyes widened. "But this is preposterous," he sputtered when he'd finished. The article described a discovery by an Emory graduate student, Grant Matthews, in a country Brady had never heard of. The manuscripts found by this student purported to explain the missing years in the life of Jesus in a way that Brady immediately understood was very un-Christian. A chill crept up his spine. The claims being made by this kid were much more serious than any of the drivel he'd seen published about Jesus in the past few years.

"Who's going to read, much less believe, this crap?"

"This article has been online less than a day and over two hundred sites have already linked to it." Jennings handed Brady another printout of an email message. "Even your parishioners are beginning to ask about it."

The reverend glanced at the email's *from* line: *Tim Huntley*.

"Tim Huntley? The man who sends me all that conspiracy theory nonsense from the Internet? I delete his messages without opening them." Brady recalled something he'd scanned not too long ago from Huntley about Americans being the real lost tribe of Israel. Huntley made him uncomfortable—the way he sat ramrod straight in the front row every single Sunday, the awful rashes that distracted Brady during his sermons each week, the way the man didn't seem to get that his minister wouldn't want to be troubled with conspiracy theories. After the man began to send him daily messages, each one more strident than the last, Brady added his name to his junk mail filter. Tim Huntley was one of those parishioners who took Brady's sermons about becoming a soldier in God's army of the righteous too literally.

"Read this one."

Brady sighed and glanced at the page from Huntley. The tone was similar to his previous emails: urgent, as if the church's very existence depended on the lunatic's theories. As Brady reached the middle of the page, however, he began to fear that the church's future, *his future*, might indeed be threatened. Tim Huntley outlined how the discovery of the texts called into question the very nature of Jesus Christ. If the texts were to be believed, Jesus was a man with fears, insecurities, and questions, a man who developed his own view of God after studying other religions in India, where he spent a majority of his life traveling. For once, Brady agreed with Tim. This view of Jesus was wholly incompatible with the teachings of the Bible, *with his own teachings*, that Jesus was divine from birth, sent to earth as the incarnation of God himself to judge and to save us. *These texts call into question the very nature of the divinity of Jesus*, Brady realized, fuming.

The hairs on Brady's neck stood up when he reached the part of the email where Tim set forth his concerns about how this discovery, were it to be accepted by the public, would also directly refute Brady's recent book. People would claim that the influence of other religions was not the cause of the country's current problems, as Brady wrote, but that Jesus himself became who he was because of his contact with other religions.

"Brian, this story will spread and come out big." Jennings continued to click his pen through his fingers in time with his speech. "If this kid's story pans out, the media will portray this find as far greater than the Dead Sea Scrolls."

God almighty, Brady thought. If the media seized on this story, the negative effect it could have on Christians everywhere was frightening. He knew that few Christians had the strength of faith that he had—a faith that could stand up to ridiculous claims like this. He flipped back to the first printout. Halfway down the page his eyes caught the reference to the "secret teachings" that Jesus had supposedly learned during his travels. Brady knew that every New Age flake would seize upon the idea of ancient texts containing secret teachings and make a big deal of it. He shook his head. The only ancient text with true teachings was the Holy Bible.

"But," Brady said, "certainly this has to be a hoax. There's no way these texts could have remained undiscovered for centuries. They simply can't be real."

"Brian, this is the opportunity you've been praying for." Jennings finally stopped twirling his pen and instead began to pace around the office. "We should preempt the news. God is giving you the chance to stand up and speak, not just to your congregation, but to the country as a whole."

Brady held his thick fingers to his chin, studying Jennings. He rarely saw his number two excited. Brady felt that Jennings lacked a certain spark, as if the Holy Spirit was having a bad day when it touched him. Jennings's emotions were about as upbeat as his wardrobe—old, tired, conservative. But the reverend recognized that he would never have made it this far without Jennings's ability to see opportunities that others could not.

"We could use some positive publicity right now," Brady said, more to himself than to Jennings.

"This story will dwarf anything about the financial situation at New Hope."

"But my book—"

Jennings grinned, something he rarely did. "If you take the lead on this, your book sales will go through the roof. Our financial stresses will be solved."

"You think so?" Usually the optimist, Brady had become increasingly disturbed by the tone of the last few development meetings. Even Jennings now spoke of delaying certain phases until they received the rest of the funding from the banks.

"I do, but we need to move quickly and control this story ourselves. We will establish you as the voice of opposition—the voice of the believers."

The voice of the believers, Brady thought. He liked the sound of that. Someone needed to protect the true Christians from the threat to their faith that academics like Grant Matthews posed. "How do you propose I do it?"

"I have a few ideas."

Brady glanced at the page in his hand. The final paragraph contained an offer of help from Tim Huntley, who suggested that with his military background and his faith, he was the perfect soldier for Brady's and God's army. The man suggested that the world would be better off if the texts just disappeared.

"You aren't going to rely on this nut job?" Brady held up the page. Although Huntley had outlined the dangers of the texts accurately, everything about the man made Brady cringe. With the endless emails and the intensity with which the man stared at him on Sundays, Brady felt as if he were being stalked, like a woman trying to escape a jealous lover. Brady conjured up the image of Huntley in the first row and involuntarily recoiled at the thought. His face was always peeling, scaly, like a sunburned serpent. He again thanked God for his own flawless complexion.

Jennings began to rotate the pen between his fingers again. He shook his head. "I have something better in mind. Something public."

CHAPTER 18

⬥

ATLANTA, GEORGIA

TIM CLICKED THE CAR door closed and scanned the parking lot. Two in the morning on a weeknight. The apartment complex was quiet and dark. Dressed in black cargo pants and a black sweater just as he was a week earlier for his op at the CDC a few miles from here, he blended into the shadows. He pulled a black stocking cap over his ears and strode to a staircase at the end building. An abundance of landscaping, particularly the freshly planted annuals, diverted attention from the cheap construction of the vinyl-sided, three-story building.

Although it was late, Tim was alert without being jittery—as if he'd consumed just the right amount of caffeine, although he never touched the stuff. Didn't believe in putting any drugs into his system, legal or not. His rush came from being back in the game. Tim was now part of something bigger than himself. He thought his missions with Johnny and the bombings they had planned throughout the Southeast would make a difference, but now he heard a clearer message from above. As he'd suspected, Johnny Meckle wasn't cut out for this type of work. Johnny had avoided Tim for two days after the bombing, and when Tim finally cornered him in the parking lot, Johnny broke down.

"No one was supposed to be hurt," he'd cried.

"Johnny, every war has its casualties."

"I'm sorry, I just can't do this."

They'd parted and hadn't spoken since. Tim wondered whether he should let Johnny live. He was a loose cannon, capable of turning himself in over guilt. In the end, Tim decided that Johnny was too much a wimp to take responsibility. Plus, he could never handle jail. Only Tim had the requisite faith and strength for the plans God had.

Tim's discovery on one of his favorite blogs had changed everything. Now he understood that the bombing had been a warm-up. The danger presented by this new discovery was much greater than that posed by the scientists in their labs. Tim had heard how the CDC scientists experimented with viruses like Ebola and AIDS. They claimed that they did this to learn about the diseases, but Tim knew better. His new discovery, however, revealed a danger more deadly than the potential to use a virus as a weapon: the research being done by Grant Matthews was aimed at attacking not people's bodies but their souls. He'd sat in disbelief, staring at the article that described the texts Matthews found in the Himalayas. *How can this guy make such a claim?* he'd wondered.

Reverend Brady's sermons came to mind: this was precisely how Satan worked. Just as Satan periodically threw temptations his way that he struggled to resist, the Dark Lord sent people like Grant Matthews to undermine people's beliefs. Tim took two hours to calm down after reading the article and then began to hatch his plan. First he'd emailed the reverend. He recalled the words from Brady's short reply, "My son,"—Tim must have read the salutation fifty times—"I deeply appreciate your commitment to the Lord and our community at New Hope. Fondly, Rev. Brady." Then Tim began his preparations.

Returning to Atlanta so soon after the bombing carried certain risks, but he'd covered his earlier tracks well, and implementing God's will wasn't supposed to be easy. He had to move quickly. Tim would play a role in history—God's history. He would find salvation for his sins.

Tim located the tarnished brass numbers on the second floor. Apartment 208. From his right pocket he produced a small leather case containing the lock pick set he'd kept from years earlier during his spec ops training. It had served him well during his brief job at the hospital, but now he understood that God had been paving the road for this mission all along. He worked quickly until he felt the pins click into place. The door swung open with only a slight creak.

After replacing the lock pick into the long cargo pocket, he pulled his Glock forty-caliber semiautomatic pistol from the nylon holster hidden under his sweater. The Glock, with its extended fifteen-round magazine, was his favorite close combat weapon. While the 9mm model was widely used by police forces, Tim had heard enough stories of amped-up perpetrators taking multiple body shots without falling that he preferred the more powerful forty. The gun's composite parts made it lightweight and easy to handle. In addition to being simply camouflaged when disassembled, the gun had no safety to disengage, which ensured that lethal seconds wouldn't be lost during a firefight.

Tim stepped into the apartment and closed the door behind him to keep the cold air from waking the sleeping occupant. A small foyer opened to a living room, which was dimly lit from the kitchen to the left. He advanced with the Glock in front of him.

Approaching a futon in the living room, he noted that it had been pulled out into a bed, a pile of laundry scattered on top.

The pile of laundry shifted.

A surge of adrenaline pulsed through Tim's veins. He swung the pistol toward the futon and froze.

For the next two minutes, neither Tim nor the laundry budged. He crept to the edge of the futon without letting the gun barrel waver.

Grant Matthews lay sleeping on his side. Matthews had bunched a heavy comforter over his legs and waist, giving the illusion of laundry from across the dark room. He slept alone. But why was he in the living room? Tim glanced to the closed door ahead of him. Maybe Matthews had a guest.

Tim studied the profile of the man who had discovered the heresy that Tim knew, from the moment he read it, it would be his mission to stop before it could spread like a virus through his country. The various articles he'd read online were essentially the same: each contained a forwarded copy of an email that Grant Matthews had sent to a professor at Emory. In addition to a translation of the heretical texts, the email had information that Tim would exploit this evening. Matthews had written that the texts were still in Bhutan but he was bringing back photographic proof. Since no photos had been posted and Matthews's flight had arrived earlier that evening, Tim hoped that he was in time. One of the rules of combat was that acting first gave you the upper hand. Now Tim was acting first.

Although the face on the pillow was relaxed in sleep, Matthews had a strong jawline that terminated in a cleft chin partially obscured by a couple of days' worth of stubble. Tim recognized the grad student from his Facebook page. He slept shirtless, and Tim's eyes traced the twist of his torso, which accentuated the V shape of his lat muscle as it tapered to his trim waist.

Tim's right arm began to tingle. The feeling was almost pleasurable. He bit his lip. What was he doing?

Then he understood. He was being tested. *Tempted.* Underneath his sweater the tingling became an itch and quickly a burning. For once, he relished the burn: the distraction from his sinful thoughts. Instead of scratching, he extended the arm until the muzzle of the gun was only a foot from the luxurious dark hair on Matthews's head.

Tim caressed the trigger with his index finger. Just a slight pressure would splatter chunks of brain matter and shards of skull onto the white pillowcase. He savored the image of this quick solution to his problems. Then he crept away.

Confident that Matthews slept soundly, Tim silently searched the apartment. He found the first two items on the kitchen counter—an expensive Nikon camera and Matthews's cell phone, which was plugged into a charger. Before taking them, Tim studied their exact positions on the countertop. Then he switched the phone to vibrate, stuck it in his pocket, and slung the camera over his shoulder.

Not seeing the third item anywhere in the kitchen or living room, he inched the bedroom door open and stepped inside. As he expected, he saw the outline of a body on the bed. Matthews had company. Then he spotted what he'd come for: Matthews's laptop, on a chair to the right of the door. He should have taken it then and left the apartment, but a force out of his control drew him further into the room.

She lay sleeping, tangled in the bedsheets. He shuffled to within inches of the bed. Her long, black hair fanned out over her pillow like the plumage displayed by a peacock. From her facial features he guessed that she was a halfbreed. He studied the roundness of her breasts, outlined against the fabric of an oversized T-shirt. Her bare right leg was draped on top of the sheets while she grasped at the rest of the bedcovers like a child holding on to her blanket. Tim followed the sweep of her leg from the arch of her foot, along the line of her calf muscle, up to the taut skin of her thigh.

Tim swallowed, aware that he'd been producing copious amounts of saliva. Who was she? A girlfriend? But why weren't they in bed together doing it? A lover's quarrel, perhaps?

He urged his body to turn and leave, but instead he leaned forward, his face inches from hers. He held his breath to avoid any sound that might wake her. He could hear her steady breathing and see the slight flare of her delicate nostrils with each breath. Tim then inhaled deeply but slowly, drawing her fragrance into his lungs as if she were an exotic dish that he was savoring before tasting. He felt nothing.

The itch began as a crackling sensation along both arms and radiated to the core of his body. He straightened and backed toward the bedroom door. He lifted the laptop from the armchair and placed it under his left arm, keeping his right hand free to maneuver his pistol.

Less than two minutes later, Tim sat panting in the front seat of his car.

"Idiot!" He banged the steering wheel.

He'd been stupid, but lucky. His actions in the apartment could have compromised the entire mission. Only he had the smarts and skills to accomplish a task of this sensitivity and this importance, yet he'd just risked everything. *For what?* He would make them both pay for the trouble they were causing on so many levels.

Tim glanced at the clock on the dash: 2:30. He began his work. Once again, the cyber ops training he'd received during his time with Army Intelligence at INSCOM would serve him well. God had been planting the seeds even then.

CHAPTER 19

※

CANDLER SCHOOL OF THEOLOGY EMORY UNIVERSITY, ATLANTA

G RANT MARCHED UP THE stone stairs toward Bishops Hall, the main administrative and classroom building of the Candler School of Theology, located just off the central quadrangle on the Emory campus. Even though he was still in the cast, his pace forced Kristin to hurry to keep up. He tried unsuccessfully to erase the image in his mind of the hundreds of emails from the previous night. He was so discouraged, he hadn't even bothered to turn his laptop on that morning. Kristin now carried it in her backpack along with the camera.

"Impressive campus," she said, wearing jeans that hung low on her hips and a faded Johns Hopkins sweatshirt. "The limestone walls and terra-cotta roofs remind me of a village in Tuscany." The warm southern sun highlighting the fall hues on the campus oak trees added to the picture. "This where you take your classes?" she asked.

"Just a couple." He jerked open the heavy door. "Candler's a Methodist seminary. My PhD program falls under Emory's Graduate School of Arts and Sciences, but the Division of Religion shares some classes and faculty with Candler. Professor Billingsly's office is here."

When they reached the door with the nameplate reading "Harold Billingsly," Grant didn't so much open the door as burst through it. Startled, the professor jumped in his seat before rising to greet them. With his thinning gray hair, half-moon reading glasses perched on his nose, blue oxford shirt with its sleeves rolled up, and striped tie, Billingsly appeared like the professor he was. But his usual jovial expression had been replaced by red, swollen eyes.

"Welcome back," Billingsly said.

The sadness in his mentor's voice halted the momentum of Grant's anger. "Are you okay?"

"You haven't heard about the bombing?"

"Bombing? We just returned late yesterday."

Billingsly described the attack on the campus the previous week that had cost Professor Martha Simpson her life. "We hadn't been dating that long"— his voice cracked—"but I really felt a connection with her." He shuddered. "When I close my eyes, I can still smell her perfume."

"I had no idea." Grant approached his mentor. Lines of concern replaced those of anger on his face. "I'm so sorry. Do they have any leads?"

"Not yet. All the FBI will say is that the van that contained the bomb was stolen from Birmingham Airport."

"I guess that explains the security," Kristin said. Just a few minutes earlier, a guard at the parking lot had examined Grant's student ID before allowing them to enter, and they'd passed numerous police patrolling the campus on the short walk to Bishops Hall.

"Ah, you must be Ms. Misaki, the lovely journalist Grant spoke so highly of in his voicemails to me." Grant felt the back of his neck flush. The professor extended his hand. "Harold Billingsly."

"Please, call me Kristin." She held the professor's hand in both of hers.

Billingsly motioned to two black wooden chairs with the Harvard crest on the backrests in front of his desk. Kristin hopped into one with her legs folded underneath her, while Billingsly pushed aside a stack of journals and sat on the edge of his desk. Grant remained standing.

"How could you, Harold?" he asked. "I trusted you."

"Whoa. Slow down a minute. I was shocked to see the story published too."

"But you were the only one I sent the email to!" Grant spat out the words.

Billingsly shifted his weight on the desk, suddenly seeming very uncomfortable. "After Martha's death, I was a little out of it. I forwarded your email to a couple of people in the department. Thought I'd line up resources for the work you had ahead." He cast his eyes to the floor. "After Martha's funeral, I drove to my cabin in the mountains for a few days alone. I returned yesterday to a deluge of voicemails from people wanting to speak to you." He looked back up at Grant. "Someone in the department must have inadvertently let the email out."

Grant massaged his temples with his fingers.

"Grant." Billingsly leaned forward and placed a hand on his student's shoulder. "We don't have the luxury of time. For all we know, your monk friend has shared these texts with other tourists too."

"Not Kinley."

"Maybe, but realize that you have a career-making opportunity here— greater than anything you could have dreamed up."

Grant lifted his head. On the flight back he'd indulged in the daydream of talk shows, book deals, and lecture circuits. He settled into the hard chair, extending his leg with the cast to the side. He felt his leg begin to throb. He couldn't wait to get the damn cast removed.

"So what do we do next?"

"Professor Singh has agreed to review your pictures of the texts. He can give us a quick read on the accuracy of the translation."

Grant glanced at his mentor. As supportive as Billingsly had been over the years, he'd always been cautious about Grant's research. Grant reached into the backpack Kristin had set down at his feet and removed his laptop. He noticed Billingsly studying his unshaven face.

"You need some cleaning up," the professor added. "The press will want to speak with you."

"The press?" Grant pressed the power button on the laptop. "Harold, you know I don't like public speaking."

"You mentioned that in Bhutan," Kristin said. "I still can't picture you tongue-tied."

"Groups." He shook his head. "I get nervous with everyone staring at me."

Billingsly threw back his head and released a guffaw. "I remember the look you used to get on your face in class whenever I approached your seat. Here's this man, Kristin, who over a cup of coffee is never shy about telling me, a tenured professor, when I'm clearly wrong on an issue, but in a class of fifty of his peers he would shrink into his chair, hoping I wouldn't notice him."

"I know it's not logical." Grant shrugged, feeling his neck grow hot. "But this feeling of dread would come over me, and then suddenly I'd forget whatever I knew about the topic."

"I've seen you mature into a first-rate student, and I'm confident you can handle the press." Billingsly's tone took on a more serious note. "But they're not the ones I'd worry about."

"So now you're saying I should be worried?"

"The existence of these texts won't be received positively by everyone." The professor stood from his desk and began to pace in front of them.

"But don't you think these texts could have a unifying effect?" Kristin asked. "Bring people of different religions together, rather than push them apart? These texts show a much closer connection between the Eastern and Western religions than was ever before considered."

The professor shook his head. "Many people will feel threatened by your discovery. Consider how disturbing it will be for people to change the image of Jesus they've held for their entire lives. It will rock their very concept of who he was—maybe lead to an ideological war."

Grant flicked his hand, then booted up his laptop. "I can handle the theological objections from those people. I'm looking forward to writing a response to them in the journal." The memory of the heated debates he'd had as a teenager with his fundamentalist father again flashed through his mind. "But what about you, Harold? You're a traditionalist scholar."

Billingsly removed his glasses and cleaned them with his striped tie. "But I am skeptical. Until we study the texts themselves, I'll hold off any commentary on their legitimacy. Frankly, I doubt the manuscripts are first-century as your monk friend claims, but even so, they'll provide useful background for your dissertation on the legend."

"But doesn't it make sense that Jesus gained his spiritual wisdom from somewhere?" Kristin asked.

"Not necessarily," the professor replied. "The New Testament describes Jesus' baptism around the age of thirty by John as the turning point in his life that led him to begin his ministry. Jesus gained his unique insight through the power of the Holy Spirit that was latent in him from birth, not from some Indian guru teaching him to meditate."

"What about the specifics of his teachings?" Kristin pressed.

"Must Jesus have traveled to India to discover certain truths about the world?"

"Oh my God," Grant interrupted. Staring at the computer balanced on his thigh, he felt the blood drain from his head so quickly he feared he might lose consciousness. "The pictures—they're gone."

Kristin craned her head over his shoulder. After a glance at the blank folder on his desktop, she snatched her camera from the floor by her chair.

Fighting the nausea creeping into his throat, Grant began a search of all his files. The response came back too quickly. Other than a few logos and some stock photography, his hard drive contained no pictures, not even ones he'd had for years. *But they were there last night!* his mind screamed. He was planning to upload them online when his discovery of the publication of the Issa texts distracted him.

"Grant." Kristin's voice trembled.

He looked from his computer screen. Her eyes were welling up. She held a tiny plastic case in one hand and her camera in the other.

"My camera. The memory card. It's empty."

Grant's mind raced. The leaked email. The computer. The camera. Somehow his discovery had been compromised. *But how?*

CHAPTER 20

⸺ ∞ ⸺

EMORY UNIVERSITY
ATLANTA, GEORGIA

THE MERCEDES PULLED to the curb in front of a white stone building whose rows of Doric columns gave it the appearance of a Greek temple: Emory University's Glenn Memorial Auditorium. The driver cut off the ignition, opened his door, and walked around to the rear passenger side.

Sitting in the back seat, William Jennings turned to his boss and said, "This is the moment you've been praying for, Brian."

Brady stared out the window. The fading light from the setting sun cast a fiery glow over the majestic oak trees rising from the lawn in front of the building. Two dozen people carrying signs marched along the sidewalk. A white truck with red lettering on the side and satellite antennas on the roof was parked directly in front of the Mercedes.

"CNN." Brady grinned broadly. "And protestors!"

"From the congregation. A bus arrived from Birmingham two hours ago. Unfortunately, the university won't let them into the hall itself, which is open only to those with Emory IDs after that bombing two weeks ago, but they'll make good news coverage."

Brady nodded. He could always depend on Jennings. In the two days since his number two had explained his strategy for boosting Brady's public profile and book sales, Jennings had worked tirelessly to pull off the event that would take place this evening. *The voice of the believers.* That would be Brady's role. Eyeing the news truck and the protestors, Brady was anxious to greet his fans.

"Now, did you review the dossier on Grant Matthews I prepared?"

"I flipped through the stuff, but come on. Regurgitating a prepared statement will make me seem stiff. I do this every Sunday in front of thousands. I can handle a discussion with a student."

"I'm sure you'll be brilliant as always, but don't underestimate him. These PhD candidates are well versed in their biblical history, and giving a sermon in front of an adoring audience isn't the same as debating an academic in a university setting."

"Who do you know who can quote scripture like I can? So he may have more fancy degrees than I do, but he lacks the most important factor."

"What?"

"Faith. Faith, my friend."

"Then I'm sure you won't need these notes." Jennings patted the leather satchel in his lap. "But I'll leave them by your seat, just in case."

Brady glanced out the car window at the auditorium. "Let's get on with this."

"Hold just a minute. I've planned an entrance."

"Well, I'm ready, and . . ." Brady's voice trailed off when the protestors congregated in front of his driver, exactly as Jennings must have instructed.

The chanting of the voices in unison was music to Brady's ears: "Reverend Brady, save our Jesus!" An intense light washed over his parishioners; a camera crew had emerged from the CNN truck. As soon as the crowd noticed the presence of the camera, their chanting grew to a roar.

"You never cease to amaze me, William."

"That's my job."

The driver opened the car door. Reverend Brady paused just long enough for the camera lights to swing in his direction. He then rose from the car to the cheers of his people. He wore a smile on his face as comfortable as his perfectly draped Armani suit. The rush of the crowd's adulation flooded his body, much as it did each Sunday when he stepped into the spotlights on the church stage. But tonight would be different.

Tonight he would be seen by millions.

CHAPTER 21

GLENN MEMORIAL AUDITORIUM ATLANTA, GEORGIA

"I CAN'T BELIEVE I agreed to do this." Sweating in the cool evening air, Grant unbuttoned his Banana Republic blazer.

Although he wasn't yet used to his new cane, he kept a brisk pace along Fishburne Drive heading toward Glenn Memorial Auditorium. When the orthopedist removed his cast that morning, he'd pronounced that Karma had done a first-rate job setting the bones, but Grant was shocked to see how much his leg had atrophied since the accident six weeks earlier.

With the chaos of the past two days, Grant had almost forgotten about his leg. After overcoming the shock of finding that Kristin's photos had ceased to exist, he'd thrown himself into the task of figuring out what happened. He was off to a slow start. The Atlanta police were unimpressed with Grant's theory that someone had somehow stolen their electronics, erased the pictures, and then returned the computer and camera. Even as Grant articulated the idea, he heard how ridiculous it sounded: his apartment evidenced no signs of forced entry, nothing was missing, and the computer and camera hadn't been out of their sight. Maybe the annoyed officers were right. Could he have made a mistake downloading the pictures? He ground his teeth as he realized he had no leads to go on.

A few hours following his discovery of the missing photos, he called Karma to arrange a delivery to Kinley. He planned to purchase an inexpensive digital camera and FedEx it to his Bhutanese doctor to take to Kinley. *But will Kinley agree to take a new set of pictures?* The question played over and over in his head until Karma came on the line. The doctor's words opened the chasm in Grant's stomach even wider: Kinley had departed "on a trip" earlier that same day. To where, the doctor had no answer.

Grant picked up his pace and tugged at his collar button, which was suddenly restricting his airflow. Kinley must have heard what was happening. Why hadn't the monk contacted him? What if the lama had reacted negatively to the publicity about the Issa texts? He could have sent Kinley away. *And the texts themselves?* He tried not to think of what happened to Notovitch's reputation a hundred years earlier after the manuscript from the Himis monastery in India was never found. At least in all the publicity about the texts Grant had discovered, the monastery in Punakha had never been mentioned. But how long until that was uncovered too? Most disturbing, still, were the missing pictures. *What had happened to them?*

"Grant—" Kristin's voice interrupted his thoughts. "You've rehearsed your talking points for I don't know how many hours. You'll be great."

Kristin's high heels clicked down the sidewalk beside him. Grant turned his head to her but kept his nervous pace. He'd never seen her without a bohemian skirt or faded jeans and hiking boots, but she carried the professional look equally well. The beige tailored suit she'd purchased at the mall for this occasion complemented her figure—conservative without hiding her athletic frame. Following their discovery that the pictures of the texts were missing, she insisted on staying longer. After emailing her delinquent article to her editor, she'd helped Grant prepare for this night. Even Billingsly had underestimated the degree to which the press would be interested in Grant's discovery. As his mentor also predicted, the backlash from evangelical circles was already taking form. The loudest voice came from a church in the neighboring state of Alabama, a megachurch called New Hope. Why had he agreed to this event with the head pastor of the church denouncing his discovery?

He glanced again at Kristin. Not only was he thankful for the help, he admitted that he felt calmer when she was around. She exuded a quirky energy, but she was also grounded. She didn't have as much at stake as he did, but she was definitely invested.

"I'm just better with one-on-one discussions, not this circus atmosphere," he mumbled.

"Just think of it as training for the day you'll stand in front of your own class of eager college freshmen."

"Well, my classroom won't have TV cameras." He jabbed his cane on the sidewalk with each quick-paced step. His mouth had gone dry the previous morning when Billingsly announced that his first exposure to the press, if he accepted the invitation, would be a discussion with Reverend Brian Brady of New Hope in front of an audience of hundreds of Emory students and faculty and broadcast to millions. He'd had only a day to process the problem of the missing photos, and now he had to cram for this. At first he said no, but Kristin had convinced him otherwise.

"I agree with Professor Billingsly," she said. "The best way to persuade the monks to release the documents will be to generate a groundswell of international pressure. We can't do that without the media."

"But why not have a panel discussion among scholars?" His voice rose despite his efforts to control it. "Why am I debating a fundamentalist preacher who thinks I'm the mouthpiece of Satan?"

What he'd read about this man seemed all too familiar to Grant. He was reminded of every Sunday of his childhood: sitting in the front pew of the small church and watching his father's face red with passion, spit flying from his lips as he urged the congregation to give up their sinful ways.

"He's popular and quite controversial. The scholar versus the preacher." Kristin smiled at him. "It'll make great TV. Why do you think CNN wanted to host the event?"

"You make it sound like a prizefight."

They were almost to the auditorium, and Grant was getting overheated. He paused to take off his jacket and toss it over his shoulder. He didn't want to appear any more nervous in front of the cameras than he already was.

Grant now understood that the fundamentalists would try to turn this event into a circus, the very thing that Lama Dorji wanted to keep out of his bucolic monastery. His best option would be to try to subdue the opposition early on. That was the only reason he'd acquiesced to this rushed-together debate.

Kristin touched his elbow. "You've worked your ass off for so many years preparing for this moment. Don't worry about style or theatrics, because that's all this guy is about. You have something much more powerful: substance."

Grant stopped abruptly. "Where did they come from?"

At the base of the steps leading to the auditorium, twenty protestors chanted. His eyes paused on one of the signs held by a middle-aged woman: a poster depicting the figure of Jesus (with long blond hair, like the woman with the sign, he noted) with arms raised, standing in a graveyard. The tombstones listed the deceased: Muhammad, Buddha, Moses, Lao-tzu, Confucius. Scrawled across the top of the poster in blood red ink was printed, "Only Jesus Still Lives."

"They don't look like college students," he said.

Grant had greeted a few friends and colleagues on his way into the building, but now he fidgeted in his seat behind the rectangular table on the auditorium stage. The forty-foot vaulted ceiling above the rows of tiered white pews made the obvious point: he was out of his element. Glenn Memorial was not only the largest auditorium on campus, it also doubled as the sanctuary for the Glenn Memorial United Methodist Church, which had opened there in 1931.

The last time Grant had set foot in a church was ten years earlier, at his father's funeral, but that had been a small gathering after the scandal, just family and a few close friends. On this night, the auditorium was packed with hundreds.

Grant tried to focus on the faces of the faculty and students filing into the pews. A few waved to him. The hum of the many voices echoed in his head. He straightened the yellow legal pad filled with careful notes in his precise handwriting, and Kristin poured him a glass of water from the pitcher on the table. Watching the beads of condensation roll down the outside of the pitcher, he regretted his choice of the blue oxford shirt: it would show the sweat he felt start to form on his torso. Kristin wiped a finger along the pitcher, drawing a smiley face.

"Here, drink this." She handed him the water. "And don't forget to breathe, like Kinley taught you."

"Thanks."

A bright light blinded him momentarily. Shielding his eyes, he saw that a camera on a large tripod in the center of the front row had been turned on. A technician scurried about, making adjustments.

"Mr. Matthews?"

A man in his midfifties, with groomed silver hair and a tailored suit, approached. Grant recognized him immediately, although he couldn't recall his name. He wore more makeup than Kristin, who, incidentally, he'd never seen in makeup before tonight.

Grant took the outstretched hand. "Hello."

"So pleased to meet you too. Charles Dawson, your moderator tonight."

Yes, Dawson. The CNN weekend news anchor's smooth baritone voice was immediately familiar.

"Nice to meet you, Charles. Easy on me. I'm a TV virgin." He somehow managed a laugh.

"Nothing to worry about. We're not live. We'll edit out the boring parts." The anchor precisely enunciated every word that came out of his mouth. "Fascinating discovery, by the way. Looking forward to hearing about it."

Remembering Kristin's advice, Grant took a deep breath and released it, trying to will the muscles in his shoulders to release. *Maybe this won't be too bad*, he thought. Dawson seemed nice enough, and he'd certainly be more sympathetic to Grant's position than he would be to that of some fundamentalist preacher from Alabama.

A commotion erupted at the rear of the hall. Several of the protestors entered and began to argue with the two campus security guards stationed at the door. Dawson nodded to his cameraman, who swung the bulky TV camera in the front row to film the disturbance.

"Never know when you'll get interesting footage," the anchor quipped.

Grant watched the bodies jockeying for admission to the closed event. Among them a single figure slipped by the distracted guards and slid into a seat in the rear pew. Short, but broad-shouldered, he wore a crew cut and sat with a military posture. His complexion appeared flushed, as if he'd just run to the auditorium. *He doesn't look like faculty, and he's too old to be a student,* Grant thought.

Just as quickly as the disruption began, the group hushed. They parted to allow a figure to emerge from the darkness of the night. The camera's spotlight glinted off the man's silver belt buckle, which held up his generous but tailored suit pants. The man said something Grant couldn't hear to the people around him. They beamed at him like groupies coming face to face with a rock star. The protestors then filed silently out the door, with the exception of the military-looking man who remained in the last pew. Grant considered alerting someone, but then he became distracted by Reverend Brady, who strode down the steps toward the stage. Before Grant had entered the building ten minutes earlier, he'd noticed that Brady was speaking to a second camera crew on the building steps. The scene could have come from one of countless movies in which prosecutors postured outside the courthouse before a major trial. Grant had lowered his head and hurried past, unnoticed.

The chatter of conversation in the auditorium cut to a silent anticipation. Brady shook hands with the audience members in the rows nearest him as he passed, while placing his hands on the shoulders of others, reminding Grant of the president entering the House of Representatives before his State of the Union speech.

"He certainly can make an entrance," Dawson said. "This should be fun."

Grant was certain that "fun" would not have been the word he would've chosen. The brief moment of calm he'd felt a minute ago quickly dissolved.

"Just keep breathing," whispered the voice in his ear. He felt Kristin's warm hand gently squeeze his before she released it to take her seat in the front row beside Professor Billingsly. They were positioned directly in his line of sight.

"Good day, ladies and gentlemen. I am Charles Dawson, and this is CNN." Dawson spoke to the camera rather than the audience from behind the lectern next to the table where Grant and Brady sat. "Today we bring you an exclusive discussion from Emory University in Atlanta on an explosive new discovery about one of the world's most sacred books, the Bible. Could a set of ancient documents discovered in a remote monastery in Asia change the way we think about Jesus of Nazareth? Let me introduce you to our guests."

Grant heard little of the introduction Dawson gave. Instead, he concentrated on the notes on the yellow pad in front of him. His mouth was dry again. He reached for the glass in front of him. Out of the corner of his eye, he noted the relaxed way the reverend reclined in the chair at the other end of the table, as if he'd just enjoyed a large meal.

"Let's begin first with our doctoral candidate, Mr. Matthews. Would you tell us please about the discovery of the texts."

"Okay. Um," he stammered. "Well, you see . . ." A wave of heat rose through his body. Although he couldn't see past the first few rows with the bright lights in his face, he sensed each of the hundreds of people staring at him. He found Kristin and Billingsly, who simultaneously nodded their heads. He glanced again at his notes but had trouble reading his neat handwriting. What had been a clear outline moments before had turned blurry.

"Excuse me," Dawson interrupted, "would you move your microphone closer; we're having trouble picking up your audio."

Thankful for the brief respite, Grant reached for the microphone on the table in front of him, but in doing so, he bumped his water glass. With a quick move, he grabbed the glass before it toppled. Only a few drops sloshed out, but the commotion of his reflex caused the microphone to fall to its side, sending a loud pop through the auditorium. After moving the glass a safe distance away, he righted the microphone and moved it several inches closer to his face. The fear of forgetting what he wanted to say was quickly replaced with a new source of embarrassment. He heard giggles throughout the room.

"Nice save, Grant," came the smooth voice from the lectern. "No worries. We're taping. Let's do it again." The anchor paused, smiling at the camera until he received a nod from the producer standing by the cameraman. He continued, as if Grant's clumsiness had never interrupted the show, "Would you mind starting us off with the story of how you found these texts?"

Grant stared into the audience. Kristin still wore a calm expression, showing none of the panic he felt. He met her eyes. Realizing that he was holding his breath, he slowly exhaled. Leaning to the microphone, he forced a smile that he hoped didn't look fake.

"Yes, well, Charles," he began, and then launched into the brief synopsis of his trip and the discovery in the monastery's library without mentioning either the location in Punakha or Kinley's involvement.

The words seemed to come from somewhere deep inside him, more as a distant echo in his head than from his mouth. He'd rehearsed this speech at least a dozen times the previous evening with Kristin. To his surprise, the more he talked, the easier it became. He unclenched his hands from his lap and began to make small gestures. He described the condition of the dusty books with their thick parchment.

"How can we know if these documents truly date back to the time of Jesus?" Dawson asked.

"As of today, we can't," he replied to the expected question. "I want to emphasize that what's been posted on the web is only a preliminary translation of the texts. Drawing any conclusions about their authenticity or age at this time is purely speculative."

"Well then, why work everyone up into a frenzy over what might be some monk's overactive imagination or, worse, an outright fraud?" Reverend Brady boomed. The steely look in his eyes, coupled with a grin that was even whiter than Dawson's, reminded Grant of one of those Discovery Channel shark shows. *Just breathe*, he thought. He wasn't going to be intimidated.

Grant willed himself to return Brady's smile. "It took decades after the Dead Sea Scrolls were found before many scholars had access to the texts jealously guarded by a few. But we want scholars to make up their own minds in real time, not after the fact."

"Then why haven't you released the actual manuscripts yet?" the reverend shot back.

He measured his words carefully. "They're being kept safe in the monastery where they've been for hundreds of years while we discuss with the authorities the procedures for sending a team of experts to study them." The tension crept back into his neck.

"Reverend, I take it you have some doubts about the authenticity of the texts?" Dawson asked.

"Ever since the time of Jesus, people have tried to hijack his name for their own agendas. Just look at the nonsense written about the so-called Gnostic Gospels. This recent find is no different. Just as the Gnostic Gospels were written by heretics well after the events took place, I have no doubt that these Issa texts will be shown to be the same."

"But Reverend, how can you make that claim until the manuscripts have been studied?" Dawson asked. "What if they prove to date from Jesus' time?"

"Charles, you're speaking in wild speculation. To date, we've seen nothing of these writings. We don't even know if they exist." He gave Grant a studied look before continuing. "The whole idea of Jesus learning his divinely inspired teachings from some guru in India is preposterous."

"Preposterous?" Grant responded. "Nothing in the New Testament directly contradicts what we found in the Issa texts."

"As I clearly outline in my book, *Why Is God So Angry?*"—Brady lifted a copy of his book from the table and held it directly in the line of the camera— "Christianity is the unique, one and only path to God and to salvation. As it is written in John, chapter fourteen, verse six: 'I am the way, the truth, and the life: no man cometh unto the Father, but by me.'" Brady sighed deeply. "I'm afraid that over these past few years we have been witnessing the consequences of disobeying God's wishes."

Grant felt the blood rise to his head. The pastor had just used the occasion of the first public discussion on the Issa texts to plug his own book! Grant opened his mouth to respond with a few historical examples of the influences of earlier religions on the development of the writings of the Bible, such as the flood story in the Epic of Gilgamesh that was centuries *older* than the similar Noah story in Genesis, or the liberal borrowing of Canaanite characterizations of God in the early Hebrew conceptions of their own deity. In his mind the Issa texts were no different. After all, Grant thought, *religions were created by humans to serve our insecurities and explain our existence, and these creations never occurred in a vacuum.* But then another idea came to him.

"Reverend," Grant asked, "I take it you consider yourself to be an expert on the Bible?"

"Son, I've been studying scripture since you were in diapers."

"Then maybe you can point out for us where it describes what Jesus was doing between the ages of twelve and twenty-nine."

Brady opened his mouth to respond, closed it again, and then glared at him. He said, "Jesus grew up with his family in Nazareth, learning to be a carpenter like his father, Joseph."

"But the Bible doesn't actually say that. Does it, Reverend?" Grant relaxed the hands that had gripped his thighs moments before. "Actually, the Bible is completely silent about those years of his life, isn't it?"

A quiet murmur spread through the audience.

Brady's face reddened, but his voice remained steady. "The Bible is silent on those years because nothing noteworthy happened. But the Good Book is very clear on the most important fact: Jesus was born to the Virgin Mary, as the Son of God, which is why he had no need to travel afar to become inspired. But then you probably don't believe in the virgin birth either. Do you, son?"

"I understand that his birth stories were written in an age when people had little understanding of the science of reproduction." Grant gestured again with his hands as he spoke. He was on familiar territory now. "The woman was seen only as a vessel for the man's seed and not as a contributor to the child's genetic makeup. Now, Reverend, in the Gospels, isn't Jesus referred to as both the Son of God and the Son of Man?"

"Those terms aren't mutually exclusive."

"Yet you refer to him exclusively as the Son of God, but he only refers to himself that way six times, and that's usually after someone else uses the term first. On the other hand, Jesus calls himself the Son of Man *eighty-five times*. Shouldn't we be emphasizing the humanity of Jesus: the man he was in history, the influences that led him to his ministry?"

Brady folded his arms across his chest. "Jesus was a man, yes, but he was the incarnation of God himself, sent here to save us."

Grant leaned forward on the table, angling his body toward both Brady and the audience. "Caesar Augustus was regularly referred to as a son of God and as a divine ruler, as were Alexander the Great and King David. Roman mythology, derived from the Greeks, had many stories of gods impregnating women. For example, Heracles, or Hercules, was born from a mortal woman but fathered by the god Zeus—a story the New Testament authors would've known."

"Nonsense," Brady sneered. "I think we all know the difference between the word of God and the silly stories of a pagan people."

"Do we?" Grant asked. "You're aware, I assume, that the oldest writings in the New Testament, Paul's letters and Mark's gospel, never mention the virgin birth?"

"Of course I am."

"Right, the story only appears in the Gospels of Matthew and Luke, written some eighty years after this miraculous birth supposedly took place, when the authors, who never themselves met Jesus, were trying to establish a community of followers. Oh, and the details of the birth story itself vary significantly in those two gospels."

Brady raised his hand, as if to silence him. "A tired argument from the nonbelievers. Look, each New Testament author merely focused on different aspects of Jesus' life. Just because one author chose to concentrate on different facts than the others doesn't mean anything."

"Or if they chose to omit Jesus' travels during the missing twenty years?" Grant added.

"That's not my point!" Brady raised his voice for the first time. "You're twisting my words."

"Well, Reverend," Dawson interjected smoothly, "isn't Mr. Matthews just demonstrating that because the Bible contains gaps in the story of Jesus' life, as well as tales about him that some could interpret as mythology, then—"

"Mythology?" Brady boomed. "What you both fail to comprehend is that these other stories—be they pagan, Hindu, or Buddhist in origin—are irrelevant because the Bible is the only writing that contains the actual word of God!" He snatched his book from the table and shook it over his head as if he were brandishing a Bible. "I explain it all here."

"I'm sorry"—Grant leaned into his microphone—"but that's too convenient for me. The Bible is one hundred percent accurate, and any evidence suggesting otherwise is Satan at work?"

"Finally, we agree on something," Brady quipped. Scattered laughter from around the audience returned him to his more relaxed demeanor.

"How can you say that?" Grant asked.

"I can say that, young man, because I have faith. Faith that the Bible is the absolute and inerrant word of God. I know that *faith* is anathema to you academic types, but faith guides my life. Faith lets me sleep soundly at night, knowing that God takes care of me."

"Having faith in God is one thing, but taking the Bible literally as the only and infallible way God has spoken to the world just doesn't—"

"It may not make sense to you," Brady smoothly interrupted, causing Grant to shoot a quick glance at Dawson, "because you've closed your eyes to the truth. You come to the Bible with your preconceptions of the way the world should be. You either accept the Bible as is, or you don't. It's really that simple."

"Reverend," Dawson said, "how do you know the Bible is the one and only literal word of God?"

Without missing a beat, he responded, "Paul, in the first chapter of Galatians, verses eight and nine, wrote, 'Though we, or an angel from heaven, preach any gospel unto you than that which we preached unto you, let him be accursed.'"

"Can't you see your argument is completely circular?" Grant said. "You say the Bible is accurate because it's the word of God, and you believe that it's the word of God because it says so in the Bible. You rely on the document itself for its own authenticity."

A look of irritation crossed Brady's face, but he spoke again in a measured tone, "No, son, I'm relying on my faith."

"So every word in the Bible concerning Jesus is one hundred percent true and accurate?"

"Now, you said something intelligent." Brady displayed his gleaming teeth. "But you forgot to add that it is also complete. If God had wanted us to have other information about Jesus, he would have guided the authors to include it."

Grant shook his head. Arguing with Brady was like a distant echo of his adolescence. "The Bible must be read in the context of the age in which it was written," he pursued. "During biblical times, earthquakes, droughts, floods, and windstorms were all believed to be caused by angry gods, not by changing weather patterns. People had no concept of microbiology, of germs. Disease was seen as God's punishment for the sinful. Schizophrenia and other mental diseases were not viewed as imbalances of brain chemistry but as possession by demons who must be cast out."

Brady raised his voice. "I've seen people with my own eyes who've been healed from these physical diseases by their faith in Jesus."

"Doctors would call that the placebo effect," Grant said. "Isn't that why new drugs undergo double-blind research studies? If you give a sugar pill to a sick person and tell them it's medicine, they'll get better merely because they believe they are being healed."

Brady's ingratiating smile was still plastered on his face, but now Grant thought it looked strained. Small beads of sweat were starting to form along his well-coiffed hairline. He was human after all.

"Maybe in your world you can convert everything to a scientific theory or a mathematical formula. But I don't want to live in a world where God becomes an equation. I see miracles every day in the lives of people who have accepted Christ. The proof is not just in the Good Book, it surrounds us today."

"But even today, voodoo doctors in Haiti and medicine men in Africa are revered in their cultures because they perform healings similar to those you claim Jesus performed."

Brady pulled a pale blue handkerchief from the inside pocket of his jacket and wiped his brow. Replacing the cloth in his pocket, he took a long drink from his water glass, the first time he'd touched it the entire night. His voice turned venomous. "What you seek is the lust for knowledge of that which should be left unknown. You desire another bite of the apple."

A murmur spread through the crowd at Brady's last comment. Dawson raised his hands to quiet them. Grant knew he'd rattled the reverend.

Dawson cleared his throat and leaned into his microphone. "So, Mr. Matthews, your point is that the New Testament was never meant to be either a complete history or a scientific text about Jesus?"

"Precisely." The words rolled off Grant's tongue. He could feel his peers in the audience drinking in each of his arguments. He realized that he'd stressed over Brady for nothing. "Leaving aside both the missing years and the scientific problems, the Gospels also contradict each other about the details of Jesus' life. In John, for example, Jesus' ministry lasts three years; in the other Gospels it only lasts one. In John, Jesus cleanses the Temple in Jerusalem in the beginning of his ministry, but in the others, he does so at the end of his ministry. Even the details of the resurrection differ significantly from gospel to gospel."

Grant expected the reverend to jump on his last comment, but instead he bent over and searched through the leather satchel by his chair. When he removed a file folder and began to flip through the pages, Grant taunted him, "So which gospel is correct, Reverend?"

Tim reached underneath his shirt sleeve and began to scratch. The burning on his arms almost matched the fire in his chest. How could this guy treat the reverend with such disrespect? At that moment, Tim regretted not having pulled the trigger when he stood over Matthews's sleeping body a few nights earlier. Then he thought of the bombing at the CDC and its less-than-spectacular effects. Surveying the unbelievers in the audience, he realized a bomb in this auditorium would have yielded a more satisfactory result.

Blasphemy, he thought, *every word out of the grad student's mouth is blasphemy.* Jesus wasn't a man; he was God. That's what Tim had learned as a child and what he knew was true. It had to be true. You don't worship a man; that was idolatry. Tim vividly recalled the reverend's description of God's fate for blasphemers. Tim wanted nothing more than to kill Matthews at that very moment.

Watching the audience's pleasure in the reverend's obvious discomfort, he thought how he'd predicted this reaction in his email to the reverend and Jennings. Tim saw things that others were too dense to comprehend. From the moment he came across the web posting about these hateful Issa texts, Tim heard the calling. The voice he heard was one he'd been waiting his whole life to hear: the voice of Jesus leading him to his destiny.

He removed his hand from his arm and attended to his forehead. Hooking his thumbnail under a piece of loose skin just over his eyebrow, he pulled the prize away and allowed it to drop to the floor. The itching subsided.

For the first time in his life, he understood his purpose—his larger part in God's plan. And now he had supporters much more powerful than that doofus Johnny. He would achieve the redemption and recognition he'd prayed for. Erasing the photographs was just the first step.

"Well, Reverend," Dawson asked, "why isn't there room in the silence of the Gospels about Jesus' young adult life to accommodate a spiritual journey to India?"

Brady turned his gaze from his paper to Dawson and then to the camera. "The Gospels simply cannot accommodate Mr. Matthews's New Age fantasy. When the angel Gabriel came to Mary in a dream, the Gospels clearly state that Jesus was born the Son of God. The Only Son didn't discover his spirituality from some Eastern mystics. I may not have the answers to every question that can be posed by twisting around the teachings of the Bible, but where Mr. Matthews looks at those questions and chooses to disbelieve, I simply choose to believe."

Grant was surprised at how quickly Brady recovered the calm confidence with which he'd begun the evening.

"Mr. Matthews," Dawson asked, "does this debate about your discovery boil down to faith in one's religious beliefs versus faith in the scientific method?"

"Absolutely not. The reverend misuses faith to hide behind a wall of ignorance. It's one thing to have faith in those fundamental questions to which we can never know the true answers: What is the nature of God? Is there life after death? But refusing to accept archaeological or other scientific evidence because it conflicts with one's belief system is not faith. That's called ignorance. Real truths, as opposed to imagined ones, are able to stand up to rigorous debate and questioning. What I sense in you, Reverend, is a deep and powerful fear."

"Fear! With faith in Christ, I have nothing to fear!"

Grant resisted a smile. He'd achieved a similar reaction from his father many years earlier with the same statement.

Grant leaned toward the microphone. "If you were truly confident in your faith, you would welcome any evidence that might shed light on the life of Jesus. Instead, you seek to persuade people to reject without any study what we have found, because you fear where it may lead."

"I have no such fear," Brady said coldly, "because I already know that you have cooked up this entire spectacle as an elaborate hoax: either these texts do not exist or they were fabricated."

"How can you say that!" Grant burst out, letting his frustration show for the first time. "We haven't even begun to study them yet."

"All we have to show from your so-called discovery are *your* own writings of what *you* claim to be a translation."

"As I said earlier, we are very early in the process of—"

"We know you don't possess the texts themselves; what proof do you have that they even exist?"

Grant hesitated. He thought he'd avoided this line of questioning earlier. Only a handful of people—he, Kristin, Billingsly, the police, and Karma—knew about the missing pictures. "We are still in the process of working through our notes, and—"

"More doublespeak. If you had proof, you would've published it. All we have to go on is your word right now. And we both know you have problems in that department."

Grant froze. Brady couldn't possibly know. A wave of nausea crept from his stomach into his throat.

Thankfully, Dawson intervened. "That's a bold statement, Reverend Brady."

"What Mr. Matthews hasn't told you is that over a hundred years ago, a Russian journalist named"—Brady referred to the paper he had taken from his folder—"Nicholas Notovitch made a very similar claim to what Mr. Matthews has made today, but then the book he claimed to have seen mysteriously disappeared." Brady now appeared as relaxed as if he were giving his Sunday sermon.

"Actually, the Notovitch report just supports our case," Grant said, relieved that Brady wasn't going where he feared. "But anyway our findings are different. You see—"

"My child, my child." Brady held up his hand to quiet him, shaking his head. "Isn't it time to give up this ruse? Confess that this ordeal was a mistake that just got out of hand."

"What are you talking about!" Grant exploded. Refusing to accept the evidence of his findings was one thing, but accusing him of making it up was too much.

"I think you know what I'm talking about." Brady stared at him with a smug expression. "This may be painful for you, my son, but if I don't rescue my people from your shamefulness, then the blood of your sins will be on my hands too." Brady pointed a finger at Grant like a criminal prosecutor pointing out the defendant and declared to the audience, "You see, Mr. Matthews here has a history of academic fraud."

The blood rushed out of Grant's head, causing a powerful vertigo. His mind screamed at him to run before Brady could complete his accusation, but every muscle in his body was paralyzed. A murmur broke out among the audience.

Brady waved the sheet of paper he'd studied moments before. "When Mr. Matthews was in college just a few years ago, he plagiarized an entire paper for a class. Copied someone else's work as his own. Were it not for him pulling some strings, he would've been expelled. What we have here with all this Issa nonsense is just another example of his scholarly dishonesty."

Grant sensed every head in the audience turn toward him, but he only saw Kristin's horrified expression in the first pew. The weight of the silence in the hall as they anticipated his response squeezed the air out of his lungs like a straitjacket cinched too tight. He tried to swallow, but his tongue stuck in his mouth as if it were a foreign object.

How was he to explain?

His mind searched for the words, but he might as well have been randomly flipping through a dictionary. Nothing came to him. His eyes darted between Brady and Dawson—both wore curious and, he thought, amused expressions.

CHAPTER 22

⸺◦∞◦⸺

BIRMINGHAM, ALABAMA

THE COMPUTER'S LED screen cast a blue glow around Tim's cubicle in the otherwise dark office. Tim had left Atlanta at the end of the debate and returned to Birmingham around midnight. After four and a half hours of sleep, he was the first one in the office, as usual. Today was special, however. Today would be his last day working for his imbecilic boss, Duncan Summers, and the other losers of the IT group. He'd been called upon to carry out a mission of supreme importance. He felt almost giddy when he thought about how far he'd come in just two weeks: from having to partner with a lowlife like Johnny to becoming a true soldier in God's army.

He clicked through the airline's website. His travel schedule over the next week would be grueling, but then he'd flown around the world in military transport planes for a decade. The passenger seat of a commercial airliner would be luxurious in comparison. He thought through the checklist of what he'd need for his travels. Some of the more specialty items he already possessed, but he had a new idea he was excited to explore after he finished his tickets. Tomorrow morning he'd fly to DC. Once there, he'd hurry to the Indian embassy for his travel visa. The following day he was scheduled to fly to New Delhi via London.

His online searches had revealed only two paths into Bhutan: fly through either India or Thailand. From the east coast of the United States, the India route was faster. Plus, he admitted to himself, Thailand held certain temptations for him—temptations that he would not expose himself to now that he was doing God's work. Unfortunately, when he arrived in India, he couldn't just continue straight into Bhutan. The Bhutanese government was stingy in handing out travel visas. The backlog in their New York consulate could take several weeks, he'd learned with a quick call. He didn't have that much time. The firestorm over the heretical Issa texts was heating up. Even after Grant Matthews's humiliation last night, the media would be clamoring to get to the texts. Tim had to find them first. Fortunately, he'd discovered he could obtain a visa from the Bhutanese embassy in New Delhi in only a few days. He would wait there, and once he had the visa, he would be much closer to his destination.

He clicked the onscreen button to finalize his itinerary.

"Damn it, William." Brady slammed his open palm on the top of his nineteenth-century English desk. "You should've prepared me better. I looked like a fool up there. Look at me sweat." He hit the pause button on the remote, freezing the image on the forty-two-inch flat-screen mounted to the wall between the cherry bookcases in his church office. The monitor depicted the reverend with a furrowed brow, flushed cheeks, and sweat-soaked temples.

"I warned you he'd be well prepared. But that's irrelevant now. The focus of this story hasn't been on the substance of the debate but on your revelation of his cheating."

Brady clicked on the play button of the remote, and they watched the concluding scene of the previous night's debate for the fourth time that day since CNN aired it at eleven AM.

"That was masterful, wasn't it?" Brady grinned.

"We've received dozens of calls from news organizations wanting to interview you."

Finally, Brady thought, *I'll receive the exposure I deserve.* How else could he spread God's word, if he was limited to one state? God had given him a gift and meant for him to share it. "Make sure you schedule the TV reporters before the newspaper ones."

"Already done." A smile spread across Jennings's face, an unusual occurrence. "Our publisher has rushed more copies of your book to print. Sales will skyrocket."

Brady relaxed into his leather desk chair. His election to the presidency of the NAE was now almost assured.

CHAPTER 23

∞∞∞

ATLANTA, GEORGIA

Sitting at the round dining table in his apartment, Grant swirled the Absolut and tonic in his glass. He watched the lime spin in the clear liquid, just as the thoughts spun in his mind. After CNN aired the previous night's debate that morning, his apartment phone had rung constantly. He'd answered over a dozen calls from reporters asking the same questions; then he finally unplugged it. He still couldn't shake the image of his pale face frozen on the TV, his mouth moving wordlessly. Dawson had stepped in, giving Grant an opportunity to rebut Brady's charge, but Grant had only managed to mumble something about having gone through a difficult period in college. Then it was all over, except for the replays of his embarrassment that the news network seemed to show continually. Kristin and Billingsly had both tried to comfort him, but he'd just withdrawn into silence. He suspected that Billingsly had given her a quick summary of what had happened his sophomore year, and so far she hadn't pried. Looking across the table as she began to eat, he knew that would change.

Grant took a mouthful of the pasta Kristin had cooked for dinner. *Not bad*, he thought, *but lacking a key ingredient—meat.*

"How can you be a vegetarian?" he asked, hoping to delay the other conversation he knew would follow. From their time together he had noticed that she never touched meat. He always thought that vegetarians missed out on key amino acids in their diets. Anyway, he liked a good steak too much.

"One day my mom bought a basket of blue crabs for dinner. We lived in Baltimore; my dad was an ob-gyn professor at Johns Hopkins. We ate crab

once a month, but on this occasion, watching her drop the squirming creatures into the boiling water nauseated me. When we sat down at the table and
my dad cracked the shells with a mallet, I began to cry. I still remember the
splintering sound. Some juice squirted me in the face, and I announced that I
wasn't going to eat any. He got furious and told me I wasn't leaving until I
finished my crab. He said that his, and by that he also meant my, Japanese
heritage had always valued seafood."

"He had a temper?"

"Not when we were younger, but when my sister died, he changed." She
shook her head as if to clear it. "So we sat there for two hours, not speaking.
Finally, I looked him in the eyes and took a mouthful of crab."

"So it was over?"

"I ran into the bathroom and threw up. Haven't touched meat or seafood
since."

As if to emphasize the point, she picked up a piece of mango from the top
of her salad, rolled it between her slender fingers, and then placed it in her
mouth. Grant couldn't help but notice the way her full lips pulled the fruit
from her fingertips. She had a way of touching everything around her, whether
it was her food or his arm, like a blind person discerning the appearance of
something from the way it felt. She was so different from him in that respect,
yet he found her movements sensual. He had the urge to reach out and take
her hand. Instead, he clasped his together and rested them on the table.

"Can I ask you about your sister?" Grant asked, hoping he was broaching
the subject at a good moment. "What happened?"

For once, she glanced at the table instead of his eyes. Her normally relaxed
posture stiffened, but she began to speak. Grant listened in silence to Kristin's
story of how Isabelle, her older sister, as a freshman in high school had attended a party and gotten drunk on wine coolers. She was raped by five senior
boys in an upstairs bedroom. Isabelle had confided in Kristin but refused to
tell their strict, Catholic parents what happened, much less go to the authorities. Her sister said it was her fault for getting drunk. Isabelle was never the
same after the assault, withdrawing from her friends and struggling in school.
Their father responded by taking away her privileges and making her work

harder. Rumors spread around school that Isabelle was easy. Two years later, when Kristin was a freshman, Isabelle killed herself by swallowing a bottle of their mother's sleeping pills one night. Kristin was the one who tried to wake her the next morning.

The embarrassment Grant felt from the previous night's debate suddenly seemed petty compared to her story. Not knowing how to respond, he chose to say nothing. He extended his hand and brushed away the tears rolling down her face. She rested her cheek in his palm.

Within a minute she regained her composure and wiped her face with her napkin. "Enough of my history." She perched herself on the edge of her seat and leaned in close enough for him to catch the faint fragrance of her curly hair. "Time for yours."

Grant reached for his damp glass, swirled the drink again, and said, "Spring of my sophomore year. Pretty stressed. Working two jobs to pay tuition and taking extra hours. For some stupid reason, I thought graduating early would be a good idea. Did well at first. Made straight As. That is, until I received the call."

He gulped his vodka tonic, tasting the hint of lime in the cold drink that warmed his stomach. "Dad was in the hospital—heart attack."

"You mentioned in Bhutan that your dad was a preacher, like Brady. Right?"

"We hardly spoke anymore. When I went to UVA and rejected his funda-mentalist teachings, he cut off communication. In his eyes I was going to a godless institution. I'd told him I wanted to study religion as an academic; he knew I would never enter the ministry as he did."

The two of them had a shared passion in religion, but the fire that woke Grant up every day was in direct opposition to his father's goals: Grant wanted to demystify religion, at least Christianity, to uncover its historical roots and origins. By the time he'd entered grad school, he'd grown out of believing in the myths his father had taught him as a child. He'd learned to study the Bible as one would critically examine any ancient text. The books were written by real men, and the words didn't just appear on paper by God's sending a bolt of lightning from the sky. The authors would have been influenced by their own personal agendas, and their views were colored by living in an ancient world. That didn't even begin to cover the editing that happened over the centuries.

"Your mom?" Kristin's voice snapped him out of his brooding.

"She was the only real link we had. I drove to Richmond, where he'd been flown in a Life Flight helicopter from our small town. When I arrived, he was in intensive care, unconscious. My mother was by his bed, but she couldn't even speak." For the first time, his voice faltered. "Just a shell of a woman."

"Seeing her husband like that must have been difficult."

He shook his head. "Dad's heart attack occurred while he was in bed—at Lorraine's house. The twenty-four-year-old church secretary."

"Get out!"

"All his talk of sin and righteousness—" Grant grimaced. "In this small town, you can imagine how quickly word spread after the ambulance pulled up to Lorraine's and carted the minister out in his underwear, while the paramedics—two of his parishioners—pumped away on his chest."

"Your mom had no idea?"

"Not until the hospital called." Telling the story brought everything back to Grant. He shivered at the memory of the cold hospital room, listening to the beeping from the machines, and breathing in that hospital disinfectant smell. His larger-than-life father had tubes snaking out of his nose and mouth, and his face had assumed a pallid blue tint. His body seemed shrunken.

Kristin's hand on his arm returned him to the present. "That's awful," she said.

"All I could think of was the arguments we'd had: about his sermons, about the church, about my education. When I stood over his bed and my mom cried in the chair beside me, I wished for his death." Grant locked on to her eyes. "He died that night."

Her grip on his arm tightened. "You felt guilty?"

"Thought I handled the death well. The day I returned to school, I started to swim—a mile every morning. Two weeks later I ended up in the infirmary with an ulcer. But the medicine took care of that, and I threw myself into my classwork, determined more than ever to pursue my degree in religious studies. But the harder I studied, the more difficulty I had focusing. I fell farther behind, rewriting papers endlessly and rereading texts I'd already read twice. I panicked when finals approached, thinking I didn't have enough time to study for all my classes."

"So you took a shortcut?" she guessed.

He nodded. "Intro to Western Philosophy. Instead of an exam, we had a final paper. I'd already composed an extensive outline. My girlfriend at the time offered to write the paper for me." He swirled his drink again. The ice had almost melted. "A week later, I received a voicemail from my professor, requesting a meeting. Hardly slept that night. You see, I'd been in such a mental fog, I never even read the paper my girlfriend did for me. I just turned it in."

"When I arrived at the professor's office, the department head and the dean of students were sitting with him. They weren't there to discuss my unique theories. Instead of using my outline to write the paper, my girlfriend simply downloaded one from a site selling college research theses. As bad luck would have it, the paper I turned in as my own work was an assignment a grad student had written three years earlier for this same professor. I broke down in the office with these three men staring at me. I told them the story about my father. Looking back on it, I wish I'd been stronger."

"Don't be so hard on yourself. You were still suppressing grief from your father's death, maybe even some humiliation too. When your academic world then came crashing down on you, it was only natural for you to react like that."

"Dad brought on his own suffering. But my academic reputation—" His face hardened. "I knew what I did was wrong, but I rationalized I'd already done the intellectual work on my outline."

"How did they respond?"

"Because of the extenuating circumstances and my previous high grades, they allowed me to remain in school. I wrote the paper I'd already outlined and turned it in a week later. I received an A on the paper but still failed the class, and the incident was kept on my record. I'm pretty sure that's the reason I didn't get into Harvard for grad school."

"And your girlfriend?"

"I left her role out. Dumb of me for agreeing to the idea in the first place, but we did break up because of it."

"In Punakha you mentioned that Billingsly helped get you admitted to Emory."

Grant nodded. "The plagiarism incident was a red flag in my file from UVA. After I explained to Billingsly what had happened, he went to the admissions committee and vouched for my integrity and qualifications. I owe him everything."

Kristin reached across the table, unhinged his fingers from his tumbler, and interlaced them with hers. The warmth from her skin was comforting. "How could Brady have dug up that information?"

"Several of my friends knew about it. But what concerns me is that it isn't just this one incident. The photos vanished from your camera and my computer, the translation was leaked, and Kinley has gone missing. Are we involved in some sort of conspiracy?"

She sat up straighter. "I just don't see how that's possible. Those events are unrelated to each other. Sometimes bad things just happen at the same time."

He dropped her hand as a thought passed through his head. One common thread was woven through these events: the pictures, the email, the debate, even his relationship with Kinley: *Kristin.* Was it possible that this beautiful woman he felt so connected with, this journalist, had something . . .

No, he didn't believe that. *But,* the voice returned, *I've only known her a short time.* He shook his head. Something else was at work here. Billingsly had warned him that people would be threatened by his discovery. *But who?*

He pressed his fingertips into his temples. "No one will take our discovery seriously any longer."

Grant's self-pity quickly morphed into anger. Someone was trying to destroy his life. Blood flushed his neck and his pulse pounded even harder in his head than it had moments earlier. Just when he caught himself clenching his jaw and grinding his teeth, he heard a voice from his memory. It was Kinley speaking a single word: *dukkha.* Grant's cart had certainly come unhinged. *Actually smashed to smithereens was the more accurate analogy*, he thought.

Broken cart, broken leg, wild horses returning with a herd, fingers pointing to the moon—all Kinley's quaint aphorisms and parables, not to mention his meditation techniques, wouldn't resolve his current predicament. Grant realized that he couldn't accept this situation. He needed to do something.

He felt Kristin's gaze, waiting for him. "We just need to bring back the real texts," he said.

"But how? You've called Karma twice a day, and he has nothing on Kinley's whereabouts."

Grant stood from the table. She was right. He didn't like having to go through an intermediary to contact his monk friend. But he had no other choice for now. "It should be morning in Bhutan. I'm calling Karma again."

While Kristin carried their dishes to the sink, Grant followed with the glasses. He then unplugged his cell phone from the charger on the kitchen counter.

After a ring that sounded as if it came from inside a shoebox, the doctor answered.

"Karma, it's Grant. Any news?"

The disposal growled loudly.

Kristin glanced up from the dishes. "Sorry," she mouthed, cutting the switch.

Grant waved for her to continue. He walked through the living room across the Berber carpet, past the futon that was doubling as his bed, to the sliding glass door.

"Nothing new from yesterday, my American friend." A pause longer than the distance of the call warranted followed before Karma's voice came over the line again. "But now it seems Jigme has left the monastery too. It's possible he left with Kinley."

Grant stepped onto the small wooden balcony overlooking a mass of pine trees. The night had turned brisk, and he wore only a T-shirt and jeans. The cold sharpened his senses. He unsuccessfully tried to push away the thought that was intruding into his mind. Kinley and Jigme left the monastery the moment news of the texts became public. Certainly the monks couldn't have been playing him all along—or could they have? What if Brady was right?

He inhaled the crisp, pine-scented air, and sighed into the phone. "Karma, it's imperative that I to speak to Kinley."

After clicking his phone closed and stuffing it into his jeans pocket, Grant leaned on the wooden rail and peered into the darkness. He could see only the outline of the trees ahead of him. He suddenly shivered against the cold of the night.

He heard Kristin's footsteps behind him. Before he could turn, she slipped her bare arms around his waist. Her hair caressed the back of his neck. He could smell its floral fragrance. He felt the tension ebb from his body.

"Beautiful night." Her warm breath touched his cheek.

"Quite beautiful." He turned to her.

Her blue eyes searched his with the purposeful intensity that had both excited him and made him uncomfortable when they first met. He felt a powerful urge to kiss her. *But what if I'm just misinterpreting her touchy nature?* he worried. He didn't think he could handle getting rebuffed now. He needed Kristin as a friend more than ever.

To his surprise, she rose on her toes so that her face was inches from his. She slid her hands from his waist, grabbed the back of his neck, and pulled herself into his body. She kissed him hard, yet her mouth was soft. A tremor passed through to his core.

After several minutes of the wood railing digging into his back, he reluctantly broke the embrace. "It might be more comfortable inside," he said.

Without speaking, she took his hand and guided him, limping beside her, into the living room. She pushed him to the firm cushion of the futon, lowered her body on top of his, and brushed her lips along his neck. Grant traced his fingers from the delicate line of her neck to her collarbone and then down her spine. A sigh escaped her lips when he slipped his hands underneath her shirt and brought them to her breasts. She responded by biting his lower lip with enough force that he feared she might draw blood. He quickly forgot about his lip, though, when she pressed her pelvis into his, gently rocking her hips.

Barely able to contain himself, Grant dropped a hand to the front of her jeans, struggling for a moment with the button in his quivering fingers. Just when he succeeded, Kristin gently moved his hand from her waist up over his head, where she pinned it to the futon with her own.

"Not yet," she whispered.

His mind raced. Did she mean, "Not yet at this moment" or "Not yet today"? He'd never experienced a woman as independent or as passionate as

Kristin, and maybe this accounted for his insecurity, but she'd sent him mixed signals as well.

After another half hour of alternating tenderness and urgent passion, Grant sensed that "not yet" had become "okay now" when she pressed her body more firmly to his. He untangled his fingers from the soft curls of her hair, which had become damp with perspiration, and slid his hands down her sides to her lower back. Her nails bit into his shoulders. He slipped his fingers just underneath the waistband of her jeans. She ground her hips into his.

This is going to happen, he thought. He hadn't been with a woman in months and he hoped he wouldn't disappoint her. The brief doubts that flitted through his head were quickly replaced when her open mouth found his again. He liked the way she tasted, the way her hair fell around his face, the way her smooth skin swept in a graceful arch from her lower back to the top of her buttocks.

"I want you," he whispered, sliding his hands further down.

That's when she abruptly pushed away.

"I'm sorry," he said, quickly moving his hands. "Did I do something wrong?"

"No. No. My fault. I just let things go too far."

"That's okay. We don't have to have sex," he said, which was true, but he was disappointed to be saying it nonetheless.

"I know. I'm sorry, Grant. I got carried away."

She shifted off him and sat on the edge of the futon. Her disheveled hair fell around her face in damp strands, making her appear even more beautiful in the unkempt way of a fashion ad. She no longer stared into his eyes but instead gazed somewhere deep into his chest.

"So, what . . ."

"Ever since Isabelle's death, with guys—" She brushed her hair out of her face. "I mean, I'm not a virgin. It's just that if I really like someone, I can't—"

"Hey, don't stress about it." He took her hand. "I understand."

"It's getting late." Kristin stood, tucked in the shirt she normally wore loose, and buttoned her jeans. "We need to get some sleep before we get back to work on your situation tomorrow."

His humiliation at the debate, which he'd briefly forgotten until this moment, seemed to have brought them closer, but now she wouldn't look him in the eyes. Kristin moved toward the bedroom door, her back now toward him. He felt an insecurity expanding within his chest as questions danced in his head. *Was it really the memory of her sister that caused her to pull away or was it something else?* After everything that was going wrong, he wasn't sure he trusted his own judgment. He couldn't afford to have things weird with Kristin. He needed her now as much as he'd needed her camera in Bhutan.

She turned toward him and said, "We have plenty of time to talk later." The bedroom door closed behind her.

CHAPTER 24

~⚬~

EMORY UNIVERSITY
ATLANTA, GEORGIA

WHAT DOES BILLINGSLY WANT? Grant paused outside his mentor's office door.

The professor had called an hour earlier on Grant's cell just as he and Kristin were finishing breakfast. In an unusually strained voice, Billingsly asked him to come alone, so he'd dropped Kristin off at a Starbucks near campus. He thought the professor's request odd, but it was just as well. An awkward tension hung between Kristin and him that morning. Neither had mentioned the events of the previous night.

Reaching for the door handle, Grant wondered whether the professor had made progress with the government of Bhutan through his university contacts in the Emory-Tibet Partnership, a program of study in Tibetan Buddhism. He also hoped that his mentor would have some advice on how he should handle the fallout from Brady's attack. Today Grant needed his counsel more than ever.

As Grant opened the door, a powerful sense of déjà vu sucked the breath from his lungs. Billingsly sat at his desk wearing a stern expression behind his half-moon glasses. Perched in one of the two black maple chairs and dressed in gray wool slacks and a wrinkled blue blazer with brass buttons was Chair of the Religious Studies Department Edward Flannigan. Wisps of white hair were combed over a pale scalp. The hazel eyes behind the horned-rim glasses surveyed Grant as he froze in the doorway.

Sophomore year again.

"Please, Grant, have a seat." Billingsly motioned to the other empty chair.

Grant limped to the center of the office but felt as if he'd left his stomach at the door. He lowered himself into the hardwood chair and stretched out his right leg, which had begun to throb.

"Have you seen this?" Dean Flannigan tossed a newspaper into Grant's lap.

Grant had meant to pick up a copy with his nonfat latte at Starbucks, but he had been running late. The paper was folded open to an article with his picture embedded in the copy. The emptiness in Grant's stomach deepened when he began to read.

Emory University doctoral candidate Grant Matthews and travel journalist Kristin Misaki stunned the theological world with the Internet release of what they claimed to be a translation of seven ancient books discovered in the tiny Buddhist kingdom of Bhutan in the Himalayas. The manuscripts purported to describe the so-called lost years of Jesus, the period in his life from ages 12 to 29 on which the Bible is silent. In a lively debate broadcast by CNN from the Emory campus on Wednesday, the Reverend Brian Brady, Pastor of the Alabama-based New Hope Church, shocked the crowd, as well as an unsuspecting Mr. Matthews, by revealing that Matthews had been found guilty of plagiarism during his sophomore year at the University of Virginia.

In an exclusive telephone interview yesterday, Lama Dorji, Senior Monk in the Punakha Dzong Monastery where the alleged manuscripts were supposedly discovered, denied the existence of any books in the monastery describing the life of Jesus. "Our library contains the sacred Tibetan Buddhist texts used by our monks. We would have no need to keep Christian writings here," the lama said through his translator. "If such texts [about the life of Jesus] existed, we would have turned them over to Christian scholars many years ago."

When asked whether he knew of any activities of either Mr. Matthews or Ms. Misaki at the monastery, the senor monk confirmed that Mr. Matthews had stayed at the monastery for a number of weeks, recovering from injuries received in a kayaking accident, but that he had been "under strong pain medication from a local doctor and confined to his room for the duration of his stay [there]." Lama Dorji had no recollection of meeting Ms. Misaki but did say, "Each week a few Western tourists walk through the grounds of our goemba [monastery], but they are always escorted by a guide. A lay person, especially a non-Buddhist, would not have access to many of the areas within the goemba, including our library."

Repeated calls to Mr. Matthews in Atlanta were unreturned.

Grant's fingers shook as he finished the article. Resisting the temptation to hurl the paper across the room took every bit of his self-control. A torrent of questions flooded his mind. How did the reporter discover they'd found the documents in Punakha? Up until this moment he'd believed the monastery to be the one thing the press didn't have a lead on. He'd been careful in the debate not to give any clues that might lead to the dzong. The more important question pounding behind his temples, however, was *where were the texts?* Were they being hidden by Lama Dorji? What had happened to Kinley? He felt the pressure in his head begin to build. Not only was he unable to answer these questions, he was powerless to do anything to get the answers. Bhutan was half a world away.

Then, for the second time in as many days, a more disturbing thought arose. If he was honest with himself, he really didn't know whether the documents were authentic. He'd implicitly trusted Kinley. But Kinley had vanished. And even if the texts were legitimate, no one would take him seriously after the lama's denial. Was it possible that the skeptics in his department were right? Had he thrown away a promising academic career to chase some Holy Grail quest?

"What do you have to say for yourself, Mr. Matthews?" Dean Flannigan interrupted the tornado of thoughts in his head.

"You have to understand,"—Grant's voice rose an octave—"Lama Dorji is very much a traditionalist. He doesn't want Westerners in his monastery, and particularly not in the library. He has no interest in cooperating. I just never thought he'd lie about it. He must be covering up to prevent a deluge of media attention on the monastery."

"Have you spoken with Kinley yet?" Billingsly asked.

Grant dropped his voice and his head. "I'm still waiting to hear from him."

"So you have no independent verification of the texts?" Flannigan asked.

Grant stared at the floor.

"And the pictures you said you had of the books somehow mysteriously vanished?"

Grant nodded.

Professor Flannigan cleared his throat. "Mr. Matthews, the school is uncomfortable with the current situation. This publicity reflects negatively on all of us, especially in light of your past problems."

"Wait! I have an idea." Grant knew he sounded desperate, but then again he was. "I'll just return to Bhutan and find the texts."

The department chair shook his head. "In two weeks you'll be given a formal disciplinary hearing. Until then, I have no choice but to suspend you temporarily. Your stipend for living expenses will continue, but your scholarship and any travel-related reimbursement will be curtailed pending the results of the hearing."

"Harold." Grant pushed himself halfway out of his chair. "You know this is bullshit. I just need more time."

His mentor refused to meet his eyes as he replied, "I know this is difficult, but our hands are tied. I think a couple weeks' break from school will be best for everyone."

Grant couldn't believe what he was hearing. *How am I to defend myself without the time or the resources to do so?* The premature release of the texts, the missing pictures, Kinley's disappearance, Brady's revelation, and now his suspension. The throbbing in his leg had migrated up his hip and combined with the pounding behind his eyes; he was barely able to stand. He no longer saw either of the professors: the obstacles before him obscured everything.

CHAPTER 25

———∞∞∞———

STARBUCKS, BRIARCLIFF ROAD
ATLANTA, GEORGIA

A SCREECH ECHOED THROUGH the coffee shop as Grant dragged a wood chair from a table over to the plush green armchair where Kristin sat on her knees with her tie-dyed silk skirt tucked under her legs. He noted how the turtleneck clung to her curves as he collapsed into the chair beside her. She wore her hair in pigtails.

"Your meeting?" she asked.

"I've been suspended, pending an emergency investigation."

"Because of this?" She rotated the laptop he'd lent her. The website displayed the same article he'd read in Billingsly's office minutes earlier. Her blue eyes blazed with an anger he hadn't noticed when he first sat.

"UVA all over again," he said through gritted teeth.

"Your case doesn't look very strong from an outside perspective."

"No, but they're not even giving me a chance." He stood. "Drink?"

She shook her head and pointed to the untouched cup of tea on the small round table beside her.

When he returned with his second nonfat latte of the day, they sat in silence. Sipping from his cup, Grant recalled the pages of notes he'd taken and the outlines he'd typed when he was in Bhutan. He thought he'd planned for every contingency, but nothing was turning out the way he expected.

He gulped his drink and winced when the hot liquid made direct contact with his throat. He removed the white plastic lid, releasing the pent-up steam. Swirling his drink, he watched how the frothy bubbles of milk clung to the sides of the cup. A memory stirred within him: lying in the monastery bed, his leg propped on blankets, Kinley offering him a cup of water.

Grant brought the latte to his nose and inhaled the rich aroma. He took a more cautious sip, savoring the layers of flavors. He thought about the coffee beans, the plants growing in the tropical sun, nourished by the soil and the rain. He placed his cup on the round table beside his chair and looked to the laptop resting on Kristin's knees.

This was easier in Bhutan. Without Kinley's guidance, he felt lost putting into practice the monk's techniques.

He glanced out the coffee shop window. The chatter of the other patrons became white noise in the background of his thoughts. Across the parking lot, a lone maple tree grew out of an island within a sea of asphalt. Its branches were bare.

Naked in the autumn wind. Like he was.

The potential unknowns scared him—the changes in his life he couldn't control. But then he recalled Kinley telling him that the future would always be a potential unknown. The essence of life was change, the monk had taught. "Even what you think of as the fixed entity that is Grant Matthews," Kinley had said, "is an illusion. Physically you are not the same person you were when you were ten years old. Every day, cells in your body die and are replaced with new ones. The neurons in your brain form new connections, as the old, unused ones die away. Memories fade, but are replaced by new ones. The thoughts and worries you have today are different from the ones you had then, just as the thoughts and worries you will have ten years from now will be different from those you have now."

Suddenly Grant knew what he had to do. He pushed aside his teacher's voice. He decided to make the proclamation he'd made in Billingsly's office a reality. The more he thought about it, the more convinced he became. He would prove to the professors, to the Bradys of the world, to his dead father, that he was right. He had one problem, though.

"You can't give up," Kristin said suddenly, mirroring his thoughts. "You need those texts even more than you realize. Since your accident on the river, you've been on a quest as well. Maybe there's something you're supposed to learn from Issa."

Grant cocked his head. *My own quest?* He hadn't thought of it in those terms before. "My only option is to return to Bhutan and bring back the texts, but I spent my savings on my last trip. Now with my suspension—"

"Look, I'm pretty frugal abroad. I still have some unspent travel funds, and my next story won't be overdue for another month."

"You'd do that?" He didn't add *after last night*, but he thought it.

"Of course." She grabbed his arm and shook it. "For some reason, you're getting royally screwed here. I helped you get into this mess by taking the photos, and I'll help you get out."

The computer in her lap beeped, causing both to jump.

"Email," Kristin said.

Grant reached across her and clicked on the mail icon at the bottom of the screen. Several seconds passed before he realized who the sender, jigme-monk, was.

"I don't believe it!" Grant exclaimed loudly enough that a young couple at the next table glanced over. He lowered his voice. "Jigme."

"Kinley's apprentice? The one who never spoke?" she asked.

"Yeah, check this out."

Grant read the email aloud:

Greetings Grant and Kristin, I have completed my retreat in silence, and am once again permitted to communicate via more conventional means. I apologize for taking so long in returning your messages. Since you left our humble country, our life has become more complicated, requiring that we take time to travel.

Have you practiced the techniques you were taught during your stay? Knowing how much you enjoyed our teacher's koans, he also asked me to pass along the following one for you to ponder:

The student asked his master, "Is it true that Isa built his monument to mankind as a crown, not of thorns, but as a palace of grief?" To which the master replied, "Only through death can we see his symbol of eternal love, reflected in a pond by the light of the full moon."

We do miss seeing you and hope that you will be able to visit at the very first opportunity. Peace to you.

"I don't get it," Grant said, rereading the email to himself. "With everything we've been through, the first we hear from them is another one of Kinley's mind twisters."

Kristin continued to stare at the email.

"Well?" Grant said, growing agitated in spite of himself. Suddenly he became aware of the sound of grinding coffee beans. The noise grated on his nerves. He felt himself falling back into despair, indulging Reverend Brady's accusation that he was being messed with. He'd spent the past week pleading with Karma through phone calls and emails for a glimmer of information on either Kinley's whereabouts or the status of the texts, and until this vague email he had nothing.

"I don't think it's really a koan." Kristin's voice grew animated. "It's a riddle or a clue!"

Grant stared at the screen. A spark of hope ignited within his chest. He knew that the witty but confusing stories Kinley had delighted in posing to him in Bhutan were not true riddles, because the questions they posed didn't have a single solution. The stories were called *koans*—sayings made popular by the Zen schools of Buddhism in China and Japan that were meant to shock the mind into thinking outside its usual boundaries.

"Look at the final sentence. She pointed to the computer. "He wants us to visit ASAP."

"You think Kinley was nervous sending us explicit meeting instructions after the negative publicity we've received and his problems with the lama?"

"I do."

Suddenly the lack of communication from Kinley and the lama's claim that the library held no texts on Issa made sense to Grant: Kinley must have taken the texts with him when he left, and now he was ready to meet with them.

Grant sipped his latte. "Okay, the clue seems to refer to Jesus. We have the reference to Issa, and the crown of thorns that Jesus wore at his crucifixion, and then the idea that his death brings eternal life through God's love." He paused for a moment, furrowing his brow. "But I don't see how that leads us anywhere. The palace of grief? Does that mean something to you?"

Kristin reread the email, her lips silently mouthing the words. She then pointed to the first line. "Here: '*Isa built his monument to mankind as a crown, not of thorns, but as a palace of grief.*' Jigme spells the name 'Isa' with one *s*. When used as the Indian name for Jesus, didn't you tell me it was spelled with a double *s*?"

Grant nodded. "I assumed he just misspelled it, or used the Islamic form, which has only one *s*."

"Look at the rest of the sentence: the *crown* refers to a *monument* which is specifically *not of thorns* but is related to *a palace of grief.*"

"Not of thorns." Grant pictured Kinley's twinkling eyes. "A misdirection. How like him. The riddle isn't about Jesus at all." Then he saw the clue. "*Monument!* It's about an actual monument, not a metaphorical one. And the monument has something to do with grief. Like a cemetery or something?"

Kristin smiled broadly. "The most recognizable monument in India is *a palace of grief*. The Taj Mahal."

"It is?" The spark of excitement flamed within him. "I never had time to visit Agra when I was in India."

"I spent a week there writing about the Taj," she said. "Emperor Shah Jahan commissioned the monument in sixteen thirty-one, not as a palace in which to live, but as a mausoleum for the remains of his second wife, Mumtaz, who died while giving birth to their fourteenth child."

"Fourteen kids? That's one dedicated mother."

"As dedicated as the emperor, who loved her above all his other wives. So the grandeur of the Taj came to symbolize his eternal love."

Grant read aloud from the email, "'*Only through death can we see his symbol of eternal love.*'"

"Exactly. Also, the name Taj Mahal translates literally as 'Crown Palace.'"

"Just like the riddle says, but"—Grant sat up straighter, the pain in his leg and his troubles at the university momentarily forgotten—"what about *Isa*?"

"The Persian architect who designed the Taj was named Ustad Isa, spelled with one *s*."

"You're amazing!" He leaned over and wrapped his arms around her in an embrace that almost knocked the computer from her lap. The couple beside them glanced over again. He didn't care that he was making a scene. For the first time since they'd left Bhutan, they were a step closer to reaching the texts. He noticed Kristin was beaming at him. "So we meet Kinley and Jigme at the Taj Mahal, but when? I assume the last phrase about the full moon has something to do with meeting them at night?"

Kristin traced her finger along the final phrase: *reflected in a pond by the light of the full moon.* "That makes perfect sense," she said.

"It does?"

"In front of the monument are two long reflecting pools where you can see the image of the Taj. When Kinley and I were chatting in the courtyard before we went up to the library, he asked me about my travels through India. One of the highlights for me was seeing the Taj at night under the full moon. You see, the Indian government strictly regulates access to its World Heritage monuments, but on one night per month, during the full moon, they open the grounds of the Taj for a few hours to tourists."

"So all we have to do is to find the next full moon," Grant said.

Kristin typed "lunar phase" into the browser's search field. Seconds later they had their answer. They had to hurry. The next full moon was in four nights, and it would take two days to get there. Fortunately, he thought, their visas were still good.

Then the thought of the hearing at Emory that would determine his academic fate in two weeks flashed through his head. He would forward Jigme's email to Billingsly, but he doubted Dean Flannigan would grant him a reprieve. Could they travel to Agra and meet Kinley at the Taj and then return to Atlanta with proof of the texts in time?

CHAPTER 26

---ooo---

AGRA, INDIA

FORTY-FIVE MINUTES behind schedule. *Did anything in this filthy country run on time?* Tim shifted uncomfortably on the train's hard plastic seat. At least he'd paid the extra rupees for the first-class car on the Shatabdi Express from New Delhi to Agra. His stomach had turned two hours earlier when he saw the coach cars pull past him on the New Delhi station platform: humans packed like livestock, standing in the stench of their unwashed countrymen. At least his first-class car had working AC, and no one had tried to bring chickens or goats into his compartment.

After flights from Birmingham to DC and DC to London, Tim had finally arrived in New Delhi yesterday, exhausted but exhilarated. He had waited his life for an opportunity like this. What he'd been searching for in the Army—belonging to the team protecting his country—had driven him until that was taken away. Now he understood that he'd suffered then for a reason: to gain the skills and the fortitude to face the opportunity before him. He was now part of something bigger than his country—he was an agent in God's plans.

After he'd arrived in New Delhi, he picked up several emails on his phone. The first was a copy of a coded message from the monk Kinley to Grant Matthews, and the second was a translation of the code that gave him a new destination: the Taj Mahal. Tim congratulated himself on his foresight to travel halfway around the world to wait in India for his Bhutanese visa. They were now coming to him. Tim stopped at Bhutan's consulate in New Delhi to apply for his visa—one could never overprepare—and then he left for Agra, the city made famous by one of the world's most recognizable monuments.

Glancing at his fellow passengers, Tim noticed how dark-skinned they were, not quite black, but not far from it either. The men looked halfway respectable, dressed in business suits, but the saris the women wore looked like silk curtains wrapped around their bodies. Colorful, but as ridiculous-looking as the odd nasal piercings and red smudges on their foreheads. During the time he'd spent in Iraq and Afghanistan, he'd never become accustomed to the primitive habits of Third World people. Indians, Afghanis, Iraqis: they were all the same to Tim. As Reverend Brady had emphasized many times, these people, the non-Christians, would all end up in hell.

He checked his watch again. He was anxious to arrive in Agra before Grant Matthews and Kristin Misaki. He'd been closely following their every move for days now. The software he'd installed on Matthews's computer worked perfectly. A copy of every email Grant sent or received was covertly forwarded to an anonymous account Tim had set up. He'd taken an additional precaution by activating the E911 microchip in Grant's phone. This chip transformed the phone into a GPS receiver, and once activated, the cell phone's location could be pinpointed to within a few yards with a web browser. Based on the emails he'd intercepted from their online bookings, he knew that Grant Matthews and Kristin Misaki would arrive in Agra late the following day, giving him little time to scout the city and plan his operation.

As the train pulled into the Agra Cantonment station, Tim hoisted the straps of his olive green backpack onto his shoulders and pushed past the other passengers. He stepped onto the concrete platform with its open-air corrugated metal roof. The stench of urine immediately assaulted his nostrils. At least the fall weather was sunny and warm, not like the scorching summers he'd spent in the Middle East. Swatting at the flies swarming his face, he shoved past a thin man wearing torn navy pants and a soiled polyester shirt.

The man, who carried a blackened rag and a can of shoe polish, followed beside Tim, tugging his arm and repeating, "Shoeshine, mister?"

Tim's hand instinctively went to his hip, but the reassuring bulge of his Glock was missing, packed into his backpack. Before leaving the States, he had carefully disassembled it, concealing parts in a fake alarm clock and a converted shaving cream can. Many parts of the gun were made from a composite plastic, which made his job all the easier. Tim had checked his only bag, knowing how lax airport security actually was in light of all their self-congratulatory efforts post-9/11.

Undaunted, the man pleaded, "Twenty rupees. Good shine."

Tim briefly considered punching the scrawny man in the face, but then he pictured the man's blood and saliva on his hands and thought better of it. Who knew what kinds of diseases these people had? Instead he glared at the shoeshine man, who, Tim realized, was not even wearing shoes himself.

"They're hiking boots, you fucking moron," Tim spat out. Although the barefoot man may not have understood the exact words Tim used, he got the message and moved to the next travelers departing the train.

As he continued along the platform, the smell of deep-fried food awakened Tim's stomach with a growl. He passed a vendor selling a breaded ball of something cooked in a murky vat of oil from a metal cart. As hungry as Tim was, he imagined the gut-wrenching diarrhea this food would probably give him. He would wait until he arrived at his hotel to find something safer to eat. He remembered that he had a handful of protein bars in his backpack too.

Reaching the end of the platform, Tim climbed a metal staircase leading to a catwalk that crossed over the train tracks to the street exit. From the group of taxi and rickshaw drivers haggling for his business, he picked the least offensive, an elderly man dressed in a frayed white shirt, who at least wore a tie. Tim tried to touch as little as possible while sitting in the interior of the dented white van. He caressed his forearms as he gazed out the window.

During his brief layover in Delhi, he'd noticed that the Indian government had made an attempt to cover up some of the squalor with wide tree-lined avenues and modern-looking office buildings in the newer parts of the capital city. After just a few minutes in the taxi, he could see that Agra was a different story. Decrepit wood and stone structures stood next to concrete buildings that had not seen a coat of paint in decades. Every few blocks, he passed communities of tent cites that had sprung up outside the walls around the buildings. Entire families lived under lean-tos made of rusted tin. Mud covered the ground and the people. The squalor here dwarfed anything he'd encountered before.

How do they steal our fucking jobs? he wondered, shaking his head. These people had no respect for themselves or their city.

Garbage littered the sides of the street, in places three feet deep. The aroma of this teeming city was a far cry from the clean pine scent of his home. As the van rounded a bend, he spotted two young children, standing in a heap of garbage by the side of the road. The older child, a girl of seven or eight, was dressed in a tattered dress that hung loosely off her shoulders. Tim watched her search through the trash, perhaps for something to eat. The younger child, a boy about four with greasy black hair and no shirt, probably her brother, squatted on his heels while lifting his hand to his mouth.

Tim swallowed back the acid taste of bile when he realized the boy was scooping brackish water from a stagnant puddle to drink. No sign of parents anywhere: they were like stray dogs on the street. As the car passed within a few feet of the children, the girl lifted her head and made direct eye contact with Tim. Behind the unwashed bangs that fell in front of the young girl's face, Tim saw only a vacant look in her eyes.

"Not even human," he muttered.

As if to confirm his thoughts, the slow movement of a hulking shape twenty meters down the road from the children caught his attention. As the car drew closer, Tim recognized the shape to be two large pigs rooting through the same continuous line of garbage that the children had been digging through down the road. Both were heavier than the boar he was used to hunting in the Alabama woods, and their wiry gray coats were covered in the same mud covering the people who lived along the road.

This place turned his stomach. He felt himself losing focus on the task ahead, so he closed his eyes and went through his mental checklist. Once he unpacked, he would reassemble the Glock. Then he would need to find some ammunition. Despite his feelings that most baggage screeners were complete morons, he wasn't confident he could adequately conceal the chemical trace of gunpowder or the unmistakable shape of a bullet. But he knew that anything could be bought in a place like this, for the right price. Forty-caliber bullets would be a cinch.

In addition to the gun, Tim's pack contained one of his most creative ideas. Just thinking of his cleverness made him grin. Inside a nylon case were six EpiPens, plastic shots of self-injectable doses of epinephrine delivered via a concealed spring-activated needle. Tim had easily obtained them from a drugstore with a forged prescription he'd photoshopped. Many people carried these single-use shots in case of emergency allergic reactions to bee stings or food items.

But Tim didn't have any allergies. Allergies were for sickly people. Instead, Tim had modified the EpiPens, none of which contained epinephrine any longer. Three now contained Versed, a benzodiazepine drug doctors often injected into patients immediately before surgery to induce a twilight state of consciousness. He recalled his own experience with Versed in his twenties when his wisdom teeth were removed. He'd pocketed the vials the day he was excused from his hospital job. *You never know when certain drugs might come in handy*, he'd thought, and Tim was nothing if not patient. So many of the things he'd done over the years, not knowing for what outcome, were starting to fall into place, further convincing him that God had held this plan for him for many years, perhaps his whole life.

Tim smiled when he thought about the effects of jabbing someone with one of his modified EpiPens: the person would be rendered helpless within seconds. Barely conscious, his victim would follow his instructions clumsily and, owing to the drug's amnesiac effect, remember nothing once the drug wore off.

The other three EpiPens were marked with a red line. He'd used a Sharpie so he wouldn't mistake them for the Versed-filled ones. The red-lined shots would act as quickly as the other three, but with far more dramatic results. These were filled with hydrocyanic acid, a chemical related to cyanide but with an even higher toxicity. The victim stabbed with one of these would go into immediate cardiac arrest. This chemical had been even easier to obtain than the Versed; he'd ordered it from an online chemical supply company.

Within a day's time, he anticipated testing both types.

CHAPTER 27

———✿———

UTTAR PRADESH, INDIA

GRANT GAZED OUT the car's window at the flat, arid land whose sandy soil was tinted with red. He wondered whether Issa had crossed this land on his way to the Himalayas. The car jolted as it hit a pothole. Calling the road to Agra a "highway" was someone's wishful thinking. Its lanes needed a complete repaving, instead of haphazard patch jobs. The bumpy ride might have bothered him were his attention not drawn to the inevitable head-on collisions their driver miraculously avoided every few minutes when he swerved into incoming traffic to pass a slow-moving tractor or an even slower-moving camel-pulled cart.

They'd spent no time at all in New Delhi, where they'd arrived yesterday after eighteen hours of flying, including a layover in Paris. The road conditions combined with their jet lag made the four-hour drive between cities seem even longer than it was. Grant marveled at the large diversity of travelers on the streets of the towns they'd passed through—cars whose drivers seemed oblivious to the rules of the road, buses with as many passengers riding on the roof as inside the vehicle, three-wheeled rickshaws whose drivers peddled furiously in the heavy traffic, camels pulling carts loaded with construction materials, and swarms of motorbikes darting in, out, and around like hornets circling their nest. Neither traffic signals nor the concept of right of way existed here, yet in the chaos, these travelers somehow managed to dance around each other as if they were performing an elaborate ballet to the sounds of the ever-present symphony of car horns.

"What're you thinking about?" Kristin asked through a yawn.

"You're awake. Oh, nothing. Just the symphony."

Kristin gave him a confused look as she stretched her arms over her head. As if on cue, their driver blared his horn and swerved around an emaciated spotted cow standing in the middle of a busy village intersection, one of many their driver had blazed through in the last three hours. The cow seemed stoned, perhaps from breathing in too many exhaust fumes, and it didn't bother to look up at the SUV as it passed within inches of its hindquarters. The aggressive maneuver pressed Kristin into Grant's side.

Before righting herself, she whispered into his ear, "There's a saying in this country that drivers only need three things: horns, brakes, and good luck."

"Fortunately, we've had an abundance of all three," Grant replied. He leaned forward and asked their driver, "Hey, what's the deal with all the cows in the road?" On his previous trips to India, he'd been quite amused by the cattle who roamed freely in the middle of the road and slept on the medians.

Their driver, whose collarless white shirt contrasted with his dark complexion and jet black hair, explained in accented English, "People keep cows for milk. Use dung for cooking fuel. But the cow is sacred animal to Hindus. We do not butcher them for meat. When the animals are too old to make milk, the owners let them go into the streets."

"Instead of stray dogs, you have stray cows?" Grant smiled.

"Oh yes. Many stray dogs here too." The driver chuckled.

Although Grant had witnessed in India the most abject poverty he'd ever seen, he also marveled at the energy of the people and the richness of the culture. The people they'd encountered so far had been extremely friendly and helpful.

Kristin checked Grant's watch. "We should be in Agra soon."

"Well, tonight's the night." He rubbed his palms on his khakis. They had replied to Jigme that they'd be there at eight PM under the full moon—the one night a month the Taj Mahal was open—but Jigme hadn't responded. Now Grant hoped for the best. He couldn't help but wonder whether the cloak-and-dagger charade was really necessary. The frenzy of publicity surrounding the initial publication of the Issa translation had died and been replaced by headlines highlighting Grant's humiliation. But then he thought about Kinley and all the trouble he must have gone through to make a reunion possible.

"You think they'll be there?" Kristin asked.

"Let's hope so." Grant felt confident about their interpretation of Jigme's email. *But what if we're wrong?* They didn't have much time, and they would deplete Kristin's travel money within a week.

CHAPTER 28

─────⬥─────

AGRA, INDIA

THE SHADOWS OF DUSK concealed the small skiff motoring east down the Yamuna River. Tim's fingers tingled from the vibration of the throttle on the fifteen-horsepower outboard attached to the stern of the flat-bottomed boat. Finding a boat for hire had not been a problem: finding one with a motor instead of an old man with a pole had taken some effort, and four thousand rupees—just under a hundred dollars. Fortunately, Tim had been given a generous cash allowance for this mission. He was thankful again for his foresight and well-planned operation. Had he not left early for India, he never would have had time to prepare after he'd intercepted the coded email and its translation. One of the key lessons from his military training had been the importance of preparation and planning.

With the skiff humming across the placid water, Tim removed his phone from the backpack by his feet. The one redeeming aspect of this filthy country, he thought, was its kick-ass digital cell service. In under thirty seconds, he connected to the Internet through the phone's browser and had access to a color map of the city of Agra. Tim tapped the screen, zooming in until he saw the flashing red dot. Matthews's cell phone. He marveled at how easy it was to follow someone's every move. The government claimed the mandated E911 chips were for public safety: a panicked motorist calling 911 after an accident could be instantly located. The cell phone companies also pitched the technology as an additional benefit to those who enjoyed using GPS, and they even sold a service to parents to make their kids safer. For a small monthly fee, parents could log on to a website at any time and pull up a city map showing their children's exact location. But Tim knew what the technology was really for—just another way for the government to control its citizens. And tonight he would use it to his advantage.

Tim's pulse quickened. His targets were on the street, near the entrance of the Taj Mahal. An hour earlier than their eight PM meeting time. He cranked the throttle to the full open position.

As the skiff rounded a wide bend in the river, Tim caught his first glimpse of the immense sixteenth-century Agra Fort with its monumental sandstone walls rising from the far riverbank. Tim allowed himself to admire how the medieval Muslim fortress was strategically located along the banks of the river, making one flank impervious to attack, while also providing outstanding views across the flat land on the other three sides—a textbook military location. Seeing the Agra Fort, Tim knew that the Taj was close; his anticipation grew.

Then the itching started. He scratched his arms. *Damn*, he thought. Why did his fucking eczema act up at times like this? While his right hand continued to steer the skiff around the river bend, he used his left hand to scratch furiously, even though he knew that scratching only made the itching worse.

The moment the river straightened, however, he forgot about the itching. The Taj Mahal itself came into view on the southern bank. Its marble, onion-shaped dome rose over sixty meters into the night sky, glowing an iridescent bluish white from the light of the full moon.

Then Tim encountered his first unexpected problem. He slowed the motor, unconsciously scratching his arms again. In addition to the full moon, floodlights illuminated the two stone plazas surrounding the Taj. Unfortunately, the bright lights also glared on the flat grassy bank that extended from the red walls of the lower sandstone plaza to the river's edge like a giant stage set.

During his scouting trip the previous afternoon, he'd chosen the river as his access point because of the Kalashnikov-toting security guards gathered at the main entrance gate. But how was he to complete his mission illuminated by these spotlights?

cℐ๏

After enjoying a hurried dinner of chicken and vegetable curry, along with ample helpings of rice and naan to calm the effects of the spices in their stomachs, Grant and Kristin walked past the closed merchant stalls lining the narrow road leading from their hotel to the main entrance of the Taj Mahal complex. Grant enjoyed the relative peacefulness of the cool night. Only a few dogs barked in the distance. As they stepped over the papers that fluttered across the paved road from the stalls, Grant imagined the chaos during the day: merchants hawking fruit, bottled water, T-shirts, and cheap plastic models of the Taj. Now that the shop owners were at home with their families, only the debris from the day's activities was left.

Grant checked his watch. "We're early."

She grabbed his hand and squeezed it. "I can't wait."

"Tell me about it."

Ten minutes later, after stepping through a metal detector that beeped at everyone and receiving a pat down more intimate than an airport security line, they entered through the gate and into an expansive grassy courtyard. The change of scenery immediately struck Grant. The stench from the sludge running in the gutter outside the exterior walls disappeared while the garbage, dirt, and grime omnipresent throughout the rest of the city were also wiped away. The grass and hedges were meticulously manicured. This country, he realized, really did encompass two vastly different worlds.

"Where is it?" he asked. Nowhere in the courtyard larger than two football fields did Grant see any sign of the Taj Mahal itself.

"We just entered the outer courtyard." Kristin gestured to their right, where an immense red sandstone building with white marble accents rose seven stories into the sky. From both ends of the building extended a low single-story structure defined by its cloisterlike arches. "That's the main gate to the inner courtyard and the Taj itself."

She pointed to the gate's multiple pointed arches. "Islamic architecture is characterized by its perfect symmetry."

Like souvenirs on a store shelf, a row of eleven marble domes sat on top of the tall building, mimicking in miniature the shape of the main dome on the Taj Mahal itself. The entire picture seemed to Grant like a medieval Islamic castle.

"So, if that's the main gate, then what are those buildings?" Grant nodded to their left across the lawn to a long, red single-story building whose arches matched those on the low building wings attached to the main gate.

"Those are the barracks that held the workers who built the Taj. Over twenty thousand labored for twenty-two years. Legend has it that the emperor had the hands of the most skilled amputated once construction was completed so that they could never again create something as magnificent."

They walked over red sandstone pavers to the main gate. A few dozen tourists, speaking Hindi, Japanese, and German, walked along with them. *Much better,* Grant thought, *than the thousands during the day.*

Kristin stopped outside the arched opening in the center of the gate, which Grant guessed to be over fifty feet in height. "See the black writing within the white marble surrounding the arch?"

Grant craned his neck. "Arabic lettering."

"The letters are black onyx inlaid in the marble walls of the gate—an Italian process called *pietra dura.*"

"Any idea what it says?" The languages he could read—ancient Greek, Tibetan, French, and German—didn't include Arabic.

"On my last trip here, my guide translated the verse for me. It's from the Koran, and it invites God's servants to enter his paradise."

The Koran? Grant's interest was piqued. Shah Jahan, who built the Taj, was a Mughal ruler, Grant recalled. He'd brushed up on some Indian history before their trip and remembered that Muslim armies invaded India beginning in the early sixteenth century. The Muslim emperors who then ruled the country, known as the Mughal Empire, went to great lengths to destroy the ancient Hindu culture they encountered when they arrived. They forced many of the people, whom they considered to be heathens for their polytheistic religious practices, to convert to Islam.

"Like the Christian Crusades and the Inquisition," Kristin said, "convert to Christianity or be executed."

"Ironic, isn't it, for religions centered on a merciful God? The crusaders, be they Christian or Islamic, believed they were saving the people they were conquering by torturing and killing them."

Kristin hooked her arm through Grant's, leading him under the arch of the main gate. "Are you ready?" she asked.

When they passed under the archway, Grant stopped. The vision ahead of him rendered him speechless.

Tim maneuvered the skiff to the northern bank of the river opposite the Taj grounds and out of the exposure of the floodlights. Once he passed the Taj complex, he spotted his landing: on the northeast corner of the property, a construction site he'd seen on his morning scouting trip. He relaxed. The site was shrouded in shadow. The authorities must not have wanted to highlight the mess of the renovations taking place at the edge of the complex. He turned the skiff and doubled back to the opposite bank.

Just ahead, Tim found the low floating dock where the construction crews unloaded their materials from the river barges. Tim twisted the throttle, slowing the motor from a roar to a low gurgle. Not that he was really worried about alerting the security guards, from what he'd seen on the Taj grounds during the day. After the initial vigilance at the security entrance, the guards supposed to be patrolling the grounds had congregated by the monument while they chatted among themselves instead of surveying the crowd for potential terrorists. Their Kalashnikov rifles were slung too casually on their shoulders. With his forty-caliber Glock, which now rested comfortably on his hip under his untucked safari shirt, Tim could take out an entire group of the slackers before any one of them would be able to chamber a bullet.

Tim tied his skiff to the dock. Just beyond the construction debris littering the grass and adjacent to the plaza walls was scaffolding that rose at least forty feet in the air. Apparently the Indian government was in the process of restoring many of its national monuments, and here they had provided Tim with an easy means to scale the walls and to avoid the barbed wire that ran along all but this ten-meter section of the grassy riverbanks by the complex. Tim was pleased to see that the mechanical lift running up the side of the scaffolding appeared to be in working order. He'd spotted the lift on his recon trip, guessing that the crews used it to haul up the stones and cement needed for the renovation. Though it was no more than a few boards strapped together and raised and lowered by hand ropes attached to pulleys, the crude lift would suffice to lower a semiconscious body to his skiff.

He patted his oversized cargo pants pockets that held the specially modified EpiPens and smiled to himself.

From the steps atop the main gate, Grant gazed across two long rectangular reflecting pools that stretched end to end for two hundred meters. Surrounded by formal gardens planted in symmetrical quadrangles, the pools terminated at the base of the pale marble structure of the Taj Mahal.

"Much bigger than I expected."

"Pictures don't do it justice, nor do written descriptions. Even mine." Kristin pulled him down the steps to the red stone walkway alongside the first pool. Out of the corner of his eye, Grant watched her face glow with excitement.

As they strolled closer to the monument, Grant realized that what he originally thought to be a rectangular building was actually an octagon. Unlike the other buildings in the complex, which were built of red sandstone with white marble accents, the Taj itself was constructed entirely of white translucent marble. In the center of the monument a two-story pointed arch mirrored the arch he'd just walked through. Pairs of smaller arches were also set into the walls on either side of the main arch in a display of Islamic symmetry and ideal proportion. Topping off the building were five domes— smaller ones on the outside corners and the largest one in the middle. Completing the picture, slender minarets as tall as the monument itself rose from each of the four corners of the raised marble plaza on which the Taj building rested.

After pausing for several minutes to absorb the majesty of the architecture before him, Grant gestured to two identical red sandstone buildings that flanked either side of the Taj on the edge of the wide sandstone plaza below the marble plaza on which the Taj itself sat. "Are those mosques?"

"The building on the left is a mosque. The one to the right was a guest house, built to preserve the symmetry of the design."

When they reached the end of the first reflecting pool, Grant spotted a solitary figure sitting on a stone bench on a raised marble observation platform between the two reflecting pools. The man wore jeans and a short-sleeved, collarless cotton shirt. He appeared to study the sight in front of him. Grant and Kristin climbed the three steps to the top of the platform. Without turning his shaved head, the man called out, "From here, you can see a perfect reflection of the building in the water."

"Jigme!" they both screamed in unison.

Jigme rose and embraced Grant and Kristin. "So good to see you," he said with clear diction, but in an accent slightly stronger than Kinley's.

"I almost didn't recognize you without your robes," Kristin said.

"It has been quite a while since I have worn layperson's clothing. I must say that these jeans are quite comfortable. Considering the commotion you two have caused lately, I thought our meeting might be less conspicuous this way."

"You know," Grant said, still grasping Jigme's arm, as if he were afraid to let him go, "this is the first time I've actually heard you speak." The monk sounded more mature than his twenty years.

"Please sit and enjoy the view." Jigme motioned to the bench beside them. "Yes, I completed my retreat in silence. I never realized how much I missed, because I was too busy listening to my own voice."

Grant was reminded of how his own mind was rarely quiet and how Kinley had taught him to pay attention to the cycle of unproductive thoughts that often consumed him, a lesson that he hadn't been heeding lately. He explained to Jigme the mysterious disappearance of the pictures they'd taken in Bhutan.

"Quite strange," the monk said.

"We've had a difficult time contacting you," Kristin said. "Is everything all right?"

"Word of the controversy reached the dzong quicker than Kinley expected. Lama Dorji received many phone calls about the documents after you left."

"The reporter who interviewed him?" Grant asked. He wondered how this person had tracked down the lama.

"At first, Lama Dorji was confused. He'd never heard of the Issa books in our library."

"The lama had limited his studies to the Tibetan Buddhist scriptures?" Kristin asked.

Jigme nodded. "After receiving the first phone call, the lama went to Dawa, the monk who keeps the archives, and asked him about the books. I think you can imagine his reaction when he pieced together that Kinley must have brought the two of you into our library."

"That's why he lied to the reporter about the existence of the texts?" Grant asked.

"Well, technically, by the time the reporter called back, the books were no longer in the dzong's library." A mischievous grin spread across the young monk's face.

"What happened to them?" Grant asked.

Before Jigme could respond, Kristin interjected, "And Kinley?"

"To answer both your questions, both Kinley and the manuscripts are safe, but as to their respective whereabouts, I am in the dark."

"You don't know—" Grant began, fighting back a frustration so acute that he nearly screamed the question.

Jigme held up a hand. "Kinley did not want to put me in the position of lying to protect either him or the texts. But he did pass along a message."

A familiar twinkle appeared in the monk's eyes.

Tim spotted Matthews and Misaki sitting on a stone bench between the reflecting pools fifty meters from him. After tying the skiff to the dock, he'd easily scaled the scaffolding and followed the signal on his cell phone's browser that led him to the formal gardens. The technology had served him well, exactly as he expected.

Tim moved closer, sticking to the shadowy areas between the landscaping lights that illuminated the garden's ornamental trees. He tried to appear casual, like a tourist exploring the grounds.

A bald man sat on the bench with the couple. Tim noted his medium dark complexion, and a face that was rounder and more East Asian than Indian. Tim's heart rate quickened. Although he wasn't dressed in robes, Tim felt sure this was his man: the monk Kinley who had shown the texts to Matthews. The monk had met them just as the coded email message had said.

Tim stepped closer, angling his head to see around the bench, as if he were looking past the three people sitting there in order to view the mosque on the other end of the gardens. A brief disappointment passed over him. The monk carried nothing with him. No bag of ancient books in sight. Not that he really expected the monk to bring the Jesus books to this place. Anyway, while grabbing the manuscripts here would have been easier, he was up for the challenge of getting his hands on them no matter what measures he had to take.

"You have a message from Kinley?" Grant asked after the young monk had sat in silence for another few moments after the revelation.

"Let us walk first," Jigme said, rising to his feet. "You have traveled all this way to see the world's grandest monument to true love. You might as well get your money's worth." He stepped off the platform and headed toward the Taj Mahal. Grant glanced at Kristin, who grabbed his hand and pulled him after Jigme.

Grant called out, "Why Agra? And why didn't Kinley meet us here himself?" With the planning and travel time, he'd already lost four precious days.

"I see you have learned patience since returning to America," Jigme said over his shoulder.

Gently chastised by the young monk, Grant held back further comment, quickly limping to keep up with Jigme's brisk pace. Grant's mind raced as fast as his legs. What other purpose did Kinley have for bringing them here, if not to give them the texts? Grant had risked his reputation and his academic career for these texts. Then another thought occurred to him: Kinley also had taken a huge risk. The monk had removed the manuscripts from the library and incurred the disapproval of the lama. But now he had disappeared.

What if Kinley has changed his mind? What if he no longer thinks I'm worthy of the secret? The doubts began to multiply in his head. Their journey had better turn out to be more than a simple riddle leading them to a famous tourist site. He didn't have time to play games, especially when his name was already a joke around the halls of the religious studies department. When he'd stopped in his office to collect some papers before leaving on the trip, he could hear the whispers of his fellow grad students behind his back.

Several minutes later they climbed a shadowy stairwell that led from the garden level to the immense marble plaza on which the Taj Mahal stood.

"Ah, here we are," Jigme said.

The sight of the architectural feat before him immediately distracted Grant's thoughts from the texts and his troubles. Standing within fifteen meters of the monument, he understood the magnitude of the accomplishment of Isa, the Taj architect, and his workers three hundred sixty years ago. The smooth marble structure towered almost ninety feet over them, while the plaza stretched out over a hundred feet in each direction. Grant realized that the marble was not purely white as it appeared in the distance, but veins of beiges and grays ran through the blocks. Similar to the main gate, the massive stone walls contained squiggly Arabic text inlaid with black onyx, but on this monument the *pietra dura* assumed an even grander scale: a rainbow of semiprecious stones was also inlaid within the marble, forming vines and flowers that appeared to climb the sheer walls.

"Jigme!" a voice called from behind them.

Grant spun on his heels.

A broad grin broke out on Jigme's face. "Razi!"

A man who appeared to be a few years older than Jigme but younger than Grant embraced the monk. The man was dressed all in white—cotton pants and a long-sleeved shirt—with the exception of a black knit cap over his head. He smiled behind a neatly groomed mustache and beard, black like the hair that peeked out from under his cap.

"Kristin and Grant, please allow me to introduce you to my new friend, Jamil Razifar. He gave me a tour of the monument a few days ago."

Days ago? Grant thought.

"Good to see you again, my friend," Razi said. "So my tour didn't drive you away?"

"Quite the opposite. I enjoyed it so much, I returned with my friends."

Razi held out a hand to Grant. He spoke in a fast, clipped English with a distinct Indian accent. "Pleased to meet you, friends of Jigme." He then gave a courteous bow to Kristin, who returned it.

"Are you a tour guide?" she asked.

He laughed. "Not officially. Just a student—studying to be a mullah one day. As a student of Islam in India"—he gestured to the monument before them—"I often enjoy visiting one of our most spectacular architectural accomplishments."

"Do you have a minute to walk with us?" Jigme asked.

Grant tried to catch Kristin's eye. *Sightseeing?* They needed to hear Kinley's message about the texts. But she gazed at Razi with an anticipatory expression, as if she'd come halfway around the world just for this tour.

Then an idea interrupted Grant's impatience. He looked at the two men standing before him and realized that they were three students of religion: Christianity, Buddhism, and now Islam. *Peculiar coincidence.* Although he knew that for Kinley there were no coincidences.

Razi guided them to the left side of the building's arched entrance, where he rested his hand on the stone. "The marble is called Makrana, one of the hardest and least porous, which is why the building has remained in such good condition for so many centuries. The inlay work you see consists of fourteen types of semiprecious stones such as coral, onyx, malachite. The stones are only three or four millimeters thick, and yet the workmanship is so detailed, you will not see any gaps or seams between the stones and the marble."

"The Islamic script around the arches, it's from the Koran like on the main gate?" Kristin asked.

Razi nodded. "The text on the building describes the damnation that awaits those who do not follow the will of Allah, as well as detailing the paradise that the faithful will experience."

"Isn't it true that the Koran is the collected visions of Muhammad?" Jigme asked. Grant glanced at his friend. *Jigme knows this to be true*, he thought. He had the distinct feeling that this encounter had been planned. *But why?*

Razi nodded. "The Prophet lived about five hundred years after Jesus. Unlike the Bible, which is the collected writings of many authors over many centuries, the Koran was a series of visions that came to Muhammad in bits and pieces over a twenty-three-year period. Many of its stories and themes overlap with the Bible. We Muslims see the Koran as completing the trilogy that began with the Old and New Testaments—the culmination of Allah's word as spoken through Muhammad."

"So do Muslims view Muhammad like Christians view Jesus?" Jigme asked.

Grant leaned against the cool marble wall of the Taj, resting his aching leg. *We really don't have time for this,* he thought. Jigme was delaying telling them about Kinley and the texts for a reason. The doubts began to creep back into his mind again.

"Not exactly." Razi traced the black Arabic script in the wall with a finger. "Muhammad was never deified like Jesus was. He was considered to be God's spokesman, but not an incarnation of God himself. We consider Muhammad to be the last and greatest in a long line of prophets that began with Adam and continued through Abraham, Moses, and Jesus."

"Wait," Kristin said. "My Old Testament knowledge is pretty fuzzy, but wasn't Muhammad actually related to Abraham?"

Grant pushed himself away from the building and began to walk along the wall, hoping that his movement might encourage the others. But as much as he wanted to steer the conversation back to the Issa texts, he couldn't resist responding, "When Abraham and his wife Sarah were unable to conceive a son, Abraham took a second wife, Hagar, with whom he had a son named Ishmael. Later Sarah had Isaac. According to Jewish scripture, Hagar was a concubine, and thus Ishmael was not a rightful heir to Abraham."

"But we Muslims," Razi interjected, "see Ishmael as Abraham's firstborn. Sarah didn't like the idea of wife number two hanging around with the competing son, so she convinced Abraham to exile them from the tribe. According to the Koran, Hagar and Ishmael traveled to the town that would become Mecca in Arabia."

Grant completed the thought, "So we have the descendants of Abraham's son Isaac becoming the Jews, while the descendants of his son Ishmael, including Muhammad, became the Muslims in Arabia."

"That puts the whole Arab-Israeli conflict in perspective, doesn't it?" Kristin said. "But how does Jesus fit into the picture?"

"The Koran speaks of Jesus' birth from a virgin," Razi said, "and so many Muslims see Jesus as a creation of God, just as Adam was, but they reject his deification as being an idolatrous creation of man. Instead they see Jesus as a great prophet, the teacher who brought us the Golden Rule, for example."

"'There is no god but Allah,'" Grant said, watching Razi expectantly. The reasoned manner in which this Muslim scholar presented his knowledge impressed him.

"Yes!" Razi clapped his hands together. "In Arabic the prayer is '*La ilaha ila Allah*.'"

Then Grant remembered something. He had difficulty controlling the excitement in his voice. "Isn't Jesus known as Isa in the Koran?" *And with one* s *like in Kinley's riddle*, he added to himself.

"Indeed." A sly smile spread across the man's face, as if he understood the implications of the question.

Who was this Muslim?

Tim watched him apprehensively, following the group as they circumambulated the monument. Tim was careful to keep his distance, while pretending to be interested in the marble castle in front of him. From their interactions, Tim guessed that before tonight Matthews and Misaki hadn't known the man, whom Tim immediately identified as a Muslim from his dress and beard. The monk must have brought some muscle with him. *How appropriate*, he thought, *to bring another heathen into their plot to confuse the world*. His hand slid absentmindedly into his right pocket. He twirled one of the EpiPens between his fingers.

Had the monk already communicated to his friends the hiding place of the books? While he could use his cell phone to follow Matthews to the texts, he wanted to get there first. He couldn't risk the chance that they might slip out of his grasp or that Matthews would photograph them again before Tim could control the situation. Tim had seen the smug attitude Matthews had taken with the reverend the night of the debate. His blood ran hot at the memory. But Reverend Brady had triumphed in the end, shown him for the liar he was. Now it was Tim's responsibility to flush away this poison for good.

After he rounded the monument's southeast corner, Tim paused. He saw no sign of his targets anywhere on the plaza.

Maybe, he thought, *they've descended the stairwell to the ground level.* Hurrying to the front of the marble plaza, he shielded his eyes from the lights blazing up from the ground twenty feet below.

Damn!

As he scanned the pathways along the reflecting pools, he began to rub his forearms. How could he have let them out of his sight for even a few seconds?

He turned to run around the edge of the plaza, when a shape at the front of the monument caught his eye. Sitting on the ground in the shadow of the entrance into the Taj Mahal was Kristin Misaki, unlacing her hiking shoes. He instantly understood his mistake. When he rounded the building's corner, he hadn't anticipated their bending over to remove their shoes before entering the building.

Tim walked to about twenty paces from the monument's entrance. When Misaki leaned forward on the balls of her feet to stand, Tim studied her well-defined calf muscles partially exposed from her jeans. He remembered the night when he'd stood inches over her bed. He waited for the stirring in his loins to begin, but again nothing happened. He examined her more intensely. Then a thought occurred to him: *Maybe she is also a part of God's plan for my redemption.*

Distracted by his thoughts, Tim didn't notice her turn her head in his direction.

When he scanned up the length of her body, his eyes met hers. He almost stumbled backward from the force of her glare. Tim quickly looked upward at the illuminated marble above her head. Walking sideways, he pretended to follow the black Arabic text surrounding the opening arch. His sweat turned cold. The force of her stare continued to pummel him. He tried to appear nonchalant, but he knew he'd been caught.

CHAPTER 29

⸻

AGRA, INDIA

"WHAT TOOK YOU SO LONG?" Grant called when Kristin walked into the dim inner chamber of the Taj Mahal.

"My boots. And then some creepy perv was staring at me."

"Well, I can't fault him for that," he said, earning a slap to his shoulder.

Proceeding further into the dim light of the mausoleum, Grant strained to see the details of the walls around them. The interior had no electric lights. As his eyes adjusted, Grant noticed that the main chamber was an octagon. An arch accented each of the eight walls, which were decorated with the same intricate *pietra dura* inlaid stonework as the exterior.

The glare from several flashlights glinted off the semiprecious stones embedded in the walls. Grant noticed that the green vines climbing the walls bloomed into various multicolored flowers. In a country with as many destitute people as India, he was surprised that millions of dollars in gems could remain in the walls of a building for so many centuries.

"Exquisite, isn't it?" Razi said. "See that flower there?"

Grant followed Razi's finger to the wall beside them. "The one with all the petals?"

"Sixty-four to be exact. The national flower of India. Do you know the species?"

"A lotus," Kristin said. She ran her fingers along the semiprecious stones as if she were reading Braille.

Jigme approached the wall. "The Buddha is often depicted as sitting on lotus petals. The lotus can grow in the most stagnant of waters, yet no matter how muddy the conditions, the flowers themselves rise above the dirty water, producing beautifully pure blossoms."

"So there's hope for us yet," Grant said. He noticed that Kristin didn't react to his comment but instead gazed intently at the jeweled flower.

Her voice was barely audible. "So . . . peaceful."

The young Muslim said to Kristin, "Islam."

"What about it?" Grant asked, when Kristin didn't immediately respond.

"The literal meaning of the word *Islam* is 'peace,'" Razi said. "Not peace in the sense of world peace, but in the sense of an inner peace that comes from surrendering your life to Allah. That is the main thrust of Muhammad's teaching, as well as the invitation of the script embedded in the walls outside this monument."

"Similarly," Jigme added, "the word *Buddhism* is from the root word *budh*, which means 'awakening.' The Buddha also taught his followers to awaken themselves by surrendering to the present moment, so that they could free themselves of *dukkha* and find everlasting peace."

Grant drummed his fingers on his chin. Meeting Razi was no longer nagging at him. He was convinced that the young Muslim was there to teach him some sort of lesson. "Kinley explained to me that 'the Buddha' was not another name for Siddhartha but a title that meant 'the Awakened One,'" he said.

"Razi," Jigme said, "please tell my friends what you explained to me earlier: how Muhammad first began receiving the visions that became the Koran."

"As a young man," Razi said, leading them along the interior wall in a clockwise direction, "Muhammad began visiting a cave on Mount Hira, just outside Mecca, when he needed to escape from the duties of his life. He would sometimes stay up all night praying to Allah to guide him. Late one evening as he lay on the ground deep in prayer, he was visited by the angel Gabriel, who told him that his mission would be to speak to the people about Allah."

"Curious," Jigme said. "The Buddha, just before he reached enlightenment and began his ministry, sat beneath the Bodhi tree, meditating day and night. Instead of an angel, he was visited by the Evil One who sought to distract him from his path with threats of violence and offers of lust. The Buddha continued his course, deep in meditation, and then he reached enlightenment."

A light flicked on in Grant's head. He spoke with his hands as quickly as with his mouth. "Around the age of thirty, Jesus, after his baptism by John and before beginning his ministry, went alone into the desert and sat in deep prayer for forty days and nights. The Gospel of Luke describes him being tempted by Satan, and just like the Buddha, he resisted." His hands dropped to his side. "In fact, this practice of retreating by himself to pray intensely characterized his entire ministry. In the garden of Gethsemane on the night of his betrayal by Judas, Jesus sat in deep prayer again, while his disciples slept."

Kristin stared at Jigme. "So what you're trying to tell us is that Muhammad, Jesus, and the Buddha each experienced a spiritual awakening through their practices of deep meditation?"

The true implication of the message contained in the Issa texts suddenly became much clearer to Grant. Jesus had studied meditation during his travels through India. Then another realization hit him. Moses had also had a similar experience. The Jewish prophet spent forty days and nights on the top of Mount Sinai experiencing a vision of God that resulted in the Decalogue, the Ten Commandments.

"But certainly," Grant said, "you're not suggesting that Muhammad also traveled to India?"

Jigme shook his head. "Why must religion be a history lesson? How the Buddha, Jesus, or Muhammad learned these techniques is irrelevant. Why not focus on what their common experiences teach us about our own lives?"

Grant leaned toward the monk. "But we can't ignore their actual histories. How can we truly evaluate their teachings without stripping away the myths created around these men by their later followers?" He felt his pulse beating in his neck. By trivializing history, his monk friend was coming close to the path Reverend Brady advocated—the path of closing one's eyes to facts. That was why finding the Issa texts was so critical. Sure, he had personal reasons, but this journey was so much bigger than him. It was also about those who were held hostage by the misinformation of people like . . . *well, like my father*, he admitted to himself.

"Understanding is a fine goal," Jigme said, "but it is not enough. If all you do is seek with your mind for knowledge, you will never be satisfied."

"Are you advocating ignorance as the solution to our problems?" Grant asked.

"No," Razi interjected. "Jigme and I only ask you to go beyond mere intellectual understanding of these men's teachings. What the Buddha, Jesus, and Muhammad experienced is available to you as well."

"How is that?"

Jigme replied, "Have you not been practicing what Kinley taught you?"

Grant averted his eyes. When he was stuck in his bed in Bhutan, he found the various meditations Kinley taught to be relaxing at times, but since he'd returned, too many things had happened to him. He didn't have time to sit around and watch his breath or pay attention to the directions of his thoughts.

Jigme placed a hand on his arm. "The truth you seek is not a lesson you can learn, it is one you must experience."

"But—," Grant began.

"Oh my!" Razi exclaimed, checking his watch in a manner Grant thought to be a little too obvious. "How late it has become. I should be leaving." He nodded to Jigme. "And I know you three have other business to conduct."

Other business? Grant wondered. Did Razi know the real reason they were there?

After they shook hands all around, Razi turned to leave. Before he exited into the artificial light of the plaza outside, he called over his shoulder to Jigme, "And please, give my regards to Kinley. You have a special teacher."

Tim watched the Muslim leave the interior of the Taj Mahal alone. The man stepped into his sandals, but instead of walking toward Tim and down the stairs, the Muslim began to stroll around the exterior of the building another time. He craned his neck at the walls above him, and his lips moved subtly, as if reciting a private prayer.

Tim waited for the others to exit. Concealed in shadow, he sat with his back against the minaret on the southeast corner, where he could observe the monument's entrance. To one of the lazy guards who infrequently patrolled the area, he would appear as a weary tourist enjoying the view of the Taj Mahal silhouetted against the black sky.

⌘

"Razi knows Kinley?" Grant asked.

"Speaking of Kinley," Jigme said, as if Grant had made a statement rather than ask a question, "I suppose the two of you are anxious to hear his message?"

"I thought you'd never bring it up," Kristin said, smiling.

Jigme lowered his voice and nodded toward the multicolored lotus blossom inset in the wall. "Grant, do you remember the stories of the Buddha's birth?"

Grant studied the stone flower. "As a newborn, Siddhartha walked outside, and lotus flowers bloomed on the ground at his feet."

"Very good," Jigme whispered. "Now you are close to discovering the next stop on your journey."

"We have to go to the Buddha's birthplace?" Grant asked. "Isn't that in Nepal?" Then another question occurred to him: *What journey?*

"Is it the birth of the man that is significant or the birth of a movement?" Jigme responded.

"Sarnath!" Kristin exclaimed. "The town the Buddha traveled to after becoming enlightened."

After a moment, realization dawned on Grant also. "Where he gave his first public lectures?"

Kristin nodded. "I've been there. Sarnath is just a ten-minute drive from Varanasi."

"Isn't that where you were writing an article before you came to Bhutan?"

"Kinley asked me about my travels there."

Jigme leaned close to them and whispered, "Visit the Mulgandha Kuti Vihar temple."

"I saw it on my trip," Kristin said.

"He remembered you saying so," Jigme replied. "You will find your answer inside the temple."

"What does that mean?" Grant asked a bit too loudly. He couldn't help but let the frustration creep into his voice. They had traveled halfway around the world to meet Kinley, only to be told to go to another city. "Will Kinley be there to meet us? Are the texts being kept in the temple?"

"I'm sorry to disappoint you, but that is truly all I know. As I said earlier, Kinley wanted to protect me from knowing too much."

"But Jigme, I'm really short on time here. In eleven days I'm supposed to go in front of a disciplinary committee at school that thinks I made this stuff up." Grant stopped himself from going any further. He imagined that Kristin had heard him complain enough about his reputation by this point.

"Do you remember Kinley's words to you in the library?"

Grant recalled Kinley's analogy of climbing the steps, but he wondered how Jigme knew since he had waited outside, distracting the guard. *Each step must be used and then left behind to reach the top.* But what relevance was that now? He had climbed more than his fair share of steps, and he needed to reach the top.

The young monk continued, "When you are ready, you will find what you are searching for."

"Ready?" Grant sputtered. He cut off his next comment when he felt Kristin squeeze his arm.

"You'll be coming to Sarnath with us?" she asked.

Jigme shook his head. "You won't need me. Only the two of you can complete this journey."

Tim watched Matthews and Misaki exit the monument. The monk remained inside. He looked to the side of the building and didn't see the Muslim either.

Matthews and Misaki crossed the plaza and descended the steps. Indecision struck Tim. He hated to lose track of those two, but he could always locate them again via Matthews's cell phone. He made a split-second decision. Flexibility in the midst of an operation was the hallmark of a good combatant, he knew. He was tiring of the cat-and-mouse game. He suspected that Matthews and Misaki would be heading for the texts soon. Tim would extract the same information from the monk and then beat them there.

After a full two minutes passed, the monk still hadn't appeared. Growing suspicious, Tim stood and strode toward the entrance of the Taj. The monk emerged from the darkness. Tim slowed, reaching into his right pocket. He grasped the EpiPen in his fingers. He was at most twenty meters from the monk. A quick glance around the near-empty plaza confirmed that neither the guards nor the Muslim were in sight. The few other tourists were widely scattered.

As the monk approached, Tim stopped and pretended to admire the pointed dome on top of the building. His thumb flicked off the cap of the EpiPen into his pocket. He withdrew it in a clenched fist. The young monk walked with an erect but relaxed posture, his hands clasped behind his back. When the monk passed within ten feet of him, Tim fought the urge to strike. They were bathed in floodlights on the exposed plaza. He turned and followed his target to the stairway.

After the monk descended several steps, Tim, a few paces behind, took a final survey of the landscape. No one in sight, and the stairway itself was satisfactorily hidden in shadow.

"Excuse me, sir. Do you speak English?" Tim called.

The monk turned. "Yes, may I be of some assistance to you?"

"I hope so. I got separated from my tour group. We're supposed to meet up in front of the guest house."

He moved to the step immediately above the monk.

"Of course, my friend, I will take you there now. It is on the opposite side of the Taj Mahal from the mosque."

The monk turned and started down the steps.

"Thank you. Are you from around here?"

They were near the bottom of the stairwell, shielded from view of either plaza.

"No, I'm from a small country between India and China called Bhutan."

Tim struck with the speed and determination of an anaconda capturing a hare. His left hand darted out and around the monk's bald head, covering his mouth and jerking him backward at the same time. The monk lost his balance on the narrow step and fell into Tim, who braced himself against the stone wall of the stairwell. In a swift sweeping motion, Tim jabbed the EpiPen clenched in his right fist into his target's thigh. He felt a slight click as the spring-loaded needle pierced the monk's jeans, instantly injecting the Versed into his victim.

Only after Tim replaced the spent EpiPen in his pocket did the monk overcome the initial shock of the attack and begin to struggle. But Tim had the advantage. With his right hand free, he snaked it around the monk's torso and grasped him tightly. His prey shook and wriggled in his arms but had no leverage. Less than a minute passed before the flailing legs and muffled cries subsided.

When the monk became more of a heavy weight than a trapped animal in his arms, Tim relaxed his grip. The monk struggled no more.

"Can you hear me, Kinley?" Tim slipped from behind his victim, allowing the body to slump to the steps.

An unintelligible groan emerged from his lips, in addition to a long string of drool. Tim squatted in front of his subdued prey, lifting the head, which lolled side to side. The eyes were open, but no one was home. Tim glanced at his watch. They needed to move quickly. It was only a matter of time before someone else decided to walk down the stairwell.

As if on cue, Tim's luck changed.

A voice from behind him called out, "Jigme!"

Tim turned his head. The Muslim stood at the top of the steps.

CHAPTER 30

NEW HOPE CHURCH
BIRMINGHAM, ALABAMA

WILLIAM JENNINGS SHRUGGED off his suit jacket while cradling the telephone on his shoulder. "Yes, I understand these last few years have been very difficult for you," he said.

"The entire country has turned against the evangelical movement!" Reverend Jimmy Jeffries, current president of the NAE, exclaimed on the other end of the line.

As Jennings listened to Jeffries rant about how no one appreciated the challenges he faced running the organization, Jennings hung his jacket on a wooden hanger and then placed the hanger on the back of his office door. Walking to his chair, he was careful not to let the extralong phone cord disturb the neat stacks of documents organized on the leather surface of his desk. What he really needed, he thought as Jeffries babbled on the other end of the line, was one of those cordless headsets.

"Your man seems to be doing well these days," Jeffries said, "in spite of the rumors of the financial difficulties at your New Hope development."

How transparent, Jennings thought. Jeffries was obviously fishing for details about his boss's campaign to unseat him from his position. "A minor hiccup we've moved past. The bank loans are being finalized as we speak, and the book sales are beyond our expectations. The country seems to be responding to Brian's warnings: the economy, the natural disasters, the terrorist incidents are all evidence of God's displeasure with our direction."

"The timing of that spectacle of a debate last week must have helped."

Jennings thought he detected a note of resentment in Jeffries's tone. The release of the texts followed by the debate had been a publicity coup. Brady's press appearances had dwarfed Jeffries's that week. Jennings was particularly pleased with the upcoming issue of *Christianity Today* with Brady on its cover under the headline THE NEW VOICE OF EVANGELICALS. With all the media attention, sales of Brady's book had jumped 63 percent. The timing couldn't have worked out better for them. Jennings thought about how Brady had almost blown the debate when he'd veered from his script. Fortunately, he recovered and concluded it as Jennings had planned. The mainstream press had lampooned the student in the days that followed while the Christian media had hailed Brady as a hero.

"Brian just responded naturally to the situation," Jennings replied.

"What will you do if that Grant Matthews character actually produces some ancient manuscripts?"

Jennings opened his desk drawer and removed a box of antacid pills. He popped two of the tiny pills into his mouth and downed them with a swig of lukewarm black coffee.

"Won't happen," Jennings said more confidently than he felt. He wiped his palms on his trousers. "The texts are just as fake as Grant Matthews is."

"Yes, of course. The whole idea of Jesus becoming inspired through his studies of false religions is preposterous."

As Jeffries continued to ramble on, Jennings began to scroll through his email. The important update he was waiting for hadn't arrived yet. Nothing bothered Jennings more than dealing with incompetence, except maybe stupidity. Although he was only half listening to Jeffries, the NAE president's next words caught him by surprise.

"William, I plan to announce next month that I'm retiring from my position as head of the NAE."

Jennings almost dropped the phone. In all his strategic planning, this was one contingency he hadn't dreamed of. With Jeffries out of the way, Brady would be a shoo-in.

"And," the subdued voice on the other end of the line continued, "if everything is still moving in the right direction over at New Hope, I'd like to offer my support to Brian's campaign."

After they discussed the details of how such an endorsement would work and exchanged pleasantries, Jennings hung up the phone, still in shock from Jeffries's offer. He had begun to scribble notes on a white legal pad when the door to his office flew open. Brady stood there, his face glowing red and the armpits of his tailored French-cuffed shirt soaked through with sweat.

"William, explain this phone call I just received!"

CHAPTER 31

‒‒‒∞∞∞‒‒‒

TAJ MAHAL
AGRA, INDIA

STARING AT THE MUSLIM, Tim felt his mind racing. He now faced two new problems. First, the Muslim would have to be dealt with. Second, the monk in his arms was named Jigme, not Kinley.

The man ran down the steps. "What happened?"

"Uh, I don't . . . I don't know," Tim stuttered. "I saw this young man lying here. He must have tripped and hit his head. Can you help me?"

The Muslim bent over the monk, who stared vacantly. "Jigme, can you hear me?" he asked loudly. An incoherent moan escaped the monk's lips.

"Is he a friend of yours?" Tim asked. His hand slipped into his left pants pocket, which still contained three full EpiPens—the ones he'd marked with red stripes.

"I only met him recently," the Muslim said. He leaned close to the monk's head and felt for injury. "He's a monk from Bhutan. I met his teacher earlier. Will you find one of the monument guards while I stay with him?"

"Sure." Tim made his best attempt at looking concerned.

When the Muslim turned to tend to his friend, Tim struck.

Using his entire body weight, he fell on top of the Muslim, pushing him to the steps. Before his victim could react, Tim grabbed his head with one hand and jerked it backward, exposing the man's neck, just as if he were going to slice his throat with a Ka-Bar knife. Without hesitating, he rammed the EpiPen into the exposed bulging vein, injecting the entire dose of hydrocyanic acid.

The man thrashed underneath him. An elbow caught Tim in the ribs, momentarily taking his breath away, but he held on to his target with both hands, pushing the man's face into the marble. The Muslim was larger than the monk and almost succeeded in throwing Tim off him, but Tim spread his legs to distribute his weight. He knew the Muslim fought a losing battle.

Twenty seconds later, the man's breathing became more rapid and shallower, as if he were hyperventilating from the effort of the struggle. Tim knew that it wasn't the effort affecting his breathing. Another twenty seconds later, the Muslim went into convulsions. His limbs flailed about like a fish pulled from the water and tossed onto a hot dock in the summer sun. Finally, the poison completed its journey to the man's heart.

Tim rose and brushed off his clothes. Flushed, his breath came in short bursts. He replaced the plastic cap to the EpiPen and returned it to his pocket. He surveyed his handiwork: the Muslim lay next to the semiconscious monk. A red welt had formed on the man's neck, and a white froth bubbled from his mouth. Tim would be gone before anyone suspected foul play.

Standing over the two bodies, Tim realized that for the first time in months his skin didn't itch. In fact, it felt silky. Then the reverend's words came to him: "Aliens as well as citizens, when they blaspheme the Name, shall be put to death."

Grasping the monk's right arm, Tim tossed it around his neck. *Jigme*, he thought, *not Kinley*. But the Muslim mentioned a teacher. He would just have to extract the information from the student.

"Walk with me now," he said, as he half carried his "drunk friend" onto the lower sandstone plaza.

Grant and Kristin reached the halfway point between the monument and the gate—the raised marble platform where they had encountered Jigme just an hour earlier.

Kristin shivered slightly. "I never think of this area of India getting cold." She moved closer to Grant.

"Why didn't Kinley meet us in Agra himself?" he asked, enjoying the closeness of her body. "I hate to think we're some pawns in an elaborate game."

"You know Kinley better than I. Do you really believe that?"

Grant thought for a moment. "No."

"Me either. Let's see . . ." She gazed across the reflecting pool beside them, scrunching her brow in concentration. "First Kinley sends us to the most famous Islamic monument in India."

"And next he sends us to Sarnath, the birthplace of Buddhism."

"Right, and Sarnath just happens to be located next to Varanasi, where he knows we will stay because of my contacts there."

"Hold on. Varanasi is the holiest city to the Hindus."

She nodded. "The Ganges River flows through the city. Thousands of Hindus make pilgrimages there every year to purify themselves in its holy waters."

"So Kinley has sent us from an important Muslim site to a Hindu one and then to a Buddhist one—all in the search for information about the origins of Christianity?"

"Wait!" Kristin stopped.

"What?"

"I can't believe I didn't make the connection earlier." She tugged on his sleeve. "The Issa texts describing his travels through India—"

"Jesus may have traveled to Varanasi and Sarnath too!"

"Varanasi was considered a pilgrimage destination even during his day. And if he was on his way to the Himalayas, as described in the texts, the waters of the Ganges originate in the mountains there. Following a river in a hot climate would have made sense."

"So Kinley wants us to retrace a key path on Issa's journey?" Grant turned to face the Taj Mahal.

The strange movement of two figures heading across the wide sandstone plaza toward the immense guest house building on the east end of the grounds captured his attention. He raised his hand in front of his face attempting to block out the glare of the landscape lighting against the white marble.

"What . . ." He pointed, unable to decipher exactly what he was seeing, but a growing feeling of dread rose from his gut. Squinting his eyes, Grant recognized the figure being dragged along—the one wearing blue jeans and an untucked white shirt. The one with the bald head.

"Oh my God," he said.

"Jigme!" Kristin shouted a second later.

Grant grabbed her hand and broke into a sprint toward the plaza. It was the first time he had run since his accident, but he felt no pain in his leg.

Sweating from the effort of dragging the monk across the plaza, Tim realized that the drug had worked too well. He'd hoped for the monk to be able to walk with assistance, but instead he only moaned and drooled. Tim must have put too much Versed into the EpiPen, and now he would have to wait for the effects to lessen before he could effectively question the man.

The open-air guest house, built from massive red sandstone blocks, lay a short distance ahead. He coaxed his burning thighs onward. Unlike the Taj, this building was open to the sandstone plaza via several vaulted arches rising to their pointy apex thirty feet off the ground. Once concealed within the building's shadows, he would rest a minute before transporting his prize down the construction lift at the building's side wall. When they were safely away on the skiff, he would question the monk without being interrupted.

They were making slow progress when Tim sensed a commotion behind him. He turned his head toward the noise.

Oh shit.

Running across the grass were Matthews and Misaki, yelling and pointing wildly. They would reach him before he could drag the monk to the scaffolding.

Tim pumped his legs, ignoring the intense burn from the effort. Then he heard new voices, but this time in an unintelligible tongue. Swiveling his head, he cursed loudly.

Two of the Indian security guards hustled toward him from the upper marble plaza. The idiots still had their Kalashnikovs slung, bouncing across their backs.

Tim pressed on. If he could just reach the scaffolding, he could dump the monk on the lift and lower it to the riverbank. The guards wouldn't know what was going on until he'd left. He glanced over his shoulder again.

He wasn't going to make it.

Matthews and Misaki were now on the sandstone plaza and closing quickly, the guards forty meters away. Tim made a decision. The open-air building was only ten paces in front of him.

Although Matthews and Misaki were closer, they were not as dangerous a threat as the two men with automatic rifles. With his free right hand, Tim reached underneath his shirt to the holster hidden in the small of his back. Both guards stopped in midrun when he drew the Glock. Tim raised the gun to eye level. The guards struggled to swing their rifles around.

Tim squeezed off four shots in succession. Forty meters was a long distance for a pistol in a combat situation, especially when he was dragging a man, but Tim didn't need to actually hit the guards for his shots to be effective. As he expected, both guards forgot about their rifles and dove for the ground behind the knee wall that separated the upper plaza from the lower one. Tim relished the rush of combat that he'd missed for years.

The gunshots surprised Grant. Although his eyes registered the pistol in the man's hand, his brain hesitated before interpreting that Jigme's kidnapper was actually shooting at people. His paralysis evaporated as the guards hit the plaza for cover. He jerked Kristin's arm toward him, pushed her to the ground, and fell on top of her. He winced when his right leg collided with the stone.

"No!" she cried.

"Stay down!"

With Kristin protected by his body, Grant focused on his friend fifteen meters away. *Something's wrong with him*, Grant thought. The gun's explosions inches from Jigme's face had only caused him to blink rapidly. The man with the gun then rotated the monk's body to face Grant and Kristin. The man's face was red and sweaty with effort but his gray eyes didn't hold the look of a crazed lunatic. He had a military demeanor to him: efficient and quick. Something struck Grant as familiar too. Then he remembered. The night of the debate he'd been concerned when this same man slipped into the auditorium. *He was one of Reverend Brady's followers.* The shock of this new reality weighed on Grant. This man had followed them halfway across the world, he was trying to kidnap Jigme, and he'd just shot at two guards with machine guns.

Kristin whispered into his ear, "He was the one staring at me outside the entrance to the Taj."

Her words solidified Grant's suspicion: *He's after the Issa texts.*

"Follow me and I'll put a bullet through the monk's head." The man's voice was even but strong with an American accent from the South.

"Don't touch him, you son of a bitch!" The furor exploded from Grant involuntarily. After the words escaped his mouth, he realized the barrel of the gun was pointed at them.

"I think it's you and your girlfriend you should be worried about now."

Grant's attention now focused only the gun. He could almost sense the man's finger tighten on the trigger. Kristin's body tensed under his. The hollowness of fear quickly replaced the heat of anger. Grant knew he was helpless to protect either of them.

Tim was now faced with his second opportunity to scatter this trouble-maker's brains. But as tempting as the idea was, he still wanted them alive, at least until he secured the texts. He turned and dragged the monk toward the guest house. The two poorly trained guards would keep their heads down for a few minutes, but the shots would draw the attention of more guards.

He entered the first arch of the red building and turned left toward his escape route. Every few paces, he checked behind him to see if they dared follow him into the open-air structure. After two exhausting minutes of hauling his prize through the building's shadows, he approached the wall at the north end where the construction work was taking place.

Tim hesitated.

He would have to step out onto the open plaza again to reach the scaffolding on the other side of the wall. He let the monk fall to the ground with a thud and gripped his Glock with both hands in front of his body. Pressing his back against the rough sandstone wall, he slid to his left until he reached the edge of the last archway.

The moment he stepped outside, the distinctive chatter of automatic gunfire rattled across the plaza. Shards of stone exploded from the wall inches from his head. He dove back into the building.

"Shit!" he exclaimed.

Tim crawled on all fours across the stone to where he'd dropped the unconscious monk. The incompetent guards had gotten their act together quicker than he'd expected. He didn't have much time before the guest house was surrounded. His handgun was no match for automatic weapons.

"Damn it!" he cursed to himself. He scratched his forearm with the butt of his pistol.

What was supposed to have been a stealthy grab and run had somehow turned into a firefight. *Stop and think*, he told himself. A quick survey of the dark interior of the building didn't reveal any openings along the rear wall where he could slip out unnoticed. His only escape was onto the plaza, over the wall, and down the scaffolding.

A groan beside him brought his attention to the monk.

The monk would be his ticket out of there.

He lifted the monk's stubble-covered head. Shaking him, Tim asked, "Where are the Jesus books?"

The monk emitted an unintelligible noise, but his eyes remained closed. Tim slapped the face, stinging his own hand as the sound echoed in the vaulted ceiling above them. The monk's eyes fluttered open.

"Grant Matthews and Kristin Misaki—where are they going?"

On his left side, Grant felt the cool, hard stone of the lower plaza; on his right was Kristin's warm, soft body. With the assailant's gun no longer pointed at him, his anger returned like a fire rekindled from hot coals by a breath of air.

He had to do something. *But what?*

The man was armed, and Grant's only combat experience consisted of a fifth-grade brawl on the playground that resulted in both him and Kyle Mills being sent to the principal's office with bloody noses and busted lips.

The two guards had shot at the assailant from behind the knee wall on the upper plaza. *Why don't they come down here and storm the building?* he wondered. If they didn't move quickly, the man might kill Jigme.

Presumably thinking the same thoughts, Kristin rose to her knees. Before she could stand, the man appeared at the far archway with Jigme held in front of him.

Grant grabbed Kristin's sweater and pulled her back to the ground.

Tim stepped into the plaza using the monk's body as a shield. The guards held their fire. He spotted them immediately crouched behind the knee wall; the floodlights silhouetted the two green uniforms against the white marble of the Taj Mahal. One of them yelled something to Tim that he couldn't understand, but he wasn't planning on following the directions, whatever they were. He dragged the monk toward the scaffolding at the edge of the plaza. He was only a few feet from safety.

"Please don't hurt him. He's just a monk," a woman's voice pleaded. With his attention focused on the two automatic weapons, Tim had momentarily forgotten about Matthews and Misaki. They were still lying on the ground.

Just as he opened his mouth to respond to the girl, something sharp poked him in the back.

He froze.

He rotated his head slowly. Then he relaxed. He'd reached the edge of the plaza and hit one of the metal supports of the scaffolding. His escape was almost complete. Continuing to hold the semiconscious monk with his left arm, he stepped over the low stone wall and onto the scaffolding. His feet now securely on a wood plank, he glanced at the mechanical lift. Taking the monk with him would be impossible. The guards would be there before he could lower the lift halfway to the ground. But if he went alone, he could drop the twenty feet to the riverbank instantly. The ground below him was hidden in shadow. He would be motoring down the river before the guards could reposition themselves for a clean shot.

Why aren't the guards doing more? The thought raged through Grant's mind. His first instinct was to stay on the ground, but now he saw that the man was getting ready to climb over the low wall with his friend, and the guards were still doing nothing. *Where's their backup?*

He glanced at the guest house in front of him. Maybe he could run there while the assailant was distracted by the guards. The options swirling in his head stopped when the man raised his gun and fired three shots. The first two hit the knee wall in front of the guards, causing them to duck out of sight.

Time stopped for Grant with the third shot. The man directed it into Jigme's back.

CHAPTER 32

—∞∞∞—

GANGES RIVER, INDIA
TWO THOUSAND YEARS AGO

T HE EARLY MORNING SUN crested the distant mountain peaks, its rays casting an orange glow through Issa's closed eyelids. Sitting with his legs
crossed on the ghats, the wide stone steps that led to the river below, Issa heard
the world around him awaken: monkeys bickering over food, the call of a
hawk soaring, the distant sounds of the town beginning its day, the splashing
of those bathing in the river. With each slow breath, he inhaled the mingled
smells of spices and smoke drifting from the town's cooking fires. As he sat in
relaxed stillness, each of these sensations washed over him like the wind passing over a field of wheat—bending and flowing with the breeze before returning to its natural upright posture.

Following his teacher's instructions, Issa focused his awareness on the
moist air moving from the tip of his nose on his inhale, down his throat, and
then filling his lungs. His *nephesh*, his breath. He felt alive, as if each breath
radiated an energy into his soul, as if his skin itself breathed for him.

"Issa!" An urgent voice beside him interrupted his meditation.

The speaker's hand roughly shook his shoulder.

Issa opened his eyes and blinked at the silhouette of a man outlined by the
morning sun.

"They're coming, Master," his student said, out of breath. "I ran to beat
them here. You must leave now."

Remaining seated, Issa raised his hand and shielded his eyes from the sun's
reflection. A man of about twenty years, his own age, but who looked much

older from a life of hard labor, stood in front of him in the dirty rags he wore for clothes. His student, one of fifteen he'd recently been teaching, practically danced from agitation. Issa placed his own hand on top of the one tugging at him to rise and pulled the man down next to him.

"Vinay, sit and calm yourself. Who is coming?"

Issa surveyed the ghats. Most of his other students were seated several steps below them and interrupted their own meditation practice to watch the discussion. He would correct them for that later. The others looked up at them from where they soaked in the cool waters of the holy river. Issa had found it interesting that the people here believed that dunking oneself in the river washed away one's misdeeds, just as the priests in his homeland bathed to purify themselves before entering the temple.

"Issa, the Brahmin priests are coming to arrest you. Oh, this is my fault. If I hadn't agreed to let you teach us . . . Please leave now." Vinay tugged on his teacher's tunic.

"I have done nothing wrong. I am not afraid to speak to them. Now sit still beside me."

"But, teacher, seeing me with you will only anger them."

"Let me handle that."

Having heard Vinay's warning, the other students stood in alarm; they were all untouchables. Not even considered worthy to be a *Shudra*, they were a people outside caste in a society where position was even more rigidly defined than in his own. Issa raised his hand, signaling them to stay where they were. This entire caste system had disturbed him from the moment he'd first learned of it on his journey with the merchants.

The caste one was born into determined one's fate in this world: at the top were the *Brahmins*, the priests like Issa's teacher, who guided the people in their spiritual lives; the next level were the *Kshatriyas*, the government officials and the warriors; third were the *Vaishyas*, the farmers and the merchants; and last the *Shudras*, the peasants and the laborers. The untouchables did the work, when they could find it, not even suitable for the *Shudras*: preparing bodies for cremation, handling refuse, cleaning animal dung from the streets. Early on, Issa noticed that the top two castes rarely spoke to the *Vaishyas*, except when they needed something. As Issa had experienced on his journey, the treatment of the *Shudras* was worse, but the members of the four primary castes didn't even consider the untouchables human.

Ever since he'd arrived in this land, Issa had been curious about the untouchables, but they seemed afraid of him, averting their eyes when he approached and hurrying away upon realizing he wanted to talk rather than give them work to do. Although Issa was a foreigner, he was studying with the Brahmins, and thus off limits.

One day Issa encountered Vinay carrying wood to a small shop that made furniture. Issa stopped him and spoke of his own experience building tables with his father. Vinay explained that he was not a craftsman; he only carried wood for the man who made the furniture. Issa made an excuse to wander by the shop each day for the next several weeks to talk to his new friend.

Issa learned from Vinay that the untouchables were not permitted to worship in the temples with the Brahmins, nor were they taught the Vedas, the ancient scriptures which were to these people what the Torah was to his. In Issa's own country, the Pharisees who governed the Temple lived as well as the Romans who ruled his land, but even the laborers were allowed to worship and were taught the law of Moses. When Issa confronted his teacher with this observation, his teacher looked at Issa as if he'd just asked why they did not teach the Vedas to dogs. He then refused to speak of the matter again.

Issa decided that he would take on the responsibility of teaching as many untouchables as he could. Only a student himself, he might not have the skills or the knowledge of a Brahmin priest, but he figured that some spiritual guidance would be better than nothing. After much persuading, Vinay became his first student, and gradually he brought his relatives and friends along. They met along the banks of the holy river before the sun rose or after it set, when they were less likely to be noticed by the Brahmins. Issa wasn't ashamed of his actions, but he thought it best not to advertise them either. Inevitably, word of his associations with the untouchables reached Issa's teacher, who refused to listen to Issa's explanations. He simply told him to stop the nonsense and focus on his own studies. That was two weeks ago.

Issa rose to his feet when he saw the four Brahmin priests dressed in white tunics and sandals approach from the dusty road. Leading the group, with his long white hair flowing behind his back and an equally stark white beard, was Swami Gundalini, the spiritual leader of the temple. Behind the swami, Issa's teacher stared at the ground alongside two other stern-looking older priests. Most troubling, however, were the two soldiers walking behind the four priests.

Maybe Vinay is right, he thought. *Why did I think I could challenge these men in their own community?* The soldiers wore smug smiles as they strutted down the road in their leather boots and vests. At least their swords were still in their scabbards.

When the group reached the steps where Issa stood, trying to appear relaxed, he bowed deeply from the waist. "*Namaste*, Swami Gundalini. I am honored by your visit."

"*Namaste*," replied the swami with a nod of his head. "I've heard disturbing reports about you, young Issa."

"What reports might those be? I have worked diligently since my arrival here. My teacher has told me I am the quickest learner he has taught." Issa noticed his teacher refused to look at him.

The swami grinned at Issa, displaying white teeth that matched his hair. The grin held no compassion. "I have heard of your quick tongue as well. My young student, we generously opened our doors when you arrived in our land, teaching you the ways of the Vedas. I understand that your practice has become quite advanced. Yet you continue to disobey us by teaching these—these untouchables," he said, spitting the last word out in the direction of Vinay as if he were trying to rid himself of a bad taste.

"Are the untouchables not also among Brahma's creations?" Issa asked in an innocent tone.

"Do you dare to debate me, boy?"

"I mean no disrespect, Swami, but I am just following what I have been taught."

"And you have the knowledge to teach our ways, when you are only a recent student yourself?" Without waiting for a response, the swami continued, "But even a great guru would not waste his time on these creatures. It is not their place in life to worship, nor to understand the eternal; they do not have the mental faculties to comprehend the holy teachings."

"Swami, I do not pretend to be a master of what I teach. I only share my own experiences with them. But if Brahman, if God, exists within each of us as I have been taught, then he exists in the untouchables as well as the priests. Why shouldn't they discover the same spirit inside of them that is inside of you?"

"Because they do not have the ability to do so. Maybe in a future life, when they have advanced farther, they may be ready for such a difficult task, but today they are simply not suited for it."

"Have you ever spent time with an untouchable, Swami? I think you underestimate them. In fact, their simple lives may allow them to reach Brahman more easily than either you or I."

"What! I refuse to listen to such nonsense." The swami's tanned face turned several shades darker, contrasting even more with the snow white mane falling around his shoulders. Issa knew he was pushing his luck, and he glanced nervously at the two guards.

"I've seen it myself," Issa said. He'd never before heard anyone contradict the swami, but the truth was as clear as the sun on a cloudless winter day. "Men like Vinay here," Issa continued, putting a hand on his student's shoulder, which caused Vinay to cringe as if he hoped to disappear, "are not caught up in the trappings of your society. By the simplicity of their existence, they have already peeled back many of the layers that separate them from Brahman."

"How dare you," the swami said with a coldness that sent a shiver through Issa. "They carry out the garbage and feed the swine. I have dedicated every moment of my life to studying the Vedas!"

Issa glanced at his teacher, who continued to gaze at the ground. Issa suspected that his teacher agreed with him. "You have dedicated your life to worship, Swami. But have you truly touched the eternal: do you live with it every day? If Brahman is the center of peace, why are you filled with anger? I have seen these untouchables stand waist-deep in the river early in the morning, when the town is still, and I have seen the expression of joy on their faces. I think they are the ones touching Brahman, Swami."

Rather than respond, the swami turned and marched to the two guards, who straightened to attention. Issa's pulse increased when he saw the one closest to him rest a hand on the hilt of his sword.

"Why do you feel the need to bring soldiers with you, Swami?" Issa asked quickly. He wiped the perspiration from his hands on his cloak. "Have I done anything to suggest violence? Would you have me arrested for bringing a moment of peace and good news to these people's difficult lives?"

When the swami turned to respond, his mouth opened, but no sound came out. He looked not at Issa but past him. Puzzled, Issa turned his head. His breath caught in his throat when he saw that all fifteen of his students had come out from the water and up from the steps. The untouchables now formed a protective semicircle behind him.

Issa released his breath and turned to the priests. He fought the urge to glance to his teacher for direction and instead fixed his eyes on the swami, who now seemed unsure what to do. Issa felt the rising sun on the back of his neck; he hoped that the swami didn't see the sweat that had started to trickle down his temples.

The swami inclined his head toward the nearest guard and whispered something Issa couldn't hear. The guard, whose hand still rested on the hilt of his sword, ran his fingers down the side of the leather scabbard hanging by his leg. After the swami finished speaking to him, the guard looked at Issa and smiled, revealing stained and crooked teeth. Not sure how else to react, Issa returned the smile.

Opening his arms in a welcoming gesture, the swami spoke to the untouchables. "I am happy to see each of you so loyal to your teacher. Although Issa is one of our most gifted students, I am sure you understand why he can no longer instruct you, since he is not a priest himself." The swami then directed his ingratiating tone toward Issa. "What is this talk of arresting you here? I only wanted to make sure that you understand our culture and how you are expected to behave, if you are to study with us. We would not want a misunderstanding to result in any unpleasant situation, would we?"

Seeing that he was being offered a temporary reprieve, Issa bowed his head. "No, we would not want an unpleasant situation, Swami. I understand."

"Good, then." The swami spun on his sandals and started down the dusty road, his white robes trailing behind him.

The guard with the hungry smile hesitated a moment, watching Issa, before he turned and followed the swami. Only with their backs to him did Issa relax and allow himself to wipe his brow. As the priests walked away, his teacher turned his head and caught Issa's eye for the first time. His grave expression spoke more than any words. He inclined his head toward the mountains on the far side of the river. Issa understood. First checking that the other priests were not watching, Issa pressed his palms together in front of his chest and bowed deeply.

It was time to leave this village and to continue his adventure. As much as he loved his students, Issa wasn't ready to become a martyr for them.

CHAPTER 33

New Hope Church
Birmingham, Alabama

"**I**'VE BEEN ON THE PHONE for forty-five minutes with the bankers," Brady bellowed. "What's wrong with our loans?"

"The bankers?" Jennings repeated.

"Yes, the bankers. They called for you, but you've been tied up on the phone all afternoon, so they asked for me. I felt ambushed. They're suspending the next drawdown on our loan pending an audit of our financials and our construction process. Can you tell me what the hell is going on here?"

Jennings massaged his temples with his fingertips. "Brian, you know we've been having budgetary issues. Ever since we fired Carla, our cash management has suffered."

"But I've raised millions through donations, and now the book is taking off. The cash should be rolling in. How could we have a money problem?" Brady lowered himself into the upholstered chair opposite Jennings's desk. He thought he detected Jennings suppressing a sigh.

"As you know, we began construction before we raised all the equity needed for the project. The bank permitted us to begin borrowing under the loan, but our continued ability to do so has been dependent on raising more money. The economy has hurt presales of the homes. Now the book is exceeding our expectations, but we won't see the next royalty check for another four months."

"Well, isn't the fact that we're going to have the money good enough?" He knocked on his forehead. "We're raising the money; it's just a timing issue."

"I suspect that their concerns stem not just from the cash flow but also from our latest budget increases."

"Oh yes, they started questioning me about that." Brady threw his hands up in the air. "They wanted to go item by item through the latest expenditures: seventy thousand last week to the grading contractor, forty to the architect, and twenty in cash a few days ago for I don't know what. I looked like a fool, William. Handling these details is your job, not mine!"

Jennings stiffened at the mention of the numbers. Brady noticed that his already pale complexion turned even whiter. He liked making Jennings uncomfortable, and he wondered if maybe he shouldn't start taking a greater interest in the financials with so much at stake.

"I'll call and explain right away," Jennings said, regaining his composure. "The grading expense is directly in our budget. But Brian, we've exceeded the design fees by a factor of three. You can't keep making changes." He paused and added, "As for the cash, you know how some of these good-old-boy subcontractors are: they don't even have bank accounts to deposit checks into."

Brady leaned back in the chair, propping his feet up on Jennings's desk. "No one ever said this project would be easy, but we cannot give up faith just when things get difficult. When the Israelites wandered in the desert for forty years, what were God's instructions? I'll tell you what: stay faithful, and the Lord will deliver you to the Holy Land. That's just what we must do now."

Jennings seemed to relax again. "I think our deliverance may be coming sooner than we expected." Then a broad grin spread across his face. Brady sat up straight as his number two detailed the conversation he'd just had with Jimmy Jeffries.

"It's really going to happen," Brady said, more to himself than to Jennings. "I'm going to be next head of the NAE. I'll be the public face of millions of evangelicals across the nation."

"These next few weeks are critical. We can't afford to have anything hurt your image. Once Jeffries announces his retirement and endorses you, we should be home free until the election."

"Well, whatever you do"—Brady pointed a finger across the desk at Jennings—"just make me look good. God help us if those heretical texts turn up anywhere. I Googled myself this morning, and the Evangelical blogs are still praising my handling of that Matthews kid at the debate."

"I don't think the texts will ever surface."

Brady hauled himself out of the chair and bent over Jennings's desk. "I need more than what you *think*, William. I need certainty on this. For the good of my reputation, for your job, for the faith of our community, those texts can never turn up."

CHAPTER 34

⸺ ❦ ⸺

VARANASI, INDIA

GRANT RECALLED A SCENE from a movie he'd first seen when he was twelve. His father had forbidden most movies in their home, especially anything with an R rating, but that night he'd slept over at a friend's house. The movie, *A Clockwork Orange*, gave him nightmares for weeks. In one particularly vivid scene, a character being brainwashed was tied to a chair. His eyes were taped open while he was forced to watch disturbing video images flashed onto a screen.

For the past day, Grant couldn't turn off the images flashing on the screen behind his eyes: the moonlit plaza of the Taj Mahal; Razi's gruesome death; Jigme's shooting; Grant himself lying impotently on the ground.

Staring out the taxi's filthy window, Kristin sat in silence beside him. He opened his mouth to speak but closed it silently. They'd arrived in Varanasi an hour earlier after a short Indian Airlines flight from Agra. Because Kristin had spent two weeks living and researching this ancient Hindu town on the banks of the Ganges River, they would use it as their home base for their trip to nearby Sarnath, just as Kinley had anticipated.

"It sickens me," she said quietly, "to think how easily he could've died. If the shot had been a few more inches . . ."

"I don't think killing Jigme was the goal of that lunatic. Jigme was only a foot away; he let Jigme live."

The doctor at the hospital in Agra explained that although Jigme's wound was serious, the bullet had passed straight through his shoulder. The distraction had worked. Whoever the shooter was, he'd disappeared down the river in the confusion that followed.

When they left Jigme at the airport earlier that morning for his return to Bhutan and their trip to Varanasi, the young monk was in better spirits than either Grant or Kristin. With his arm in a sling, he joked, he would be excused from dormitory cleanup for the next few weeks. He added that his injured shoulder would also keep him out of trouble. During his recovery, he couldn't sneak away, as he often did during a free period, to practice his secret hobby. Monks, he explained, were forbidden from participating in the national sport of Bhutan—archery.

But Grant was too distracted by the many unanswered questions to appreciate Jigme's attempt to add levity to the situation. Now in the taxi, he caught himself having asked these questions so many times that he attempted to use one of Kinley's techniques. He turned his attention to his breath: it was shallower than it should be. He exhaled fully, and on the following inhalation, he watched the air move from the tip of his nostril until it filled his lungs completely.

Continuing to breathe, he followed Kristin's gaze out the window. Although Varanasi was smaller than Agra, the town teemed with the same chaos of vehicles, people, and animals vying for room on the narrow streets. When the taxi slowed to turn at the busy intersection of Aurangabad and Durgakund roads, Grant noted how daily life was lived on the town's streets: women in kaleidoscopic saris perused tables on the sidewalk where vendors sold everything from fresh fruit to blue jeans and cell phones; elderly men chatted while getting haircuts and shaves from roadside barbers who set up shop with nothing more than a chair, scissors, razor, and bucket of water. He rolled down the dusty window and inhaled a perfume of exotic fragrances.

Kristin touched his arm. "You know, I can't stop thinking about Razi . . ." Her voice caught in her throat.

"I know." He turned to her. He'd already gone over at least a hundred times the mental checklist of all the things he could have done differently to save Razi's life and prevent Jigme's shooting. "But what we need to do now is to focus on the future. We need a new road map." He unzipped the daypack at his feet and removed a small spiral notebook. "I've jotted down some notes, and—"

She snatched the notebook from his hand and tossed it on the vinyl seat between them. "Must everything boil down to a list or a flowchart? Razi is dead! Jigme almost died!"

He took the notebook from the seat, replaced it in his pack, and grasped her hand. "I know. I'm just not sure how else to do this."

She turned to face the window again, her voice softening. "Grant, I'm scared. Who was that man?"

Grant knew that the little information they'd been able to tell the authorities wouldn't help catch the guy. Kristin recognized him as the one who'd watched her in front of the Taj, and Grant knew he was the same man who had struck him as a shady character at the debate. *Not that the police even gave a damn,* he thought. He sensed the authorities had wanted to get them out of the police station as quickly as possible; they would cover up the incident to protect tourism to the country's most famous site. Although shots were exchanged, the events happened at night and the only death was Razi, a local Muslim student. Nothing had appeared in the press about the incident, and Grant doubted it ever would. Then he recalled the police in Atlanta who had refused to believe his theory on the missing photographs. As he turned the memory over in his mind, he couldn't help but think that the two events had to be related. He'd seen that man in Atlanta, and now he'd followed him halfway around the world in an attempt to—*what?* Get his hands on the manuscripts? Stop their meeting with Kinley? Grant had called Billingsly after they'd left the police station, and his mentor had shared his concern that he was involved in something more dangerous than they'd expected. Grant, however, refused the professor's advice to return home.

"How did he find us in Agra?" she asked, not for the first time over the past two days.

"We don't even know he's after the texts."

"But what else could he possibly be after? And who is he?"

The second question troubled Grant the most. The image of the assassin's smug expression burned into his mind. *Was the shooter a lone fanatic?* Grant doubted it. He was more likely part of a larger group threatened by the release of the Issa texts.

Kristin dropped her head. "Is it even worth it?"

"We can't let this guy, whoever he is, prevent us from moving forward; that's probably exactly what he wants." He sounded more confident than he felt.

Kristin motioned out the window. "Hey, we're here."

Grant glanced at his watch. Almost five. They would travel to Sarnath first thing in the morning. He'd wanted to rush there immediately, but she explained that the temple would be closed by the time they arrived. Instead she'd insisted that they stop first at Banaras Hindu University to visit a friend, a professor of Hindu studies who had helped provide her with background research for her article on the Hindus' religious pilgrimage to the Ganges River.

The taxi turned underneath a salmon-colored stone gate. Entering the campus reminded Grant of stepping onto the grounds of the Taj Mahal and finding peace from the bustling city of Agra. Leaving the chaotic streets of Varanasi behind them, they drove down a wide, tree-lined avenue. Conspicuously absent from the university grounds were the city's stray cows, dogs, and pigs. Only a few students and professors on bicycles pedaled calmly down the road. Grant thought that Banaras University could have been any college in the States. To their right, classroom buildings were set back from the main road by expansive lawns, where students sat, studying textbooks under the shade of mature hardwood trees. To their left, they passed the athletic fields where other students played soccer and cricket.

"It's not quite what I expected," Grant said.

"Something smaller, more Third World?"

"Yeah, I guess so."

"BHU is one of the largest universities in India, over twenty thousand students. See that building?" Kristin pointed to a classically designed red brick building. "That's the law school. Over there"—she pointed to a peach-colored plaster building with brick accents on the cornices and along the main entrance—"that's the nursing school. The university is divided by academic fields; each has its own building. Religious studies is up ahead."

Five minutes later, they ascended a worn marble staircase to the second floor of one of the brick and plaster buildings. Proceeding down the hall past several classrooms, they arrived at a wooden door. A nameplate on the wall read "Professor Deepraj Bhatt."

In response to Kristin's brisk knock, a scratchy voice on the other side called out, "*Hahn?* Yes?"

Kristin opened the door into an office that could have belonged to Grant's own mentor. Books and periodicals were piled on the desk and overflowing from the bookcase behind it. A small desk lamp was the only other illumination in the room aside from the single window's natural light. A blast of cool air from the AC unit mounted underneath the window greeted them as they entered from the humid hallway. A small Indian man with silvery streaks running through his jet black hair peered over a stack of documents from behind the desk. His eyes opened wide, and he leapt from his chair.

"*Namaste*, Kristin! So happy to see you again." The professor, who was about an inch shorter than her, embraced her like a favorite relative he hadn't seen in years.

"Professor, this is Grant Matthews."

"Ah yes, Grant, I have heard good things about you." He extended his hand to Grant.

"Likewise, Professor Bhatt," Grant replied.

"Please, call me Deepraj." The professor cleared off a pile of journals from the two mismatched wooden chairs in front of his desk. He then wheeled his own chair from behind his desk so that all three were facing each other and motioned for them to sit.

Grant took a seat, but Kristin opted to hop onto the edge of the desk, swinging her legs like a school kid. Grant couldn't help but catch a glimpse of her legs underneath the lime green cotton skirt. He was reminded of their passionate night in his apartment that ended so abysmally. Since then, she'd been friendly, even flirty at times, but she kept her distance.

"So, Grant, I understand this isn't your first trip to my country?"

"On my first trip, I was on the coast, in Kerala studying the spread of Christianity eastward. My research focused on the Apostle Thomas's travels here in

AD fifty-two. With my second and now third trips, I'm chasing the possibility that Christianity may have spread from East to West with Jesus' travels. Ironic, isn't it?"

"Ah, but my friend, whichever way you travel, east or west, you will always end back where you started, if you travel long enough."

"Professor—I mean, Deepraj," Grant said, "you sound like a friend of mine, a monk in Bhutan who started me on this journey."

Professor Bhatt clapped his hands together. "That wouldn't be KG, would it? I hear you've become one of his favorite students."

"KG?" Grant's eyebrows rose. "You know Kinley Goenpo?"

Deepraj chuckled. "Oh, we have quite a history together."

CHAPTER 35

—⚬⚬⚬—

OLD VARANASI, INDIA

*N*ASTY.

The word came to Tim as he searched through his duffel bag in the rented flat. The same word had come to him as his rickshaw driver had driven him through the streets of Varanasi yesterday. To him, the word accurately described this country, this city, this room, and now the way he felt.

Tim removed the large pink bottle from an inside pocket. Not bothering to read the directions, he chugged a third of the medicine. Anything to quell the explosive feeling building in his bowels. He'd been careful with what he'd eaten so far, but something had caught up with him. In the Army he'd been protected from the local cuisine with MREs. He wished now that he'd brought some with him.

Tim replaced the bottle in his bag, which he then dropped onto the room's dusty floor. Reclining on the hard, lumpy mattress, Tim cursed the rickshaw driver who had found the flat. The formerly white plaster of the walls and ceiling of his room had turned a dull gray from years of grime and pollution. Chunks of it had peeled back, hanging loosely like the leaves of a giant plant, revealing the concrete block of the structure behind it. On the trip from the train station, his driver had promised the flat to be just what Tim wanted—quiet, with a private first-floor entrance through a nondescript alley in the heart of the Old City of Varanasi.

Tim recalled the man's rapid-fire English. "I negotiate very fair deal from owner," he'd said. An owner, Tim suspected, who was no doubt a relative of the driver's. What sealed the deal for Tim, though, was when the man asked with a mischievous look, "You don't mind sleeping near the path the corpses take on their way to the cremation ghats?"

"Cremation ghats?" Tim asked, his curiosity aroused.

"Yes, along the banks of the Ganges River, stone steps, the ghats, lead from the city streets to the water."

"Are you telling me they cremate bodies outside on these steps?"

The driver glanced over his shoulder at Tim and laughed. "Every day."

The disgusting image of bodies cooking like hot dogs on a campfire confirmed for Tim the primitiveness of this society. Unfortunately, once he'd engaged the driver in conversation, he couldn't shut the man up. Over the whine of the motorbike's engine pulling the creaky rickshaw, the man droned on, explaining that Varanasi was to Hindus what Mecca was to Muslims: a holy pilgrimage site to be visited during their lifetime. The Ganges was believed to have cleansing powers both spiritually and physically for those who bathed in its waters.

"We Hindus believe," the driver had said, "that Varanasi is the ultimate place to die. By dying here, we are released from the endless cycle of reincarnation and death."

The extent of the superstitions and bizarre beliefs of non-Christians never ceased to surprise Tim, but he would use their perverted ideas to his advantage. He would be able to carry a semiconscious person to his flat without arousing suspicion; the sight of a weak, terminally ill traveler who had come to die in Varanasi wouldn't raise an eyebrow.

CHAPTER 36

VARANASI, INDIA

DEEPRAJ SMILED AT the astonished looks on Grant's and Kristin's faces. "Kinley and I overlapped at Oxford for two years. In a sea of Anglo-Saxons, I was comforted to find a friend from my part of the world."

Closing his still gaping mouth, Grant asked, "Have you spoken with him recently?"

"Have I spoken with him? He was sitting just where you are two weeks ago."

Grant and Kristin looked at each other for a second time. Kristin leaned forward. "We've been told to go to Sarnath. Did he mention that to you?"

"No. He only told me to expect you. I learned many years ago not to push Kinley when he's not inclined to talk."

"Do you know about the texts he showed us while we were in Bhutan?" Grant asked.

"I've been following the news online. I was even able to watch the video of your TV appearance at Emory."

Grant's face fell.

Deepraj patted his shoulder. "Don't be so hard on yourself. You were quite good actually. Poised, intelligent, knowledgeable. You were just ambushed. I can't fault you for your reaction."

"What do you think about the texts?" Kristin asked.

"As a young man, I heard the stories of Jesus' travels through my country. Many Indians are familiar with his trek."

Grant's face hardened. "But the key question is whether these texts just chronicle a legend that developed later, or whether those events actually happened as recorded."

"Does it really matter?" the professor asked.

"Of course it matters. If Jesus' experiences with Hinduism and Buddhism shaped his understanding of God and formed the basis of his own teachings, then we have a very different understanding of him as a man."

The professor nodded his head, although to Grant it looked like he was nodding not in agreement with his argument but in understanding of a larger issue. "Kinley and I discussed how you see the world in such black-and-white terms."

Grant was reminded of this same critique that Jigme and Razi had made of him. Then an idea came to him. Just as he had realized at the Taj that the encounter between the Christian, Muslim, and Buddhist students—he, Razi, and Jigme—was not a coincidence, he thought about the professor standing in front of him: a professor of *Hindu* studies. Then a single word popped into his head—*connection*. One of Kinley's favorite teachings was that life was not a series of individual incidents but that we live in an web of interconnections.

He spoke quickly. "I know the texts are more important than just revealing the nonsupernatural aspects of Jesus' life." He tapped on the professor's desk. "They show the *connections* among the various world religions in a way that previously was less apparent." He leaned back in his chair and smiled.

Rather than applaud Grant's insight, Deepraj rose from his seat and pointed to the darkening skies outside the small window above the humming AC unit. "Care to join me for an early dinner?"

"We're starved," Kristin replied.

Deepraj led them out of the main university entrance and down Assi Road, negotiating a path through sidewalk tables overflowing with fresh fruits and vegetables, many of which Grant had never seen before. The professor stepped into a small store that sold perfumes and tonics stored in hundreds of unlabeled bottles on wooden shelves. Before Grant could ask what they were doing in the place, Deepraj led them through the rear door of the store into a dark and dank alley behind the crumbling concrete building.

Grant's instincts immediately kicked in. Since the attack in Agra, his senses had been alert for any sign of danger. He scanned the shadows. Nothing but the stench of rotting garbage. He watched Deepraj climb a shaky metal staircase that led to the second floor.

"Don't worry, my American friend," Deepraj said, laughing. "Very fresh food. We won't drink water, however, just beer." He held open a rusty door.

As soon as he stepped inside, Grant relaxed. In contrast to the grimy alley, the restaurant was colorful, clean, and infused with the smell of turmeric, cumin, and baking bread. Fabrics in a rainbow of silk billowed across the ceiling from the center of the room and then draped down the walls, creating the illusion that they were in some maharajah's tent. The restaurant held only seven tables, and they were the first customers of the night to arrive. The host, a slight man who was a full head shorter than Grant, greeted the professor by placing his hands to his chest in prayer position and bowing deeply.

While the host sat them and brought naan and cold bottles of Kingfisher beer, Grant studied Deepraj. Kinley had planned for them to meet this Hindu scholar, just as they'd met the Islamic student in Agra. Based on what he knew from Karma and now Deepraj, Kinley had left the monastery immediately after Grant and Kristin had flown back to the States and had traveled to Varanasi. Jigme had followed shortly afterward. After he'd visited with Deepraj, Kinley must have gone to Agra, where he'd met Razi and planned Grant's trip there. *But what's waiting for us tomorrow morning in Sarnath?* he wondered. He hoped to find Kinley and the texts there.

"Now, Deepraj," Kristin said, "the books Kinley showed us described Issa first studying the Vedas when he arrived in India, before he continued on his travels and focused on Buddhism." She tore off a piece of naan slippery with butter and waved it in the air as she spoke. "I understand that the Vedas are the sacred scriptures to the Hindus, but the Issa texts are not entirely clear on what Issa would have learned from them."

The professor set his glass on the table. "I cannot even begin to summarize a religion as diverse as Hinduism over dinner, but let me give you a few thoughts to ponder. We don't have a founding date or figure for our religion, but it is certainly among the oldest surviving religions in the world today. In existence for thousands of years, Hinduism has survived occupations by Muslim and Christian rulers because of its adaptability. You see, we do not believe in only one spiritual path. In fact, our religious scriptures, the Vedas, describe multiple paths to God—intellectual, physical, spiritual, emotional. Just as my students all have different learning styles—some are more visual and learn through reading texts, others must hear my lectures to learn, while others must experience the reality of my teachings themselves before they accept them—each person has a different proclivity toward the best path to his or her spiritual center."

"But," Grant said, swirling around the Kingfisher in his tall glass, "if there really is just one ultimate truth—call it God or whatever—why wouldn't one spiritual approach or paradigm of beliefs work for everyone?"

"If different nations speak different languages within their borders, why wouldn't God speak in different religious contexts to different cultures?"

A look of confusion passed over Grant's face. "You speak of God in a mono-theistic way, like a Christian or a Jew, but doesn't Hinduism recognize literally thousands of deities?" He asked the question rhetorically, pointing to a bronze statue that rested on a shelf near the entrance to the restaurant. The figure had a portly human body, four arms, and an elephant head. Then Grant turned and gestured above the kitchen door to a tapestry made from shimmering red and gold threads that depicted another god who had six arms and a wide human face with a third eye peering out from the center of his forehead.

"Ah, your Western mind-set at work." Deepraj chuckled. "The world is not so dualistic: what you see as black may really also be white and vice versa."

"I don't mean to be disrespectful, Professor, but that sounds awfully New Age. In today's world, we can prove scientifically that something is black or white."

"Can we? Now, I'm not a scientist, but my understanding is that modern physics—quantum mechanics, relativity—rests on the very notion that reality is not always fixed or measurable. Light, for example, can act as a particle or a wave; subatomic particles can behave as if they are in more than one place at the same time; and even time has no absolute value but can speed up or slow down depending on certain variables."

The food arrived without Grant even having seen a menu. They spooned the steaming items out of shiny metal bowls that kept appearing on their table, one after the other. Grant lost track of the number of courses the owner s wife, a quiet round woman, brought to their table, but he was relieved to find the food fresh, tasty, and most important, thoroughly cooked. The dishes were as colorful as the room décor: carrot and coriander soup, orange peppers and bright green beans in red curry, potatoes in green curry, tandoori chicken cooked to a brick red from the spices in which it had marinated, and long-grain white basmati rice.

After swallowing a mouthful of curry, Grant tried again. "But what does that have to do with Hinduism's view of God?"

"Hinduism is not monotheistic, it's true, but contrary to your impressions from having seen our many temples, or even these representations dedicated to the various Hindu deities"— Deepraj gestured to the elephant-man statue and the colorful tapestry—"we are not polytheistic either, at least not in the sense that the Greeks or Romans were."

"What are you then?"

"Ah." Deepraj chuckled. "How do you describe the infinite, the indescribable, that which existed before words, before matter, before the universe?"

"Through analogy and metaphor, I guess," Kristin said.

"And through mythological tales," added Grant.

"Right on both counts. Even we Hindus find it easier to visualize God in various manifested forms than as some undefined concept. So while we have the concept of God, or *Brahman*, as the infinite power behind existence it-self—an omnipresent but formless and inconceivable presence—we visualize this power and influence by its various manifestations. You see, the cosmo-logical questions of the existence of the universe and our purpose in it are not issues we deal with every day like the joy of birth, the emotional closeness felt between lovers, or the pain of sickness and death. So to express these influ-ences of God, we see the manifestations of Brahman in deities such as Lord Vishnu, who protects and watches over us, or"—Deepraj nodded to the color-ful tapestry with its figure whose penetrating third eye seemed to focus on their table—"Shiva, the destroyer, who incidentally is seen as the deity who rules over the city of Varanasi. Of course, our most popular god, Lord Ganesh"—he now pointed to the bronze elephant-headed statue by the door—"is the god of good fortune and prosperity."

Grant eyed the figures again, taking a swig of his Kingfisher. At home he usually preferred darker stouts, but tonight in the warm restaurant with the food whose spices accumulated with each successive bite, the cool lager helped to quench the growing fire in his mouth.

"Indeed," the professor continued, "we have a saying that Hinduism is a religion of one God but many faces."

"But isn't the danger of this approach," Grant asked, keeping his tone reasonable so he wouldn't sound like he was trying to debate this man's religion, "that people lose sight of the purpose of these myths and that religious practice becomes merely idol worship, praying to a deity to provide whatever it has control over?"

"True." The professor stroked his chin. "The excessive focus on rituals designed to influence the gods was one of the reasons the Buddha distanced himself from some of the practices of Hinduism."

"Much like Martin Luther sparked the Protestant Reformation by speaking out against the excesses of the Catholic Church," Grant added.

"Wait. You're losing me," Kristin said. "I thought that Hindus saw the Buddha as one of them, that they absorbed Buddhism into modern-day Hinduism, which is why Buddhism as a separate religion is not heavily practiced in the country of its origin."

"Yes, a good observation," Deepraj said. "In fact, Hindus see the Buddha as an incarnation of Vishnu, which leads us back to your original question concerning Jesus."

Grant frowned in confusion, not sure how the discussion had returned to its origin. Just as he turned to Deepraj to pose his next question, the small restaurant plunged into total darkness.

CHAPTER 37

⚬⚬⚬

VARANASI, INDIA

TIM GLARED ACROSS the flat's small sitting area to the bathroom at the far end of the room. *Why did I rent this pit?* An extended acidic burp erupted from his mouth. The coming night wasn't going to be pleasant.

His "private bath" was hardly large enough to turn around inside. It didn't even have a separate shower or tub—only a hand-held nozzle attached to the wall and a floor drain in front of the porcelain sink whose layers of brown mold and mildew obscured its original white color. Most disturbing to Tim, though, was the toilet, or lack thereof: a hole in the floor with two indentations on either side to place your feet.

"How the hell am I supposed to take a crap like that?" he mumbled.

He suspected he would be finding out very shortly. At least he'd had the foresight to buy some toilet paper from a small market down one of the maze-like alleyways that surrounded his flat. Eyeing the bucket that sat next to the Indian toilet, he told himself there was no way in hell he was going to forgo the rough paper and wash his ass with his bare hand and water from that thing.

Tim wiped his clammy forehead with the back of his hand. So far his plan was not following his expectations. He'd hoped to grab the Jesus texts in Agra, or at the least discover their precise location. The grab and run with the monk had gone to hell. He knew that covert operations were unpredictable, but he'd handled the Muslim efficiently. Then he'd been only a few yards from disappearing into the shadows of the guest house when Matthews and Misaki ruined his plans. The memory of Matthews's defiant stare made Tim's pale face flush with anger. Temporarily forgetting about his growing nausea, Tim anticipated the time when he would put a bullet through the grad student's brain.

He snatched his phone from the table by the bed and checked the browser. *Nothing, again.* He hadn't picked up Matthews's cell phone in over a day, which most likely meant he'd turned off his phone or the battery had died. Fortunately, Tim had another option. The latest intelligence he'd received revealed that Misaki had previous ties in Varanasi, a Professor Deepraj Bhatt. Tim wondered whether he held the clue to the texts. He'd spent the past day scouting the university where this professor worked. He'd planned to pay a visit that afternoon, but now with his protesting stomach, he'd be forced to wait until the morning.

Tim knew that no covert op was foolproof, but the uncertainties here ate at him. This was supposed to be his moment of glory.

With little warning, his stomach violently lurched, sending him hurtling to the bathroom. He barely made it to the hole before dropping to his knees and vomiting out his stomach's contents.

Grant froze where he sat.

He could no longer see either of his dinner companions or anything else in the restaurant for that matter. The clatter of cooking in the kitchen ceased along with the quiet chatter among the other patrons. The silence weighed on Grant as much as the darkness. He reached his left hand until he touched Kristin's shoulder and the soft hair that fell around it. Her hand found his and closed around it. With his right hand, he felt around the table for his knife. Blunt, it wouldn't make much of a weapon, but it was the only protection they had.

Finally Kristin broke the silence in a whisper. "Probably just a power outage. Happens randomly a couple of times a day in the city." Grant felt some relief at Kristin's explanation, but he detected a note of concern in her voice as well.

"Nothing to worry about," Deepraj added more confidently. "We're quite used to these little interruptions."

"How long do they last?" Grant called out in the darkness. He felt odd talking to someone he couldn't see. Nothing shone from the single window either. The entire block must have lost power.

"Sometimes three minutes, sometimes three hours," Deepraj replied.

A small flickering light danced from the kitchen door toward them. The hostess placed a small candle on their table.

Grant relaxed. No sign of anything sinister. No psycho with a buzz cut waiting to jump them in the darkness. Kristin released Grant's hand and then proceeded to recount for the professor the events that had taken place in Agra.

"That is truly horrible." Deepraj shook his head. "Well, you will be safe here. Varanasi is not an easy city to navigate, and anyway I'm sure that, whoever that man was, he is hiding out from the authorities."

"Let's hope so," Grant said, unconvinced.

Deepraj lifted his leather satchel from the floor. From inside, he withdrew a yellowed paperback book. "Have you read this?"

Grant squinted at the cover. *The Bhagavad-Gita.* He had a copy on his bookshelf at home but had never gotten around to reading it. "Been meaning to. It's one of Hinduism's most sacred texts, right?"

Deepraj nodded. "I always keep a copy with me."

"Wasn't it composed around the time of the Buddha?"

"Probably just after. Some scholars suggest that the text could be four thousand years old, but I think the more probable date is around five hundred years before Christ."

"What's it about?" Kristin asked.

"The title translates literally as 'Song of the Lord.' It's an epic Sanskrit poem that tells the tale of a young prince, Arjuna, who rode in his chariot to a major battle between two competing sides of the royal family. He told his charioteer to stop between the two armies where his brothers and cousins prepared to kill each other. The prince's driver, Krishna, then engaged him in a discussion about life, death, and reality itself. As it turned out, Krishna was none other than Lord Vishnu, who had manifested himself as a man—God incarnate."

Interesting, Grant thought. The professor had chosen another example of an ancient people's believing in God taking the form of a man. "So for Hindus, the *Gita* is a poem about the word of God as spoken through Krishna, while for Muslims the Koran is the word of God as spoken through the prophet Muhammad?"

"As I said earlier, God speaks to different cultures in the language with which they can best identify. How else can we interpret an infinite and indescribable God but through the lenses of our individual cultures, histories, and languages?"

"Do you think Issa would have studied the Gita on his travels through India?" Kristin asked.

"Most certainly."

Grant leaned forward in his seat for a better look at the book. "So what would he have learned?"

"Ah, for that you will need to read the text for yourself." Deepraj patted the book on the table. "But for a taste, imagine God not as a being who exists in some other place called heaven, but as the formless power underlying existence itself, as vast as the universe. God is a presence within every living thing." Deepraj lifted the glass bowl that held the dripping candle. "Imagine a tiny spark of the essence of God existing deep within each of us, like a tiny flickering candle within this dark room. If our minds and emotions are distracted by the competing spotlights of greed and wealth, jealousy and lust, pain and depression, elation and euphoria, or even thought itself, we become blinded from seeing the tiny flickering candle in the center of our *atman*, our soul."

Grant sat in silence, tracing his finger along the faint checkerboard pattern of the vinyl tablecloth. A voice from his childhood came to him. He was sitting on the hard church pew on a humid Virginia summer morning. His father strode in front of the altar, sweating more from the passion of his sermon than from the still air in the church without air-conditioning. Nine years old, Grant was captivated but afraid as he listened to his father's words. With a fire in his eyes, his father depicted God sitting upright on his heavenly throne judging the newly deceased as they stood quivering in front of him. Those who had not accepted Christ were condemned to an eternity of damnation. Young Grant was determined that he would never be subject to that fate. His faith would remain strong.

Kristin stirred in her seat. "Deepraj, that's quite beautiful. What an expansive and, at the same time, personal view of God."

"Grant." Deepraj rested his elbows on the table, a gleam in his eyes. "Doesn't Christianity speak of God in equally ethereal terms?"

Grant touched his fingers to his lips. "The Holy Spirit," he said, more to himself than to the others at the table. "One third of the Trinity—the Christian concept of God's presence within us as a spirit that can be felt and experienced but not seen."

"But wasn't the concept of the Trinity developed much later, after the life of Jesus?" Kristin asked.

"In the fourth century, as a formal doctrine, yes, but the term, 'holy spirit' had its origins in the Jewish writings of the Old Testament. In Hebrew the expression *ruah hakodesh*, or 'holy spirit,' was used as a description of God's presence as it empowered the prophets. *Ruah* translates literally as 'wind,' but in earlier biblical translations like the King James version of the Bible, it's mistranslated as 'ghost.' In other passages God's presence is described with a similar Hebrew concept—*nephesh*, which means 'breath.'"

"Hmm," Kristin said, reaching her hand toward the candle in the center of the table. Grant watched her rub a finger along the liquid wax that dripped down its side. She brought the finger to her lips and blew on it. "The breath of God." She pulled the hardened wax from her fingertip and rolled it into a ball. "It's the idea that God is what animates all life."

Grant stared at her. An idea clicked into place. "In Genesis, God literally breathes life into Adam, a metaphorical representation of the concept you just described."

She smiled while still rolling the wax ball in her fingers.

Grant thought about the various meditation techniques Kinley had taught him in Bhutan. *Techniques that centered on the breath.*

Grant's eyes narrowed. "If Jesus learned this lesson in India, it could have profoundly influenced his view of God, especially since he would have known, as a Jew himself, about the concepts of *ruah hakodesh* and *nephesh*."

"Every so often in history," Deepraj said, "a great prophet will arrive—a Buddha, a Jesus, a Muhammad—who can not only see this spark of the divine within himself but focus on nothing else but that spark, fanning the tiny flame into a roaring fire, until the fire itself becomes the guiding center of that individual."

As Grant contemplated the professor's comments, the power flickered back on. He blinked while his eyes adjusted to the light. "If what you say is true," he said, "wouldn't such a prophet exude this fire to those around him? It's not surprising that his disciples would want to deify their teacher if they witnessed the presence of God in that person."

Deepraj, finished with his meal, pushed his chair back from the table and clapped his hands like a child opening a present. "KG was right. What a wonderful student you are!"

Grant felt the warm feeling of pride wash over him. He'd already grown fond of this diminutive man with the expansive mind. He realized that receiving the respect of a professor he'd met only a few hours earlier meant more to him than the meager words of encouragement he'd received over an entire childhood under his father's judgmental eye.

The good feelings were short-lived, however. Grant mentally shifted gears; as enlightening as the discussion with Deepraj was, he was anxious to get on with finding the texts. The images from the past weeks returned to him: the dusty covers of the manuscripts nestled in the plain pine box, Reverend Brady's smug expression after he'd revealed Grant's past, the death at the Taj Mahal, Jigme crumpling to the ground after being shot, the man with the steel eyes and fiery expression.

Grant's tone turned businesslike. "Well, this discussion just underscores the importance of locating the Issa texts."

Kristin turned to Deepraj. "We're driving to Sarnath in the morning."

Grant glanced at his watch. "We should probably get going."

Deepraj pulled a five-hundred-rupee bill from his wallet and laid it on the table.

"Please, let me." Grant reached for his own wallet.

"I wouldn't think of it. It was such a treat to have the two of you for company in my city."

Grant sensed he was engaged in an unwinnable argument, and a quick calculation revealed that the entire meal had only cost twelve dollars. He nodded in appreciation to the professor and then stood. Walking to the door of the restaurant, he removed his cell phone from his pocket and turned on the power that he'd kept off for the past day to preserve the battery.

"Can I get your cell phone number, Deepraj? We may want to reach you when we're in Sarnath tomorrow."

Grant again pondered what lay in store for them the next day. *Will Kinley be waiting in Sarnath with the texts?* He was running out of time at Emory, and Kristin's money wouldn't last long. Then a darker thought intruded: *The man from Agra. Could he have followed us here?*

CHAPTER 38

———⊷———

VARANASI, INDIA

"**W**HICH WAY'S THE RIVER?" Tim muttered.

He poked his head down yet another dark alley. Negotiating the labyrinth of six-foot-wide streets near his rented flat was more difficult than he'd expected. The streets ended or doubled back without warning, and he struggled to avoid touching the dirty people, stray dogs, and homeless cattle that congested the narrow passages.

He glanced at his watch. Eleven fifteen in the morning. The previous night had passed in a blur of misery. He'd lost precious time, but conducting his mission then would have been impossible. Tim had never been so sick in his life. Placing his hand on his side, he could feel his protruding ribs; the muscles around them were still tender.

After consuming a double dose of the antibiotic Cipro and the antinausea medication Phenergan, Tim slept for ten hours straight—double his usual time. He congratulated himself on coming prepared with his own medicines. Who knew what kind of doctors practiced in this place. When he woke at nine thirty, his legs were still shaky, but he was back among the living. He'd even nibbled on some hard bread.

More encouraging than his improved health, Tim had learned from his phone's web browser that Matthews had finally turned on his cell phone. Selecting the history icon, Tim saw that they had arrived in Varanasi late yesterday, a day earlier than he'd expected. They traveled from the city center to Banaras University, where they must have met with Misaki's professor friend, and then to the outskirts, where they'd remained for the night, about a mile and a half from Tim's flat. A quick flipping of pages in his guidebook revealed that they were staying at the Hotel Taj Ganges, a hotel that read like an oasis compared to the scum pit he called a room.

Tim shook his head. If it wasn't for this country's unsanitary conditions, he'd have been waiting at the university yesterday when the targets arrived. He'd have to make up for it today.

He picked up his pace, turning east down another unnamed alley, carefully stepping over the cattle dung in the center of the street. He swatted at the flies swarming from the feces to the people around him and back to the shit piles again. He was only a couple of miles from the university, and so he decided that walking there would give him a chance to scope out the city, in addition to clearing his head. He absentmindedly caressed his forearms, more out of habit than any feeling of itchiness; he'd applied his lotion before leaving the flat.

"Fresh air?" he said to himself before letting loose a wad of spit to the stone by his feet. "What was I thinking?"

How could anyone ever get used to the stink in this country? To Tim, the stench of Varanasi overpowered even Agra's. It was like nothing he'd experienced in his travels before. He concentrated on taking shallow breaths to lessen the impact of the nauseating cloud of incense emanating from the closet-sized stores lining the alley, the cooking stove fumes from the streetside stalls, the garbage strewn along the streets, and the human and animal urine flowing along the dips and cracks in the sidewalk. Although he'd showered an hour earlier, if you could call it that, Tim felt dirty, as if the essence of this city were polluting him.

He removed his phone from the inside pocket of his black windbreaker. Tapping the screen, he pulled up a map of Varanasi. After tapping the screen three more times and waiting for it to refresh, the map zoomed out, and the red dot appeared. About ten kilometers north of him, the dot blinked above the icon for a small town labeled Sarnath.

A call to the Hotel Taj Ganges earlier had revealed that the couple had paid for two more nights, and both the train station and the airport were in Varanasi, not Sarnath, so he was in no danger of losing his targets. He would first question the professor, and then he would properly greet Matthews and Misaki when they returned to their hotel.

Tim finally emerged from the claustrophobia of the alleys into the daylight. One block later the street terminated at fifteen stone steps—the ghats he'd heard about—leading to the water of the Ganges River. Tim turned right and walked along the top of the ghats, which stretched along the riverbank as far as he could see.

He welcomed the view across the river. Unlike the crowded and crumbling city around him, the far bank contained a stretch of grassy marshland that terminated in the foothills of mountains on the distant horizon. The suggestion that nature once ruled this area reminded Tim of how far he was from the woods and creeks of Alabama where he'd spent many an afternoon hunting. A few minutes later, he passed sewer pipes emptying a foul-smelling dark sludge into the river. He had to stifle his gag reflex when he saw the groups of men bathing waist-deep in the same water.

"Holiest river in India?" he said to himself.

Just when he thought the city couldn't disgust him any more, he reached a three-story brick building extending from the street over the middle of the ghat in front of him. On the steps around the building, seven bonfires burned in various stages—some were smoldering coals, while others blazed fifteen feet in the air. The sickly sweet odor of the smoke mixed with an unfamiliar aroma caused an unpleasant feeling in his stomach. Drawing closer to the building, he saw a group of eight men dressed in white standing in a circle next to an unlit bonfire of stacked wood six feet in height. Tim slowed his pace. When he stopped parallel to the men, he noticed that seven of them stood in a semicircle while the eighth stood back with a camera gesturing for them to move closer together. Lying on the ground in the center of the smiling men was a corpse draped in a white sheet.

After the cameraman shouted new instructions, two men in the center bent over and propped up the corpse into a semisitting position. One of the men pulled back the shroud, revealing the lifeless head of an elderly Indian man. Something about the casual nature of the men drew Tim into the macabre photo op: was it the way they handled the corpse, the smiles on their faces, or the knowledge that in a few minutes the body would be cooking on top of the pile of wood like a hog on a spit?

Walking around the end of the brick building, Tim came across bundles of wood stacked against the wall and extending a block down the street. Scrawny Indian men dressed in tattered clothes and worn sandals carried logs from the street to the brick building. Tim figured a few rupees would get one of these guys to build a cremation pyre.

He wondered whether anyone could bring a body here wrapped in a bed-sheet and plop it on a fire.

CHAPTER 39

⊷⊶

SARNATH, INDIA

THE MORNING SUN BURNED brightly in the cloudless sky as Grant and Kristin hustled down the dusty road leading from the public parking lot to the ancient ruins of Sarnath, the tiny town where the Buddha gave his first lectures twenty-five hundred years ago. Grant anxiously anticipated what they might find when they reached the temple where Jigme had sent them.

"You think Kinley has been hiding out here?" Kristin asked, the exact question that had weighed on Grant's mind all morning.

"Don't know." After the disappointment of not finding him in Agra, Grant tried to suppress his expectations that their friend was waiting for them here. He was convinced, however, that their travels to Agra, then Varanasi, and now Sarnath—three holy cities for three different religions—was part of a larger lesson that Kinley had planned for them.

Grant waved off two teenage boys who trotted up to them. Undeterred, one boy held up a souvenir book for them to see, flipping through the colorful pictures of ruins, monks, and pilgrims.

"You English? American?" The boy asked.

"No thank you," Grant replied.

"Only thirty rupees."

Grant grabbed Kristin's hand and continued down the road. As far as Grant could tell, Sarnath wasn't a town as much as it was a collection of ruins, temples, and monasteries.

"Twenty rupees. Good buy!" The boy still followed beside them holding up the book.

The second boy then took his cue from Grant's lack of interest in the book to say, "You like Buddha? I give good price." He held up a handful of carved Buddha figures. "Made from ruins."

"Sorry," Grant said, picking up his pace. The dirt road ended at a large field of short green grass, flowering trees, and red brick ruins. Closer inspection revealed that the brick walls, most of which were only a few feet in height, were the excavated footings of buildings whose rectangular patterns suggested the busy complex of temples and courtyards that must have existed here long ago.

"Looks pretty old," Grant said.

Kristin nodded, surveying the field herself. "The oldest layers date from the third century BC, during the reign of Emperor Ashoka, a Buddhist who made his religion the centerpiece of his enlightened rule. The monasteries and temples flourished for fifteen hundred years, but then several generations of Mughal rulers destroyed the city and its temples."

"What a shame. Quite peaceful here, especially compared to Varanasi."

"The name Sarnath actually means 'deer park.' Even before the Buddha arrived, this place was a refuge where its residents and visitors could contemplate the natural surroundings."

Grant realized that he could use some time for rest and contemplation, but only after they had the texts. He recalled their conversations with Jigme before they left Agra. The young monk was vague about what they were supposed to do at this temple in Sarnath. If they were to meet Kinley, they had no specific time to do so, unlike their meeting with Jigme at the Taj.

They followed a gravel path through the ruins and approached the one monument from antiquity left mostly intact, a phallic-shaped pillar, which Grant guessed to be over a hundred feet tall. In front of the pillar he saw five monks in flowing tangerine-colored robes sitting in the grass silently contemplating the brick monument.

He hurried forward, searching the faces. They looked Japanese and Kinley wasn't among them.

"On my last trip here," Kristin said with a note of disappointment in her voice that reflected the way Grant felt, "I photographed a contingent of Tibetan monks worshipping at the Dhamekh Stupa too."

"What is it?"

"It was built in the sixth century AD, and the stupa supposedly stands on the exact spot where the Buddha gave his first lecture."

"Kinley chose this location for a reason." He scanned the tourists and pilgrims walking the grounds.

Kristin nodded to a cypress-lined stone path that ran along the ruins and ended at a temple whose multiple spires pierced the cloudless sky. "That's where Jigme told us to go."

He took her hand and started toward the temple.

Sick of walking, Tim started to signal for one of the ever-present rickshaw drivers to pedal him the rest of the way to the university when a curious sight caught his eye.

A man who appeared about seventy, or maybe a hard-lived fifty, sat cross-legged on the top level of the ghat just ahead, staring vacantly over the river. Wiry white hair peeked out from under a blood red turban, while a beard of the same color and consistency as his hair fell down the front of his robe. At first Tim suspected the man to be just another of the old men he'd seen sitting along the steps leading to the water, but while the others seemed oblivious to their surroundings, this man turned toward Tim with yellowed and bloodshot eyes. A drugged-out distance in the man's expression registered Tim and looked beyond him at the same time. Normally Tim would have ignored a street person, but he was drawn in by a covered straw basket about eighteen inches in diameter and twelve inches tall sitting in front of the man. Tim suspected what it contained, and the thought excited him.

The man forced a smile, revealing a mouth whose few remaining teeth were blackened and jagged. He then gestured to the basket with some sort of homemade instrument—a flared wooden recorder.

"Twenty rupees," the man croaked.

"Twenty rupees for what?" Tim asked.

The man jabbed the basket with the instrument. "Twenty rupees."

Tim thought he saw the basket continue to shake after the jabbing stopped. He dug out a twenty-rupee bill from his pocket and handed it to the man. Although he had his four remaining EpiPens—two of each type—in the pockets of his cargo pants, the quivering basket gave him a delicious idea.

The old man stuffed the bill inside his robe and then raised the recorder to his mouth. The instrument produced a hypnotic, melancholy tone. While he played with one hand, he flipped the lid off the basket with the other. Tim stepped backward when a black cobra popped out of the basket, its body splayed out in its aggressive posture. As the tip of the recorder swayed in front of the hissing creature, the snake danced to the music, following the motion of the recorder. Tim watched, transfixed. To his disappointment, the snake seemed too mesmerized to attack.

After the man finished his song, he started to close the basket's flat top over the snake's scaly head. Then it struck. The snake hit the woven reeds of the top, missing the man's hand by mere inches. Tim's heart lurched. The elderly snake charmer, however, never flinched, closing the lid over the creature. He then returned his vacant gaze to the river, as if a snake hadn't just popped out of his basket and as if Tim were no longer there.

Tim surveyed the area around him. Away from the busier cremation ghats several blocks behind him, only a few people bathed in the disgusting water at the river's edge below, and they paid no attention to Tim and the old man. This was too good an opportunity to pass up. He reached into his pocket for a handful of bills.

CHAPTER 40

⚬⚬⚬

SARNATH, INDIA

"Is that Mulgano . . . ?" Grant asked.

Kristin laughed. "Mulgandha Kuti Vihar. A shrine. Tibetan."

Grant thought the temple looked like a Buddhist version of Cinderella's castle.

After climbing a short flight of steps, they entered through the stone archway of a cloistered hallway. Grant felt the anticipation building within him.

Turning left, they followed the cloister to a heavy double wooden door, which opened into a spacious hall. The polished marble floor contrasted with the rough-hewn blocks of the shrine's exterior. Grant's attention was immediately drawn to a life-sized golden Buddha at the opposite end of the room. The statue sat on an altar adorned with freshly cut roses and lilies.

"Now what?" Kristin asked. The hall was quiet and mostly empty.

"Jigme didn't give us much to go on."

"Maybe we should ask someone if they know Kinley?"

An elderly Tibetan man, dressed in work overalls rather than a monk's robes, was pruning dead flowers from the arrangements on the altar. Two Italian tourists examined a fresco that covered the entire perimeter walls of the hall.

Grant stopped.

The fresco was immediately familiar. He'd seen a similar one during his stay at the monastery in Bhutan. *Another coincidence?* He walked to the left wall where the mural began. The story of the painting started with the birth of a baby.

"Kristin, look. This fresco is almost identical to the one in the Punakha Dzong temple." He recalled the large hall with the twenty-foot columns and the monumental statues.

She stood by his side. "When we were standing together that day before the lama summoned us, I mentioned to Kinley I saw this work here."

Instead of the primary colors and hard lines of the painting in Bhutan, Grant noted that this one had a more ethereal quality with softer pastels, yet both told the same story: the life of the Buddha.

"I think it was painted by a famous Japanese artist," Kristin said. "'A poor country's version of stained glass' is how Kinley put it, but I find it quite beautiful." She turned from the mural to Grant. "Did Kinley ever tell you the story in the painting?"

"He did." Grant scanned the temple again for Kinley and then pointed to the first scene on the far left. "This palace is in Kapilavastu, near the Indian and Nepalese border. Siddhartha Gautama was raised there as a prince in the middle of the sixth century BC. This is his mother." He pointed to an elegantly dressed pregnant woman sleeping on a raised bed, with the image of a white elephant floating above her. "The elephant spirit came to her in a dream and told her that she would give birth to a unique son. The spirit then entered her womb. Next you see the crowd gathered to look at the blessed baby. This old man is speaking to the crowd. He makes a prediction that the baby will grow into the spiritual leader of the people. The Buddha."

"When I was here last, I never knew the details." Kristin stepped closer to the wall. "But hearing it from you, the parallels seem so obvious."

He nodded. "The birth of Jesus."

She raised her fingers as if to touch the painting but stopped an inch short of the plaster. "The angel Gabriel coming to Mary in a vision. The virgin birth. The wise men."

"Religious myths often share similar archetypes." Grant stepped to his right. "Next we see the baby Siddhartha taking his first steps. Lotus flowers blossomed in his footprints."

"Like the jeweled flower inside the Taj that led us here!"

Grant again considered what Kinley would want them to find here. He continued, "By the age of twenty-nine, Siddhartha had grown restless with the easy life of a prince. When he left the palace gates one day, he encountered sickness and death for the first time." A realization occurred to him. "The same age Jesus was during a pivotal point in his life: his baptism by John."

"Didn't know that," she said, bending close to the painting of the colorfully robed prince walking among pale figures hobbling in old age. Next to the path, an ox-drawn cart overflowed with dead and decaying bodies.

"The shock that life was not all beauty and youth had a profound impact on Siddhartha, and so he abandoned his princely possessions and left on a spiritual quest. He lived in the wilderness as an ascetic, spending his days in silence, fasting, and meditation. But after six years, he realized that renouncing society was not the solution either. He decided that there must be a middle way."

In the next scene Siddhartha sat in the classic meditation pose underneath a tree, the same species of tree, Grant realized for the first time, that he'd been lying under in the dzong courtyard when he met Kristin. He turned to see the back of her head with its wide curls flowing down her back. She was studying the depiction of four scantily clad girls dancing around the left side of the seated man, while to his right a group of demons threatened him with swords, spears, and torches.

Grant touched her shoulder. He enjoyed having Kristin's undivided attention as he retold the stories that Kinley had recounted to him. "Here we have the temptation of the Buddha by the Evil One as he sat underneath the Bodhi tree in meditation. First, the Evil One appeared as Kama, the god of desire, and then as Mara, the god of death, to disrupt his concentration. But none of these temptations drew him away from his path."

"At the Taj, you mentioned how Jesus was similarly tempted in the desert during a spiritual retreat before he began his ministry."

Grant smiled. "After one night, the Buddha saw the light, a path that would lead to inner peace. He became, as we say today, enlightened. Thus, we now refer to Siddhartha as the Buddha which translates literally as 'the Enlightened One.'"

The next scene depicted the Buddha standing on a small hill. "After becoming enlightened, the Buddha traveled here to Sarnath, where he gave his first lecture."

"At the stupa outside?"

"I guess that's the legend."

"Do you think this has something to do with the Issa texts? Why else would Kinley have sent us here?"

"That's what I've been trying to figure out." He cast his eyes to the ground. Kinley wasn't there waiting for them as they'd hoped, but the monk had sent them to a mural nearly identical to one he'd shown them in Bhutan for a reason, just as he'd led them through the three sacred towns of Agra, Varanasi, and Sarnath. Did Kinley simply mean for him to draw a comparison in the similar stories of the lives of Jesus and the Buddha—the birth myths, the spiritual practices, the temptations, the parables, and the disciples? *There has to be more than that*, he thought.

Kristin turned back to the fresco. "So Buddhists worship the Buddha as a god, like Christians believe in Jesus?"

"A complicated issue." Grant recalled Kinley's love of such complications. "Throughout his life, the Buddha's followers tried to deify him, but he resisted. He insisted that he was nothing more than a man who understood the truth. He had been enlightened, and he taught that others could become similarly enlightened."

They reached the end of the long wall, stopping in front of the altar and the statue of a golden Buddha sitting on a lotus petal throne, his eyes half closed, one hand resting on a knee and the other raised in a blessing.

Kristin whispered, "I suppose it's only natural for people to want to worship a concrete image rather than an abstract ideal."

"Like Christians kneeling before the cross at a church altar." Grant then recalled Kinley's words: *But the true nature of Buddhism lies in how we apply its teachings to our lives today, not in worshipping an individual from the past—no matter how great he may be.* Kinley taught his students that drawing guidance and inspiration from the Buddha was fine, unless Buddha worship became an end in itself.

He felt Kristin tug on his sleeve. "If Issa did indeed travel here, what would he have learned that could have changed his spiritual being?"

Grant shrugged. "According to Kinley, the Buddha's early lectures here were about human suffering, what he called *dukkha*, and how we can move beyond suffering to find peace—eternal nirvana."

"I guess we could all use a little less *dukkha*."

"The Buddha realized that our unhappiness or discontent, if you will, results from our cravings, our grasping at the things we desire."

"Like more money, a better job, more friends?" Kristin asked.

"Or the Issa texts," he added and then stopped. Grant suddenly recognized how much he'd been grasping at the idea of finding the manuscripts. He'd imbued their quest with the power to determine his future purpose in life, his security, and his happiness. He looked to Kristin and saw that she was waiting for him to continue.

"Our cravings come in different forms: we seek sensual pleasures—food, alcohol, sex, excitement; we seek to obtain what we don't have—a bigger house, a new car; or we seek to get rid of something we don't want—annoying people, extra pounds, a physical ailment. The origin of *dukkha* comes down to wanting what we don't have or trying to become what we are not."

"So Buddhism doesn't rely on supernatural explanations for our current state or, I assume, our salvation?"

He nodded. "The Buddha laid down certain steps to break out of the cycle of *dukkha*."

"And the steps are?" Her blue eyes appeared to Grant as if they were lit from within. She didn't blink as she waited for his response. He realized how much he'd assumed Kinley's role in the past few minutes, relaying the monk's teachings to Kristin.

"First, you must have the correct mental framework to start down the path. You have to understand intellectually the origins of suffering. Next, you should strive to live a clean, moral life, treating others with compassion and speaking well of them; many of these teachings closely parallel the lessons in Jesus' parables, which came five hundred years later. Finally, you must practice meditation diligently in order to train the mind to move past the clutter of thoughts that lead to grasping and craving."

Kristin furrowed her brow in concentration. "So the path to salvation for Buddhists contains an intellectual, a moral, and a spiritual practice."

Watching Kristin make sense of it all, Grant noted how his transformation from student to teacher energized him. Then he realized how much he missed Kinley.

"Black and white," she said suddenly.

"Huh?" The painting was multicolored.

"Kinley and Deepraj. Both said we view the world too simplistically. What if the three spiritual paths—the Buddhist, the Hindu, and the Christian—are interrelated?"

"I've been thinking along the same lines these past few days." A pang of sadness shot through him as he recalled meeting Razi at the Taj. Then their conversation with Deepraj the previous night replayed in his head. *Connection.* He repeated the word to himself. Not only were these events connected, but the teachings were as well.

Kristin grasped his arm. Her fingers radiated an electricity that seemed to run through her entire body. "What if following the Buddha's path—the practical steps that help us to eliminate suffering—also provides a mechanism to cultivate the divine spark within that Deepraj discussed? Issa learned both of these traditions during his travels. His spiritual practices may have involved aspects of both Hinduism and Buddhism."

Grant nodded. "In Agra, we learned that the Buddha, Jesus, and Muhammad each engaged in similar meditative practices. Maybe those practices allowed them to shed their external cravings, to move past their inflated views of their own selves, and brought these men into direct contact with the presence of the divine within themselves: that inner spark of God, Allah, the breath of the spirit, nirvana."

He recalled Deepraj's comment that each person would interpret the ultimate divine reality according to the lens through which they viewed it. The Buddha, Jesus, and Muhammad were three separate men who lived in different cultures and times. Each of their experiences of an infinite divine would be understood by them and then expressed in different ways.

"Take away the supernatural but leave the spiritual," she said.

Grant stared at her for a full minute. "What I'm still struggling with, though, is the ultimate conclusion itself—the ability to touch the divine. What Deepraj and Kinley have said makes sense from a certain perspective. I just—" He frowned. "I'm just not sure that I believe that."

"I think if Kinley were here, he would say that you're not supposed to believe."

He shook his head. Understanding wasn't enough for him. He needed physical proof.

He turned to the next scene: a pale Siddhartha lying on his deathbed, surrounded by his weeping disciples. He recalled Kinley's explanation of how the Buddha instructed his disciples not to mourn the death of his body because the body of his teachings would live on. He also told them that one day he would return to them in a different form. How eerily similar it was to the concept of the resurrection of Jesus and predictions of a Second Coming.

"Grant, over here!" Kristin no longer stood beside him but waved from the far side of the room at the end of the mural.

He approached her. "What?"

"This section of the fresco is new."

He saw that the segment of the painting she was standing in front of was brighter than the rest of the mural.

"When I was here a few months ago, it ended there"—she pointed to where he'd just been standing—"with the Buddha's death."

"Just like in Punakha."

"Right, but now . . ."

Grant studied the scene. It wasn't part of the story he'd learned in Bhutan. A group of monks were crossing a mountain range.

"A depiction of the spread of Buddhism east?" she asked.

"They must be monks from India heading into Tibet across the Himalayas. Look at this monk." He pointed to a seated monk on top of a forested mountain in a land divided in half by a long wall. "That must be the Indian monk who brought Buddhism to China." He thought about his own journey to India in search of the history of Christianity.

"This Buddha-looking guy riding an elephant probably represents Thailand," he continued, "and this island must be Japan."

Then he saw it.

"No way," he said. Out of the corner of his eye, he saw Kristin staring at the same section.

Near the top of the fresco, painted above the other scenes, was a man in flowing robes flying on the back of a tiger toward a cave opening on the sheer side of a cliff. Grant had not thought about this strange tale in weeks, but now it flooded back to him.

The story was one of Bhutan's most cherished: the Tibetan monk, Padmasambhava, also known as Guru Rinpoche, who flew to a cave on the side of a cliff near the town of Paro. After meditating in the cave for several months—like Muhammad did, Grant now realized—Padmasambhava hiked down to the valley and began teaching Buddhism to the people of Bhutan.

"That's the location of the Tiger's Nest Monastery Kinley told me about," Grant said.

"It's Bhutan's most-photographed site, a stone monastery impossibly perched on a narrow ledge two thousand feet up the side of a sheer granite cliff. I'd planned to go there, until I met you and saw the texts."

Grant marched to the altar. This was surely the clue they were looking for. "Excuse me, sir, do you speak English?" he asked the old man arranging the flowers.

"Yes, may I help you?"

"We were wondering about the addition to the mural there. When was that done?"

"Wonderful, yes? Finish just two days ago. We have painter young in age, but very talented."

"Yes, very talented. Why was this section added?"

"We have need for money for renovations some time now. We receive generous donation from fellow Buddhist country Bhutan."

"Do you know the person in Bhutan who gave you the money?" Grant asked.

"No, I only clean here and lock doors at end of day. You may talk to our director or one of his assistants."

"That would be great," Grant said. "Where can we find them?"

"Oh, they not here now. Gone to Dharamasala until next week."

Grant and Kristin strode down the dusty road from the temple to the parking lot in silence. On the one hand, Grant was disappointed that Kinley hadn't met them in Sarnath, but on the other hand, he had a hunch that they would find what they were looking for at Tiger's Nest. *What better place for Kinley to hide the texts than in a monastery perched on a granite cliff in his own country?* The texts would be out of the lama's reach, but Kinley would not have had to violate Bhutanese law by removing them from the country. Grant also now understood Issa's travels in a new light.

One question nagged at him, though. Someone from Bhutan had arranged for the mural they just saw to be painted, and they knew from talking to Professor Deepraj Bhatt that Kinley had recently been here. But how had Kinley come up with that kind of money, not to mention the political pressure it must have taken to accomplish this feat so quickly?

"Hey, do you have your phone?" Kristin asked, interrupting his thoughts. "Left mine plugged in at the hotel for when the power comes back on." Another of the city's frequent power outages had left the hotel dark for an hour that morning.

"Yeah, here. Who're you calling?" Grant waved to the front taxi queued along the dirt road.

"I want to let Deepraj know we're stopping by. We have to tell him about the new section of the mural."

After holding the phone to her ear for a minute, she gave up. "No answer. He must have stepped out of his office."

CHAPTER 41

VARANASI, INDIA

Tɪᴍ's ᴀʀᴍs sᴡᴜɴɢ ʟᴏᴏsᴇʟʏ by his sides as he hurried out of the salmon-colored gate of Banaras Hindu University. He was relieved to be free of the basket containing the cobra as he headed straight on Assi Road. He wanted to distance himself as much as possible before the authorities arrived, but he didn't want to draw attention by running. A brisk walk would do him good anyway. His interrogation methods had been brilliant but had yielded an unsatisfactory result. The effete professor hadn't told him much he didn't already know. Misaki and Matthews had traveled to Sarnath, and then they would return to Varanasi.

A motorized rickshaw waited on the street corner just ahead. He would intercept them at their hotel.

"He's still not answering." Kristin returned Grant's cell phone.

"It is Saturday. Maybe he's taking the day off."

"No, he practically lives in his office, even weekends." The taxi driver turned down the university's tree-lined road, following Kristin's pointed finger.

"Why don't we come back later? I'm anxious to get to the hotel and see if we have power yet. Email Jigme about our travel plans back to Bhutan."

She shook her head. "Drop me off at Deepraj's building. If I can't find him in the lounge, I'll check his office."

Grant hesitated a moment before saying, "After what happened in Agra, wouldn't you feel safer if we stayed together?"

"Grant Matthews, I've traveled around the world for the past three years on my own."

"Okay." He tried to catch her eye, but her gaze was focused outside the window. "After I email Jigme, I'll book our flights."

"Stop here please," Kristin said to the driver. The car pulled to the curb. The building was quiet without the frenzy of students attending class.

"Here, take this." Grant handed her his cell phone. "Call me at the hotel after you speak to Deepraj. I can send the car back to pick you up."

Kristin opened the car door, but before she stepped out, she leaned in and kissed him on the check. The brush of her lips against his skin sent an unexpected electricity through him. "See you in an hour." She winked and closed the door behind her.

Tim reclined on the torn vinyl bench of the motorized rickshaw, trying to ignore the annoying whine and noxious fumes coming from the small engine just beneath the driver's seat. The driver gripped the handlebars of his cycle with one hand, while he used the other to hold a cell phone underneath a wide hat that flopped in the wind. Tim removed his phone from the inside pocket of his jacket and flipped open the leather cover. The red dot representing Matthews's cell phone flashed at the university entrance he'd just left behind. His targets were heading to the professor's office.

Knowing that adaptability in a field operation was a hallmark of an effective combatant, Tim didn't hesitate to modify his plan. The professor's building was deserted, whereas their hotel would have workers and other tourists around.

"Pull over there," he yelled to his driver, pointing to a side street just ahead. Between the engine noise and his own screeching into his cell, the driver didn't respond. Tim whacked him on the shoulder, and yelled louder, "Stop there!"

Startled, the driver hung up the phone and slowed the rickshaw. Tim reached for one of the EpiPens but then decided that he didn't need to waste one. Instead he drew his Glock from the holster hidden under his shirt and flipped it around in his hand, gripping the barrel. The driver stopped beside a building abandoned for so long the boards covering the windows had rotted. He turned to face Tim with a stupid grin on his face. Concealing the gun by his hip, Tim nodded that the location would work. He climbed out of the seat, placing his free left hand on the back of the cycle for balance. The only person he saw nearby was a toothless man squatting in a stoned stupor across the street.

Tim's left hand then bumped into his driver's hat, knocking it to the ground.

"Sorry," Tim said cheerfully.

"*Theek hai*, okay," the driver responded, bending forward.

Tim attacked swiftly and efficiently, much the way he'd attacked the Muslim on the steps at the Taj Mahal. The gun cut a wide arc through the air before cracking into the skull of the rickshaw driver, who collapsed to the ground. *Not dead*, Tim thought, *but out for now*. He picked up the driver's hat. As he climbed on the cycle, he began to anticipate what lay ahead for him at the university. As soon as he pulled away from the curb, however, the itching began.

Kristin's hiking shoes squeaked in the empty hallway. The building seemed unnaturally quiet without students. She walked up to the closed door of the faculty lounge and pushed it open.

Unlike the dark classrooms she'd passed in the hallway, the lounge had fluorescent ceiling lights illuminating two worn couches, a leather armchair, and a wooden coffee table. Steam rose from the teapot on the counter in the corner. *He must have been here recently*, she thought; his was the only faculty office on this floor.

When she reached his office door, she knocked firmly. "Deepraj, it's Kristin," she said, not sure why she felt it necessary to announce her arrival. Her voice echoed down the empty hallway, but only silence came from behind his closed door. *Maybe he left for home early today*, she thought.

Kristin tried the doorknob. "Professor?" It turned in her hand.

The blood drained from her limbs. Professor Deepraj Bhatt sat behind his desk. He was slumped over, his head resting on a woven basket in the center of the desk. The normally neat but crowded office was in disarray. His papers lay scattered, as if someone had quickly searched them.

"Oh, God!" she cried, running to him.

Please let him be alive, she prayed. But her gut told her to expect the worst. When she reached his side, she saw that Deepraj appeared to be inhaling deeply from the interior of the basket, but he wasn't breathing. His body was frozen.

"Deepraj?" Kristin placed a hand under his shoulder and lifted his head out of the basket.

The professor's body flopped back into his seat, his head lolling to the side. She screamed. His naturally dark complexion had turned a creamy white with the exception of the fiery welts covering his face. Terribly swollen, his face appeared like an inflated blowfish covered in chicken pox. Deepraj's lifeless eyes bulged out of their sockets.

Kristin shivered involuntarily. She placed her hands on the desk in an effort to keep her entire body steady. Deepraj had been one of the most gentle men she'd ever met. He was the last person in the world who deserved to die like this.

She squeezed her eyes closed and shook her head, trying to clear the image now burned into her memory. *I have to call the police.* Opening her eyes, she avoided the professor's face and reached for the phone on the desk. Her hand paused over the open straw basket. *Why was his face in there?* Her instincts told her to run from the office, to call the police from outside, but the seeds of anger and frustration within her started to sprout.

Kristin bent over the desk and peered into the basket. Empty.

Her mind raced. *Who could have done such a thing?* Then a nausea rose from her stomach. *The man from Agra.* Could he have tracked them to Varanasi? Had he tortured Deepraj? And for what? She didn't want to believe that she'd been responsible for her friend's death, but the two attacks couldn't be coincidence. The painful irony was that Deepraj was less involved with their search than Jigme.

Her next thought sent a new shiver across her skin. *What if he's still in the building?*

She held her breath, listening, but heard nothing other than the percussion of her own pulse.

Then the sensation of movement near her right ankle caused her to shriek and jump backward. Darting her eyes to the floor, she half expected to see the man from Agra with his crew cut and leering eyes staring up at her from the shadows under the desk. What she saw, however, chilled her even more. A black cobra flared up in the exact spot where she'd just been standing. With its tail tightly coiled in a circle on the carpet, the snake's head stood a foot and a half off the ground, its neck spread in the shape of a deadly diamond. Kristin froze, fighting every urge in her body to scream again and run. The snake emitted a menacing hiss. Its head swayed back and forth, as if challenging her to pick a direction to move toward.

Barely breathing, Kristin inched her left leg, now the closest to the snake, backward. The snake continued its bob and weave but didn't strike. After seconds, which felt like hours, Kristin had backed away a couple of feet—out of striking range, she hoped. She slowly turned her body away from the animal but kept her eyes on it. Once she faced the door, she bolted, running faster than she had since her days on her high school tennis team.

Kristin didn't stop running until she broke through the main doors of the building, stumbled down the stairs, and collapsed on the lawn. After catching her breath, she peered over her shoulder at the building's entrance, now anticipating anything. And yet the building looked as peaceful as it had when she'd arrived.

She had to escape.

Rising to her feet, she brushed off the blades of grass that clung to her jeans. Then she remembered the cell phone in her pocket. Her fingers fumbled with the phone. *What's the number for the police?* She didn't think 911 would work, but tried it anyway.

Rapid beeping. *Wrong number.*

Swiveling her head frantically, she saw a rickshaw parked on the curb. She broke into a full sprint toward the only means of transportation currently on the campus road this quiet Saturday. She hoped it wasn't occupied.

Kristin leaped into the back seat without bothering to ask the hunched-over driver in the floppy hat if he was waiting for anyone.

"Hotel Taj Ganges."

Collapsing onto the worn vinyl, she pressed the menu button on the phone. Grant had the hotel's number stored. They could connect her with the police. Scrolling through the list of numbers, she felt the vibration of the rickshaw's engine, but the driver hadn't pulled away from the curb.

"Please, quickly. This is an emergency!"

She found the number and pressed send.

The driver swiveled in his seat to face her. "Yes, it is."

The sight of the man from Agra sitting inches away paralyzed her with a fear deeper than any she'd ever known. Before she could react, the man's hand darted out as quickly as she'd assumed the snake would have struck had it been given the opportunity. His fingers cinched her throat. Instinctively, both her hands flew to his, clawing at the fingers which cut off her air, but he held on to her with a power that belied his size. The man then raised his free hand, balled into a fist. She flinched when he struck. But the expected impact to her face never came. Instead he punched Kristin on her upper thigh, delivering an unexpected sharp, stinging blow.

Her brain screaming for oxygen, Kristin kicked out with both feet and twisted her body, but he held on with his python's grip. She couldn't find any leverage in the rickshaw's cramped back seat.

A disembodied voice called to her in the distance, "*Namaste*. Hotel Taj Ganges."

She still held the cell phone in her right hand. Gripping it tighter, she thrust her hand forward straight into the face of her attacker. The phone struck him squarely on the nose, which made a crunching noise as it snapped sideways. The man let out a yelp, relaxing his grip on Kristin's neck at the same time. She moved instantly. Dropping the phone, she catapulted herself out of the rickshaw, landing hard on the asphalt.

"You fucking bitch," the man screamed from behind her.

Bruised and off balance, Kristin rose to her feet, ignoring the pain in her knees. *I have to run!* her mind screamed.

But something was wrong with her legs. She couldn't move them. Like a tree rooted into the road, she swayed, struggling to maintain her balance. She looked down at the capri-length cargo pants she wore. *Move!* But suddenly her legs no longer even supported her own weight.

Overcome with vertigo, she collapsed to the asphalt.

What's wrong with me? Her mind pleaded with her to escape. Her hands and elbows scraped against the rough pavement. But her attempts to crawl were futile. She rolled onto her back. Confused, she sensed the overcast afternoon quickly fading to night. Kristin lay helpless on the warm ground, peering through the dark tunnel that had become her disappearing vision. At the end of the tunnel was the face of the man who had shot Jigme and killed Deepraj and Razi. Blood streamed from his nose.

She succumbed to the blackness of the tunnel.

CHAPTER 42

⸻

HOTEL TAJ GANGES
VARANASI, INDIA

G RANT SAT ON THE BED'S burgundy cover with his laptop open before him.
Too many thoughts raced through his mind. He felt that they were closer
to the texts, but now they had to travel to another country, his hearing at Emory
was only a week away, and some fanatical man seemed to be following them.

Then he thought of Kristin: *What's going on with her?* God, she was beautiful. He'd noticed that from the moment they'd met, and despite his initial
impression of her as the flighty, artistic type, the more time they spent together, the more he admired her. She liked him too; she'd even just kissed him.
But ever since that uncomfortable night at his apartment, he couldn't help but
wonder where they were heading. He'd been careful not to push things with
her physically since then, not that he didn't want to, but after the tragedy in
Agra, the timing wasn't right either. Once he had the Issa texts safely in hand,
he would focus on figuring her out.

Grant rubbed his hands on his jeans, observing the sweaty imprints left
behind on the laptop's keyboard. He could feel the tension creep from his back
to his neck. The uncertainty of the future ate at him.

He closed his eyes and inhaled the air-conditioned hotel room air. He recalled Kinley's words from one of the days he lay trapped in the monastery
and struggling with his predicament. "You have a strong intellect, Grant—too
strong. You've become a slave to your mind, so much so you don't even realize
it. Your mind causes your unhappiness, leading you down multiple paths of
uncertainty and fear."

"Don't our minds control all of us?" he'd asked.

"Only if we allow them to. The carpenter should be master over his tools; the tools should not rule the carpenter."

Grant inhaled again, attempting to remember more of his friend's advice, but Kinley's voice faded into the distance of his memory. At one moment the path in front of him looked so clear, but then without warning the way became obscured. He returned his attention to his breathing. Exhaling, he felt the tension in his body subside marginally.

Opening his eyes, he typed "Druk Air," the national airline of Bhutan, into the browser. While he waited for the flight schedules to load, he glanced at the series of icons at the bottom of his screen. He squinted.

Both his virus protection and spyware software programs were deactivated.

He sat up straighter. Had he deactivated them recently in order to install new software? He didn't remember doing so. He closed the airline schedules, reactivated both programs, and downloaded updates for them. He didn't like surfing the web in a foreign country unprotected. After the software finished scanning the hard drive, he scrolled down the list of its discoveries. In the middle of a list of advertising cookies were two programs, MailTrac.exe and GhostKeys.exe. He reopened his browser and ran a search of both names. His mouth went dry. The first file was an email spying program popular with hackers, while the second recorded whatever was typed into the computer and then covertly transmitted the data to the person who installed the program. Grant selected the entire list and clicked on the button that read "Clean."

His computer had been hacked. Someone was reading his email.

The realization of the most likely culprit nauseated him. *The assassin in Agra.* That's how he'd tracked them to the Taj Mahal. The questions Grant had been repeating to himself played again: *Is this man trying to prevent the Issa texts from revealing the truth about Jesus? Is he a lone psychopath who believes he's on a divine mission? Or is he part of a broader conspiracy?* None of the possibilities appealed to Grant. He wondered how much the murderer knew about their quest for the texts. Then a single thought froze all the others swimming in his mind.

Kristin.

He snatched the hotel phone from the bedside table and punched in his cell phone number. After an interminable wait while the signal traveled in search of his phone, he heard his own voice telling him to leave a message. His cell phone was turned off. But he knew that it had been on when he gave it to her. Something was wrong. He dropped the receiver on the bed and ran from the room. He had to get to the university and Deepraj's office.

CHAPTER 43

⸻⸱⸺

OLD VARANASI, INDIA

THE SHRILL SOUND OF HINDI music grew in the darkness like a movie soundtrack fading in at the beginning of a film. The world was dark, distant, and cold. Only the music provided evidence to Kristin that she was still alive. Gradually the fog in her mind began to clear. She blinked her eyes at the increasing light. She was shivering.

The space around her came into focus. She was sitting on a wooden chair in the center of a small living room in a run-down apartment. The chair creaked in protest as she shifted her weight and glanced up. A single bare bulb hung from the ceiling, casting a harsh light on the gray plaster peeling from the walls. A simple wood-laminate coffee table sat beside the only other piece of furniture, a ragged sofa. The screeching music she heard came from a clock radio on the bedside table in the bedroom just ahead of her. She was alone.

Where am I? She shook her head, trying to rid it of the sluggishness she felt. Her whole body was limp, and she had to fight the urge to close her eyes and return to sleep. She licked her lips. She was parched.

Then the memories flooded her mind. *Sarnath. Deepraj's office. The snake. The man from Agra.* The final thought provided the jolt of energy she needed to wake up. She willed her body to rise from the chair but discovered she couldn't move. Panic quickly replaced the lethargy she'd experienced moments before. She shook her limbs, scraping the rickety chair against the floor. She looked to her arms. They were duct-taped to the armrests.

The horror of her situation came to her: *I've been drugged and kidnapped, like Jigme.* Thrashing anew in the chair, she realized that her legs were free to move; they were unbound. She awkwardly stood, hunched over, and began to shuffle toward the door on the room's left wall. She had to escape, before the man returned.

"Going somewhere?" the voice behind her asked.

She stumbled and fell forward, hitting the wood floor with the chair on top of her.

"I step in the bathroom for two minutes, and you wake up."

"What are you doing with me?" Her words came out slurred.

Kristin's breath quickened at his approaching footsteps. He lifted her off the ground. The old chair protested when he set her down hard, back where she'd started.

"Since our chat earlier, I've been debating what to do with you." He spoke in a southern twang, but his words were short and clipped, in military style.

What chat? she wondered. She'd been unconscious. But before she could pursue the thought, he bent over, covering her taped-down arms with his rough hands. He leaned close enough that she felt his stale breath on her cheeks. As terrified as she felt to be helpless in front of this man, she refused to turn away from his leering face. Her captor appeared to be in his late thirties, with a forehead creased into a permanent frown between his steel gray eyes. His complexion was fiery red and flaky, and he looked as if he were peeling from a severe sunburn. His crew cut had sprinkles of premature salt through the dark pepper. His nose sat slightly askew and a hint of crusted blood poked from his nostrils.

He broke the stare-down first, dropping his eyes down the length of her body. Feeling his gaze linger on her breasts before moving to her stomach and legs, she shuddered. She recalled his giving her the same look in front of the Taj Mahal: a look not really of lust, but of study—like a butcher pondering a cut of prime beef to decide how best to carve it into the most succulent pieces. She felt exposed under his gaze, as if he could see through her clothes to the bare flesh beneath.

"What do you want?" She struggled to keep her voice from wavering. By engaging him, maybe she could buy herself more time to think of a way out.

He cocked his head. "Why do you think I'd reveal my mission to you?"

"I think that you feel threatened that Grant's discovery will shake your faith." She was surprised by her own brazenness.

His voice was controlled. "You're slippery, aren't you? Just like your boyfriend was with the reverend." He stood and paced in front of her.

The mention of Brady surprised her. *Is this man one of his fanatical followers?*

He spoke as if lecturing to a group of military recruits. "That's the way you work, isn't it? You redirect the debate from your wrongdoing to the other person. I've studied psychological warfare, and your tactics won't work on me. The Angel of Darkness masquerading as an Angel of Light." The man began to lightly scratch his forearms.

She had no idea what paranoid fantasy her captor entertained, but at least he was talking instead of mentally undressing her. She wondered how long she'd been unconscious. *When will Grant realize I'm missing?* She shifted her weight in the creaky chair and softened her tone. "All Grant wants is to bring out the facts about what made Jesus the man he was. His journey is truly uplifting, you see—"

"The facts! For too long you atheists and agnostics have dominated the media, turning our country away from the principles of Christianity—the same principles our forefathers fought for." He began to scratch his arms more vigorously; flakes of dead skin fell like snow flurries to the floor. "But you've underestimated us true Christians."

Kristin had the impression that this man wasn't speaking to her at all but to someone else.

"But the time has come to take preemptive action," he said, no longer scratching but instead gesticulating with his arms to an imagined audience. "A David to take on Goliath." In a quieter voice he concluded, "Then our sins will be forgiven."

The lunatic propped his right foot on the coffee table and hiked up his pants leg. Kristin's eyes widened when he withdrew an eight-inch serrated military knife from the sheath attached to his calf.

"Please, don't hurt me." The words escaped her lips before she could stop them. Her attempt at bravery evaporated upon seeing the glint of the blade. This man had tortured Deepraj and now appeared ready to do the same to her. "What do you want to know?" she asked, following the knife with her eyes as it approached her.

"I have what I need to know." The man lightly traced the sharp point of the commando knife down the center of her shirt. His leering expression had returned. Reaching buttons, he hooked the knife under the bottom one. With a flick of his wrist, the button flew off. One by one, each of the next four buttons sailed across the room, making soft clinking noises when they scattered on the wood floor.

A deep nausea rose within her. He opened her shirt with the knife's edge, revealing a black sports bra now damp with perspiration. Her breathing came in quick and shallow gasps. She was unprepared for the tears that involuntarily fell from her eyes. His free hand reached toward her. Her stomach turned at the vision of the red scaly skin on his forearm. He pushed the shirt off her shoulders.

"Please, don't."

He didn't respond. He seemed transfixed by the honey complexion of her torso and shoulders.

Kristin knew that begging wouldn't stop this man; he might even enjoy it. His calloused fingers traced the flesh of her bare arm to her collarbone, raising chill bumps of revulsion on her skin. When the fingers moved down her chest, she snapped her eyes closed, wincing. His hand paused at her left breast, cupping it through the fabric of her bra with enough force to bring discomfort, but not enough to cause true pain. Kristin thought of her sister. The memory of the night her sister described her own rape seemed to reach up to strangle her.

She forced her eyes open. The man released her breast and let his fingers trail down her stomach to the waistline of her capris. She no longer felt his touch. She seemed to look at herself from a distance. His fingers quivered, fumbling with the top button.

Kristin moved without warning. She kicked her right foot out as hard as she could from her seated position. Her powerful leg muscles were magnified by the pent-up rage at her helplessness. Her foot connected with the man's groin. She felt the soft, squishy flesh give way to the pubic bone beneath.

The effect was instantaneous. Her captor dropped to his knees. A low moan escaped his lips. The knife clattered to the floor beside him as he grabbed his crotch with both hands. Her second kick was as effective as the first, but this time her foot connected with the crooked nose she'd broken earlier in the day. He howled as blood sprayed across the floor.

Kristin jumped to her feet and hobbled to the apartment's door with the chair attached to her back. She desperately tried to work her hands free, but they were secured too tightly. She reached the door. Turning her body sideways, she grasped the knob with her fingertips. She turned the knob and pulled.

"You bitch!" the hoarse scream came from the floor behind her.

Hunched over and still pulling on the door, she glanced at the man crawling toward her. He left a trail of blood and curses behind as he moved closer.

The door was locked. Releasing the knob, her fingers searched the metal plate.

There! A deadbolt. Just above the handle. She turned the lock and heard the click. She cut her eyes to the floor. He was almost to her. She grasped the knob again and turned it. The door opened.

"You're not leaving!" he wailed.

The door stopped after only a few inches. She jerked it harder, but it wouldn't budge. *The chair.* It was still attached to her back, and it was blocking the door. Frantically Kristin stepped away, giving the door room to swing out. It didn't. The man rose to his knees, just out of range from her legs. She looked back to the door, and then her heart sank.

The chain lock was attached two feet higher than her bound arms could reach.

"Help! Help me!" she screamed through the small opening.

She angled herself to grasp the handle again and tried to jerk the chain out of the wall.

The door slammed shut. Her captor pushed in front of her, blood and rage dripping from his face.

"Nice try."

He punched her hard in the jaw, snapping her head sideways. Her skull thudded against the door. She crumpled to the floor, and the lights around her again faded to darkness.

CHAPTER 44

———⟨∞⟩———

NORTHERN ALABAMA AIRSPACE

THE WHINE OF THE TURBINE engines on the Hawker 800 series aircraft subsided as the plane leveled off at cruising altitude. William Jennings loos-
ened his lap belt and relaxed into the plush leather seat. He'd never enjoyed
flying, especially takeoffs and landings. He knew his fear was irrational, originating from a lack of control over the giant tube of metal's capacity to stay up
in the air, but he still avoided planes as much as possible. Although the aircraft
was technically considered a luxurious midsized private jet, it felt small to
him. He would have preferred sitting crammed into the coach section of a 767
rather than being surrounded by the creamy leather and walnut trim in this
cabin where he had to duck to avoid bumping his head on the Alcantara-up-
holstered ceiling.

"I need a Coke!" Reverend Brady bellowed from the sofa where he slouched.
A notepad rested in his lap, and he chewed on the end of his ballpoint pen
while he worked on the speech he was to give the next morning at the annual
meeting of the National Association of Evangelicals.

Jennings knew that Brady was anxious because his breakfast address would
be his first step in taking the reins of the organization. In the keynote that evening Reverend Jimmy Jeffries would be announcing his retirement and his support of Brady in the upcoming election. Word of the announcement had already
leaked on the blogs, and many were already crowning Brady the heir apparent
after the trifecta of his bold announcement of the New Hope Community, his
best seller, and his public leadership in the recent charge against the Issa texts.

Jennings better than anyone understood how each of these public relations gold mines worked to reinforce each other. *After all*, he thought, *I planned them all.*

Jennings knew that Brady's more confrontational style and substance suited these uncertain times better than Jeffries's feel-good message of redemption through Christ's sacrifice. While Jeffries had grown his Texas-based church into one of the largest congregations in the country over the past two decades—he claimed a membership of an astounding fifty thousand believers—the NAE had lost its power and influence in American politics while under his control. The media loved to portray evangelicals as uneducated buffoons, often choosing the dumbest ones among them to interview. Jeffries's strategy had been to coddle the media, to show a softer and gentler side of their movement focused on outreach programs to the less fortunate, humanitarian trips to Africa, and even a recent move toward environmentalism in the name of protecting God's creation.

Jennings, however, had anticipated the folly of this strategy from the beginning. Just as one didn't negotiate with terrorists, playing into the mainstream media's hands had only weakened them. No longer were they feared as an organization that could deliver millions of Christian votes on election day. But he and Brady were close to changing the rules. Brady's recent media exposure had now propelled him to prominence in an organization restless for a new vision. Jennings had carefully crafted Brady's message so that it didn't shy away from blaming the country's problems on its sinful direction. Just as children craved firm rules and discipline, the country needed to be taught the Bible's message clearly, without reservation. Jennings had shaped the content of this message through his influence over the reverend's sermons and the hours he'd spent with the ghostwriter of Brady's book. *Maybe even more hours than Brady himself has spent,* Jennings mused.

They were so close to achieving their dreams. Now he needed to get his boss under control for the final stretch. The stakes were too high for any missteps. *Or*, he thought, *any bad publicity.*

"Here you go, Reverend." The perky blond assistant secretary from Brady's office placed a glass filled half with Diet Coke and half with Regular Coke, cold but no ice, on the polished table beside the sofa.

Jennings pulled an overflowing file folder from the worn leather briefcase at his feet. He flipped through the first few pages, spreadsheets containing the church's current financial statements. As positive as Brady's media attention had been recently, the reality of New Hope's finances was another matter. He knew that this moment was not a good time to bring up a financial discussion with his boss, but Brady had avoided the topic for the past week, and now Jennings had him alone.

"Brian, the outside auditors required by the bank come on Monday."

"Yeah, so deal with it." Brady made notes in the margin of his pad without looking up.

"We need to prepare for their questions. Our loan is contingent on this audit. We've never had an outside audit before, and I'm concerned about how some of our expenses may be perceived."

Brady sighed, finally looking up. "William, I'd love to be more involved now in the financial details of the church, but I've got to prepare for the most important speech of my career. Just do whatever you need to do to make the auditors happy and send them away."

Jennings clenched and unclenched his jaw. This reaction was typical of Brady. The reverend delegated the financial and other day-to-day operations of the church to Jennings, but when the time came to make tough decisions about controlling the expenditures, every line item in the budget was sacred, part of the "necessary operations of the church" or part of God's "vision for the future." How was he to make the bankers happy when the New Hope Community's projected construction costs were now 35 percent over a budget they'd already increased three times—and his hands were tied when it came to cutting costs?

The empty club chairs around him were a perfect example. The short roundtrip flight to Little Rock was costing the church eight thousand dollars for the three of them. Their one-quarter interest in the fractional jet owner-ship program provided the flexibility of having a plane at their disposal on a few hours' notice anywhere in the world, but at an extravagant cost. When Jennings had tried to discuss the economics of flying commercially rather than privately, Brady dismissively replied that he could perform God's work much more efficiently from the private plane: he saved time by avoiding ticketing, security, and luggage lines. He'd also told Jennings that the bank president didn't fly commercial, so why should he?

Jennings knew that trying to budge his boss on the topic of saving money was an exercise in futility. They'd prospered as a church only because of their ability to continually increase revenues. If Brady excelled at one God-given ability above all others, it was raising money. Had the reverend not received the calling to become a preacher, he would've made millions in the business world. Brady was the most natural salesman Jennings had ever met. It didn't matter whether Brady was selling a parable from the Bible, the vision for the new church development, or his book, he had the gift of generating an infectious enthusiasm among those around him. Twenty years ago, Jennings himself had been persuaded by the same charisma. If only he'd been born with such a gift.

"Look," Jennings persisted, "the bankers don't look at the world in the same way we do. If we can't show at least a trend of increasing our revenues beyond the temporary spike in book sales—either through home sales or growing our congregation—we risk the bank cutting off our funds permanently and possibly even taking over the project."

"What!" Brady went red in the face. "New Hope is my vision, not the bank's! How can they even think they could execute a project like this?"

"They could never execute the project like you, but that's never stopped lenders in the past from foreclosing on developers who cannot make their payments."

Brady wiped his brow. "The national media will cover my speech tomorrow, just as they've been following me since the debate. Won't that help? I'm the one, after all, who showed the world that those Jesus texts were a fraud."

Actually, Jennings thought, *he* had given Brady the information about Grant Matthews's past plagiarism. He'd long ago become used to Brady taking credit for his work, but as long as their end goals were reached, he didn't care.

"That's exactly why you have to hit it out of the park tomorrow. Let me see what you've got." The right speech covered by the national media would drive more people into the church, onto their website, and into bookstores to buy

Brady's book. The uptick in sales of the book after the debate had been huge, just as Jennings had anticipated, but he knew that that effect could only last so long.

"Okay," Brady huffed. He handed Jennings the legal pad with the scribbling that was the beginning of his speech.

After a glance, Jennings said, "Not bad, Brian. I like how you speak out against all of these so-called self-help gurus who encourage people to find peace within themselves with their watered-down references to Eastern religions."

Brady nodded. "True peace *only* comes through acceptance of Jesus Christ as our Lord and Savior, not from within. That is the lesson that our country is missing today."

"I agree, but what if we also hit people where they are really hurting."

Brady templed his fingers under his chin. "Their pocketbooks?"

"Exactly." The slow economy had not only hurt home sales in New Hope, it was dragging down contributions to the church as well. Jennings figured they could turn their problems to their advantage. "What are the two countries that are doing well economically today while the U.S. and Europe suffer?"

"China and India, but those are not Christian countries."

"That's your point. You make the argument in your book that God punished Israel, even though the Jews were the chosen people, by allowing Rome, a pagan empire, to destroy the Temple in seventy AD. Why? Because the Jews had rejected Jesus as the Messiah. Well, take this one step further. China and India are countries controlled by people who believe in heathen religions, yet even as they take our jobs, our businesses form subsidiaries there, moving even more of our production offshore, which is destroying our nation."

Brady's eyes lit up. "Just as Paul wrote in First Corinthians, chapter ten, verses twenty–twenty-one: 'You cannot drink the cup of the Lord and the cup of demons too; you cannot have a part in both the Lord's table and the table of demons.'"

Jennings smiled. The reverend hadn't lost his touch.

"I can give a hundred sermons like that in my sleep."

"Your speech will be great, Brian. After the CNN debate, the media will be anxious to see what you have to say."

Jennings glanced at his watch. They would be landing soon. Thinking about the debate, he was reminded of the phone calls he needed to make. In addition to the financial problems at New Hope, the other occurrence that could discredit Brady and upset his bid for the presidency of the NAE would be the sudden appearance of the texts he'd condemned as fraudulent. Jennings believed that the Internet release of the texts had been both a gift and a test sent by God. His strategy of using them to create controversy and drive more people to Brady's book was exactly the kind of response that God had wanted from them. Only when the texts disappeared for good, just as they had done a hundred years earlier in the case of Nicholas Notovitch, would God's will be done.

CHAPTER 45

─── ∞ ───

VARANASI, INDIA

KRISTIN STIRRED AND opened her eyes. Her head throbbed. *Where was she?* She lay on her side on a dusty wood floor, her arms bound to a chair attached uncomfortably to her back.

Then the horror of her entrapment overcame her.

She attempted to move her head, but a lightning bolt of pain convinced her to keep it resting on the floor. *How long had she been unconscious?* The room had no windows to the outside, so she had no idea if it was night or day. She blinked at the bare lightbulb in the ceiling above her. When her eyes refocused on her surroundings, she realized that she no longer lay by the door to the apartment where she'd fallen. Her captor must have dragged her back to the center of the room. She also noticed, with relief, that her pants were still on. Her shirt was open, exposing her sports bra, but it was in place too.

The pain in her head radiated outward from her jaw. She had a vague memory of the blur of a fist before passing out. She tried to open her mouth, wondering if her jaw was broken, but immediately realized that something was wrong. A stale dry taste pervaded her mouth, and her tongue felt as if it had ballooned to twice its normal size. After a moment, she realized it wasn't her tongue that was swollen but that her mouth was stuffed with some kind of cloth. She tried to spit it out, but it wouldn't budge.

She was gagged. Immediately the sensation that she was suffocating overwhelmed her. She forced herself to inhale deeply through her nose. She didn't want to be the cause of her own death from choking.

Her sinuses were clear. She could breathe. *Just relax and keep breathing*, she told herself.

"I'm in Varanasi." A muffled voice drifted across the floor to her. "I have the girl."

Straining her eyes to look up without moving her pounding head, she saw her assailant sitting on the edge of the bed in the next room. His head inclined away from her, he spoke into a cell phone.

"Don't worry about that. You don't need the details. Just give me what I need and it will be taken care of."

Either sensing or hearing her, he swiveled his head in her direction. His nose, while crooked on his face, was no longer bent at the right angle she'd last seen it following her kick. He must have set it himself. Both of his nostrils were packed with tissue, the bloodstained tips of which dangled out. He paused the conversation to smile at her, a cold, predatory smile.

"I'll call you back," the man said and then hung up his phone. He then lifted his feet to the bed and began to unlace and then remove his black boots. Then he unbuckled his belt.

Kristin watched the monster, knowing she was helpless to prevent him from abusing her. Then she heard a voice. It came not from the room but from deep inside her, like a single candle flame flickering faintly at the far end of a dark cave.

"It's only your body. It's not you." Her sister's soft voice spoke to her in the gentle tone Kristin missed desperately.

Through the throbbing in her jaw and head, Kristin came to the simple understanding that this man could do nothing to her. He might rape her, he might kill her afterward, but he couldn't take from her something deeper, something that only she could relinquish. She recalled Deepraj's words and the image of the single candle flame on their dinner table, the tiny flame which she now understood also burned inside her own body. Whatever happened, she would not relinquish that. Kristin's realization had an unexpected effect on her. Lying on the ground and staring at the man removing his pants, Kristin became aware of a calmness that rested deep within her. Her breathing slowed. The air slowly passed through her nostrils and filled her lungs, the air that fanned the tiny flame inside of her.

Nephesh, she thought. The breath of God.

Kristin still felt the physical pain in her body. The fear of what lay in store for her still produced adrenaline coursing through her veins, but now she watched these sensations as an outsider. The sensations were dulled, like someone had turned down the volume of a loud stereo to the point where she was aware that beyond the noise was a silence, a peace that the noise could mask but not reach.

With the pain in her body now a dull echo of its former strength, she gathered her legs underneath herself and rose to her knees. The pervert on the bed looked startled at her movement. He quickly finished removing his pants, as though he didn't want to be caught tangled in case she tried a new escape tactic. But Kristin merely stood and then sat back in the chair. For a moment, she wondered whether the old chair would support her weight as it creaked and wobbled under her.

He stared at her with a new curiosity. She held his gaze, not in angry defiance, and not in fear, but as a gaze.

He didn't move immediately toward her. He cocked his head, puzzled. As they continued to stare at each other, the lightbulb above flickered on and off twice in rapid succession. *The ever-present Varanasi power fluctuations*, she thought.

Her captor glanced at the ceiling and then rose from the bed. The smirk had returned to his face.

Blackness engulfed the room.

"It's *M-I-S-A-K-I!*" Grant spelled for the third time to the two police officers standing in the hallway in front of Deepraj's office.

"Your wife?" the shorter one, who looked barely old enough to shave, asked.

"Not my wife, my . . . girlfriend." He paced in the empty hall, his footsteps echoing off the plaster walls. The shock of finding Deepraj murdered and a four-foot long cobra curled under the professor's desk almost did him in. Grant knew immediately that this was the work of the man from Agra. He was still tracking them. Grant didn't have time to grieve for the kind professor, though, because his greatest fear had been realized. Kristin was missing. He'd called the police from the phone in the faculty lounge. They had arrived quickly but slammed shut Deepraj's door as soon as they saw the snake. They called for backup.

"When did you last see her?" the senior officer in the ill-fitting blue jacket asked.

"About two hours ago, when I dropped her off here."

"Was the professor alive then?" His pen paused above his notepad.

"I dropped her off outside the building and then returned to the hotel." He wrung his hands together. They should be sending out search parties to scour the neighborhood, not standing here talking. The older officer continued to stare at him. "Wait. I hope you're not implying that Kristin may have had something to do with his death!"

"I'm not implying anything. Just gathering information." He scribbled something on his pad. "Had they argued recently?"

Grant threw his hands up in the air. "No! They were very close. We had dinner last night. Deepraj was helping us."

"Where do you think she might have gone?"

Grant put his hands on his hips and let out a breath so that he wouldn't begin screaming at the officers. "That's what I need your help with. She's been kidnapped. By the same man who did that"—he pointed to the closed office door—"and the same man who murdered one of our friends in Agra!" He had already told the story of the events at the Taj Mahal twice to these two.

"Our office will check into that. But now we have the problem that one of our distinguished professors is dead in his office under suspicious circumstances."

"Suspicious circumstances! Have you been listening to what I've said?" He took another breath and tried again. "If you want to find the man who did this, we need to find Kristin."

The younger officer tapped his superior's shoulder. "While you wait here for backup, I can take him to his hotel. We'll be around if the woman shows up."

Grant looked back and forth between the officers as if he were watching a bad comedy routine. Standing around, whether in the university building or at the hotel, would not find Kristin. His heart ached for her. He had seen with Razi and now Deepraj what this man was capable of doing. He forced from his mind the possibilities of what Kristin might be enduring. But how could they begin to find her in this crowded, teaming city? He felt bile rise to the back of his throat and swallowed hard. *Why did I let her go alone?*

Then the hallway's fluorescent lights flickered on and off in rapid succession. The three of them glanced around. Another power outage. The overhead lights stayed off, but the emergency floodlights at the end of the hall by the stairwell popped on. The sharp light from the halide bulbs cast daggerlike shadows across the wood floor. A deep unease gripped Grant's gut.

This time the power remained off. Kristin could see nothing.

She moved without thinking. She pushed her legs as forcefully as she could with the chair attached to her back, but she didn't run in the direction of the door. Instead, she hurled herself toward the opposite wall. Her captor lunged a second slower than she did.

He must have anticipated she would try another escape attempt, because she heard him yell from the direction of the door, "Come here, you bitch!"

Kristin hit the opposite wall violently, twisting her body at the moment before the expected impact. She hadn't been able to see the approaching wall, but she'd felt its presence. A loud splintering sound echoed through the room. The chair shattered and fell from her body in pieces.

"Huh?" the man called out in confusion.

Now free from her seated prison, Kristin squatted and groped in the darkness until her hands closed on one of the chair's legs. Still taped to her forearms were foot-long pieces of wood, but they no longer impeded her movement. Ignoring the stiffness in her back, she stood with her newly acquired weapon in her right hand, ripped her gag out with her left, and began to make her way around the perimeter of the room. She kept her left hand in light contact with the wall, while her right gripped the chair leg above her head.

The sound of her assailant stumbling over the wreckage of the destroyed chair echoed from behind her. He'd moved quickly. Kristin turned. She strained to see in the darkness, but the absence of light was complete. Instinct told her to raise her left arm protectively in front of her face. She shuffled backward, facing the direction of the expected imminent attack.

A sharp metallic edge pressed into her spine.

She froze.

The image of the blade of the commando knife blazed in her mind. She shifted her body weight to her left, preparing to swing her weapon toward the new menace. The edge rotated with her, now pressed against the length of her back. It wasn't her attacker but the bathroom door.

Before she had time to experience any relief from this realization, the actual attack came. She sensed rather than saw the quick movement in front of her. She still held her left arm high in front of her face while her right held the chair leg suspended over her head. Kristin heard the sound of metal striking wood at the same time she felt the ringing vibration run from the armrest taped to her forearm through to her bone. He'd struck with the knife.

She wasn't going to give him the chance to adjust his aim. Kristin brought the chair leg she was holding down in a forceful arc in front of her body in a movement that reminded her of serving for match point. Her hand stung when the wooden leg cracked loudly against a hard part of his body. A howl went up in front of her. Kristin knew she needed to press her advantage.

She regripped the chair leg, now with both hands, and swung back across her body with every bit of power she could generate. During her tennis-playing days, she'd hit thousands of balls with her powerful two-handed back-hand. Swinging from her hips as she'd been taught, she now put her entire body into this swing, aiming for the spot where the howl had just originated. Her coach had trained her to see nothing but the markings on the ball during the point she was playing, regardless of what had happened on any of the previous points. At this moment, Kristin saw nothing but the target in the darkness in front of her.

The wooden leg connected with a stomach-churning crunch. No howl escaped her captor this time; the only sound was the thud of his body hitting the floor. The impact of her strike tore the chair leg from her hands. She stood in the blackness, hearing only her own panting. She bolted in the direction of the door.

Slamming into the wall, her hands fumbled with the locks. She frantically turned the smooth knob that opened the deadbolt and then whipped off the chain that had frustrated her earlier escape attempt.

She flung open the door, letting in the cool evening air infused with the pungent city smells. A gas lamp attached to the building's exterior illuminated the narrow alleyway outside the door with a flickering yellow light. The alley was deserted.

Grant. She had to get to Grant.

Kristin lunged through the door to her freedom. Once outside, however, she couldn't resist a glance into the apartment behind her. The gas lantern cast a pale glow into the room. Her attacker lay unmoving on the dusty wood floor, the side of the chair leg embedded in the man's gaping mouth where she must have struck him. A dark pool of blood spread outward from his head.

Oh God, she thought, *I've killed him.*

Kristin ran as fast as her legs would take her. From the maze of narrow streets she knew that she was in Old Varanasi. If she kept heading in one direction, she would eventually hit either the river or the main road at the edge of the small town. In either case, she would be able to find her way back to the hotel, which was within a mile or two of the city center. She ignored the bewildered stares of the shopkeepers, pedestrians, and pilgrims. In a city where amputee beggars, corpses, and stray livestock all competed for space on the street, the sight of a bruised and battered Asian American woman running in an open shirt with wood handles taped to her arms couldn't have been too great a shock.

When she finally burst through the lobby doors of the Hotel Taj Ganges twenty minutes later, the first thing she saw was Grant talking animatedly with a short uniformed police officer and the hotel manager by the reception desk.

☙

Grant had accompanied the younger officer back to the hotel. He'd held out a slim hope that she would be there waiting for him, but they found nothing. He explained to the officer and the hotel manager that he needed a driver to go with him into the city to search for signs of her. He had a picture of her on his laptop that he could print in the business office, but the manager explained that with the power failure, the hotel's generator only ran the lights in the lobby.

A commotion at the lobby entrance caused them to turn.

The sight hit him like a shot of adrenaline directly into his heart.

"Kris!"

She ran across the marble floor, collapsing into his arms.

"What happened?" She had pieces of wood taped to her arms. "Are you okay?" With a quivering hand, he lifted the chin buried on his shoulder. The side of her face was blue and swollen. His voice was barely above a whisper. "What did he do to you?"

He repeated the questions over and over as if his own voice would make the answers okay. But rather than respond, she just gripped him tighter. Grant had a vague awareness of those around them watching the bizarre scene in the hotel lobby, but that didn't matter to him. His senses narrowed to Kristin. His hands pressed into the smooth skin on her back, damp with perspiration; he inhaled the scent of her hair; he felt her breath on his neck.

Then he gently pulled her arms from around him and carefully removed the duct tape and wood sticks from her forearms.

"Kris," he repeated, "please talk to me."

Keeping her silence, she tilted her face to his and kissed him deeply.

PART THREE

⊸∞∞⊸

THE FIRE

"If your leaders say to you "Look! The Kingdom is in the sky!" then the birds will be there before you are. If they say that the Kingdom is in the sea, then the fish will be there before you are. Rather the Kingdom is within you, and it is outside you. When you understand yourselves, you will be understood. And you will realize that you are Sons of the Living Father."

Jesus, *The Gospel of Thomas,*
AD 1st–2nd century

"Anyone who withdraws into meditation on compassion can see Brahma with his own eyes, talk to him face to face and consult with him."

The Buddha, *Digha Nikaya, Sutta Pitaka,*
2nd–3rd century BC

CHAPTER 46

⁕

NORTHERN HIMALAYAS, INDIA
TWO THOUSAND YEARS AGO

ISSA STARED UPWARD at the moon; only a faint glow emanated from the edge of the dark disk. Issa sat on the damp leaves in the mountain forest that he'd been traveling through the past forty days and nights since he'd left the town by the holy river. He was hungry. Before leaving the town, he'd packed his sack with bread and a skin of wine. He didn't expect to be traveling this long. He'd encountered a few camps of monks along the way who generously shared their food, but he knew if he didn't make it to another town soon, he would starve to death.

Issa pulled his cloak tighter around him. The wind, the *ruach*, whistled as it moved through the canopy of pine needles draped from the trees like a disembodied spirit circling above him. Glancing around in the faint light of the stars, he sensed that the forest had taken on a different character in the night than during the day. He felt its aliveness, a presence in the plants and the creatures that moved in the shadows.

Issa knew that he was on the verge of a breakthrough, an understanding that had eluded the rabbis at home, a discovery that would justify his journey and the hardships he had endured. Sometimes when he was practicing the techniques he'd learned by the river, he caught a glimpse of this understanding—like the flicker of a single candle flame from across a nighttime field. But the light was always out of his reach. Just when he thought he was close, his thoughts would intrude, jumping from one inconsequential topic to another. His teacher had called this his monkey-mind.

Issa thought back to a lesson his teacher had taught soon after he'd arrived in the town by the sacred river. "So my atman is like my soul?" Issa had asked.

"Originally the word *atman* meant breath, but today we use it to signify the force that brings you life and animates your actions," his teacher replied, reminding Issa of a lesson the rabbis at home had taught.

"In the tongue of my scripture, we call that *nephesh*."

"Your atman resides deep within you, eternal and unchanging. But more important to realize is that the atman deep inside you also contains the light of Brahman."

Issa struggled with the strange idea that a piece of God, or Brahman, as the people of this land spoke of him, was present in every living thing. "If God is more than just the creator and protector of the world but is part of life itself, why have I never recognized this presence inside myself?" he asked.

Before his teacher could respond, Issa added, "For that matter, with God present in all living creatures, why do we see death and sickness around us?"

Amused by Issa's rapid-fire questions, the teacher responded, "Being able to debate about God doesn't mean you understand God. Your atman is hidden deep inside the layers of what you consider to be your self: your thoughts, your personality, your emotions, your memories. You, my son, are a child of God. You just do not yet see this."

"But how is that possible?"

The teacher considered Issa for a moment and then pointed to a magnificent tree about fifty paces down the bank of the river. "Bring me a fruit from the banyan tree."

"A fruit? I don't understand."

"I know." The teacher pointed to the tree again.

Issa stood and jogged down the riverbank to the solitary tree whose branches extended the length of the entire clearing and whose multiple twisted roots grew from the high limbs to the ground like gnarled fingers reaching for the dirt. Issa stood on his toes and reached for one of the lower-hanging fruits. He picked it and then examined its firm and wrinkled flesh. It was burnt orange in color but had no discernible scent.

He carried it back to his teacher.

"Break it open."

Issa tore into the fruit. The stringy flesh stuck to his fingers.

"Now open a seed."

The seeds were tiny and the juice of the fruit made them slippery. After several tries, Issa grasped one between his fingernails and snapped it in half.

"What can you see?"

"Nothing." Issa shrugged.

"Exactly!"

Issa didn't try to hide the look of confusion that passed over his face.

The guru pointed to the split seed. "From that nothingness that you cannot see, we get the mighty banyan tree. That which you cannot see in the seed exists within you too. It also gives rise to the universe around you."

"If I cannot see it, how do I know it's there?"

"Eternal and infinite, God cannot be comprehended, but you can touch and experience your own being directly. Once you understand your own nature, only then will you understand God."

As the memory of his teacher faded from his mind, Issa leaned backward against the trunk of a pine tree. He closed his eyes and inhaled deeply. The aroma of damp earth filled his nostrils. He allowed this to pass through him. Issa lost track of time; he was relaxed but not sleepy. Then the flicker appeared to him. The dancing flame was faint but steady in the darkness of his mind. This time Issa didn't strive for the flame; he just allowed it to be.

Suddenly Issa understood. He understood that the truth lay not in the religious texts that he'd studied—the Torah, the Vedas. Nor did it lie with the teachers—the gurus of this land or the rabbis in his own—but it lay deep inside him, just as its presence also surrounded him. He'd just never known where to look before.

Issa was filled with an energy unlike any he'd ever experienced before. As he continued to breathe, he felt the candle flame within him grow into a raging fire.

CHAPTER 47

PARO, BHUTAN

GRANT TIGHTENED his fingers around the man's neck.

The man's red and scaly face turned a more gruesome shade of purple as Grant choked the life out of this person who had kidnapped Kristin, shot Jigme, and killed Deepraj and Razi. The feeling of the power surging through Grant's forearms was as addictive as any narcotic.

"Ladies and gentlemen, this is your captain speaking."

Grant's eyes opened. The bright lights of the plane's cabin caused the fantasy to fade. A tightness in his chest replaced the fullness in his arms. Not only was the idea of extracting revenge on this man just a fantasy, the reality was that he'd sat helplessly in a hotel room during Kristin's assault, just as he'd lain on the ground when Jigme was shot.

The pilot of Druk Air flight 203 broadcast over the intercom in a clipped British accent. "On the left side of the plane, you can see Mount Everest, at twenty-nine thousand thirty-five feet the tallest point on earth. Next to Everest you will find the ridgeline of Lhotse."

Grant peered out the window at the mountain range beside the plane. They'd left New Delhi midmorning, on the flight that Grant had booked two days earlier just before he'd learned of Deepraj's murder and Kristin's kidnapping. Grant had wondered whether they would even make the flight, but the interviews with the police had been almost as brief as they had been in Agra. The authorities seemed to be happy when he told them they were leaving the country. After a short stopover in Katmandu, Nepal, to let on new passengers, they were now en route to Paro, Bhutan. At cruising altitude, the snow-covered peaks were almost parallel to the plane's wings. The cloud ceiling was thousands of feet below them, obscuring the ground, but the view of the highest summits in the world thrusting up through the clouds was clear.

"Which one?" Kristin asked. She leaned across Grant's lap to look out the window with him. He tried not to stare at the purple bruise along her jaw.

"That one. In front of the wing." He pointed to the pyramid-shaped mountain, steep black rock on one side and brilliant white snow covering the rest.

"Magnificent." She raised her camera to the Plexiglas and snapped a series of pictures.

An unexpected emotional response from seeing the tallest mountain in the world displaced Grant's fantasy of revenge and his memory of helplessness. The thought of the forces of nature that had created this mountain over billions of years put some perspective on their travails. As he watched a wispy plume of snow rise from Everest's summit, he thought of the men and women who had struggled past physical and mental exhaustion on their quest to reach the peak, and of the many others who had perished trying to do so.

"Do you think he'll be waiting for us?" Kristin asked.

"Jigme's last email said he'd meet us outside baggage claim."

"I wasn't talking about Jigme."

One look at her furrowed brow and tight lips cleared up the misunderstanding, and he understood which "he" she meant.

"I don't see how," he said, taking her hand. "Since I erased his spyware programs from my computer, he can't track us anymore."

"I don't know what I might have told him when I was drugged."

That thought had worried Grant as well, but he didn't want her to know that. "This flight was the next one out of India for Bhutan. The train would take much longer. And you know how difficult it is to get a visa." *But*, he thought, as soon as he spoke the words, *that madman has been remarkably persistent in tracking us so far.*

"I hit him so hard, and lying there . . . he looked . . . so dead."

"He's probably holed up somewhere nursing his wounds."

"I don't know. He isn't really the nursing type. He was like one of those pit bulls bred for fighting. You know, those animals don't give up until they're killed."

Grant squeezed her hand. "If you want to stay at the hotel tomorrow while Jigme and I hike up to the Tiger's Nest Monastery, no one would blame you."

Without hesitation, she shook her head. "I won't give in to fear. I won't grant him that victory."

"I didn't expect you would." Although the bruise ran from her jawline to under her eye and her bottom lip was still puffy, the injuries obscured neither the determination in Kristin's face nor her beauty.

She had changed during the few hours she'd been kidnapped, but he couldn't put his finger on exactly what the change was. At first, he'd thought she'd merely gained a new strength from facing and then overcoming death, but then he reminded himself that her confidence was one of her traits that had attracted him from the beginning.

Observing her—traumatized but at the same time peaceful, apprehensive yet determined, bruised but beautiful—he discovered something that was as clear as the snow-capped mountain peaks reflecting the sun outside his window. He slowly exhaled, hoping to relieve the pressure deep within his chest.

He was in love with Kristin.

✑

Tim's legs burned.

To make matters worse, every time he sucked in a lungful of the thin mountain air, the cold made his raw gums ache. Although he tried to stop himself, his tongue darted in and out of the smooth gap in the center of his lower jaw, feeling for his missing three teeth. At least her aim had been a couple of inches low. The blow to his jaw had knocked him unconscious, but he'd survived. Had that bitch hit him as hard as she had in the eyes or forehead, he'd be blind or dead.

The Versed worked exactly as he'd hoped, especially after he'd adjusted the dose following the lesson he'd learned in Agra. While she was in a twilight state of consciousness, he'd questioned her about the location of the texts.

Although deciphering the incoherent rambling that came with the drug took almost an hour, his next destination became clear soon enough.

As Tim continued his hike up the mountain trail, the pain in his jaw made him wish he could breathe through his nose. With a broken nose, bruised face, and missing teeth, Tim knew he looked like crap. But the cover story he'd given on his arrival in Bhutan yesterday—a rickshaw accident in India—had resulted in sympathetic nods from both the customs officials and hotel staff, who knew how hectic Indian streets were. Anyway, they wouldn't be suspicious of an important businessman like him. The Paro airport didn't often receive privately owned aircraft. In this small, poor country, an individual owning a plane was the stuff of movies.

The phone call Tim made after he regained consciousness had been more painful than the blows to his face. "There's been a complication," he'd said, struggling to speak into his cell phone through the tissues he'd stuffed in the holes where his teeth had been.

"We can't afford any complications!" The voice from across the globe came through all too clearly as Tim limped down the dark alley away from the flat.

"I know, but the girl escaped and is heading to the authorities now." Tim knew better than to sugarcoat his predicament. He was running out of time.

"I thought you were a trained professional! How are you letting a grad student and a journalist outwit you?"

The stinging rebuke pained Tim as much as the blow he'd received to his face had. But he felt in his gut that he would ultimately prevail. God was on his side. These texts were the work of Satan. His discharge from the army, his job troubles, his personal demons—none of that would matter once he had his hands on the texts. *I am part of a divine plan bigger than my sufferings*, he thought, *even bigger than the reverend*. Anyway, he had the upper hand now. He knew where the texts were.

"I'm going to need a plane," Tim said. "I can beat them there." He then explained that only a few commercial flights a week left India for Bhutan, and the authorities would certainly be looking for him. Flying a chartered jet was the only way to accomplish his mission.

Tim had to hold the phone away from his ear as the voice screamed at him for getting into this situation and then detailed the costs and risks of chartering a plane.

"Do you want the texts or not?"

After a full minute of silence, the man said, "If you don't get to the texts first, my future is over." He added quickly, "And the faith of millions will be shattered because of your incompetence."

He agreed to Tim's extravagant request. Fortunately, Tim's foresight in applying for a visa early paid off. It was waiting for him at the consulate in New Delhi. He would be a step ahead of Grant Matthews. This time he would be successful.

Tim trudged up the steep mountain trail, following the Bhutanese guide he'd hired from the hotel. Although the elevation was just under nine thousand feet, not high for the Himalayas, he still felt the effects of the altitude. He paused for a moment, resting a hand on the charcoal jacket tied around his waist and taking a swig from his bottled water. What had begun as a cold hike underneath the tree cover that morning had turned considerably warmer as they emerged into the sun halfway up the mountain. He was used to hiking for a day at a time in the woods in Alabama, but he'd been on this path for just two hours and he was practically wheezing.

"Just up here is cafeteria," his Bhutanese guide said, pointing through the tall blue pine trees. "We rest and eat there. Get good picture of Taktshang Goemba too."

Tim nodded at the guide, who was dressed in what Tim thought to be a ridiculous mix of a Scottish kilt and a bathrobe—something they called a *gho*. Then Tim noticed a rough narrow trail which broke off to his right and descended through the scrub brush. "Where does that go?" He cringed when he heard the words whistle through the gap in his teeth. *That bitch*, he thought for the hundredth time.

"To bottom of mountain."

"Why the hell didn't we come up that way?" This other trail looked to be a more direct route than the circuitous traversing of the mountainside they'd hiked.

"Too dangerous for tourists. Very steep. You not last ten minutes without slipping and sliding down mountain."

"Bullshit," Tim said, wondering why they couldn't hire guides who spoke proper English. "Someone's been using it." Tim had followed enough deer trails while hunting to recognize a currently used path.

"Some of the younger monks use it, when they are in a hurry."

"How much faster?"

"About half time, if you don't fall."

Tim eyed the trail again before continuing around another bend. The dirt path in front of them then opened to a small clearing, revealing the cafeteria. Tim soon discovered that the Bhutanese used the term "cafeteria" to describe all restaurants, although even "restaurant" was an ambitious description for this one-room wooden structure with a flimsy tin roof. Tim's attention, however, was immediately drawn from the nondescript building to the mountainside now visible to the left of the cafeteria. The dirt path transitioned to stone steps. The steep and narrow steps hugged the face of the mountain, weaving upward along the sheer granite cliff, which dropped to the valley two thousand feet below. The sight at the top of the steps left Tim in awe.

"Ah, Taktshang Goemba." The guide gestured toward the Tiger's Nest Monastery, a satisfied look on his face. He must have been accustomed to seeing the amazed expressions of tourists, but Tim didn't believe one could ever become accustomed to such a view. He wondered how the simple monks ever built such a thing.

The monastery balanced on an impossibly narrow ledge on the sheer side of the black granite cliff. The painted white stone blocks of the monastery walls ascended the rising ledge in a steplike fashion, as if the walls had organically sprouted from the mountain itself. While no section of the monastery appeared to be more than two stories in height, the total structure climbed five levels. Multiple red metal roofs covered the various articulated sections of the monastery, the highest of which were topped with golden pagoda-styled structures.

As physically impressive as the sight was, Tim was most impressed by the military advantages of the location. The monks would have a commanding view of the entire Paro valley from the red- and gold-painted wood windows. Furthermore, since the structure was built two-thirds of the way up the cliff, the only way to access it would be along the narrow stone steps that snaked up to the gatehouse at the base of the monastery. An army of invaders could never lay siege to the monastery from either above or below. *No*, Tim thought, *the only workable approach was a covert one at night.* He realized he had an advantage too; there would be no army of invaders when he returned later that night, but rather an army of one.

The Bible clearly declared Tim's God-fearing way of life as sacred, and Tim remembered the punishment for those who would deny Jesus—fire, suffering, and death. Once he had the texts in hand, he would take care of Grant Matthews and Kristin Misaki. This time there would be no playing around with that half-breed bitch. She and her boyfriend would not be given an opportunity to escape.

Grant and Kristin descended the metal stairs of the plane onto the tarmac of Paro International Airport. The terminal ahead of them, with its whitewashed stone walls and intricately carved wood trim, looked more like a dzong than an airport building. While zipping up his fleece against the air, which had grown considerably cooler in the time since he'd left Bhutan, Grant noticed the sleek white lines of a corporate jet parked at the edge of the tarmac, unusual in such an out-of-the-way country. Probably some celebrity or corporate tycoon hoping to escape his hectic life in the last Shangri-La of the Himalayas.

After clearing customs, Grant and Kristin emerged from the opposite side of the terminal. They found Jigme waiting for them on the sidewalk amid a handful of tour guides and drivers. Kristin dropped her backpack and embraced Jigme first, holding him for a full minute. He'd exchanged the civilian clothes Grant had last seen his friend wearing in Agra for his crimson robes.

"How are you feeling?" Jigme asked. He held Kristin at arm's length and studied her bruised face. Grant had relayed the details of her kidnapping in his last email.

"Just some bumps and bruises. At least I wasn't shot." She touched his shoulder. Jigme's arm was in a sling made of the same fabric as his robes.

"Oh, my wound is healing fine." After Jigme embraced Grant, he led them across the parking lot to a waiting taxi. "On the way to your hotel, you can tell me about Sarnath," Jigme said with curiosity in his eyes. Although Grant believed his laptop to be secure since he cleansed it of the spyware, he didn't want to take any unnecessary risks. He hadn't yet revealed to Jigme the location of their next, and he hoped final, stop.

After loading the bags in the back of a beige Land Rover and starting down the bumpy road, Grant tapped Jigme, who sat in the front passenger seat. He asked the question that had been on his mind since they'd left Sarnath. "Any word from Kinley?"

Jigme shook his head. "Rumor among my fellow monks is that he's in Bhutan."

"Rumor," Grant chided him. "I thought one of the steps of the Buddha's Fourth Noble Truth is Right Speech."

"I'm happy to see you were listening on those grumpy days of yours here." Jigme smiled. "Although gossip is frowned upon in my religion, rumors spread through the monasteries faster than fire through a candle factory."

Kristin leaned forward. "What have the monks said?"

"Before I returned, Kinley was spotted meeting with the Je Khenpo, our spiritual leader, which of course infuriated Lama Dorji. I suppose you two have a better idea where he is than I do." Jigme raised his eyebrows, not asking the question, while asking it at the same time.

Grant inclined his head in the direction of the driver. Jigme said, "A friend of mine. Doesn't speak English."

The story spilled out of both Grant's and Kristin's mouths as they recounted the discussions they'd had in Varanasi and Sarnath and the mural they'd seen in the temple.

By the end of the story, Jigme nodded. "Always the teacher, Kinley is."

"I have to admit I have a better understanding of Issa's journey," Grant said, but for him understanding alone was still not enough. He needed the actual texts.

"Yeah, me too," Kristin added, but Grant noticed that her soft tone and unfocused expression suggested that she was speaking more to herself than to them. She leaned forward. "Kinley has brought us back to Bhutan, where we began our journey, to the place where Buddhism spread through this country. A poetic climax to our quest."

"Ah yes, so like Kinley."

"Are we heading to Tiger's Nest now?" Grant asked.

"Too late to begin the hike," Jigme said. "I'll drop you off at your hotel in town. We'll meet at the Paro Dzong at dawn."

Staring out the car's window at the cottages that dotted the green hills rising from the valley like Swiss chalets in the foothills of the Alps, Grant began to replay in his mind the scene of his reunion with Kinley: the questions he wanted to ask, the experiences from their journey he wanted to relate. But his questions were secondary. *By tomorrow—*

He closed his eyes. He was speculating about the future again, he realized. Playing movies in his head. *But*, he thought, *we are so close.*

CHAPTER 48

―❦―

TIGER'S NEST MONASTERY
PARO, BHUTAN

Twelve hours after his last hike up the same mountain, Tim once again crept along the narrow stone steps, hugging the cool granite wall to his left. On this trip, however, it was pitch black, and he didn't have a guide to lead him. Tripping in the darkness would have tragic consequences; the edge of the steps dropped to the valley floor two thousand feet below him. He paused to catch his breath, which cast a light green fog through the viewfinder of the night vision monocular he held to his eye. Cocking his head to listen, he heard only the gurgling of the small waterfall he'd just passed.

One last flight of steps to go. Ahead of him, the monastery stood as dark and quiet as the night itself. He pulled back the sleeve of his black wool coat and the black sweater underneath it. It was two AM. The monks would be asleep and unsuspecting.

Before climbing the final steps, Tim reviewed his inventory. Tonight would be simple and efficient—no fancy drugs in EpiPens and no gimmicks like the snake, although holding the shaking basket over the professor's face had given him quite a rush. Tonight the only weapons Tim carried were the knife strapped to his leg and the forty-caliber Glock he held in his gloved hand. Tonight he would tolerate no mistakes, no hesitations. Tonight no one would be left alive.

A few hours earlier, Tim had stolen a scooter, one of many parked at his hotel in town. He'd hidden it just off the road in the woods, at the trailhead for the shortcut he'd taken up the mountain. Once his mission was accomplished, he would race down the trail and drive the scooter onto the tarmac at the airport. His pilot had instructions to have the plane ready to depart at dawn. Tim would be airborne before anyone realized what had happened in the remote monastery. Then he would return to Birmingham and reap the glory of his success.

∽

Grant stared at the sun yellow wall opposite his twin bed. Above a wood-laminate dresser, the painting of a three-foot-long red dragon chasing its tail stared at him. He should be sleeping, but the lights on the outside of the hotel, shining into the room with no curtains, kept him awake.

He used the time to organize the thoughts that rolled across his mind like waves hitting the beach. Although he was so close, he wrestled with a new concern. With the strict Bhutanese laws against removing historical artifacts from the country, and the obvious hostility of Lama Dorji, how would they get the texts out of Bhutan, if indeed they found them at Tiger's Nest? They had Kristin's camera and two backup memory cards, but Grant suspected that after the negative publicity, only the actual books themselves would convince the naysayers.

"Are you awake?" Kristin's voice from the other twin bed startled him.

"You too?"

A breath of cool air touched him as the quilt covering his body lifted. He rolled over to face Kristin as she crawled onto the narrow mattress beside him.

"Hi," he said, pleasantly surprised at the smooth skin of her legs next to his. He wore only boxers.

"Do you mind?"

His hand traced the bruise along her cheek. "Does it hurt?"

"Not anymore." Her body was warm, and it seemed to him that the two of them fit on the narrow bed like two puzzle pieces joined together.

He moved a few strands of hair that had fallen in front of her face, and then, as if drawn magnetically, he brushed his lips against her upturned face. He kissed the bruise, then her jaw, and then her neck just below her ear. Her body arched subtly. He dropped his hand from the soft curls of her hair to the soft curve of her waist.

"Look, Kris," he whispered. "I mean Kristin . . ."

"You called me that in Varanasi too."

"Sorry."

"No, it's okay now." Her voice was breathy. "I find it comforting. Reminds me of my sister."

She raised herself onto her elbow and then pushed him back into the firm mattress. She rolled on top of him. The only fabric separating their bodies was her thin T-shirt and the cotton shorts each wore. The sensation of her body pressed into his sent a current of electricity through his core.

Her eyes locked on to his. "I'm ready," she said.

CHAPTER 49

⊷⊶

TIGER'S NEST MONASTERY
PARO, BHUTAN

UMMON SAT ON HIS REED MAT, rubbing his eyes. He closed his crimson robes around his small body. The winter cold was moving in quickly. Soon the mountain would be covered in snow. Ummon glanced at the three empty sleeping mats in the room. He looked forward to the older monks, who should have been there beside him, returning from town in the morning. They had left earlier in the day to restock the monastery's supplies. One would bring dry wood for the stove. He glanced at the profiles of the only two other occupants in the dormitory room. One belonged to an elder monk, whose advanced age relieved him from the duty of the long hike into town. The other was Ummon's snoring teacher. Kinley was more like a father to the eleven-year-old than his own father. Since the day four years ago when his parents brought him to the monastery, Ummon had only seen his family twice a year. The youngest of three brothers, he wasn't needed on their small farm.

Although studying to be a monk was boring at times, he generally enjoyed the *goemba*. Kinley's other students had become his new family, and they didn't pick on him the way his older brothers had. Jigme was Ummon's favorite. He wondered why Kinley hadn't brought his senior student to Taktshang with them, but he knew not to question Kinley about such things. While Ummon was happy that his teacher was finally back from the travels that had taken him away several times these past few weeks, he looked forward to returning to the warmer Punakha valley and to his friend Jigme. After all, the older monks who lived at Taktshang preferred to spend long hours playing dice games instead of kicking around a ball with him.

Ummon tiptoed to a small door at the rear of their dorm room. He opened it slowly so that no noise would wake the sleeping men. One advantage of being little was that he could take the shortcut to the latrine; the door was just one meter square and meant to be an emergency fire escape. Once outside, he shuffled along the narrow ledge at the back of the building. Then he climbed the ladder to the next higher level, where the single toilet was located.

Ummon opened the red swinging door of the closet-sized latrine and flicked the light switch. Nothing. He shook his head. The bulb had been out for three days now. He would have volunteered to change it, but he was too short to reach it. He left the door open to let in the dim starlight from the clear sky. Squinting his eyes, he could barely make out the footrests in the ground. He had to be careful not to step into the hole itself. The old monks would get a laugh out of that.

The explosions that pierced the silence of the night startled Ummon so badly that he misdirected his stream of pee down the side of his robes. Terrified, he placed a hand on the wall to steady his shaking body. The noises sounded like fireworks going off inside the *goemba*. Was the monastery exploding? Ummon knew that Taktshang had been severely damaged by fire before; in fact, it had only reopened recently after decades of rebuilding.

The image of being trapped inside the *goemba* as it tumbled down the mountainside in a burning heap snapped Ummon out of his paralyzed state. Closing his robes, he raced out of the bathroom and slid down the ladder. *I have to warn them!*

As he reached the ledge at the rear of the dorm building, Ummon opened his mouth to shout for the two elders to wake up when he realized two things. First, he didn't detect any evidence of a fire. No smell of smoke, no glowing flames, nothing. Second, in place of the sounds of the explosions, which had disappeared as quickly as they had startled him, Ummon heard screaming voices through the dorm walls. Something was wrong inside the building. Ummon knelt silently outside the small door.

He heard voices in English, a language he recognized but didn't yet speak. He'd last heard it when Grant, the friendly American with the broken leg, was recovering in Punakha. Although students in Bhutan studied English in school, for a monk living in a monastery, English was not a regular subject. Kinley had promised to teach him as he grew older.

Pressing his ear to the cracked wood, Ummon heard that one of the voices belonged to Kinley, but it contained a tone Ummon had never heard before, a deep sorrow. He didn't recognize the other voice, but it sounded angry. He knew immediately that his teacher needed help.

Ummon twisted the handle of the square door, opening it a crack. For the rest of his life, Ummon would never forget the scene inside. He bit his lip to suppress the scream that desperately wanted out of his body. The old monk who had been sleeping by him lay on his back in a contorted position. A pool of blood the same color as his robe spread outward along the floor. Ummon's stomach lurched into his throat. He swallowed back the acidic bile. The gentle man's eyes were open, staring unblinking at the ceiling.

Kinley thankfully was alive. Kneeling in the center of the room, the monk faced the rear wall where Ummon watched through the crack in the doorway. The look of sadness and pain on his mentor's face disturbed Ummon almost as much as the gruesome death before him.

Ummon's heart threatened to explode out of his slight chest. Standing in front of Kinley with his back to the boy was the Dark One himself. *Mara, the God of Death.* Ummon had seen the murals on the walls of the dzong that depicted him with multiple horned heads, fangs, and flames for hair, but in person he was simpler, and much more terrifying to the eleven-year-old.

He was dressed in black as dark as the night itself from his boots to his clothes and even to the cap on his head; the only skin exposed was the demon's neck and face, which Ummon caught a glimpse of when he paced in front of Kinley. The Dark One's skin was flushed almost as red as the depictions Ummon had seen on the temple walls, and it had a scaly appearance, like a serpent's. The man yelled at Kinley with such a force that spit flew from his mouth as he shouted. A gap in the front of his mouth, where teeth should be, added to his snakelike appearance.

Watching his teacher's suffering pained Ummon deep in his chest. But what could he do? He was frightened as he'd never been in his life; he was so scared that as much as he wanted to turn and run down the mountain, his limbs were frozen where he crouched.

The slapping sound of a blow from the hand of Mara stung Ummon almost as much as it must have hurt his teacher. Kinley rocked backward from the strike. As soon as Kinley righted himself, the man struck a second time, but this time with his opposite hand, the one holding the gun—the gun which must have killed the eldest monk. This second blow landed with a harder sound that sent Kinley sprawling to the floor. A whimper escaped Ummon's lips, causing him to clasp his hand over his mouth. Kinley, on the other hand, was silent and still.

Please, don't be dead, Ummon prayed.

After a moment, his prayer was answered. Lying face down with his hands secured behind his back, Kinley stirred. He rolled to his side, gathered his legs underneath him, and rose to his knees. Ummon had never seen such a thing. His teacher must be suffering greatly. His brother lay murdered beside him; his swollen face now bled from the blows he'd endured, but he showed no outward signs of pain. Kinley gazed at the demon with the same sad but passive expression he'd worn a minute ago. When he finally spoke, he did so in a quiet, calm tone. Something about Kinley's manner angered the man even more. He hit Kinley again and again.

Ummon closed his eyes. His mind raced. He had to do something. Only he could save his teacher. He opened his eyes and searched the room. Not ten paces from him in the rear corner sat the wood-burning stove they used to cook their meals and heat their living quarters. Next to the stove was the heavy iron poker the elders used to stir the fire. It would have to do.

Kinley fell to the floor again. While he was attempting to right himself, the beast walked to the front wall, where he studied the long bow and quiver of arrows that hung by the main door. A gift from the national champion archery team, the display was merely something to enjoy, not to use. Monks were forbidden from participating in Bhutan's national sport, as Ummon had learned when he'd been disciplined for handling an arrow shortly after arriving. But the bow and arrows now provided Ummon with the opportunity he needed. The demon's back was to him. If he moved quickly and quietly, he could be inside the room and to the iron poker before the man turned around.

Ummon swung the door open slowly to avoid making any noise. Just as he ducked his head to clear the sill and enter the room, Kinley looked up. His teacher's expression changed instantly from weariness to fear. Ummon pointed to the iron poker and then back to the demon, letting his teacher know his rescue plan. To Ummon's surprise, Kinley shook his head violently. He then mouthed the words, "Bring help."

But there's not enough time, Ummon thought. His teacher must be confused from the blows to his head. He climbed through the trapdoor. Kinley's eyes grew wide. Ummon had never seen his teacher afraid before. Kinley glanced over his shoulder at the demon, who was mumbling to himself while pulling two arrows from the quiver. Ummon only needed a few more steps, and he would have his weapon.

Kinley turned to the boy. The fear vanished from his face and was replaced with the determined look Ummon knew too well. His teacher mouthed the words, "Leave. Now."

The command could not have been more authoritative had Kinley yelled it at the top of his lungs. Ummon glanced at the poker. So close. But he knew not to challenge his teacher. In a second, he was back through the trapdoor. As he reached to close it, the demon began to turn around. Ummon's breath caught in his throat. *I'll be seen!*

Kinley faced the Dark One and said something in a voice as strong as the command he'd silently given Ummon. Before the small door closed cutting off his view, Ummon watched the demon look at Kinley in confusion. Although his teacher was the one in need of rescuing, he had just saved his student.

Ummon navigated the narrow ledge faster than he'd ever done before. When he reached the front corner of the building, he climbed down the wooden structure to the rocks underneath the stairway. He stumbled a few times, cutting his shins on the sharp granite as he circumvented the section of stairs where the demon would be able to see him from the open door. Once he was clear of the dorm, he climbed to the stone stairs, taking them two at a time until they ended at the cafeteria. Then he turned down the path that would get him to the bottom of the mountain the fastest. His chances of navigating the steep trail in the moonless night without falling and breaking his leg were not good, but Kinley's life now depended on him.

CHAPTER 50

——◦◦◦◦——

TIGER'S NEST MONASTERY
PARO, BHUTAN

TIM FELT THE RAZOR TIP of the arrow with his finger. He then ran the arrow's shaft along his left forearm, which had started to itch ever so slightly. For a moment, he contemplated pulling up his coat sleeves and lightly scraping the edge of the arrow's tip across the dry scales of his skin, but he had other plans for the arrow.

Tim had grown tired of the silly mind games and doublespeak from the monk. He'd underestimated the man's tolerance for pain, but anyone could be broken. When he turned around, he glimpsed an emotion he hadn't seen yet from the monk—fear. His techniques were starting to work.

"I've lost my patience with you, monk. Where are the Jesus books?"

"I have already told you I am not in possession of them."

"That wasn't my question," Tim spat out. He bent forward so that he was level with Kinley. He brought the arrow to within an inch of the monk's eye. "Will you be so clever when I gouge out your eyeball?"

"You must do what you must do."

Tim felt a burning that radiated from his arms, up his shoulders to his neck, and then out the top of his scalp. He rotated the arrow with a flick of his wrist, and he thrust it deep into Kinley's thigh. He waited for the shriek of agony but was only rewarded with a slight tremor that passed through the monk's body. The extent to which the monk endured physical pain wasn't natural.

The monk gazed at Tim, sweat dripping from his temples. "Does causing me pain serve to lessen your own?"

Once again, Tim was confounded by this strange man. "My own what?"

"Your pain. I can sense it in you as readily as I can sense my own suffering. Your emotions have blinded you to what is good and true in the world. All you see is hatred and fear, and they consume you. But you do not have to suffer so. There is another way."

How dare this foreigner presume to know what I'm feeling! Tim didn't operate by his emotions like some helpless woman. Everything he did was planned, based on information he'd gathered and organized. If anything, he was devoid of weak emotions. To prove the point, he would teach this monk about his capabilities.

Tim grasped the arrow and, while holding the monk's gaze, he twisted it back and forth, working the razor tip further into the quadriceps muscle. Blood began to flow freely from the wound. But only silence came from his captive.

"Scream, damn it!"

Kinley's complexion had paled, and sweat now soaked his orange robes. With a final quick twist of the arrow, Tim watched the monk's eyelids flutter and then close. His body slumped forward onto the wooden floor.

"No!" Tim screamed. His only source of information about the texts lay unconscious at his feet. Tim hadn't planned on Kinley's being able to withstand torture to this extent. The monk was using some kind of mind trick to avoid the pain, just like Tim had seen in old kung fu movies.

Grimacing at the crumpled mass in a robe on the dorm room floor, Tim realized his mistake. He'd thought that shooting the old monk would lessen the risk that the man would turn on him or try to escape. The old monk was frail and no match for Tim, but he'd learned his lesson in Varanasi about the consequences of playing cat and mouse with one's victims: sometimes the mouse got away. He'd also calculated that the quick death of the other monk would make Kinley fear for his own life. Tim realized now that a more effective strategy would have been to threaten to kill the old man if Kinley didn't reveal the location of the texts. The monk was one of those soft types who cared more about those around him than himself. If all humans behaved that way, Tim thought, we would still be living in caves. Survival of the fittest. For all the nonsense Darwin wrote about, that had been one solid theory. Tim glanced at the other empty mats in the room. Kinley had explained that the other monks who usually slept there had gone into town to gather provisions for the monastery—a two-day process. At least Tim had caught a break there.

No matter, he thought. He would tear apart the monastery temple by temple, room by room. Certainly Kinley had brought the texts with him here. The cliffside monastery was the perfect hiding place. *But how long will it take?* He had a few hours left before dawn, and he wasn't sure when the other monks would return after that. But the monastery wasn't that large. He would just have to be systematic.

Tim unclipped the night vision monocular hanging from his backpack and pocketed it. Next he unzipped the main compartment, moved aside the rope he'd purchased that afternoon at the hardware shop, and grabbed the duct tape he'd brought from India. He wrapped the tape around Kinley's ankles five times, so tightly that it dug into the monk's skin. Tim didn't think Kinley would go anywhere with the arrow in his leg, but he wasn't going to take any chances this time.

Grant fumbled in the dark, randomly punching buttons on the alarm clock, trying to silence it. *Morning already?* He read the glowing green numbers on the clock: 3:16. He and Kristin had collapsed, sweaty, exhausted, and fulfilled, only an hour earlier. When his mind cleared, Grant realized that the alarm clock wasn't ringing; the hotel phone was.

"Hello?" he croaked into the receiver.

"Grant, it's Jigme. Something terrible has happened."

Grant bolted upright, flicking the switch on the cord of the bedside lamp. Kristin rolled toward him, shielding her eyes.

"What is it?" Grant asked.

"An attack on the monastery."

"An attack? In Punakha?" Grant asked, confused.

"Taktshang."

"Tiger's Nest?" The light of realization pierced the darkness of sleep in his brain. He was afraid of what Jigme's answer would be to his next question: "Kinley?"

"We don't know. Ummon was there when a man attacked the dorm. The man killed the other monk sleeping with them, and he was beating Kinley severely when the boy escaped. He ran all the way down the mountain. He thinks he saw a demon."

"A demon. Are you thinking what I am?"

"It must be him."

"Jigme, we have to go there right away."

"We're assembling a party right now. The police should arrive in a few minutes. I'm going up with them."

Grant stood and hopped into his jeans. "We'll grab a taxi and meet you there."

"Kristin?"

"As much as I'd like to persuade her to stay here," he said, turning to the bed where she sat watching him with an alarmed expression, "I don't think there's a chance she will."

"Kinley," he said when he hung up the phone. The fog of sleep had completely dissipated from his mind. Instead, a feeling of dread ached through his core. His mind raced with memories of the gentle and kind man who had saved his life, carried him from the river to the dzong, and sat by his bed each day while he recovered. A man who had carefully rescued a ladybug from the leaf of the plant in his room, a man who had patiently taught Grant about Buddhism even when Grant had resisted the teachings. Now this man, this peaceful monk, was suffering in a remote monastery on the side of a mountain, and Grant had brought the killer there. *Please God*, he prayed silently for the first time in many years. *Please let us not be too late.*

CHAPTER 51

———⟨∞⟩———

TIGER'S NEST MONASTERY
PARO, BHUTAN

"GODDAMN IT!" Tim's voice echoed through the empty worship hall.
He kicked a large chunk of plaster from the shattered six-foot-tall idol he'd just cast down from its perch on the marble altar. The statue's hand skidded across the floor. He was supposed to be long finished with his mission by now. He glanced out the temple's open door. Still dark, but first light would arrive shortly. Searching the monastery had been more of a challenge than he'd expected. Starting on the fifth level, he'd only made it down to the third in over two hours. Stairways and ladders connected a maze of rooms and temples. Concealed doorways led through windowless passages into other small temples.

He'd visited Kinley several times to no avail. Using a second arrow in the monk's other leg produced the same results as the first. Infuriated, Tim had twisted the arrow deeply, resulting in a spurt of blood that almost hit him in the face. *Must have pierced the femoral artery*, he thought. The monk was unconscious, probably for the last time.

After scratching his arms vigorously, Tim flung a copper offering bowl from the altar against the wall. *What had gone wrong?* He'd carefully planned the logistics. He had years of training, planning, and most important, God to his advantage. Even if he'd made some mistakes, he'd quickly adapted to the unforeseen and made the best out of adversity.

He shook his head. The texts must be hidden on a lower level. He knew from the early press reports as well as from the intelligence provided to him that he was looking for a number of narrow old books with wooden covers wrapped in silk scarves. He'd seen nothing like that, but he still had time. Before leaving the temple, he held the night vision monocular to his right eye. In other rooms it had revealed temperature differences in the walls, leading him to hidden passageways. Seeing none here, he turned to the door. The monocular flashed brightly.

"Shit!"

A dozen flashlights bobbed along the stairs on the other side of the cliff, just beyond the cafeteria. They would arrive at the monastery in minutes.

How?

Tim flew down the steps. He stopped just above the dormitory where the monk lay dying. If he descended the last flight, the light from the open doorway would illuminate him. He had to make a decision quickly. Watching the number of flashlights approaching, he realized he could never fight them all.

But he'd come prepared. During his afternoon reconnaissance, he'd discovered that relying on one means of egress from the monastery, the stone steps, would be foolish. He shrugged off his backpack and yanked out the hundred-and-fifty-foot-long rope. He hoped it would be long enough. He stuck his head over the stairway railing. The granite dropped for at least sixty feet, but then outcroppings of rock began to jut out. The darkness made it difficult to judge the distance, but he thought he spotted a series of ledges about twenty feet or so farther down that should lead to the other side of the cliff. If he were lucky, the ledges would go as far as the restaurant, where he could find his way to the trail below.

After pushing on the stair railing to test its strength, Tim threaded the rope through four of its thick wooden stanchions and tied off the end using a double figure eight knot. He tossed the rope over the edge of the railing and watched it disappear in the void below. Unless they shined their lights directly on this spot, they would never notice the rope until the morning.

Tim placed his hands on the railing ready to climb, but then he paused to peer at the dorm building one flight below him.

Kinley. The stubborn monk was probably still alive. Tim hesitated. He couldn't see the beams from the flashlights anymore, which meant they had rounded the crevice in the cliff where the steps crossed the small waterfall. They were very close. Could he risk a few seconds to run down and slit Kinley's throat? He was the true source of the lies about Jesus, the blasphemy that must be stopped. Plus, something about that monk wasn't natural. The last words the monk had uttered before falling unconscious were unsettling. He had looked at Tim with a strange expression: was it pity? *But why would the monk have felt pity for me when he's the one who has lost everything?* Tim figured that he was being condescended to, just as he so often had been by all the people who underestimated him. Then Kinley had said, "It is all right. I forgive you."

The shouting voices that echoed up to him from the monastery gate on the other side of the dorm precipitated his decision for him. Tim pulled on his black gloves, slung his backpack over his shoulders, swung his legs over the railing and began smoothly lowering himself down the cliff just as he'd practiced in basic training. *He'll be dead soon*, he reasoned.

Grant was out of breath, and his leg was throbbing. With the atrophy in his right quadriceps, he struggled to keep up with Kristin's athletic strides as they ascended the dark steps below the monastery. The motivation of reaching his friend in time pushed him through the pain. Four police officers and eight monks preceded them by a few minutes. The hotel's night clerk had somehow persuaded a taxi to pick them up and take them directly to the trailhead, where Jigme waited. Grant tried not to imagine what they might find when they reached the monastery. He focused on his breath, just as Kinley had taught him.

"There." Kristin pointed to the lowest of the monastery buildings, from which a glowing light spilled out through its open doorway. Grant heard shouting ahead.

"That's the dormitory. That's where Ummon left Kinley," Jigme said.

Two minutes later Grant stepped to the doorway of the one-room building, blinking his eyes to adjust to the light. At first he had trouble interpreting the chaos of activity taking place. The room was awash in the flowing crimson robes of the monks as well as the blue and white uniforms of two police officers. One of the officers spoke rapidly into a handheld radio, presumably to the other two policemen in their party who were searching the monastery levels above them. The monks shouted at each other in frightened Bhutanese.

The other officer met them at the doorway holding his arms out to block entrance into the dorm. As the officer and Jigme exchanged words, the scene came into focus for Grant. Four of the monks carried the body of their fallen brother to one side of the room, where they carefully laid him on reed mats. The other four monks circled around what had to be Kinley, dressed in orange, lying in the center of the floor. Grant's stomach lurched.

He shoved past the protesting officer who blocked the doorway. Kristin bolted into the center of the room after him.

"No!" she cried.

Grant's pulse pounded from his chest to his head. He stepped into the circle of monks. Kinley's normally robust complexion had turned ashen; his robes were soaked in blood. Two arrows stuck upright, buried inches into each thigh. Three monks knelt by his legs, pressing around the arrow wounds, while a fourth who looked to be a couple of years younger than Jigme cradled Kinley's head.

"Is he alive?" Grant croaked. For once, he didn't try to disguise the emotions welling up within him.

Jigme appeared by his side, speaking in Bhutanese to the younger monk. "He's unconscious, barely breathing."

"Can't they remove the arrows?" Kristin asked. She knelt and took Kinley's hand.

"Not here," Jigme said, surveying Kinley's legs. "The arrows are barbed. Pulling them out would tear his veins and arteries. If we could get him to a hospital, a doctor could surgically remove them."

"What if we can't get him there in time?" Grant remembered his own accident and how he had to remain in the monastery in Punakha. But surely Paro had to have modern medical facilities? Then he thought about the difficult hike up the mountain.

Jigme grimaced. "The alternative is to break the arrows in half and push them out the other side, but in his current state, doing so would cause too much blood loss. Controlling the bleeding is the best we can do for now."

The back of Grant's throat burned, making it difficult to swallow. His friend had saved his life, and now Grant was helpless to aid him. Then he noticed that the monk's ankles were tightly bound by duct tape. Grant dropped to his knees by Kinley's feet. Just as he'd done with Kristin only a few days earlier, he began to unwrap the tape. He moved slowly so that that he wouldn't disturb the arrows embedded in Kinley's thighs. He felt Kinley's calf muscle. The skin was cool to the touch. Not a good sign, he knew. The other monks cast wary glances at Grant, no doubt suspicious of the fact that he was a foreigner.

When he finished removing the tape, he balled it up and tossed it to the corner of the room. He wiped his sticky hands on his jeans and noticed that the denim was soaked through the knees with Kinley's blood. He rose and moved to Kristin's side where she sat softly crying, caressing Kinley's arm. Grant placed a hand on his friend's chest. His mind raced to figure out a way they could carry Kinley off the mountain without causing him any more harm. Then Grant felt a movement he wasn't sure was real or imagined. Kinley's chest seemed to expand, as if he was drawing in a deep breath.

Grant bent over the monk's pallid face. "Kinley, can you hear me? We're here for you."

The raspy voice that came from his teacher's mouth startled him. "What took you so long?"

Hope surged through Grant. Kinley was conscious. The monk was strong. "Well, you monks didn't exactly build this monastery in the most convenient of places." Grant smiled through his tears.

Kinley opened his eyes—eyes that were clear and knowing. Through chapped lips, Kinley returned Grant's smile. Grant addressed the young monk kneeling by Kinley's head. "Water. He needs water." He seemed to understand and jumped to search the room.

"Wait, I think I have some." Kristin pulled a half-filled plastic bottle from the daypack she'd carried up the mountain. She lifted Kinley's head and helped him drink. Tears rolled down her cheeks. "Are you in much pain?"

"No, I am not," he said hoarsely. "My body, on the other hand, has seen better times."

"I wish I could remember." She began to sob. "When I was his prisoner and unconscious, I . . . I must have said something about this place. All of this death. I'm so sorry."

"My dear"—Kinley squeezed her hand—"it is I who am sorry. When I sent you two on this journey, I meant for it to be an eye-opening experience. I was naïve, for I had no idea that it would lead to this suffering. Please do not cry for me. We will all die. My time just happens to be tonight.

"You will not die tonight," Grant said, sitting up straighter. "We are going to carry you down the mountain." Then he noticed a broom in one corner of the room. *That's it*, he thought. Knowing how fastidious the monks were about keeping the *goembas* clean, he imagined that several other brooms could be found. The plan formed quickly. They would fashion a stretcher from the broomsticks and the robes of the monks. Four men would carry the stretcher down, and the police would have an ambulance waiting at the base of the mountain.

"I think we both know that I've lost too much blood."

Grant let his eyes fall to the puddle that was still spreading around Kinley's legs, in spite of the efforts of the three monks putting pressure on the wounds. He felt the wetness on his jeans. The hope he'd held moments before began to slip away. "But you can't die," Grant said, as if the force of the words would make it so.

Kinley's eyes fluttered closed. Grant's heart skipped a beat until his friend blinked them open again. "What is the true nature of your journey, Grant?"

Grant was caught off guard. Even close to death, Kinley had not lost his knack for posing vague questions, but they didn't have time to sit here and discuss another one of the monk's koans. They needed to get him off the mountain. Grant opened his mouth to protest, but the determined expression on Kinley's face caused him to close his mouth and consider the question. The first response to pop into his head was the obvious one—to find the Issa texts—but he dismissed it as too trivial. He considered next the journey that brought him from Bhutan through India and then back again. *Is he referring to my crash course on the interconnectedness of religion? Maybe the lessons of the similar mystical experiences shared by the Buddha, Jesus, and Muhammad?*

Kristin cleared her throat and tugged on Grant's arm. He was wasting precious time. Kinley's patient expression, however, communicated that he had all day to wait for Grant's mind to churn through the possibilities. Ultimately Grant realized that each of these answers captured part of the truth but none entirely. He also knew that Kinley did not like to receive ten answers to a single question. He had learned so much since his fateful kayaking trip, but then there had been so much suffering too. *Jigme's shooting. Kristin's attack.* He thought of Deepraj, Razi, and the old monk on the other side of the room. These men had sacrificed their lives for the lessons they had imparted to him. Too high a price. *What am I doing here?*

"I don't know," he answered in a low voice.

"Exactly!" Kinley's own voice contained a strength that belied his condition. "Not knowing is the ultimate truth."

"But after everything we've experienced—"

"Ah yes, the most important lesson you have learned is that you still do not know. After a lifetime of study and meditation, I have realized that sometimes it is better to stop seeking the answers, stop asking the questions. Just be."

Grant had not expected this response. For so long he'd searched for answers or, at the minimum, for the path that would lead him to the answers he needed. Something in Kinley's simple statement, however, resonated with him. Maybe he'd been trying too hard. *Grasping.*

Kneeling beside his dying teacher, Grant felt a strong sense of déjà vu: he himself lying crippled in a Bhutanese monastery, struggling to solve riddles that had no answer. But now Grant was the healthy one, and Kinley was incapacitated. He recalled one of the koans that Kinley had posed to him in what seemed like another lifetime.

"When the tree withers and the leaves fall . . ." Grant began.

"The body is exposed in the autumn wind," Kinley finished. "The answers you seek, my friend. Look first to your questions. The source of both is the same."

Although he was still bundled up in his fleece and jacket, Grant felt naked before Kinley. He sensed Kristin's questioning expression, but he wasn't sure that he could explain to her why what Kinley said suddenly made sense to him.

Kinley drew in a deep breath, but instead of exhaling, tremors of deep coughs shook his body. He winced in pain. Kristin exchanged a worried look with Grant. "What can we do to make you more comfortable?" she asked, offering him another sip of water.

"Having my friends here is enough." They both had to lean forward to hear the monk.

Grant's throat constricted. He knew that despite his desperate wishes, his friend did not have much time left.

"The books . . ." Kinley said.

"Are they still here?" Grant asked.

"The tiger's lair."

"Huh?" Grant and Kristin said in unison.

Kinley's eyes refocused. "You came here because of the mural in Sarnath?"

"Yes," Kristin said. "We recognized the image of Padmasambhava flying on the back of a tiger to the cave on the side of this mountain."

"The tiger's lair," Jigme said, nodding his head. "Now I understand." Grant turned to him. Jigme had been so quiet that Grant had forgotten that Kinley's longest student had been observing these exchanges in silence. The younger monk continued, "What better place to store the texts that describe Issa learning the teachings of the Buddha than the place where Padmasambhava meditated before spreading Buddhism to our country?"

"The cave exists?" Grant asked. "I assumed it was just a myth."

Jigme shook his head. "We can get into it through a concealed door in one of the lower temples."

Jigme spoke in Bhutanese to the oldest of the monks who stood by Kinley. The monk responded in an irritated tone, gesturing to Grant and Kristin. Jigme started to argue when Kinley lifted his head a few inches and spoke a few authoritative words that silenced both of them. The elder monk left the room. Jigme helped Kinley lower his head to the floor. The two spoke for a minute. Jigme concentrated on every word his master said, as if each held a little piece of magic.

When he finished speaking with Jigme, Kinley's breathing became more labored. Kristin leaned forward and kissed his forehead. Tears fell from her cheeks again. Grant opened his mouth to say something comforting, but he couldn't make any words come out.

"Thank you for believing in us," Kristin said.

Kinley smiled at her and then shifted his eyes to Grant. His voice came out in a whisper. "I've always known the importance of these texts. I was just waiting for the right person to find them." He closed his eyes and exhaled.

Kristin stroked the graying stubble on his head with her hand. "Save your energy, don't speak."

But Grant knew that the energy had finally left his friend.

CHAPTER 52

TIGER'S NEST MONASTERY
PARO, BHUTAN

THE ROOM WAS STILL. As Grant watched the last breath escape from Kinley's lips, a word popped into his head. *Nephesh.* The breath of God. But the spark of the divine in Kinley was lit no more. The monk's face appeared relaxed, the corners of his mouth turned slightly upward, as if his last moment held a bit of humor for him.

Grant had just lost a friend and a teacher. Watching Kinley accept his own death with such a sense of peace brought Grant an unexpected comfort. Up to the moment of death, Kinley cared more about imparting a last bit of wisdom to his students than he worried about his own fate.

"Good-bye, my friend," Grant said, giving Kinley's shoulder a final squeeze. He stood and then helped Kristin, whose body shook with quiet sobs, to her feet. He didn't bother to disguise or to wipe the tears from his own cheeks.

As the monks began to remove the arrows from Kinley's legs and wrap him in his robes, a sound rose from the circle of men. The monks began to chant. Each monk, including Jigme, sang. Their voices harmonized, until the vibrations of the chant filled every corner of the room, and every corner of Grant's body.

"I can't believe he's gone," Kristin said, leaning on the wooden railing outside the dormitory.

"I know." Grant put his arms around her from behind. "These last few weeks I've been thinking of the questions I wanted to ask him, and now—"

She straightened and leaned her head back against his chest. To Grant, the lights of the town of Paro in the valley far below reminded him of fireflies dancing through the warm air on a summer night. A strange comparison, he thought, considering that the temperature had dropped about thirty degrees since the afternoon, and the wailing wind blowing from the valley pierced his layers of clothing.

Shuffling from the steps above drew their attention. Someone was coming from the upper levels of the monastery. Grant realized that they hadn't yet heard from the two officers who were searching the temples. He felt Kristin tense.

The figure who emerged from the darkness, however, was the monk whom Kinley had spoken to a few minutes earlier. A leather lanyard swayed from his closed fist. The monk glared at the two Americans before he disappeared into the lit doorway.

A few moments later, Jigme emerged wearing the lanyard around his neck. A single skeleton key dangled from its end. "Come with me," he said in a hushed voice.

They followed him up the staircase. Kristin stayed at Grant's side, allowing him to put a little weight on her arm. His leg had stiffened from the climb, and he was limping now.

"The texts?" she asked.

"We are about to enter the tiger's lair," Jigme replied.

After everything they'd been through, they were finally here, Grant realized. Kinley had given up his life protecting the texts. Grant couldn't help but feel that his sacrifice was too big and that the texts weren't worth all the lives that had been lost. Following the beam cast by Jigme's flashlight, they navigated around granite boulders which rose in the center of the passage. The monastery walls around them appeared to grow from the cliff itself, an illusion dispelled only by the uniformity of the masonry work and the colorful murals painted from floor to ceiling.

Stopping on the second level, Jigme turned to his right and descended a separate narrow wooden staircase, rather than continuing up the main stairs to the higher levels above them.

Another memory came to Grant. "Kristin, in the Punakha library Kinley spoke of growth being like climbing a staircase."

"That's right," she said. "After some point, we reach a landing. Some choose to remain on the landing where they're comfortable. Kinley challenged us to keep climbing to the next level and the one above that."

Jigme nodded. "That analogy was one of his favorites. Whenever I became too prideful of my progress, he would remind me that there was always another stairway to climb, another plateau to reach. Well, tonight"—he pointed to the stone landing at the foot of the stairs—"we must go down in order to go up."

Then a beam of light hit Grant square in the face.

Blinded, he simultaneously grabbed for both Kristin and the wooden railing. A voice shouted from behind the white light.

Jigme answered from the step below. The light swung from Grant's face, but the starburst pattern remained in his vision for several moments. The voice responded in a friendlier tone of Bhutanese.

"Grant and Kristin, this is Sangay," Jigme said, introducing them to the man with the intense flashlight who stood on a landing on the upper staircase. "He's the son of my mother's sister."

"Ah, your cousin," Kristin said, relief in her voice.

"That's right, cousin. He lives here in Paro. A policeman."

When Grant's eyes adjusted, he saw that two men stood on the floor above them, dressed in the same blue and white garb as the officers in the dormitory hall.

"Did they find anything?" Grant asked, also relieved.

Jigme spoke to his cousin, and then translated. "The *goemba* is empty, but someone searched the temples, leaving a path of destruction behind." He spoke again with his cousin. "Having Sangay here will help us. Come, we must be quick."

While the two officers waited outside, Jigme led Grant and Kristin through a thick red door at the bottom of the stairs into a temple not too much bigger than their hotel room. The glow of Jigme's light illuminated a blue plaster statue that Grant recognized as Padmasambhava behind a stone altar at the far end of the room. The floor was wooden and the walls were covered in silk, giving the temple a softer feel than the rest of the monastery. Jigme recited a short mantra and then prostrated himself on the ground before the statue. On rising, he went to the left wall and parted the silk fabric, exposing a heavy whitewashed door. While Jigme removed the skeleton key from his neck and worked it in the large padlock, Grant peered through the six-inch square opening crisscrossed with iron bars at eye level in the door.

"The cave?" he asked. The only interior detail he could make out in the darkness was a single candle flame, which flickered, as if suspended in midair. He thought that he could almost feel the warmth of this light, as if it burned inside him rather than in the cool air of the cave before them.

"Over twelve hundred years ago, Padmasambhava sat here for three months, alone and silent, deep in meditation," Jigme said with reverence.

"Just as Muhammad did two hundred years before him on Mount Hira," Kristin said softly.

Jigme removed the lock and swung open the heavy door. The temple walls were built flush into the rock. They stepped into a twenty-foot-deep cave in the side of the cliff. Surrounded by black granite, the air was dry and cool but not cold. Grant could now see that the candle, which had appeared to float in midair, actually sat on a small altar at the rear of the cave.

Jigme led them to the altar, which contained other unlit candles, incense burners, and a bowl for offerings. Grant examined the uneven stone floor beneath his feet. He imagined the guru sitting, legs crossed, eyes half closed, free from the distractions of life in the valley below.

Jigme disappeared behind the altar. "Here!" he cried. He bent over and lifted a wooden box.

"The box from the Punakha library!" Kristin said.

Jigme carried it to where they were standing, set it on the floor, and opened the latch.

"I can't believe it," she said. She gently picked up a narrow, silk-wrapped book while Jigme shined his light over them.

Grant's eyes fixated on the book in Kristin's hands. After all the sacrifices, they had the texts. "Jigme, do you read Pali?" he asked.

"Not as well as Kinley, but I can manage."

Grant consulted the mental checklist he'd reviewed countless times in anticipation of this moment. "We need to go through each book and confirm what we have," he said.

"Not here." Jigme closed the box and relatched it. "We need to move the texts quickly, without the other monks' knowledge."

"But I thought Kinley spoke to them about helping us," Kristin said. "The old guy even brought us the key to the cave."

"Kinley is no longer with us. Last night at the Paro dzong, I learned that the Je Khenpo himself assigned Kinley to watch over Taktshang Goemba. The other monks do not know anything about the Issa texts or why we needed the key to the cave. In light of what's happened, I think it prudent to keep it that way."

"What do you suggest?" Grant asked.

"My cousin and his partner will escort you down the mountain. They will carry the box. If anyone questions them, they'll say the box contains important evidence."

"You're coming with us, aren't you?" Kristin asked.

"As Kinley's senior student, I must stay here and help prepare his body for cremation. I will meet you in the afternoon."

"But the killer. He's still out there," she said.

"I know. That's why I want you and the books to leave with these officers. Both are armed and will protect you. I trust my cousin with my life. The other police will remain here with the monks and me."

"Where do we go?" Grant asked. "Somehow this guy knows our plans before we do. Our hotel isn't safe anymore."

"Agreed. You'll stay at my cousin's house. The man won't know to look for you there."

"Okay," Kristin said, "but somehow after all that's happened, that's not too comforting."

They descended the stone steps, leaving the monastery behind them. Jigme stopped in the open doorway of the dorm building, presumably telling his fellow monks that the Americans had suffered greatly by Kinley's loss and were being escorted down the mountain. His body obscured the view of Grant, Kristin, and the two officers passing with the box.

Grant and Kristin followed Sangay, who carried the books. His partner, a step ahead, lit the staircase with his powerful light. The image of the killer's face—the fiery complexion—burned in Grant's mind. *Who is he?* Grant wondered yet again. He glanced to his left at the void below the narrow steps. They had an hour-and-a-half hike down the mountain in the shadow of night, and this killer was out there somewhere. Although Grant was comforted that both officers were armed, he wished he were carrying a gun himself. He didn't have any real shooting experience beyond video games, but he felt the need to be able to protect Kristin and the texts himself.

Stepping carefully so he wouldn't trip on the uneven stones, Grant pondered how their lives had changed. After all they'd been through—the derision in America, the deaths of their friends in India and Bhutan—they finally possessed the books. This was the moment he'd dreamt about, a moment for which his entire academic career had prepped him. Although they still had a long way to go to bring the texts safely to the States, a new chapter of his life had begun, yet he didn't feel the excitement he'd always expected he'd feel.

His mind replayed their journey. By sending them to Agra, Varanasi, Sarnath, and Paro, Kinley had forced them to understand that neither the historical veracity of the stories of the great religions—the virgin births, the miracles, the flying tigers—nor the religious doctrines about the ancient prophets ultimately mattered. Instead the monk wanted them to learn from the spiritual connection each of these men shared through their similar mystical practices. Grant knew that Kinley wanted them to experience this same connection to the divine ground within themselves. But with the glow of the monastery fading behind him, the strange calm he'd felt at the moment of Kinley's death had passed and now he only felt regret and anger.

Why did my friend have to die?

The distant lights in the valley from the small town of Paro caught his attention. He stopped, allowing the others to proceed ahead, and followed the dancing lights with his eyes. Inhaling the brisk air, he recalled one of Kinley's favorite Chinese proverbs: "The finger pointing to the moon is not the moon itself." *Couldn't that same expression be applied to each of the prophets of old?* he wondered. Neither Muhammad, nor the Buddha, nor Padmasambhava, nor even Jesus was the moon itself. But each was a finger pointing to the moon—to the light in the darkness. Then he recalled the image of the lotus flower embedded in the wall of the Taj Mahal: beauty and life arising from the stagnant muddy water. He felt a stirring within.

Grant suddenly understood how much of his motivation in finding these texts came from a desire to prove his dead father wrong, a desire that he'd imprinted on Reverend Brady and other fundamentalists like him. Grant knew that even if scientific dating proved the texts to be of first-century origin, the Reverend Bradys of the world would still dispute their authenticity.

These narrow books are just another finger pointing to the moon, he thought.

Five minutes later they reached the last of the steps, where a small wooden building with a tin roof was perched on a spit of land jutting off the mountain. Sangay motioned to the door. "Water?" he asked.

Grant glanced at Kristin. They had a long hike back and needed to move quickly.

"Please," she said.

They entered the one-room restaurant. Jigme's cousin lowered the box of ancient texts onto the single table in the center of the room. Grant imagined how dishes would be laid out communal style on the table for the tourists who came to see the spectacular site of the monastery, but on this night the table was bare except for an oil lamp whose glass had yellowed with use. They left the lamp unlit because the three bare bulbs strung across the ceiling provided more than enough illumination. Grant watched Sangay walk to a small bar in the corner of the room by the door. He guessed that the large window to the right of the bar provided a spectacular view of Tiger's Nest during the daytime, but at night with the bulbs burning brightly, the only image in the window was his own disheveled reflection.

"The other officer?" Grant sat beside Kristin on a wooden bench against the wall. Although he was anxious to keep moving, his leg was throbbing. The hike up the mountain had taken its toll.

Sangay pointed toward the door. "Guarding outside."

"At least someone is finally taking our security seriously," Kristin said.

A thump echoed through the wall. Sangay placed the two bottles of water he'd just found on top of the bar. He called to his partner.

No answer.

Sangay drew his revolver and stepped from behind the bar. He held up a hand, indicating for Grant and Kristin to stay in place. Grant straightened, his sore leg momentarily forgotten. Sangay pushed the swinging door to the outside open with his left hand; his right held the gun by his side. The creaking of the rusty hinges was the only sound in the room.

Grant saw no sign of the other officer in the darkness. Sangay called into the night. Still no reply. He stepped outside, raising his weapon.

"See anything?" Grant asked. He stood and stepped forward.

"Nothing," Sangay said from outside. "Going to check corners. No move."

Grant opened his mouth to suggest radioing to the monastery, which was just a hundred yards away, but the door swung closed behind the officer. Grant glanced at the box on the table next to him. He made a quick decision. A half a minute later, he was back, standing next to where Kristin sat. When the door opened, Grant held his breath. He relaxed when Sangay appeared. *Maybe everything is normal.* But as soon as the thought occurred to him, he saw that everything wasn't normal.

The officer staggered into the room, a wild look in his eyes. No longer carrying his gun, he clutched his throat with both hands; his mouth worked wordlessly. A fraction of a second passed before Grant realized that Jigme's cousin had been wearing white, not red, gloves when he left the room. Kristin must have comprehended the same thing. Her scream pierced the silence.

Sangay fell to his knees. Blood ran freely from his neck down the front of his uniform like a faucet someone forgot to turn off. The officer's eyes seemed to apologize to them as his life slipped away.

The door opened again.

CHAPTER 53

⎯⎯⎯◈◈◈⎯⎯⎯

PARO, BHUTAN

THEIR PURSUER STOOD dressed in black like a shadow against the night behind him.

"Don't make another sound."

He leveled a black semiautomatic pistol at Kristin, whose scream caught in her throat the moment he turned the gun on her. In his other hand, a serrated commando knife dripped blood onto the wood-plank floor. Grant immediately saw that the killer's face had been disfigured from Kristin's beating.

Grant shifted sideways, placing his body between the gun and Kristin. "Who the hell are you?" he asked.

"Tim Huntley." The man pointed the pistol steadily at Grant's chest.

"You're one of Brian Brady's people?"

"*Reverend* Brady is a voice of God, and I am his servant!" Tim shouted. "You and your half-breed girlfriend are what's wrong with my country, poisoning people's minds. Jesus Christ is the one and only Son of God, and I will not let you take that away!"

Grant's mind raced. He needed to buy time, but he didn't want to push this man, who already seemed over the edge. *Did the officers in the monastery hear Kristin's scream?*

Kristin spoke in a remarkably calm voice from behind him. "All we want to do is to open people's minds to—"

"Shut up! I told *you* not to make another sound." Spit flew from his mouth. "Where are the Jesus books you got from the monk?"

Grant flinched at the mention of Kinley. His eyes narrowed at the man with the gun and the bloody knife. An intense heat spread outward from his core to his arms and legs. This son of a bitch had just killed Kinley and the elderly monk. He tortured the gentle professor in Varanasi and murdered Razi at the Taj Mahal. He would have raped and killed Kristin too had she not escaped.

Grant made his decision. He was going to fight back. "We never found the texts." Grant struggled to keep his voice level. He resisted the urge to glance either at the empty table in the center of the room or toward the bar in the corner where he'd moved the box. "Kinley died before he could tell us their location."

"I watched from the woods as the policeman carried a box inside here." The man sheathed the knife on his belt and strode toward them; the gun held steady in his hand. "Where is it?"

Grant felt a trickle of sweat form along his hairline, even though the unheated building was freezing. Kristin's breath came in rapid bursts behind him. He swallowed back the metallic flavor of fear on his tongue. If the man found what he was there for, he would kill them both.

Grant had only one option left. The assassin was a full head shorter, and the graying of his crew cut implied he was several years older than Grant. But he was compact, solid. Tim Huntley was obviously well trained, and Grant was just a lanky grad student; he wasn't some Indiana Jones. But he had nothing to lose.

Grant softened his knees, released the breath he'd been holding, and inhaled from his diaphragm, just as Kinley had shown him in their meditation exercises. The stale aroma of foreign spices cooked earlier in the day permeated the air. Grant felt the effects of the nine-thousand-foot elevation; his lungs craved oxygen. He anticipated that his next action would result in his being shot, but maybe he could create an opportunity for Kristin to escape.

The moment Tim stopped within range, Grant sprung. He lunged like a tiger pouncing on its prey.

Surprisingly, the gun pointing at his chest never fired. Instead their pursuer moved. Only he moved faster and more gracefully than Grant. With a twist of his body and a shift of his weight, he sidestepped Grant's hurtling mass. Simultaneously, he swung the gun.

The blow connected with the side of Grant's face while he was still in mid-air. Smacking into the splintered floor, Grant's head exploded in a shot of pain. A groan escaped his lips.

"No!" Kristin jumped to his side. Her dark hair fell around his face like a protective veil. She pulled him up by his shoulders with slender but strong hands.

Wincing, Grant rose to all fours. Pink saliva drooled from his mouth. It tasted salty. He never saw the kick to his stomach that lifted him off the ground.

"Show me the box!" Tim screamed.

Grant's vision blurred. He fought away the encroaching darkness. He had to confront the murderer.

"If you kill us, you get nothing!" Grant heard Kristin yell.

The assassin's shriek echoed through the shack. "I won't permit your heresy to destroy our faith!"

The man kicked Grant again and again.

"Stop it! Stop it!" Kristin screamed. "You're going to kill him."

To Grant, her voice sounded distant although she knelt beside him. He gasped to reclaim the wind knocked from his lungs by Tim's repeated kicks.

"Tell me where the books are!" the murderer screamed.

"We don't know!" Kristin cried, keeping up Grant's bluff.

Grant sucked in a chest full of air. "Just a minute," he grunted, pushing to his knees. The room gradually came into focus. Tim stood a safe distance from them, covering both with his gun. "Let Kristin leave. Then I'll take you to the texts."

"Grant, no!" she pleaded.

Tim swung the barrel of the gun a few degrees to Kristin's head. "You have five seconds to tell me where they are, or I blow off her face. You saw what a forty-caliber bullet did to that monk."

"Wait!" The anger that had fueled Grant's desperate lunge drained from his body. He wouldn't allow Kristin to be harmed. "You shoot her, and I won't give you shit. You can shoot me too; I don't give a damn anymore. But the sound of the gunfire will draw the men from the monastery here in a minute. You won't have time to search for the books and get away."

Tim reached his free left hand into his jacket and removed a silver butane lighter, one of the torch lighters cigar smokers used. "If that's the way you want to play, I'll shoot both of you, and then set fire to this place. The books are here somewhere. They'll be destroyed before the others arrive."

Grant hung his head. His bluff hadn't worked. Tim's finger tightened on the trigger.

Grant pointed to the bar. "Over there."

Tim's trigger finger relaxed. "Where exactly?"

"I'll show you." Grant put one hand on his knee and another on the leg of the center table, slowly pulling himself to a standing position.

"No, stay there. Tell me."

"Under the far bench, next to the bar."

"Behind the milk crates?" Tim shuffled toward the bar, but the gun never wavered.

"Yes." Grant cast his eyes to the dusty floor.

Tim turned toward the bar, searching the dark corner where the box was hidden. Grant saw Tim's left hand move to his right forearm, scratching in a slow circular motion with the edge of the lighter. The gun shook.

This time Grant reacted in one fluid motion. He didn't think or prepare himself. He no longer felt the various pains in his body. His entire awareness narrowed on the glass lantern on the table beside him. The yellowed glass felt sticky in his palm from the oil residue. He flung the lantern directly at their tormentor's head.

The glass shattered on impact with Tim's skull, peppering his face with shards and oil. Tim shrieked, bringing both hands to his eyes. Grant lunged, but on this attempt, he hit the murderer in the midsection like a linebacker sacking the quarterback on the final play of the game. They both toppled to the ground, but Grant's fall was broken by Tim's body. The murderer wheezed, trapped underneath Grant's weight. Grant grabbed the gun. Gripping it in his right hand, he thrust his left at the killer's neck. Clenching the man's throat, Grant brought the barrel of the gun to his forehead.

"You bastard! I'll kill you!" Grant screamed. The shards of glass stuck in Tim's neck cut into his hand. He didn't care. He squeezed harder.

Tim gasped for air.

The gun felt good. Grant liked its weightiness, the composite grip, the power it now conveyed to him. His index finger closed on the trigger with enough pressure that he felt it push back. Just a flinch, a quiver of effort, and he would shoot this son of a bitch. Facing Tim this closely, Grant saw an expression he hadn't seen in him before. Through the broken nose, bruised mouth, missing teeth, and the shards of glass now oozing blood and oil from the scaly skin, Grant recognized fear.

I could end it all right now, he thought. Justice for Kinley and the other monk. Justice for the two officers. Justice for Deepraj, for Razi, for Kristin, and for Jigme. Redemption for himself for not preventing these tragedies. The rage he felt toward this man flowed through him like a river of lava. His finger tightened around the trigger.

"Grant, no," Kristin said from behind him.

"After what he did to you?" Grant didn't take his eyes off the man. "What he was going to do?"

"I know." Her voice softened. "But Kinley—"

Kristin's words hit him like a glass of ice water thrown in his face. His narrowed perspective zoomed out from the gun pressed against Tim's forehead. He pictured the scene from Kristin's view: him sitting atop this bleeding man, the battle now won, but carrying out the man's execution to quench his own rage. At once he became conscious of the anger within himself: the agony over the loss of his friends, the need for revenge, the desire to remove the pain he felt deep inside. But she was right.

Killing Tim wouldn't take away those feelings, the *dukkha*.

Grant uncurled his fingers from Tim's throat, allowing the man to gulp a mouthful of air. He stood, careful to keep the gun trained on Tim's head. The anger and the pain still flowed through his body, but instead of letting his emotions dictate his actions, he merely observed the effects his feelings had. Two months ago Kinley had described this technique as shining the light of consciousness on one's own suffering. Grant became aware that he'd been breathing as heavily as Tim. Slowly the fire of his emotions dwindled.

"If you move, I will shoot you." Grant's breathing returned to normal. He backed away from Tim, but he didn't take his eyes off the man. He wouldn't be the executioner tonight, but that didn't mean Grant trusted this snake.

"Kris, grab Sangay's radio and call up to Tiger's Nest."

He sensed her staring at him. He wanted to look at her, to embrace her, but he didn't dare take his attention away from the killer. Kristin walked past him, brushing her hand across his shoulder as she did.

When she reached Tim, who lay motionless on the ground, she jumped backward.

"Grant, the other gun!"

"What?" Grant's mind raced, trying to comprehend the new danger. He tightened his finger around the trigger again, but Tim appeared not to have moved.

"Sangay's gun; it's in his belt." She pointed. Grant realized that Tim must have taken the gun off the officer after he'd killed him. He shivered involuntarily. While Tim's right hand lay by his head where Grant had wrestled his gun from him, his left hand had slid to his side, just inches from the revolver stuck in his waistband. Grant's lack of experience in these things had almost proved fatal again. He felt the anger warm his body again, but rather than fight it, he allowed the blood to rise to the surface of his skin. This time, however, its power over him was far weaker.

"Nice try," Grant said. "Put both hands up on top of your head." Tim raised his left hand and clasped both on top of his head. His face remained expressionless.

Grant debated having Tim pull the gun slowly out with his fingertips, as he'd seen on TV police shows, but he'd seen how fast and well trained this man was. He didn't doubt that Tim could turn the gun on him and fire before he realized what had happened. Grant started toward Tim. He would remove the pistol himself, and then the knife, for that matter.

"I'll do it," Kristin said. "You cover him."

Grant hesitated for a second. He didn't want Kristin near this monster again, but she sounded determined, and he could more easily cover the killer from a distance of a few feet.

"Okay, but carefully."

Kristin knelt by Tim, a look of revulsion on her face. Grant gripped the gun with both his hands and aimed at Tim's chest, where he was sure not to miss. Kristin's hand shook as she withdrew the revolver from his pants.

"Good," Grant said. "Now slide it on the floor to me, and then do the same with the knife." Kristin leaned over Tim and slid the gun, which skidded over the rough-hewn planks of the floor until it stopped by Grant's feet. He didn't look at the gun or kneel to pick it up; he kept his gaze on Tim, who returned the stare without blinking.

The mistake happened, as it had on the river many weeks earlier, unexpectedly, and at the most inopportune time. When Kristin straightened to her knees after leaning over to slide the pistol, her body passed in front of Grant's line of vision for the briefest of moments. It was enough time. Tim's unblinking expression never changed when he struck. Before Grant's brain could react, Tim simultaneously kicked a leg, sweeping Kristin off her knees, and shot both hands from behind his head.

By the time Grant realized he needed to pull the trigger, Kristin had fallen on top of Tim. One of the man's arms wrapped around her neck and pulled her tight against his body. Grant had lost the shot.

Kristin screamed, kicked, and threw elbows.

"Let her go!" Grant yelled.

He shifted the barrel of the gun but couldn't find a clear target in the thrashing of bodies on the floor. He took a step toward them.

The glint of steel flashed through the air. Grant and Kristin froze at the same time. Tim pressed the tip of the commando knife into the flesh of Kristin's neck. His other hand moved from her throat to her head, where he grasped her hair, twisted, and pulled her head back into him.

"Don't fuck with me!" Tim screamed. "I'll slice her open just like I did those cops."

Kristin's eyes widened. The tip of the knife drew a pinpoint of blood.

"Okay. Just take it easy," Grant said.

"We're going to stand. Don't shoot your girlfriend."

Tim rolled himself to the side, holding Kristin tightly as he maneuvered himself, and then her, to a crouched and then standing position. He kept her body in front of his, and only a portion of his face was unprotected. That was where Grant aimed the gun, but he wasn't a marksman. He couldn't risk either shooting Kristin in the head or missing outright and having Tim cut her throat.

"If you hurt her, I'll blow your head off," Grant snarled.

"Oh spare me. You had your chance earlier. I knew you were a pussy. You should've shot me."

"That's the difference between us."

"You're right. I win. You lose. I'm walking out of here, and she's coming with me." Although his voice was calm, Grant heard the strain. More disturbing was the wild look in his eyes; Tim was barely holding it together.

Grant's mind screamed at him. He couldn't let Kristin out of his sight. This guy had outmaneuvered them at every opportunity, and he'd never hesitated to kill. The fear inside Grant threatened to consume him, but he couldn't afford to let it. Instead, he concentrated on the dilemma at hand.

"You can go, but Kristin stays here."

"I don't make deals!" Tim's face flushed.

"The others will be here any minute. If you run now, you might escape."

The knife quivered against Kristin's skin. "One more word from you and I open up her neck." He jerked Kristin's head back, eliciting a squeal.

Tim backed toward the door. He was parallel to the large window, and almost to the bar. Suddenly Tim's scheme unfolded to Grant. The killer would continue backing up until he bumped into the swinging door, never allowing Grant a clean shot. Then he would draw the blade across Kristin's throat, severing her carotid artery and opening her windpipe. A shove on her back would send her flying into the room toward Grant, while he vanished through the door. Grant would have no choice but to go to Kristin, although saving her life would be impossible. Tim would escape through the woods. Grant had already seen a variation on this tactic at the Taj Mahal when Tim shot Jigme. Now Grant stood mere feet from the same killer, and Grant was the one with the gun, yet he knew he didn't have the skills to do what he needed to do.

Grant struggled to think of an option that didn't involve him shooting inches from Kristin's head, but nothing came to him. Tim shuffled backward toward the door. *I'm going to lose my chance,* Grant thought. He closed his left eye, and sighted with his right down the barrel of the gun. He focused on nothing but his target—the steel gray eye, now swollen and bloodshot. But the gun wouldn't remain still. He thought his hand was steady, but the target danced around the sight at the tip of the barrel. Most disturbing was the way Kristin's dark hair bounced in and out of the sight as well. Grant drew in a deep breath and held it. He tightened his index finger.

The sound of breaking glass startled Grant. His finger paused on the trigger, and he opened his closed eye. Tim appeared confused as well; his face had the wide-eyed, open-mouth expression of someone surprised by a most unwelcome occurrence. What transpired next shocked Grant. Tim released Kristin and dropped the knife, which clattered to the floor. With the blade no longer cutting into her neck, she sprang away, flinging herself to the ground in front of him. Grant now had a clear shot, but rather than take it, he relaxed his finger from the trigger. He saw that Tim was no longer a danger to them.

Rooted in place, Tim moved his hands, plucking at the metallic diamond poking out from just below his shoulder. A low moan escaped his mouth, as he rotated his torso. The graphite shaft of an arrow stuck out of his back. The shattering glass had come from the large window beside the bar and directly behind Tim—the one that faced Tiger's Nest.

Jigme! Grant thought, remembering the young monk's passion for the national sport in which he was forbidden to participate. He'd found a better use for the arrows that had killed Kinley.

Tim silently clawed at his back.

"You're going to make it worse," Grant told him.

Tim dropped his arms and hung his head. He had lost. If their assailant was lucky, he would live to be carried down the mountain and then spend the rest of his life in a Bhutanese jail. Shouts from outside filtered through the walls. The tension finally drained from Grant's neck and back muscles. He lowered the gun. They had the texts, and the man who had pursued them was finished.

Kristin was still on all fours, breathing heavily. She rose to her knees and wiped her hands, which were covered in the sticky yellow oil from the broken lantern, on her jeans.

"They're coming," Kristin said.

"Can you poke your head out and yell to them? I'm not leaving him."

"Sure."

As she began to rise, Grant noticed a subtle movement from Tim. The killer held something small and silver in his hand.

The butane lighter!

Once again, the killer's plan unfolded before Grant's eyes. He was standing and Kristin was kneeling in the broken lantern's puddle of oil that had spread out on the old wood floor. In a second they would be engulfed in flames.

Grant felt the cool weight of the gun in his hand by his side. He raised the weapon, but it seemed to move too slowly. Tim's thumb flicked the cap off.

Then another blur of movement flashed before Grant. Kristin lunged toward the man who had kidnapped, tortured, and almost killed her. She must have seen the lighter as well. A glint of silver arced through the air. She'd picked up Tim's knife when she rose to her knees. Before Tim could ignite the lighter, Kristin plunged the eight-inch blade into his chest.

Tim's body collapsed to the ground, convulsed, and went still.

Grant ran to Kristin and lifted her from the floor. She threw her arms around him as the doors to the restaurant burst open. Jigme and the other officers poured inside.

It's finally over, Grant thought.

CHAPTER 54

—⊶⊷—

NEW HOPE CHURCH
BIRMINGHAM, ALABAMA

WILLIAM JENNINGS PACED back and forth in front of his office desk. It was nine thirty at night, and he was alone again. He eyed the metal trash can beside him. The strips of paper that had just come from his portable shredder were clumped in a pile like a nest of black-and-white pasta.

Maybe I should burn it too, he thought.

Staring at the trash can, he felt that it might soon serve another purpose: he was on the verge of vomiting into it. The unease in his gut was caused by neither food poisoning nor a virus but the disintegration of his future. *Why the hell did I ever agree to use to Tim Huntley?* All his careful planning was falling apart.

While his boss might have been a visionary thinker, Jennings made things happen. Without him, the church that Brady had envisioned would never have existed. Without him, Brady's bid to lead the NAE would be nothing more than a dream. As head of the NAE, Brady would be the voice that would lead the people out of the darkness and into the light. He had that gift. But Jennings would be right behind him, running the finely oiled machine of salvation. They were so close too: construction of the New Hope Community was under way, Brady's book was a best seller, and Brady had no challengers for the upcoming election.

But now their futures were on the verge of unraveling. The bank was threatening to freeze their loan and stop construction. The cost overruns from Brady's extravagant tastes combined with the slow economy had wrecked the pro forma projections that Jennings had presented to the bankers when they'd initially approved the loan. And then there was the matter of the Issa texts.

When they'd first appeared, Jennings had turned the destructive potential that they would have on Brady's book and the faith of millions into a PR gold mine. Just as he'd been the one to encourage Brady to write a book, even securing the ghostwriter for him, Jennings had orchestrated the spectacle at Emory. The debate, the press, the humiliation of Grant Matthews had been his doing—all to wonderful results. But that strategy also depended on the real texts' never seeing the light of day.

When Tim Huntley had offered his services, Jennings had seized on what seemed to be the perfect solution to that problem. Tim was a professional, but he was also a believer. The initial misgivings Jennings had about the mental stability of the parishioner who sent weekly emails filled with all sorts of conspiracy nonsense were outweighed by the man's commitment to the cause and his military training. Jennings knew that God had provided them with a tool that they were meant to use.

What exactly Tim was doing overseas to obtain the texts, Jennings didn't want to know. War could be a messy business, especially when fighting for God. The plagues visited on Egypt, the destruction of Sodom and Gomorrah, the violence predicted in Revelation—each revealed that God recognized that force was needed to overcome evil. Jennings understood that they were in a critical time. The End Times were nearing. These heretical texts about Jesus were just another piece in the puzzle.

But now everything Jennings had worked for was in jeopardy. When Tim had called three days ago requesting a private jet to take him to the location of the texts, Jennings had originally resisted. Not only was the cost outrageous, but it would also tie the church directly to whatever the violent man did. Jennings had been careful to provide Tim only with cash that couldn't be traced back to the church. But at that point he was too far in, and Tim's insistence that he would beat Grant to the texts finally won him over.

As he continued pacing by his desk, Jennings wished that he'd listened to his initial reservations. Thirty minutes earlier, he'd received a call from the nervous pilot of the plane he'd chartered. Tim was three hours late for their six AM departure time, and the tower had radioed the pilot asking if he would come into the terminal. The police were on their way and wanted to speak to him about his passenger. Something had gone terribly wrong. Jennings asked the pilot if he could take off right then. Not wanting to get involved in a controversy in a Third World country, the pilot readily agreed.

Now Jennings had to cover his tracks. Tim would be on his own in dealing with whatever trouble he'd caused. Fortunately Jennings knew better than to charter a plane with the company that operated the fractional jet ownership program the church used. He'd turned instead to a charter service in Dubai that had grown rapidly during the boom times and were desperate for business in the slow economy. They wouldn't ask questions as long as they received the wire for forty-five thousand dollars. He'd used funds from a Panamanian trust he'd formed ten years earlier to help certain wealthy patrons of New Hope who had moved their assets offshore. These supporters could donate money to the Panamanian trust without the greedy minions of the U.S. government ever knowing that their money was offshore. Jennings would then periodically wire "contributions" from the trust to the church.

Now that he'd destroyed the copies of the faxes from the charter company confirming the deal, he had to focus on the next threat. *What am I going to do about the texts now?*

CHAPTER 55

———⊶⊷———

PARO, BHUTAN

G RANT LISTENED TO THE gurgling jade current splash over the small rapids of the Paro Chhu. Lining the riverbank, thirty monks stood in silence. Their crimson robes fluttered in the breeze as they waited to witness the ashes dissolve in the cold water. Jigme stood on the end. He held a black plastic bag—the type the women used to bring a month's supply of rice from the market. The bag held Kinley's ashes. In some cultures the ashes would be stored in an ornate box or decorative vase, but Grant knew that the monks viewed using a fancy container for ashes to be dumped into the water a waste. Another monk beside Jigme held a similar bag.

A tsunami of thoughts whipped through Grant. He and Kristin balanced themselves on the smooth rocks of the riverbank behind Jigme. If not for a simple accident that had cast him into the cold Himalayan water just a few hours from here, he would be hunched over his dissertation in Atlanta. The sun on this day shone as clear as it did on that day two months ago, but it hung lower in the sky, just above the mountain peaks that defined the green valley. The wind sweeping along the river had a bite, reminding him that winter was close by. Just as he'd lost Dasho, his kayaking guide, to the river, they were here to say good-bye to Kinley and the other monk murdered at Tiger's Nest.

The sound of tires crunching on gravel caused the monks to swivel their heads. Three silver Toyota Land Cruisers stopped on the grass shoulder. A murmur spread along the riverbank. First, three red-robed monks exited from the back seat of the lead car. Second, three orange-robed monks emerged from the last car—senior monks, as Kinley had been. One of the seniors looked particularly displeased—Lama Dorji, the conservative monk from the Punakha Dzong who feared the dangers of Western influence in the monastery. Grant reluctantly admitted to himself: the monk had been right.

The murmur grew louder when the doors to the middle car opened. A civilian dressed in the traditional plaid Bhutanese *gho* exited the driver's seat and then assisted from the rear of the vehicle a monk who appeared to be in his midseventies. Tall and thin, the monk held his posture erect but relaxed. The chestnut eyes set in the weathered face were sharp and alive as they surveyed the assembled group. He was dressed in saffron robes.

The Je Khenpo.

Only the king and the Je Khenpo, who was head of the country's monk body—the *dratshang*—wore yellow. With help from the civilian, the Je Khenpo descended the bank to the river's edge. The entire gathering of monks, including Lama Dorji and the other orange-robed seniors, bowed to him. The Je Khenpo spoke for some time to the gathered monks, who drank in every word he uttered. When he finished speaking, a melancholy chant rose from the group. Jigme and the monk beside him took turns emptying the bags of ashes into the flowing waters.

A cloud of gray dust billowed from Jigme's bag. Grant watched the fine particles cling to the surface of the water, riding the ripples over the small rapids.

Just when he was so close to true understanding, his teacher had been snatched away. Over the past day he'd been contemplating everything he'd learned from Kinley. The monk had wanted him to experience the messages contained in the Issa texts firsthand, just as Issa had done. Grant worried that he'd failed his teacher. Issa had traveled to the east; he had studied Hindu and Buddhist doctrine; he had struggled with his own teachers; he had taught the lessons he learned to the disenfranchised; he had had a spiritual awakening to the presence of God within himself and the world around him—an awakening that transcended any particular religious doctrine. But something was missing for Grant.

Now that he was in possession of the texts he'd worked so hard to obtain, he was surprised that he experienced a feeling he wasn't expecting: incompleteness. Even if he was successful in persuading the authorities to let him take the texts out of the country, Grant feared that he wasn't ready yet to assume the role of teacher. Recovering the texts was supposed to solve his problems: his dissertation, his reputation, his future, and the legacy of his past, but he felt only emptiness.

Grant glanced at the now empty plastic bag that had held Kinley's ashes. He thought of the emptiness in his own heart. He cast his eyes upward to the heavens. Not even a cloud.

Then he heard the familiar voice. It came from inside. Kinley's voice. The voice chastised Grant for looking to the sky for his answers. It chastised him for looking to the bag as well. Both revealed nothing but emptiness. The voice reminded him that the answers he sought were within, if only he would look deeply. Although the lesson was familiar to him, at this moment, the words in his mind suddenly became clear.

He was grasping. Grasping for the answers. The river water playing over the smooth pebbles reminded him of one of Kinley's earliest lessons. By looking deeply, he could understand the nature of water, but only by tasting it could he truly experience it.

He exhaled fully and closed his eyes. His teacher's voice faded and was replaced by the mournful cry of the chanting monks. Grant stood still for many minutes. He wasn't aware of the passage of time, only the sensations of his gentle heartbeat, his soft breath, and the chant that vibrated to his bones.

After the ceremony ended, the Je Khenpo walked directly toward Grant and Kristin. Jigme kneeled and touched his forehead to the ground in front of his leader, while Grant and Kristin bowed deeply. Grant lifted his head when he felt the old man's hand on his shoulder.

Bhutan's religious leader spoke in a deep baritone. "So you are Grant Matthews and Kristin Misaki."

Grant was unsure of the proper protocol when addressing the most senior monk. Should he keep his eyes averted? Kristin replied in a quiet voice beside him, "Yes, we are, sir."

"Please, call me Ummon. That was the name Kinley used many years ago, when he was my student." He gestured to the yellow robes on his body. "Before all this." Grant glanced down the line of monks now all staring at them. In the middle was the small boy, another Ummon, who'd brought him food when he was incapacitated in Punakha and who'd alerted them to the tragedy at Tiger's Nest.

"Kinley spoke to me of his fondness for both of you." The Je Khenpo spoke English with a British accent as Kinley had, and Grant was surprised by his warm, casual tone.

"You were Kinley's mentor?" Kristin asked.

"So full of energy and ideas that boy was." The Je Khenpo chuckled. "Quite a handful for his teachers. Constantly questioning, challenging them. It was I who thought a few years of regular school outside the confines of the monastery would suit young Kinley better in the long run. When he was one of only two students in the country to apply for a scholarship at Oxford, he asked me to write his recommendation. I always believed he would return one day to life as a monk."

Although Grant had a hard time picturing Kinley as a young student, the image of his friend as a rebel suited him just fine. "I'm so sorry, sir, I mean, Ummon." The words stumbled out of Grant. "Tiger's Nest. We didn't mean to . . ." How did he apologize to the country's religious leader for the death and destruction that had followed them to Bhutan's most sacred site?

The Je Khenpo placed a comforting hand on each of their shoulders. "Evil exists in the world, as does good. From what I have heard, the two of you put your own lives in danger, both physically and professionally, in order to pursue what is right. All you can hope to do is to put forward the right effort with the right intentions. The results will fall where they will."

"Jigme is the one who should be commended. He saved our lives," Grant said.

"So I heard." The Je Khenpo shot a reproving look at Jigme, who bowed deeply again. "A shame that monks are forbidden from competing in our national sport."

"I know that nonviolence is one of the key precepts of Buddhism," Grant hastily added, "but without his actions, Kristin wouldn't be with us today."

Kristin cast her eyes to the ground. Grant guessed her thoughts. While Jigme had shot Tim Huntley with the arrow, she'd been the one who actually killed him. He'd assured her that stabbing Tim had been necessary, that she'd saved both of them from being engulfed in flames, but he knew that she was still disturbed.

"Yes." The old monk reached out a hand and rested it on Kristin's shoulder, seeming to sense her troubled thoughts. "If I have a pebble in my sandal, I remove it. But I do so without becoming frustrated at the pebble itself or angry at the person who forgot to rake the ground. Sometimes turning the other cheek should happen here"—he thumped his chest—"and not necessarily here," he concluded, patting his face.

Kristin smiled at the Je Khenpo. "I see now the source of Kinley's wisdom."

Talking about the events of that night a day and a half ago reminded Grant of their narrow escape. He shuddered. Tim Huntley would never torture or kill again. After a blur of interviews with local police and the U.S. consulate, Grant and Kristin had returned to their hotel, drained. Jigme kept the Issa texts at the dzong.

The Je Khenpo's voice interrupted his replaying of events. "I have a long drive to Punakha. I wish you both the best. Jigme will see to it that you leave with everything you came here for."

The meaning of the Je Khenpo's words hit Grant. "You're allowing us to take the Issa books to America?"

The monk shrugged. "They have sat unused in my country for too long. It is time for the scholars in your esteemed universities to decide if these books are the treasures you think they are."

Grant inclined his head. "Thank you."

"Kinley said you were a quick, if hard-headed student, much like young Issa himself."

"What about your country's laws against removing artifacts?" Kristin asked.

"Hmm." The monk brought his fingertips to his chin. "Technically those books never belonged to my country; they were sent here for safekeeping." He winked at them. "An interpretation of the law, and a privilege of my position."

"How will the other monks feel about this?" Kristin asked. Grant glanced at Lama Dorji, who glared at them, as if to accuse them of bringing the very trouble to his country that he'd feared.

"I make the decisions I believe to be in the best interest of the *dratshang* and then let the others take care of their own happiness."

"Ummon, before you leave. One question has perplexed me," Grant said. "In Sarnath, we were told that your country made a generous donation to the temple, allowing them to add to the mural that led us here. We know that Kinley was behind it, but how did he arrange to fund the painting?"

"Ah yes, we had been in discussions with the temple there for several years about helping to pay for an expansion of the mural. Kinley offered to travel there himself, with the funds we had already promised, to speed the process along."

"So Kinley took advantage of the opportunity to send us to the site of the Buddha's first lectures and to give us the final clue to the location of the texts?" Grant asked.

The Je Khenpo smiled, a familiar twinkle in his eyes. "The more we open our eyes around us, the more we see how everything is interconnected."

The Je Khenpo nodded to his assistant, who held his arm as they ascended the dirt bank. He then gathered his saffron robes, climbed into the SUV, and sped off.

CHAPTER 56

⊸⊶

CASHIERS, NORTH CAROLINA

"ARE WE CLOSE?" Kristin rubbed her face with her hands.

Grant squinted to see through the fog on the road winding through Cashiers, a cozy mountain community in western North Carolina. "It's been a year since I was last here, but I think so."

He flicked his blinker, slowed, and turned left just past a farmer's vegetable stand. The three-hour drive into the Smoky Mountains should have been a pleasant one, but they had already traveled for two days without a break. After planes from Paro to New Delhi, then to Paris and finally to Atlanta, where they endured an hour-long customs line at Hartsfield-Jackson International Airport, they'd located Grant's six-year-old Audi in the economy parking lot and begun their drive north.

The anticipation of finally showing the Issa texts to Professor Billingsly kept Grant alert despite the jet lag. His mentor had been shocked when Grant called from Bhutan with the texts in hand. Issa's story—the missing years in the life of Jesus—was now complete: his journey as a teen, the teachings that affected him, and his spiritual awakening. Grant's excitement was tempered, though, not just by his exhaustion but by the knowledge of the price of obtaining the texts: Kinley, Deepraj, Razi, and the others who died.

After listening to Grant recount the story, Billingsly had said that the department chair would have no choice but to reinstate Grant's status immediately. When Grant mentioned his desire not to repeat the fiasco of the premature initial release of the Issa find, Billingsly offered to arrange a private meeting between Grant and Professor Singh of the department of Near Eastern studies in the privacy of his cabin in the mountains right away. Grant had visited his mentor's cabin several times before; each October when the turning leaves were at their most colorful, Billingsly hosted a weekend retreat for his grad students. Today, however, the golden fall hues were a month past their prime, exposing branches that were mostly bare.

They planned to spend two days in the mountains, and then they had to return to Atlanta to the FBI district office downtown. Although they had been debriefed by the U.S. consulate in Bhutan, the FBI wanted to interview them in person about Tim Huntley. Before they left Paro, Grant had learned from the consulate that Tim Huntley was in fact the man's real name. He lived in Birmingham, and he'd traveled to Bhutan on a chartered jet, but that was all the information they had. At least he and Kristin were out of danger. Grant took solace in the realization that the man would never hurt anyone else.

"How well do you know the professor coming with Billingsly?" Kristin asked.

"Professor Singh? I met with him a couple of times before I left for India. Sharp, no BS."

"Can he really validate the texts?"

"Complete authentication will take at least a year, requiring carbon dating, analysis of the ink, and study of the language, but he can give us a gut check on their age and authorship." Grant glanced in the rearview mirror at the black duffel bag on the rear seat. Inside the bag rested a plain pine box wrapped in airtight plastic wrap. "As an expert in Pali, he can also provide a more complete translation."

"So if the texts check out, you take them to Emory with the credibility of both professors standing behind you."

"And likewise, if Professor Singh believes them to be obvious fakes, we save ourselves a new round of humiliation. But my instinct tells me they're the real deal."

After another twenty minutes navigating up and then down a serpentine mountain road, they passed a chocolate brown sign with yellow lettering indicating they'd entered the Nantahala National Forest. A few miles later, Grant turned onto a dirt road. The road paralleled a noisy stream that flowed through the dense trees. After passing a lone log cabin, the road began to climb. A short distance later, a manicured gravel driveway peeled off to the right.

"That's Billingsly's." He pointed.

"Where does the dirt road go?"

"U.S. Forest Service property. Harold's parents were fortunate enough to snag one of the few lots completely surrounded by national forest."

Rounding a bend in the drive, they approached the professor's cabin, perched on a grassy clearing. Constructed of native stacked stone and large timbers with a steep-pitched shingle roof, the house looked more like a ski lodge one might find in the Rockies than a cabin in the woods.

"Wait till you see the inside," Grant said in answer to the astonishment on Kristin's face.

"On a professor's salary?"

"Family money."

"That his car too?" She pointed to a shiny black sedan.

"Must belong to Professor Singh."

Grant lifted the bag from the back seat. They'd carried the texts from Paro to this remote mountain getaway with the same care they would've given a newborn baby. Now they would see what the experts thought. Grant experienced a slight queasiness in his stomach. In his heart he believed the documents were authentic, but there were no guarantees.

Kinley. Deepraj. Razi. Grant caught himself heading down the now familiar path of playing over the events that led him to this moment. He practiced a meditation technique he'd come to rely on to get him through these mental movies: noting the memories as they arose and the resulting emotions they caused. Then he inhaled deeply, released the breath, and refocused his attention. In this case, his focus was on the reverberating pitch of the iron knocker that Kristin banged on the tall mahogany door. He relaxed.

"Grant, Kristin!" Billingsly exclaimed upon opening the door. "We're so excited you made it back safely." Then he frowned. "I'm still horrified by your story."

"You haven't heard the half of it." Grant gave his mentor a warm hug. "We'll fill you in over dinner." He nodded to the car. "Professor Singh?"

"We're waiting for you in the keeping room."

Billingsly led them down a hallway of wide-planked heart-of-pine floors, past a kitchen of old-world cabinets and modern stainless-steel appliances, and into a room that took Grant's breath away every time he saw it. Soaring above the pine floors, heavy cypress beams supported a twenty-five-foot vaulted ceiling. To Grant's left, a stone fireplace large enough for him to stand in took up the entire end of the room, but it was the view from the floor-to-ceiling glass windows along the length of the wall in front of him that left him speechless each time he saw it. The unobstructed vista of the multiple peaks and layers of the Smoky Mountains reminded him of the Himalayas surrounding the valleys of Bhutan. Taking in the wisps of fog swirling around the distant mountains, he thought of Kinley.

So engrossed was he in the juxtaposition of the memory of his teacher with the mist-covered ridges before him now that he didn't notice the silver-haired man rising from a worn leather club chair on the right side of the room. Kristin's sharp intake of breath returned his attention to the room. The sight of the man in the tailored suit caused Grant to gasp as well.

"Reverend Brady?" Kristin sputtered.

CHAPTER 57

———⊗———

CASHIERS, NORTH CAROLINA

"TAKE A SEAT." Reverend Brady waved a hand to the coffee-colored, upholstered sofa.

"Harold! How could you?" Grant's face flushed a deep crimson. "You brought *him* here?"

"I . . . it's very complicated. I think if we can explain to you the problems with these texts, you will come to agree with us."

"Explain!" Grant shouted. "You know the Issa texts are one of the most important biblical finds ever." The calm anticipation of seeing his mentor had vanished. He felt the anger boiling inside him. He didn't even try to cool it.

"Look"—the professor's voice quivered—"why don't we sit here and discuss this, before we draw any conclusions."

Watching Billingsly lick his lips and fidget with his hands, Grant replayed the events of the past month in his mind, starting from their first visit with the professor in his Emory office. The extent to which he'd been betrayed by his mentor struck him like a blow to the gut. He placed the bag on the coffee table and collapsed onto the sofa.

Kristin must have made the same connection. She sat next to Grant and said, "You betrayed us from the beginning. Didn't you, *Professor* Billingsly?" The word *professor* came out of her mouth more as an anathema than as a professional title. "The premature release of the Issa texts Grant emailed to you was no accident." She jabbed a finger in his direction. "And how else in the debate could Brady have known about Grant's academic past?"

"How could I have been so naïve?" Grant ran his fingers through his hair.

Casting his eyes to the floor, Billingsly mumbled, "I'm so sorry."

"Oh come on, Harold." Brady settled his frame into the armchair across the coffee table from the sofa where Grant and Kristin sat. "You understood the dangers of these texts, the damage they could do to the faith of millions of people around the world. We can't have the Savior of the world, the one true path to God, fumbling around in India, finding himself through other inferior religions. Believing such a thing devalues Jesus, removes his unique divinity. It destroys our religion. When you and Jennings first spoke about this heresy, you agreed that the documents were not authentic and should be left alone." A Cheshire cat grin spread across his face. "I wouldn't have expected anything different from my ghostwriter."

"Ghostwriter?" Grant's jaw dropped. "You wrote *Why Is God So Angry?*"

"And he's working on the sequel as we speak," Brady said, while Billingsly studied the floor. "He's becoming a very wealthy man. After all, the costs of keeping up this lifestyle"—Brady gestured to the room around them—"are quite high, especially since the money he inherited ran out."

Grant glared at his mentor. "You sold me out for money?"

"It's not like that," Billingsly pleaded. "I wrote the book before you even left on your first trip to India. You, better than anyone, know how I was screwed over for the dean's position at Emory. After all the years of hard work, all the papers I published in obscure academic journals, all the departmental politics I endured, I deserved that job!"

"But you wrote a book playing on the fears of the country by misinterpreting the Book of Revelation—a book written in reaction to the Roman destruction of the Temple in seventy AD and the harsh suppression of the Jewish revolt. You know that Revelation was never meant to be a prediction of events two thousand years later."

"Grant, it was a unique opportunity. My career has reached a dead end. Through these books, I can reach an audience of millions. Yes, the premise may be dramatized, but the underlying message that the only redemptive path is found in Jesus is just as valid."

"But, Harold, look at the consequences. That lunatic Tim Huntley chased us around the world. He murdered Kinley, Deepraj, and Razi!" Grant turned to Brady. "A parishioner of yours."

Brady paled but spoke confidently. "I don't know what you're talking about."

Then another disturbing thought occurred to Grant. "Kinley's riddle that sent us to India and to the Taj Mahal—Huntley never would have decoded that himself. Even though he'd hacked my email, he needed help." He glared at his professor. "I shared our interpretation of the riddle with you before we left!"

"I swear I didn't know that anything like that would happen!" Billingsly's voice became high-pitched, and he was sweating profusely now. "When William Jennings called me to help, we only planned to cause you a little embarrassment at the debate, so that you would give up the quest."

"And the documents would be forgotten, just like they were when Nicholas Notovitch discovered evidence of them a hundred years ago?" Grant said.

"Exactly. But when you returned to retrieve them . . . Honestly, I never knew about the murders. Nothing at all! We just wanted the texts to disappear."

"Keeping the truth from people is in their best interest?" Kristin blurted. "You're an academic!"

"What is truth?" Billingsly cried. "No matter how many documents turn up in desert caves or forgotten monasteries, we will never know what really happened two millennia ago. How we respond to Jesus today matters more than the specific events of his life two thousand years ago. You need to see how the people in the reverend's congregation are strengthened by their faith—the joy it brings them, the comfort it supplies in times of difficulty. Do you want to take that away by telling them that the basis for everything they believe is wrong?"

"These texts don't invalidate people's experience of Christ today," Grant said. "If anything, they provide a more spiritual insight into Jesus and the practices which led to his, and maybe to our own, spiritual awakenings."

"A man who woke up to the divinity that is inside us all," Kristin said, making eye contact with Grant. "A mystical but not supernatural Jesus."

Billingsly shook his head. "The stories of Jesus' virgin birth, the miracles he performed, his physical resurrection are all central to his divinity. Without these Christianity doesn't exist."

"Harold, during our journey I came to a new understanding." Grant leaned forward with his elbows on his knees. "Why should the spark of the divine the apostles experienced when they were in the presence of Jesus disappear with the death of his flesh? And if Jesus and his followers could experience the divine directly, why can't we too? The kingdom of God here today, within and around us, to paraphrase the Gospel of Luke."

As the words came from his mouth, Grant realized the effect that Kinley, Deepraj, and Razi had had on him. Religion was not about belief in certain historical facts; it was about experience. The Bible that he'd resisted for much of his adult life as superstitious and nonfactual had now taken on a different character for him. It spoke to an experience of a people in a particular time to the divine, an experience that he was also beginning to sense.

"New Age doublespeak!" Brady bellowed. "I knew it during our debate. First you outsource Jesus' spirituality to India, and now you hijack his divinity."

Grant stood. "I didn't expect to find you here today, Reverend, and I certainly don't expect to convince you of my views, but these texts will be released and studied."

He held a hand to Kristin. "Come on, we're going to Emory."

"I don't think so," a voice from behind him said.

CHAPTER 58

———∽∞∾———

CASHIERS, NORTH CAROLINA

GRANT TURNED TOWARD the voice and his mouth went dry. A balding man in a dark blue suit advanced into the room. He pointed a revolver with a pearl handle and a silver barrel at Grant's chest.

Brady bellowed from behind Grant, "Jennings, what the hell are you doing here?"

Rather than answer Brady, the man spoke to Grant and Kristin. "Mr. Matthews and Ms. Misaki, I presume?"

"Who are you?" Grant asked.

"William Jennings, director of operations for New Hope Church."

Grant then recognized the man who had accompanied Brady at the debate. But today the dour-looking Jennings had narrow eyes that darted around the room. The gun quivering in his hand brought a cold sweat across Grant's body. *Not again*, he thought.

Then he realized who Jennings really was. Billingsly had said a few minutes earlier that Jennings was the one who'd called him before the debate. Brady also had seemed genuinely surprised when Grant mentioned Huntley's name. Jennings was the mastermind behind all the suffering Grant and Kristin had seen.

"You sent Tim Huntley to hunt us down in India and Bhutan!" The words flew out of Grant. "A man who never hesitated to torture and kill to obtain these texts."

"I never told him to kill anyone. He was just supposed to destroy the books."

"You used that wacko?" Brady bellowed. "The one who sent me the crazy emails?"

"God presented us with a useful tool when we needed it. I was just following through with his will."

"But you never told me!"

"Brian, you've never enjoyed the details of how I operate the church, and this needed to be handled delicately."

"But you made it possible for him to carry out his violence!" Grant yelled, ignoring the gun that was pointed at him. "How is this 'turning the other cheek' to your enemies?"

"I don't need some disgraced student quoting the Bible to me." Jennings's voice rose an octave. "God's destruction of the sinful and unfaithful did not end in the Old Testament. In, um, Matthew, chapter ten, Jesus . . . Jesus himself said, 'I come not imposing peace. I impose not peace, but the sword.' The violence we will see at Armageddon will make the events you experienced look like a nursery school playdate."

While Jennings didn't have Brady's smooth delivery, Grant saw that the true architect behind the tragedies was just as well versed in scripture. He also couldn't help but think of the familiarity of Jennings's response to his father's philosophies. But on this occasion, Grant allowed the memory of his father to pass over him. *I am the one present, here and now.*

He had to think of a way to talk Jennings down. But after all he'd been through, he found himself scanning the room for anything he could improvise into a makeshift weapon just in case. The table in front of him held only the duffel bag containing the heavy box of ancient books—not even an ashtray to hurl. Then a four-foot-long iron rod with a pointed end caught his eye: a fire poker leaned against the stone fireplace. But it was a good eight feet away.

"Come on!" Kristin said, perched on the edge of the sofa as if she were a lioness prepared to spring forward and grab her prey by the throat. "In Varanasi, I heard Tim Huntley on the phone with someone when I was his prisoner. It was you, wasn't it? You must have known how violent he was."

Grant took a step toward the fireplace and turned his body so that he now faced Jennings, the sofa where Kristin and Billingsly sat, and the armchair containing Brady.

Jennings smirked. "Honey, great men must make great sacrifices at times. God did not put me on this earth to sit quietly and contemplate the nature of my existence. He put me here to be his agent of change. Just as the reverend was sent to be the voice of his gospel, I was sent to ensure that this voice of God's"—he pointed with a free hand to Brady—"will be the one to deliver millions to salvation. In a war there will be casualties. Just like there were at Sodom and Gomorrah, just like there will be on the hills of Armageddon, and just as there were in India and Bhutan."

This man is as crazy as Tim Huntley was, Grant realized. He glanced toward Brady, who for once seemed to be speechless as the events unraveled before him. The reverend's eyes were wide and his mouth agape as he watched his second in command take over the room. Grant took a step backward toward the fireplace.

"My only mistake in using Huntley," Jennings continued, "was in trusting that he would actually accomplish his mission. Sometimes to get a job done properly, you must do it yourself."

Jennings advanced further into the room toward Brady. The gun swung back and forth between Grant and Kristin. But unlike their confrontations with Huntley, the weapon didn't linger on either one of them. Huntley was a trained professional; Jennings wasn't. Grant decided that as soon as he had an opening, he would take it. He stepped closer to the fireplace.

Jennings pointed to the duffel and then to Professor Billingsly. "Do some good and toss that bag of heresy into the fire."

Grant's pulse pounded in his ears. As afraid as he was for their lives, he couldn't let the texts be destroyed, not after the price that had been paid to bring them here.

"Why don't you put the gun down, William." Brady finally found his voice. "Don't make the situation worse than it already is."

"Oh, the situation is already bad." Jennings licked his lips. The gun shook in his hand. "I'm going to have to finish what Huntley should have done in Bhutan."

Grant swallowed and wiped his palms on his jeans.

"No!" Billingsly shrieked. "There won't be any killing in my house."

"They know too much," Jennings said. "It's the only way we can be sure of our future—of the future of God's message."

"No, if you just destroy the books, they won't be able to say anything credible," the professor pleaded. "Remember, they were already disgraced once; everyone thinks they lied about the texts."

Grant was only five feet from the fireplace. If he lunged, he could grab the poker, but he wasn't sure he could make it to where Jennings stood by Brady's chair before Jennings pulled the trigger.

With a grunt, Brady pushed himself out of his chair so he was standing next to his number two. "When you arranged this meeting, you specifically said you didn't need to be here. Billingsly and I had things under control. We were explaining to these two the dangers of the texts, just as you said I should."

"They would never have voluntarily given them up."

Grant backed closer to the fireplace. *Four feet.*

"Well, then," Brady said, "we show the world that the texts are obvious forgeries or written by later authors long after the events. It will continue to be a PR bonanza for us just like the debate was."

"What if the texts actually date from the first century?" The tension in Jennings voice betrayed the strain he was under. "Anyway, the time for explanations has passed. We're in a heap of trouble."

"Trouble?" Brady asked.

"Grant and Kristin would've figured out that Billingsly leaked the texts to the media as I asked him to do, that he provided the information about Grant's past before the debate to me, and that he gave me the translation of the Taj Mahal riddle, which I provided to Huntley. The FBI would be knocking on our door within days." Jennings wiped his brow with his free hand. "I used church funds to fly Huntley to India and then to charter a plane to get him to Bhutan. I've covered our tracks up until now, but we can't afford either the texts or these two to surface."

"What is this craziness!" Brady bellowed. "If you've done things you shouldn't have, you need to repent."

"It's gone too far for that. The church, everything we've planned will be destroyed."

Grant inched closer to the fireplace. No one noticed his movements in the escalating argument. He could almost reach the poker.

"The church has overcome adversity before."

"Brian, this morning the bank called in our loan. We're in violation of the financial covenants; our cash reserves aren't sufficient to pay our debt service. The New Hope Community is on hold for now."

"How did that happen? It's God's will that New Hope be built! You've dropped the ball on this, William."

"My fault!" Jennings face reddened. "For too long, I've overlooked your shenanigans: the ego, the hypocrisy, the outlandish expenses. I fooled myself into believing those were necessary compromises in pursuit of the greater good—the growth of the church. You do have an amazing gift from God, one that I could only dream of, but you've become intoxicated on your own charisma."

Once again Brady was rendered speechless by his subordinate. After a moment of silence, Brady reached out and grasped Jennings's arm, the one holding the gun. "It's over, William. Let's walk outside."

"It can't be over!" Jennings cried. "You don't understand. Everything I've done—my whole life—has been for you, for the church, for God!" He tried to jerk his hand away from Brady, but the reverend must have gripped his arm tightly, because Jennings stumbled forward. They struggled over the gun.

Grant reacted immediately. He swiveled and lunged for the iron poker hanging by the stone fireplace.

The gunshot exploded the moment he turned his head from the men. His ears ringing, but the cool iron now in his hand, Grant pivoted toward the action. Both Jennings and Brady stood facing each other. Neither moved.

Grant noticed the dark circle of the bullet's exit wound spreading outward on the back of Brady's suit jacket. When the reverend slumped to the ground, Grant surged forward. He closed the gap in three quick strides. Jennings's eyes darted from the crumpled body to the gun. He had the look of a wild animal caught in a trap.

The shooting provided the distraction Grant needed. He raised his weapon with both hands and raced within striking range.

Jennings's face hardened as he looked up. He now pointed the gun straight ahead—at Kristin, sitting on the sofa. Jennings glared at her, hatred and desperation in his eyes, as if she were the one who shot his boss and friend.

He doesn't even know I'm here, Grant thought.

Grant tensed his muscles for the strike, and then time slowed to a crawl. He swung the poker in a downward arc, but the iron wouldn't move fast enough. Grant knew what was coming, and he knew that he would be a fraction of a second late in preventing it.

He saw the spark of a flame and the wisp of smoke erupt from the silver barrel of the gun. Before the echo of the shot dissipated, the iron rod in Grant's hands cracked on Jennings's outstretched forearm. The bone shattered on impact, causing his wrist to hinge upward. The gun dropped, landing softly on Brady's body. Jennings sank to his knees. A howl arose from deep inside his chest.

Grant leaped on him. The poker in his hand still rang from the impact.

Having learned his lesson with Huntley in Bhutan, Grant kept his attention on both of Jennings's hands as he searched for the gun with his peripheral vision. He found it lying inches from Brady's body. Grant dropped the poker and grabbed the gun. He cocked the hammer with his thumb, trained the polished barrel on Jennings's torso, and then rose to his feet. Ignoring Grant and the gun, Jennings stared at his broken arm, which he now cradled with his good arm.

Like a magnet attracting his attention, the terror of what waited for him on the sofa forced Grant's head to turn and look.

Kristin sat immobile on the center cushion, her eyes wide. Hope flooded through Grant's veins. The words barely came out of his mouth, "He missed?"

She shook her head. Her eyes fell to the figure collapsed at her feet, partially hidden by the coffee table. Keeping the gun trained on Jennings, Grant moved toward Kristin. She said in a quiet monotone, "He jumped in front of me."

Professor Billingsly's twisted body lay in a heap at her feet. A stream of blood ran along the pine flooring.

Grant bent over to check for a pulse.

"Grant!" Kristin screamed from beside him.

Grant swiveled his head. Jennings flew toward him, as if propelled by an unseen force. His face was neither contorted in rage nor pain but was calm, expressionless. He held his broken right arm to his stomach. He swung the iron poker with his healthy hand. In a second it would connect with Grant's skull.

Grant felt the smooth grip of the revolver in his hand. He raised the gun toward Jennings's hurtling figure and pulled the trigger. Both the explosion and the recoil were more dramatic than he expected. Jennings jerked as if he'd been punched. Grant pulled the trigger a second time. Jennings crashed to the ground, bouncing hard against the wooden edge of the coffee table. The acrid smell of gunpowder filled Grant's nostrils as the thunderclap of the shot faded from the room.

Jennings was dead.

Grant knew that he would have to deal with the emotional consequences of his actions, just as Kristin had with Huntley, but that would have wait. He laid the pistol on the coffee table and pushed the sofa back. He then gently rolled Professor Billingsly over. The front of his green striped Oxford shirt was soaked in blood. Grant's mentor—the man who had given him a chance at Emory, the man who had betrayed him, the man who had just sacrificed his life for Kristin's—had also died.

Grant's eyes stung and his throat burned, but his voice remained strong. "I forgive you, Harold. Thank you."

"He's alive!" Kristin shouted.

Grant turned. *Jennings is still alive?* The gun was still on the table, but Jennings hadn't moved.

"Brady!" Kristin knelt by the reverend.

Grant picked up the gun, tucked it into his belt, and hurried to her side. Brady's face was pallid and a low moan escaped his lips. Kristin snatched a white handkerchief from Brady's front suit pocket and opened his jacket. The bullet wound just below his right shoulder oozed blood down his blue pinpoint cotton shirt. Brady winced when Kristin pressed the handkerchief directly on the wound. Grant knelt beside them.

"Stay with us, Reverend," she said. "Your body is going into shock, but you're going to make it."

Brady's eyes blinked closed and then opened again, focusing on Grant. "I had no idea. Please understand that." Brady's hand grasped Grant's arm with a strength that surprised him. "All the suffering and death. That was not part of God's plan. I'm so sorry." His eyes closed again, but he continued to take shallow breaths.

"I'll stay with him," Kristin said. "Can you call nine-one-one?"

Grant walked back to the sofa, sat on the floor by the body of his mentor, and dialed from his cell phone. After explaining the events to a confused mountain emergency operator who promised to send the police and an ambulance right away, Grant hung up the phone. He rested the gun on the floor beside him, not wanting to touch it again. He then pulled the bag of texts from the coffee table onto his lap. The heaviness was comforting. Kristin still knelt on the opposite side of the table over Brady, keeping pressure on the wound and quietly reassuring him that help would be there soon. Grant felt an unexpected emotion for the man who had humiliated him on national TV.

He felt pity.

Brady was blinded by his ego, but he was also a man who believed passionately. *Just like my father*, Grant realized. Grant exhaled the air in his lungs and with it felt the tension in his body begin to ease. With a new clarity he saw how he'd harbored negative energy—about Brady, about his father—like a petri dish growing a virus unchecked by antibodies. He'd viewed himself as the victim, but sitting on the floor surrounded by death, a death that one day he would inevitably encounter personally, he understood how he had created the negative energy within himself. His father and Brady were the men they were, just as he was the man he was.

He'd wondered for so many years if he'd ever be able to forgive his father. Maybe he'd just used the wrong word. *Surrender. Acceptance.* Those seemed better.

He inhaled deeply, taking in the aroma of cool mountain air infused with the woody smoke from the fire and the sweet smell of gunpowder. The adrenaline racing through his body dissipated, and his heart rate slowed.

He turned his attention from the carnage around him to the view out the picture windows. The fog that earlier enveloped the mountains had cleared. Rays of yellow sunlight danced across the pine-covered peaks before him. Without taking his eyes from the view, he unzipped the bag in his lap and slipped his hands inside. He traced his fingers across the top of the smooth box.

He thought of the books inside, and the story of Issa.

He focused on his breath—the molecules of air moving in and out of his nostrils—just as Kinley had taught him two months earlier. He allowed his eyes to close halfway. After several minutes, Grant noticed the energy. It started as a tingling across the surface of his skin. He felt the presence of every hair follicle on his body as if they were each charged with static. He felt alive. But rather than grasp at the feeling, he simply watched it play across his person. Gradually, the energy drew inward like water swirling down a drain. He followed the energy until it coalesced into a tiny spark of light suspended in the darkness within his soul.

He focused on the spark. He breathed into it as he might fan a fledgling fire. The spark grew into a flame. When the flame began to spread outward from the core of his being, he became aware of a sense of peace that he'd not thought possible under the circumstances. Then he realized he felt another sensation washing over him. He felt love. Love for Kinley, love for Kristin, and strangely even love for Brady, Jennings, and Billingsly.

Grant now saw how they were all linked together.

He now poured his breath into the flame within his soul, fanning the fire. His breath.

Atman. Nephesh. God.

EPILOGUE

---∞∞∞---

YALE UNIVERSITY
NEW HAVEN, CONNECTICUT
FIVE YEARS LATER

A SINGLE FLOWER EIGHT inches in diameter. An abundance of canary yellow petals. The petals' edges curled up saucerlike, forming a large cup surrounded by circular, flat, forest green leaves.

A lotus.

Grant studied the flower floating in the water bowl on his desk: the tiny veins running through its petals, the yellow stamens reaching out like miniature tentacles, the hint of fragrance reaching his nose. He mentally retraced the path that brought it here: the florist, the farmer, the plant, the seed, the generations of previous plants, the water, the soil, and the light. He recalled learning five years earlier that a lotus could grow in the foulest of conditions but still rise above the surface, producing radiant blooms. Beauty from darkness. Now it rested on the desk in the wood-paneled classroom of Harkness Hall on the Yale campus.

Grant turned his attention from the flower to the view through the leaded glass panes of the window. The late morning sun brought out the warm earth tones from the Gothic arches and cathedral spires of Sterling Memorial Library, opposite the expansive green lawn from his building. The light warmed Grant as well. Although he'd just showered at the Payne Whitney Gym, Grant realized he was still sweating from his morning workout.

Her train should've arrived by now, he thought for the fourth time in the past half hour. He then smiled at his impatience. Almost two weeks had passed since they'd last seen each other. He reached for his cell phone. Maybe she'd texted. It wasn't in his pocket. He shook his head, remembering. He'd left it charging on the kitchen counter again.

Grant turned at the sound of the classroom door opening. His pulse quickened at the sight of the fifteen noisy juniors and seniors filing into the seminar room. The university had been in session for almost two months, and he still experienced a rush every day he walked into his class on comparative spirituality.

A gangly senior with shaggy blond hair and curious blue eyes spoke to him from the center of the front row. "What's up, Professor?"

"Just hangin', Mr. Hodges," Grant replied. He raised his voice over the clamor of the students dropping their book bags on the floor and talking as they slipped into their seats around the U-shaped table. "Waiting for your colleagues to decide they're ready for another inspiring lecture." A few laughs spread across the room.

Grant sat on the edge of his desk facing the semicircle of students. While he gave them a minute to boot up their laptops, he reflected on the whirlwind of the past five years that had brought him here.

The media circus surrounding the New Hope Church had required months of interviews and testimony from Kristin and him. A subsequent IRS investigation that revealed illegal contributions and misuse of funds resulted in the shuttering of the church. As William Jennings had predicted, the banks also foreclosed on the New Hope Community development and then sold the partially completed project at auction for a fraction of the construction costs to a national homebuilder who eventually made millions using the project's New Urbanism design minus the church affiliation.

After extensive investigations, the authorities decided not to charge Reverend Brady with a crime. It appeared not only that the deceased Jennings had masterminded the events leading to the deaths, but that he'd kept the details away from his boss, just as he'd done with the financial workings of the church. Brady, however, had been disgraced. He withdrew from the election for the presidency of the NAE and disappeared from public view. Grant later read that almost three years to the day year after New Hope closed, a small church opened in Montgomery whose head pastor was none other than Brian Brady.

After an extensive search of the deceased Tim Huntley's apartment and computer hard drives, the FBI also linked him to the bombing at Emory. In addition to finding gigabytes of extreme political and religious propaganda and conspiracy theory writings, the FBI also discovered that Huntley had researched other potential targets. When they looked into Huntley's military career, they found that he'd been discharged from the Army because of the "don't ask, don't tell" policy on homosexuality that had since been repealed. But his file also contained numerous reprimands for disrespecting senior officers and engaging in inappropriate speech. As part of the investigation, one of Huntley's work colleagues and childhood friends, Johnny Meckle, was arrested and convicted of the bombing and the murder of Professor Martha Simpson.

Immediately following the police investigations, Grant had been reinstated at Emory with profuse apologies from the dean. He'd earned his PhD six months later. The formal release of the Issa Gospels, as they'd become popularly known, thrust Grant and Kristin into the media spotlight. They selected Yale as the location for the Issa Project, which they co-chaired. In addition to the many world-class resources at the university, the school's Beinecke Rare Book Library served as the new permanent home of the Issa Gospels themselves. Grant found it appropriate that the documents were stored in a library that, like the monastery in which they were recovered, was itself an architectural marvel. Constructed as a giant cube of translucent marble, the library also coincidentally displayed the Gutenberg Bible, the first Western book printed from movable type.

He'd never been so busy, yet so content.

"Okay, let's get started." He knocked on the desk to get their attention. When the students turned their eyes to him expectantly, he began. "Yesterday we left off addressing some of the parallels in the life stories of Jesus and the Buddha: their birth stories, their temptations by the devil, the ability of both men to heal the sick by their touch, the resurrection and reincarnation stories, and finally and most important, how each used the practice of intensive meditation and prayer." Grant paced in front of the room. "Today, let's begin with the extensive parallels in the teachings of these two men. Anyone care to begin?"

Before the students could respond, the door at the rear of the seminar room opened. Grant watched her walk around the table. The short Burberry skirt emphasized her toned legs. Only he could detect the slight bump under her cream blouse. They hadn't told anyone yet.

"Class, I'm sure everyone knows my wife, Ms. Misaki." Kristin waved to the students. He embraced her. She responded by kissing him fully on the lips, which drew several whistles from their audience.

After he reluctantly released her, she turned to the students. "Hello, class."

A curly-headed woman dressed in sweats emblazoned with a giant blue *Y* fidgeted in her seat, as if she were in the presence of a rock star. She blurted out, "We saw you on TV yesterday!"

Grant had seen her as well. New York was the final stop on the book tour. Just three weeks earlier, they'd released their second book exploring the Issa Gospels. The first was a rushed-out translation with few editorial comments, but the new one examined the issues the manuscripts raised in their historical context. They decided that Grant would remain at Yale, teaching and overseeing the day-to-day activities of the Issa Project while she took a semester's leave from her duties to lecture on the book.

"Left your cell phone at home again?" she asked. He nodded. "So, I take it you haven't seen this yet?" She held up a folded newspaper.

He looked at her quizzically.

"Anyone?" She displayed the paper to the students but received only blank stares. "I guess you guys just roll out of bed in time for your eleven o'clock class." She hoisted herself onto Grant's desk, crossed her legs, and opened the paper to the front page.

Printed across the top right column, the words VATICAN ANNOUNCES RELEASE OF ISSA MANUSCRIPT screamed at Grant. Kristin began to read aloud:

In a surprise move, the Vatican announced late yesterday that they were releasing an ancient manuscript, which like the Issa Gospels discovered five years ago this month by Grant Matthews and Kristin Misaki, details the travels of Jesus of Nazareth to India and his study of Hinduism and Buddhism. According to

Vatican representative Cardinal Giancarlo Giovanni, the Vatican manuscript was written in Tibetan and appears to be a later compilation of the various Issa Gospels found by Mr. Matthews and Ms. Misaki. Scientists and biblical scholars have dated the Issa Gospels, which were written in the ancient Pali language, to the early first century, predating the earliest books of the New Testament.

According to Cardinal Giovanni, the Vatican manuscript has a "somewhat cloudy history." Originally discovered in 1887 by Russian journalist Nicholas Notovitch during a stay at the Himis monastery in Ladakh, India, the text was acquired in the early 1930s by a Vatican contingent visiting the Himis monastery. The document allegedly remained forgotten in the Vatican archives until it was rediscovered last month during a routine cataloging exercise. When asked why the manuscript was not released when originally found, the cardinal replied, "In addition to questions as to the authenticity and age of this document, the text was found during a time of upheaval surrounding the beginning of the Second World War. The Church decided that releasing the manuscript during this critical period would not be in the best interest of the world." Cardinal Giovanni went on to say that this news in no way affects the Catholic Church's previously stated position on the books discovered by Mr. Matthews and Ms. Misaki.

"Wow," Grant said shaking his head. "I'm surprised the Vatican didn't call us first."

"They must have wanted to control the publicity."

"What about the newspaper?"

"The reporter called to apologize this morning before I jumped on the train. They received the story late last night and had to run it before they could interview anyone, including us. But"—she checked her watch—"we have an interview scheduled in forty-five minutes that will appear tomorrow."

Grant was stunned. He didn't believe for a minute that the Vatican simply forgot the manuscript amid the tens of thousands of documents stored in their archives, especially after the publicity over the past five years. The cardinals had waited to see how scholars would handle the Issa texts. Last year the Vatican, along with a number of mainline Protestant churches, had admitted that Jesus might have traveled to India during his formative years but that such travels in no way affected his status as the Messiah, nor would such an event contradict anything in the New Testament, which was silent on those years of his life.

Most evangelical churches still referred to the Issa Gospels as "works of Satan" that should be categorically rejected along with any other apocryphal sources about Jesus. They held steadfast to their position that the early Church Fathers were guided by the Holy Spirit in choosing to include in the New Testament all the texts that were true to the word of God.

Based on numerous requests for speaking engagements, however, Grant and Kristin were encouraged at the growing number of independent churches that were reexamining the way they taught about Jesus, and even the way they conducted their services. Each year also saw a greater number of interfaith conferences taking place, some sponsored by the Issa Project. He and Kristin were scheduled to give the keynote address at one in San Diego during winter break, and Grant was thrilled to hear that Jigme, who they hadn't seen in two years, would be attending as well. Grant could feel the momentum building.

The curly-headed woman clearly in awe of Kristin raised her hand. "You have a comment on this article, Ms. Lynn?" he asked her.

"More of a question for you and Ms. Misaki," she said in a melodic southern drawl that added at least two additional syllables to Kristin's last name.

"Go ahead," Kristin said, folding the paper in her lap.

"With all the controversy still surrounding the Issa Gospels, how are we ever to know two thousand years later what the truth is?"

"Another way to ask your question," Kristin said, "is do the actual historical events even matter? Do we care whether Jesus actually learned his theology on his travels to India?"

"Don't we? Isn't that the whole point of your Issa Project—to encourage more interfaith communication and cooperation based on the commonalities of these religions rather than their differences?"

"When I was in graduate school"—Grant strolled in front of the class—"I was obsessed with distinguishing myth from history, story from fact. But during my search for the Issa Gospels, I realized that my focus was obscuring the original purpose of these stories. The Issa Gospels are more than a historical explanation of the influences in the early life of Jesus. These texts point to a deeper truth underlying religion, a truth independent of the historical details, which we will never truly know."

"And that ultimate truth is what?" Hodges called out from the front row.

Without missing a beat, Grant replied, "The answer to Mr. Hodges's question can only be answered by one person."

"Me?" Hodges answered.

"Yes, you. You do not need me, or a priest, or a rabbi to tell you what to believe. We can only provide you with the tools and the knowledge that will allow you to experience the ultimate truth for yourself."

"Don't you think that most people want to be told what they should believe in?" the student persisted.

"It's often easier to believe than to question," Grant said. "But what happens when you have an experience that shakes your belief system—you learn facts about another religion that contradict your own, scientific advancements disprove elements of your faith, or new texts like the Issa Gospels are discovered?"

Marcus Park, a dark-haired junior in ripped jeans and a black T-shirt who with his Eurasian features could have been Kristin's younger brother, raised his hand. When Grant nodded to him, he asked, "So, by studying other religions, we can expand our own spirituality, maybe even deepen our own faith, or take it in new directions?"

"Like Issa did on his journey," Lynn added.

Grant smiled at his students. "I knew I had a purpose behind teaching this class."

"But ultimately," Hodges persisted, "regardless of any common themes or practices among the different religions, they can't all be right. One has to be closer to this ultimate truth than the others."

Grant heard a familiar tone in his student: he heard himself, his own dualistic logic. He was reminded of his conversations with Kinley, while the monk patiently sat with him for weeks during his recovery. Grant could hear his friend's voice through his own when he answered, "When a deer walks through the forest, he will take a path along the ground, while the squirrel will leap from branch to branch. The bird may fly above the trees, while the worm will tunnel underneath them. Each of these animals reaches its destination, but is one way through the forest the best? Will one path even work for all the animals?"

Kristin glanced at her wrist and tugged on Grant's shirt. He looked at her watch, since he'd stopped wearing one. Class should have ended five minutes earlier, yet not a single student had started to pack his or her books.

"Looks like we ran over a bit today. I apologize if we've made anyone late for another lecture." Grant rubbed his hands together before clasping them behind his back.

"Professor, just one more question," Hodges said with his hand in the air. No one groaned at having their departure delayed again. "When you strip away the myths and the stories from a religion to access its deeper truth, do you not also take away the essence and character of that religion? I mean, what's left?"

Grant looked from Hodges to the sea of faces waiting expectantly for his answer. "A friend of mine once told me the story of a student who asked his master, 'When the leaves fall from the tree, what then?'" Grant paused and then continued, "The master replied, 'The body is exposed in the autumn wind.'"

Grant turned to his desk and reached for the leather binder that contained his class notes. His eyes caught the brilliant yellow flower floating in the bowl. He allowed his vision to linger.

He saw the lotus.

ACKNOWLEDGMENTS

THIS NOVEL WOULD not have been possible without the support, encouragement, and infinite patience of my wife, Alison, and my daughter, Gabriella. I am also deeply indebted to Chris Russell, who started me down a path many years ago through our discussions on spirituality and his meditation instruction that changed my life. Although I was a math and science geek in high school, my English teachers at the Westminster Schools (Eddie, Frank, Nedra, and John) taught me the fundamentals and appreciation of writing that have stayed with me all these years and given me the skills to complete what has been the most difficult yet rewarding accomplishment of my life. I would like to thank my early readers who provided many great suggestions: Rev. Sam Candler, Jon Ezrine, Tom Flanigan, Steve Floyd, Anna McGarrity, Dr. Art Schiff, Ambassador Raymond Seitz, and my sister Chanley Small. To my YPO Forum, thank you for believing in me and encouraging me to pursue my passion. To my parents, Jeff and Eileen, your confidence in me and your support throughout my life have meant more than I can express. To my editors Brooke Warner and Danelle McCafferty, without your attention to detail and instruction on craft, this first-time novel would be much less than it is. Infinite gratitude goes to my publisher Mark Bernstein and Hundreds of Heads Books and the folks at PGW for taking a risk on a first-time novelist. Finally, the writings of the following scholars have inspired me and contributed to many of my themes: Marcus Borg, Thich Nhat Hanh, John Hick, Stephen Mitchell, John Robinson, Huston Smith, John Shelby Spong, and Paul Tillich.

ABOUT THE AUTHOR

—⚬⚬⚬—

 JEFFREY SMALL GRADUATED *summa cum laude* from Yale University and *magna cum laude* from Harvard Law School. He holds a master's degree in the study of religions from Oxford University. Jeffrey is an acclaimed speaker on the topics of rethinking religion in the twenty-first century and the common spiritual themes in the world's religions.

For more information, please go to www.jeffreysmall.com.